I0823930

EVERYTHING LOST RETURNS

ALSO BY SARAH DOMET

The Guineveres

EVERYTHING LOST RETURNS

A NOVEL

SARAH DOMET

FLATIRON BOOKS
NEW YORK

This is a work of fiction. All the names, characters, organizations, places, and events portrayed in this work are either products of the author's imagination or used fictitiously.

 Printed in the United States of America. For information, address Flatiron Books, 120 Broadway, New York, NY 10271. EU Representative: Macmillan Publishers Ireland Ltd, 1st Floor, The Liffey Trust Centre, 117–126 Sheriff Street Upper, Dublin 1, D01 YC43.

www.flatironbooks.com

Designed by Leah Carlson-Stanisic

Library of Congress Cataloging-in-Publication Data

Names: Domet, Sarah, author.
Title: Everything lost returns : a novel / Sarah Domet.
Description: First edition. | New York : Flatiron Books, 2026.
Identifiers: LCCN 2025026600 | ISBN 9781250087898 (hardcover) | ISBN 9781250087881 (ebook)
Subjects: LCGFT: Fiction | Novels
Classification: LCC PS3604.O456 E94 2026 | DDC 813/.6—dc23/eng/20250624
LC record available at https://lccn.loc.gov/2025026600

First Edition: 2026

10 9 8 7 6 5 4 3 2 1

For Saskia and Buchanan

There is one rule to be learned. Life is not you. Life is outside you. If it is outside, you must go toward it. The essential thing to know is that life is in front of you. Go toward it.

—Stella Adler, *The Art of Acting*

Keeping quiet when I want to howl
is old work, the day labor that never
breaks me even.

—Alicia Mountain, "Train Town Howl"

EVERYTHING LOST RETURNS

PROLOGUE

August 1909

The first time Opal heard the voice she stood ankle-deep in the Ohio River. It was night, and the water was a universe of stars. Opal wiggled her toes, then dared herself farther until she was calf-, then knee-deep. Her skirt clung to her legs. She willed herself to be brave.

Above, the crescent moon looked like a sickle her husband swung to cut wheat. She could not make out the man up there. She remembered the poem her old schoolteacher once had the class recite:

Our man in the moon drinks claret,
With powder-beef, turnip, and carrot.
If he doth so, why should not you
Drink until the sky looks blue?

The poem had stirred something inside her. *Why should not you?* Someone had taken a sickle to the moon, and, like wheat, it would grow again. Opal dug her toes into the mud to steady herself. Her body felt tingly, floaty from the medicines. Since Madame de Fleur left she hadn't been herself. Her husband declared it an *unusual episode.*

Opal took a few steps deeper, pulled her legs forward until she submerged herself to her waist. Her skirt bloomed around her, petals and she was the pistil. Her husband grew medicinal crops in their fields, studying them to determine the timing of the harvest. When the pistils darkened, when they curled inward like a hooked finger, the plants were ready to be picked.

Now, she glided her hands through the water, and she felt something. Not the floating fabric of her skirt or a rock in the riverbed. No, something invisible that caused her skin to tighten against her bones, then a jolt she could only later describe as a shock of electricity.

She heard the nattering of late summer cicadas, then a rustling from the thicket of trees. "Who's there?" she called out, but darkness cloaked the world around her. Still, Opal wasn't afraid. What could she lose that she hadn't lost already? She pondered the sky for a moment, how the stars now made her think of Oren somewhere up there, among them.

Oren, her first love, gone twelve years now. The last time she saw him, he was nothing more than a bundle of sheets and wet rags, his skin waxy and gray, his eyes darting back and forth like an animal that'd been caught. How could she tell him all that'd happened since? How her grief had been ordinary—nausea, listlessness, the feeling her body had been turned inside out, like a pocket emptied of its contents—until it wasn't, until it became a fact, not a feeling, the new life inside her. How could she tell him that at sixteen her mother had taken her to see a doctor to cure her of her shame, how that doctor performed a procedure to render her sterile, how a year later this man would become her husband. How she'd lived as his wife for ten years. How she'd met Madame de Fleur and—

Those on the Other Side can see the wider scope of possibility. They're no wiser; they merely have access to the fuller story. *Souls without bodies,* Madame de Fleur had explained. Opal remembered the time she and the woman visited Mound Hill, how Opal picked a yellow mum to set on Oren's headstone, and how Madame de Fleur asked her, what comfort did she expect to find in stone? *My dear, those on the Other Side crave what we all do: contact. Touch.*

Now Opal felt that ordinary grief again. Her body was not her body. There in the river, Opal grasped for something—an object just out of reach—but found only damp night air. The current urged her deeper. She inched farther. An aura ringed the moon. She didn't see a man up there.

Still, she sensed a presence, someone calling from the distance. The field of stars looked vast and flat, but in the dark of it, she found a speck of moving light. Then another. Falling stars. The meteors from the comet all the papers talked about, still months away. Halley's Comet—a possessive phrase, as though one could own a mass of distant light, something that couldn't be held even if it could be touched.

The water sloshed beneath her chin now. The river smelled like a body in need of washing. She drifted from the shore until her toes could no longer skim the riverbed. She floated for an instant, then held her breath and allowed herself to sink.

Beneath the water, the world fell silent. Bubbles dropped from her nose like little stones. Only weeks ago, Madame de Fleur had hidden herself beneath this river, then emerged in the moonlight. After that, everything had changed.

Opal wanted to understand the woman, to feel what she'd felt. Now, the water gently pulled her, the pressure a kind of embrace. Now, the cold stung her skin. Now, her lungs began burning, and Opal longed for it, this kind of pain. She swam downward. Her fingers grazed the pebbled riverbed, but her body was buoyant. She had to keep kicking, struggling to stay beneath the water. How had the woman submerged herself for so long when hiding required this much effort?

She stopped resisting and allowed herself to rise, but then, that terrible tug. Her skirt tangled on a root growing up from the riverbed. Opal was stuck.

Frantically, she stretched her arms upward; she kicked until her thighs felt afire. Her husband had told her drowning felt like pneumonia, only quicker, but now time slowed. Dull whooshing. Heavy limbs. Her fingers worked to unfasten her skirt. The surface above appeared like a mirrored sky, impossible to reach.

Yet, a body wants to survive.

A body needs another body to do so.

Her legs heaved another kick. Her skirt ripped. An unseen force pushed her upward, toward the light of the night. Her head breached the surface, and she gasped for air, and in the coming up she knew. She *knew*. This, perhaps, marked her first true moment of clairvoyance. Her grief was not ordinary. It was not even grief.

She was pregnant.

The moon hung high. Opal floated on her back, breathless, aware of the life inside her, despite the impossibility of it. Later, she might say the baby had saved her, but it was her own body that pushed her toward the surface, wasn't it? She brought her hands to touch the flat of her stomach. And that's the moment she finally heard it—the voice the woman had told her about—thin but clear. The voice said this:

Save her.

1986

> The soap's purity is your surety.
> [I]ts whiteness cannot tell a lie.
>
> —N. K. FAIRBANK COMPANY

I am dead.

The director scrutinizes the lighting, the angle, *me,* there in the coffin. His head floats above me; his eyebrows cinch. My ruffled collar itches my chin, but I must remain still, for stillness is an actor's greatest tool.

I am never *really* dead.

I always recall the characters I've played as though I'm still playing them. *Embodying them,* my old acting teacher at the conservatory would say. *Channeling their essence.* She used to have us sit at a table with our eyes closed, our palms stretched wide. *Listen for a pulse, a voice inside you,* she'd say. *Your body is no longer your body. Your mind is no longer your mind. Now say it...* More than a decade and a half later, in that plywood coffin, I repeated those words to myself. *I am not me. I am not me.*

It was early January 1986, around the time of the comet, that nine-mile ball of light that appears every seventy-six years and bears the name of the astronomer who predicted it. Halley's Comet. Already the comet was everywhere: on ball caps and T-shirts, on magazine covers and beer ads and souvenir spoons. Each night, the local meteorologist tracked the comet's progress toward perihelion—February 9—when it'd be closest to Earth, visible to the naked eye.

There, in that box beneath the dirt—though really on the soundstage—I said it: *I am not me. I am Stella.* My body elongated and relaxed. My skin stretched. My legs became her legs. Her hands were my hands. I was full of grit, literally and metaphorically. I manifested strength on-screen.

I became Stella. I was in a box. The box was in the ground. The ground was in Port Middleton, the fictional setting of *Stars and Shadows*, the fifth-ranked soap opera in the nation, though the most popular in the regional market because it was filmed in Cincinnati, Ohio, in the studio attached to the Earthshine Soap Factory, the show's only sponsor.

Elliot yelled, "Roll sound," then I heard the click of the clapper board by the production assistant, some young intern with no panty line. I couldn't see much from where I was lying, only the bobbled heads of the makeup girl and the wardrobe assistant, the boom mic hanging above me. My stomach growled, and this felt like a betrayal because I'd eaten Dexatrim for breakfast.

I focused my mind again. I was Stella Shadow, the niece of Celeste Shadow, the wealthiest woman in Port Middleton. I'd contracted a disease so rare that only two doctors in the world had ever heard of it, and luckily one of them practiced at Port Middleton Memorial.

My body felt heavy. *I'm buried alive,* I told myself. At the conservatory, my acting coach taught me to feel my impact points. She taught me to follow the breath through my body, to extend it out of the top of my head like a whale spouting water. I began to sense the walls around me, the way my toes and arms and head grazed the wood. The dome lamp hung over me, and the heat dampened my skin, but

I imagined it'd be cool beneath the soil. I imagined earthworms wriggling outside the box, the kind Wyatt would tell me increased soil aeration and nutrient cycling. He'd once bought me a bag of worms when I'd planted a garden because that's what our marriage looked like then: possibility.

"Action," said Elliot. The camera rolled. The bulb near the viewfinder blinked red three times, then became a beady eye.

Oh, I'd died before: a boat explosion, a safari disaster, an airplane crash over the mysterious island of Notelddim Trop, which is just Port Middleton spelled backward. But I always came back. The credits list me as a recurring guest star—and I loved seeing that word beside my name, *star*, even if I wasn't technically part of the main cast.

Above me, I could hear Celeste Shadow beside my grave weeping.

"If only I'd been in time," Celeste said. She'd been in the Far East, searching for the other doctor who had the cure for the rare disease that claimed me. "I arrived with that vial just as you expired," she wailed.

I heard my cue, then I felt it: the weight of expectation, the shift of attention in my direction. So much of acting is stillness and energy combined—even when you're not playing dead. My eyes were closed but they fluttered, then opened, and then fill lights blinded me, like I was looking directly at the sun. The brightness distracted me. I began thinking about endings, about Wyatt, about how the last time I'd seen him everything was confusing again. Wyatt kissed me goodbye and said, *You're a hard habit to break,* which was just a lyric from a Chicago song, so it didn't mean anything, really. But it made me sad because, first, it was a breakup song, and, second, I wasn't a habit: I was still, technically, his wife.

And that's when I heard it first, there in that coffin. I mistook it for a horn in the distance, or a barge passing on the Ohio River nearby. The noise was staticky, faraway and close at once: just a single note, repeating.

Waaaa. Waaaa.

"Line," I said.

"Can you hear me? Can you hear me, Aunt Celeste? You *are* in time. I'm still alive," read the production assistant. The way she spoke told me she had secret ambitions.

"Cut, cut," Elliot yelled. A hand reached down for me, and I allowed myself to be pulled up. "Ten-minute break, everyone," he said, then: "For christsakes, Nona, what's your problem?"

"Sorry, Elliot," I said. I could no longer make out that strange noise. "Just give me a minute." Getting out of the coffin was like getting out of a canoe; there was no easy way. I wore heels for authenticity, even though the script called for only close-ups of my fists pounding the box.

"I know, I know," he said. Elliot was short, so I slouched to make myself smaller.

"I'm distracted is all."

"Me, too, Nona, but Christ. I'm doing *my* job—at least while I have one, which may not be long, if you've been keeping up with the news. Did you see today's paper? Another one."

He was talking about the latest article in the *Cincinnati Inquisitor*. Last month, four Jane Does had come forward with a lawsuit, claiming Earthshine Soap contained addictive chemicals of some sort, psychoactive ingredients that caused all sorts of side effects. Since then, production schedules had been all over the place; the studio was needed to shoot new commercials for the latest PR campaign. Now, according to this morning's paper, a fifth woman had been added to the lawsuit.

"Crazy," I said. "Soap crossing the blood-brain barrier. Who'd ever come up with that?" Standing there on set, my toes squeezed into too-narrow shoes, I'll admit: I didn't believe those Jane Does. I hadn't considered I could be one, too.

"I'm already getting heat. Threats of a boycott. Worse. We can't drop our only sponsor. We'd be done."

"Bored housewives would never give up Port Middleton," I said.

"Someone egged my car this morning. Those women are batshit."

"Was it one of them? A Jane Doe?" I asked.

"No. I don't know—protesters of some sort. A line of them as I drove in this morning. Didn't you see them?"

I shook my head.

He leaned against the foam gravestone bearing Stella's name but thought better of it. "I bet Bertie Tuttle's gone ballistic. That's one woman you don't want to piss off, even if she is a hundred."

"Ninety-nine," I said.

"Look," he said. "This must be extra difficult for you, you know, because . . . well, because of your involvement."

"I've got nothing to do with the lawsuit," I said.

"Well, you know. Because you're close with the Tuttles, with Halley, all that. And because your face is on the soap."

"I was a kid. I doubt anybody even remembers it's me." I sat down on the bench next to Stella's grave, still warm from Celeste. "Orthodontics and hair dye."

Even as I said the words, I knew it was a lie. Sure, I played Stella, but I was better known as the Earthshine Girl, the original Earthshine Girl, famous face of the soap. At age seven, I'd been discovered, singing at Music Hall with my school choir in the May Festival. Shortly thereafter, Bertie Tuttle herself offered me the part. It wasn't my acting that made me famous. It was the soap. It was because I'd been in *People* magazine. "It's the Earthshine Girl!" strangers would shout from their cars, even years later, even after orthodontics and hair dye. Occasionally someone would ask for a photo or an autograph.

"Look, Nona," Elliot said, changing the subject. "Last week we had to do three takes during the funeral scene. And forgetting lines? I just don't want to see you written off again."

"I'm always written off, Elliot. That's the whole point of bringing me back."

"So soon. You know what I mean. I've been talking to the writers about making you a series regular," he said. "They're considering pitching it to the execs."

"Do I get a love interest?" Stella never had a romance, no desires of her own, no storyline written just for her character. Writers easily killed her off because nobody besides Celeste ever *really* cared she was gone.

"This isn't exactly *Love Connection.* I . . . I know you're dealing with some, uh, personal stuff. You and Wyatt."

"You know about that?" We hadn't used the word *divorce.* Not yet. A month apart—*some time to think*—had turned into three. I stared down at my shoes, Edwardian oxfords that reminded me of what Virginia Woolf might have worn when she walked into that river with rocks in her pockets.

"Everyone sort of knows, yeah."

"Did Halley tell you?" I asked.

"She just wanted to help. *I* want to help. We're like family."

"Does Stella live this time?" I only ever received the script a week in advance, at the cold reads, to ensure the storyline didn't get out to the gossip rags, though *Stars and Shadows* may have benefited from that kind of publicity.

"You know I can't tell you that." Elliot sat beside me on the bench.

"I thought we were family."

"*Show* family."

"I need this job, Elliot."

"It's not up to me. I've always said I think you have star potential."

"Potential. That's what we called the girls who made chorus. At the conservatory, I was always the lead," I said. He put his arm around me, and I rested my head on his shoulder. "I was good. I was better than good."

"Word of advice?" he said. His breath smelled like the Fritos and Skyline Chili dip someone left in the green room. "This isn't the conservatory anymore. This is real life."

HALLEY WAS WAITING FOR ME in my dressing room, her feet up on the vanity to reveal the Birkenstocks she wore, even in winter. She rarely used makeup, but her lips were smeared with my lipstick—Sugared Maple—the plum tones washing her out so she looked sick.

"You okay?" I asked.

"I heard you flubbed your lines," she said. She'd been reading the *Cincinnati Inquisitor,* but now she folded it and tucked the paper beneath her arm.

Halley Tuttle was my "studio mom," we used to joke, though she was only eight years older than me. She had been hired at the studio as "Chaperone to the Earthshine Girl," her official title, and she continued in this role even after I was let go. I came of age on-screen, and it was Halley who guided me through my body's changes. When I found that first spot of brown period blood, it was Halley who rushed me to the bathroom with a Kotex, explaining to me what my own mother wouldn't because we didn't speak of such things at home. That I had to be careful because I could get knocked up, *like my mother did with me,* Halley said, even though I was only twelve and still five years away from losing my virginity on a waterbed that sloshed with each movement. Afterward, Halley would be the first person I'd call.

Halley was the one who told me the Earthshine factory was haunted by the seven women who died there in the fire that nearly destroyed the building back in 1910. She said when the factory is quiet at night, you could still hear their voices. They wanted revenge.

"On who?"

"Who do you think?" she said.

"Your family?" Halley nodded. It was no secret she was the black sheep. She claimed she wasn't a *true* Tuttle, and we all knew what she meant. "What do they say?" I asked.

"Boo!"

Sometimes when Halley laughed too hard, tears streamed down her face and she lost her breath, and I'd say: "Breathe! Breathe!" like I was begging for her life.

Her demeanor was serious now. She'd pulled her hair up into a bun. You could see her face better that way, the bulbs of her cheeks, her penetrating eyes, intense even when she didn't mean to be. "I've been fired."

"You can't be fired. Your dad is chairman of the board."

"Tell that to Bertie."

"What happened?"

She stood and turned toward me. Her lips parted like she was about to speak. She wore a long gray sweater and rooted through her woven purse until she found what she was looking for: an orange medicine vial. I shot her a look.

"Prescription. To settle my stomach," she said. "Geez, what is it with everyone?"

"We just worry about you is all," I said. I grabbed the bottle from her and checked for her name, then handed it back. "What happened this time?" Like Stella, Halley's job had many lives, on and off like even her most serious relationships. They always hired her back. She was Bertie's only grandchild, and Bertie staked her whole career on helping women.

Now Halley shuffled through a box of her effects on my vanity. I could tell something else was on her mind. "We need to talk," she said. Her eyes roamed the room like they were trying to fix themselves to a stationary object.

"About that?" I asked. She handed the newspaper to me. "The lawsuit?"

"Shhh," Halley said. I noticed then how red rimmed her eyelids were, how little rivers of veins were mapped on the whites of her eyes. She'd taken something, and not just a prescription to settle her stomach. "Not here. They're probably listening."

"They? Halley . . . You sound like *1984*."

She grabbed my hand and intertwined our fingers. When we held hands in public, we often elicited looks from strangers—remember, this was still the 1980s. But Halley and I were close like this. "My dad didn't even call me this time. I had to hear it from some smarmy executive. The one who smells like sardines. Come with me. I'm meeting my dad at the country club. We can talk on the way. It's important. It's about . . ." She nodded toward the *Inquisitor* still tucked beneath her arm.

"I've got to get back to set," I said. "Elliot would kill me."

"Please. Have dinner with us. It'll be easier with you there. He likes you better."

"Not true," I said.

Halley squeezed my hand. Her palms were clammy. "Come on. He attended every show of yours in college. He gave you away at your wedding," she said. I managed to free my hand. "Sorry. I didn't mean to bring that up. Have you talked to Wyatt lately?"

"I need to get back. I'm buried alive, you know. It takes a while."

"Meet me there."

"Celeste just missed saving my life."

"Please. We can talk after. It can't wait."

"It's hard on Celeste."

"That rich bitch."

We laughed.

"See you there," I said, and Halley left.

As I turned to go, I caught a reflection of myself in the mirror. My face was gaunt, my frosty perm poofed and feathered like Krystle Carrington, but without the look of money. I thought of the myth of Narcissus, not because I was smitten with my own image but because I didn't recognize myself. And I couldn't look away. I didn't understand yet—but I would soon—that a series of events had already been set into motion, a predictable object bound by a gravitational pull, like that comet making its way toward us.

HALLEY WAS DRUNK BY THE time I arrived at the country club a few hours later, her head resting atop the table. Charlie stood to greet me, kissed each of my cheeks in the way Celeste Shadow kisses Stella. Charlie Tuttle, Bertie's only child, Halley's father—though he'd not learned of his daughter's existence until she was thirteen years old, the product of a brief affair.

Halley raised her head. "I can always count on you," she said. She'd been crying. Salt spots crusted around her eyes. The waitstaff cleaned up a mess of lettuce and broken china from the floor, trying their best to pretend they hadn't just witnessed a scene.

"Halley is just leaving, I'm afraid," Charlie said. He winked at me, like this was all great fun.

"He has his dignity to uphold," Halley said.

"She needs some rest," Charlie said to me. "She's not thinking clearly."

"I've embarrassed him," Halley said.

"I'm worried about you," Charlie barked. He turned to me again. "She's high on something. She's talking nonsense. She told the waiter—"

"Halley's Comet, it's a sign," she said. There, in that country club restaurant, as her voice slowed and slurred, she explained the Pilgrims followed a comet to the New World. She said the Star of Bethlehem wasn't a star at all—the three wise men had followed the path of a comet to find baby Jesus in that manger. "History," she said, "is repeating itself."

"Halley," I said, taking the seat next to her. I didn't want to admit she was getting worse. I rubbed her back, small circles, like one might use to lull a sleepy child. When Wyatt had left, I called Halley first. It was Halley who came over and drank a bottle of wine with me until I had sufficiently numbed my body. She promised sleep would give me perspective. She put me to bed and stayed the night, right there next to me, to make sure I wasn't alone that first morning. "Listen to your dad. Get some rest."

"You don't know Bertie Tuttle," she said.

"She's clearly high on something," Charlie said. "She had only a single glass of wine." He ran his fingers through his hair, dark and wavy like his daughter's. When he first met Halley, even Charlie couldn't dispute the striking resemblance. Same square jaw. Same eyes the color of coal. Same manner of moving stiffly, sitting erect, like their spines were hewn from metal.

"Your head will be much clearer in the morning. Nothing seems as bad after a good night of sleep," I whispered. "Remember when you told me that?"

"I sound smart," she said.

"Halley, nobody thinks otherwise," Charlie said. "I'll talk to your grandmother. I'm sure this is all a misunderstanding." Bertie had long since retired from the family business, but everyone knew she was still in charge.

"I thought you'd be on my side," she said. She placed her hands on the table to hoist herself up, but she slumped back into her chair. She turned toward me. "You said we could talk."

"We will," I said.

"Come with me?" Her eyelids drooped now.

"I've got an early call time," I said. "Celeste is having flashbacks. A whole montage of us set to 'Through the Years.' You'd hate it. Get some sleep. I'll call you." I hugged her. I kissed her cheek. I squeezed her shoulders.

Charlie's driver had to help carry her out, her legs dangling over his arms, one Birkenstock balanced on a toe. Now, Charlie cleared his throat. He was a man of dignity—not prideful, but private. "That girl," he said.

That girl. Her head dipped back over the arm of Charlie's driver, her lips parted on the verge of speaking, though she didn't say anything. She didn't make a sound. I'll never forget how she looked, like a child who'd fallen asleep at a dinner party.

Charlie had a conference call with a PR firm—"This Jane Doe nonsense," he explained—so the driver delivered me back to the Earthshine factory, to my car parked in the studio lot. Everyone says there's no culture in the Midwest, but we had our own institutions. Earthshine had evolved beyond the brand to become the industry leader in all sorts of domestic products, from tampons to toilet paper, diapers to dusting spray. Midwestern culture is the home and the lives we make inside it.

Windows lined all four stories of the factory, and a hulk of a tower arose from the center bearing a clock and the company name: EARTHSHINE SOAPS. The stump of a chimney looked like a fat cigar, the name BREMEN spelled out in white brick. I drew my eyes to a line near the roof where the walls had been patched with mortar, where char stained the bricks.

A fire had destroyed much of the building in 1910, on the night Halley's Comet was supposed to be closest to Earth, visible to the naked eye, the same night Charlie was born. I'd read about it in *The Juggernaut*, Bertie's biography; I'd heard Bertie tell the story herself. There'd been an ongoing strike at the factory. The fire had been set by one of the workers. Several of them died. The flames reached up like fingers toward the sky. It was so noisy and hot, and she stood too close to the building, trying to call for help. That was her mistake. She felt the pang of early labor, and she doubled forward, so a group of women—Earthshine workers—dragged her away from the crowd. She could have died that night. Instead, her water broke. Help arrived. Charlie was born two months premature. She named him after his father and after the comet he was born beneath. Charles Halley Tuttle.

The factory was eventually restored.

Years later, after her husband left her a widow, Bertie took over the company. She modernized the factory—brought it into the new age, with the addition of the recording studio. To many, she's called the Mother of Marketing, the first to shift a brand's focus from product to consumer. She phased out the old bars of Earthshine Soap and brought a new powder formula to the market. The Soap for Women. I attended the Grand Re-Opening Ceremony wearing a yellow dress with a fur collar and little pompom drawstrings—a gift from Bertie herself—and it was me, the Earthshine Girl, who snipped the ribbon and watched it flutter to the ground as Bertie gave my shoulder a quick pat and said: *Soap will never be the same.*

Now the driver pulled up near the brick-lined promenade called the Plaza of Dreams that led to the front entrance of the factory. At the center stood that bronze statue of Bertie Tuttle, the one the Women's

Empowerment Fund had erected in her honor. The statue depicted a young Bertie, her arms crossed, her chin assuredly tilted. At the base of the statue stood a casting of her Saint Bernard, Sudsy, who apparently reincarnated as a puppy every time an old Sudsy died.

"It's her," Bertie had said the moment she saw me all those years ago, after my first audition. Her voice was breathy, accented like an old movie star who held her vowels just a bit longer than necessary. I knew she was important because the whole room hushed when she entered, and they pushed themselves against the walls as if Bertie needed the space. In reality, she was petite, short, compact. She marched toward me, past the cameras and the sound equipment and the wall lined with screens that still held my image, moving as I moved. "It's her," she said. Bertie was in her late sixties by then, a star in her own right. She knew Rosemary Clooney and Doris Day. She'd dined with Mamie Eisenhower. She knelt down so we were eye level. "My Earthshine Girl." She took my hand and asked: "Do you want to become someone very important?"

Already at seven, I did. I stood there transfixed, imagining my future. I'd never clean houses like my mother, who spent her days inside, dusting drapes or bent over toilets or on her knees scouring baseboards. It embarrassed me back then to tell friends what my mother did for a living, when most of their mothers didn't even have to work. "Yes," I said to Bertie. A portrait artist sketched my rendering, which became the face of the brand, printed on every canister, and, there, in that studio, I was reborn.

Bertie held out her hand, and I took it. Her hand was warm, and her bracelets jangled on her wrist. She smelled like honeysuckle, which reminded me of spring, and at that moment I would have said yes to anything she'd asked of me. That's the power Bertie had. She painted an entire world before my eyes and invited me to step inside.

You don't know Bertie Tuttle, Halley had said. But I did.

Standing there, I didn't know the name Opal Doucet. Not really.

Not yet, even though it was close to me, so close I could have almost touched it. I didn't know about her cures or the Comet Pills or the baby or the voices she heard or channeled through her own. I only knew what I'd been told. That's what history is, stories repeated until they're no longer stories, until they're monuments or books or gravestones bearing our names.

1910

At first, Opal mistook the sound for something else, a machinist ratcheting a stubborn pipe. Her hearing had grown more discerning since she arrived in Cincinnati a month ago, when every noise startled her, when her own name shouted by the foreman caused her alarm. *Cautiously alert* she might have described herself on those first few paydays, the other Earthshine Girls watching as she collected her envelope.

Now, she'd grown accustomed to the sheer volume of the factory, the layered sounds she'd learned to separate: the clanging of metal, the growling of the grinders, the hissing of steam. Madame de Fleur had told her that if you focus, you can bring distinct vibrations directly to your ear like a telephone receiver. *Listening,* she said, *is a choice.* A skill, too. Opal had been practicing. She found if she paid attention, her sense of hearing could swaddle itself around a single sound. And there, behind the background whirring of the factory, she heard it, the unfamiliar rhythmic clapping, like a metronome.

She directed her attention back to her station. She mustn't bring scrutiny to herself. She was here to work—not to practice—to earn enough money so she could leave. The job provided means, a weekly wage for her living expenses plus some for her savings tin, if she scrimped. She must keep up with her *numbers,* which is how the floor manager described the quantity of boxes each worker could fill in an hour.

The girls behind her were gossiping again, but Opal focused on the materials in front of her: the sponge pot, the sealing wax, the stack of overwrap. She wetted her thumb. She pulled a piece of paper from the stack. The uneven floor caused the arches of her feet to ache. One of the boilers in the corner kicked out heat, and she wiped her brow with her apron.

"Come on, Earthshine Girls. Pick it up. No slacking today of all days," the foreman yelled from his perch on the platform.

In front of her, the plodder machine discharged the long waxy-looking log the color of egg yolk. Then, the arm of a blade mechanically rose and fell, slicing the soap into even cakes. The machine wasn't too dissimilar from the pill cutter Jagr kept in his office, the one he'd instructed her to use from time to time. She detested this habit of hers—this thinking of Jagr, even now when she was free of him and his medicines. Would she be doomed to consider him for the rest of her life? Would that be her punishment?

Now she pulled a single bar of soap to the table and set it on the paper. Fold, tuck, flip. A dab of wax at each end. The work itself was tedious but uncomplicated. She never imagined working girls could be paid for such simple tasks, when she herself had been paid nothing for more difficult labor. She turned the Earthshine mark forward, that recognizable circle formed by a sun and a crescent moon. It was an unusual mark, not because of the merging of opposites but because the eye was first drawn to the thick, sloped line that both joined and separated the two images. Opal stacked the soap in a box and repeated the process. At night, her fingers ached, and she soaked them in Epsom salt.

When Opal had responded to Earthshine's help-wanted advertisement, the foreman asked her personal questions: about her constitution, about her ability to stand for hours at a time, about whether or not she was an againster or if she read books. He circled her, like Jagr had done the first time she'd been brought to see him as a patient, and this made her nervous. Her form was already changing. *Former work experience?* the foreman asked. His voice was gruff, but the body it came from was slender, slightly stooped. *Not formal,* Opal said.

Children? the foreman asked, and here Opal touched the curve of her stomach, the secret she was keeping, the secret she must continue to keep until she got to France. She shook her head.

Husband? the foreman asked, and Opal's mind fluttered to Jagr, to the jagged breaths he took as he lay heaped on their bed. *No,* she had said, and in that instant she chastised herself for thinking about Jagr again.

That was her old life, her old self. Now, she was what the papers would call a *self-sustaining woman.* She earned her own cash. Five and a half dollars a week, to be exact. From her check, the company deducted rental fees for the white uniform dress similar to what domestics wore. She'd overheard the other Earthshine Girls complain about this—and about low wages and the foreman and the suffocating heat—during their breaks, standing in their aprons and hair netting, taking thirsty drags of cigarettes by the back door. When the women spoke, clouds of winter breath formed, like something was smoldering inside them.

Tick, tick, tick. Now that Opal heard it, she couldn't unhear it. That noise. More like a clanging, like the pots and pans revelers banged at the stroke of midnight to ring in the new year. 1910. A year ending in zero. Opal liked the number 0, like the *O* in her name, the roundness of it, like a hole she could slip through to a place where she felt, after years of waiting, her real life would finally begin.

Soon.

There, in the factory, Opal inhaled the dusty lavender scent of Earthshine Soap. By the end of her shift, she'd reek of it. She tucked and folded. Flipped and stacked. Silently, she filled her box. At the other stations, girls spoke excitedly, for today was the day the owners would be touring the factory, along with a newspaper man from the

Cincinnati Inquisitor. Some of the girls hoped to get their picture in the paper; they'd even worn makeup for the occasion.

The newsman was writing a story about the seventy-fifth anniversary of the company, founded by the Bremen family in 1835, the last time Halley's Comet had orbited the earth. Back then many believed the fantastic flame of the comet's tail would burn bright enough to illuminate the entire world. In December of that year, the Great Fire in New York City blazed for seventeen hours, destroying nearly a quarter of the city. The papers blamed the bearded star.

And now, in this first year of a new decade, Halley's Comet would appear again. Opal thought of what hadn't existed seventy-five years ago, or even a dozen: telephones, telegraphs, automobiles, electricity. Now airplanes could power through the sky. Now X-rays could penetrate one's body to glimpse bone inside.

"They're selling the factory," the girl at the station next to Opal whispered. The two of them weren't overly friendly, but they covered for each other if one needed to run to the washroom. Maria was a girl accustomed to defenses. She planted her feet shoulder-width apart and bounced like a footballer. When she spoke, she lifted her chin as though every word were an act of defiance. "That's why they're visiting the factory, you know. I heard it was Mr. Tuttle's idea, to do the article in the paper. Free advertising."

Jagr had never allowed Opal to read the papers, said it wasn't good for her condition, for her *unusual episodes*, the ones he'd been treating her for since right after they married. Lightheadedness, dizziness, the sense that her head was a helium balloon risen very far from herself. Opal read the papers all she pleased now. During lunch breaks, the Earthshine Girls huddled around the benches in the paved courtyard out back, eating pickled eggs and reading aloud from Dixie About Town, the gossip column in the back of the *Inquisitor*. Opal listened from the bench where she sat by herself, keeping her distance.

Dixie Ellison reported stories of personal affairs: marriages, births, deaths, of debts unpaid, of miscegenation and other misconduct, of the awful streaks upon the glassware at ladies' luncheons, of the wretched color of the ladies' toilet at the Women's Club. Recently, she'd reported that Charles Tuttle was having an affair, that he'd been spotted riding with a "mystery woman" in his automobile. Dixie described the woman as "trim and salacious." All the Earthshine Girls were talking about it.

But not Opal. She read the papers, but she didn't *like* them. The papers marveled at the misery of others. They survived on fear and outrage. She couldn't let the papers override her own good sense, not when her eyes and ears worked just fine.

And then there was what the papers had said about her.

"He's selling the factory, I'm telling you. He believes the future's in appliances. Mechanical washtubs. Electric irons. That sort of thing. I read all about it," Maria said.

"Then let him sell it." Opal couldn't just ignore the woman. "What should it matter?" she asked as a means to end the conversation. She creased the edges of the overwrap and placed the soap in the crate.

"We'll all be out of work, that's why," Maria said.

What should it matter to me? Opal should have said. She didn't intend to be here for very long. A few months more and then—

Her bosoms throbbed, even though she'd bandaged them beneath her shirt to dull the ache. She needed to relieve herself, a symptom of her pregnancy that sent her to the washroom twice as often as the other girls. She eased into the discomfort. She looked to the clock and counted the minutes until their break, then she counted the number of cakes in her box. She tried to calculate how much each box was worth in wages, how many weeks it might take to save enough.

Opal was used to counting now, counting money and minutes and boxes and days, counting the weeks, waiting for a quickening, a sign from the baby. Her monthly bleeding had already accustomed her to waiting, to counting, to the keeping of secrets, to the disposal of messes.

Her body could not sustain a life, Jagr had always told her. It was too weak; her feminine organs had been irreparably altered. He should know: he was the doctor to whom her mother brought Opal for the procedure. She recalled how when he'd finished, he'd helped her sit and patted her shoulder like one might pat a horse, with consolation for being the weaker beast.

And even without that procedure, her husband had explained, she couldn't have handled a baby, not physically, not mentally, not with her *unusual condition. It's best for you,* he'd say because he was always claiming to understand her body more than she did herself. He told her stories of Ida McKinley, the former president's wife, for whom pregnancy brought on headaches, convulsions, confusion, a brink from which even medicines could not retrieve her.

As Opal lay next to her husband at night, thirty, then forty, then fifty days after her last bleeding, she believed she might burst into a billion molecules. She'd written to Madame de Fleur in France, and two weeks later she'd heard back. She hid the letter among the canned vegetables in the cellar so Jagr wouldn't find it, and each time he left to see a patient, she took secret pleasure in reading and rereading the woman's words.

Dear Opal,

The mystics say the wise men followed a comet, not a star, to Bethlehem, to that miraculous baby conceived by spirit. I am no mystic; I am a medium, a listener. It's clear now—from that voice you heard—you are a listener, too. Remember when I told you that you had it in you, this gift? That last night I saw you? By the river?

You asked me if I believe you. I do. You asked me what to do. I cannot tell you. In France they understand people like us. I know a man here with a Spirit Machine. When he connects the machine to a spiritist, a ghost becomes, in a way, incarnate. The Spirit Machine could tell us—you—more about this baby's origin. It may provide some comfort to know what you're saving, or who.

—Madame de Fleur

The owl outside Opal's window had hooted a melancholy tune: *Who? Who? Who?* Who was Opal to think such thoughts? She listened for that voice again. Already, she began to feel unfamiliar to herself. It scared her to want something this much.

Opal imagined wiping excrement from a bare bottom or holding a crying child to her breast like a farm beast. She'd helped Jagr birth foals and piglets; a mare had recently died; a neighbor, too. She knew there'd be pain. And risk. Jagr had declared her sterile, and yet now she was pregnant. She didn't have to be a seer to know how her own life would unfold if she stayed, what Jagr would force her to do with her baby.

A buzzer sounded from the foreman's platform, the release signal for a break, and the workers on the factory floor set down their materials. The foreman held a megaphone to his lips. "Earthshine Girls," his voice boomed. "Return to your stations. We'll be taking our break later than usual." His voice sounded different, stern but less insulting. A collective groan from the floor, but then two men appeared from behind the foreman, and Opal understood the delay. The owner had finally arrived.

Opal recognized Charles Tuttle from his picture in the paper. He was the kind of man who could be handsome if one squinted. He dressed smartly in a suit and vest. His features were strong but mixed up and slightly out of place: his eyes set too close together, his nose a bit too dramatically sloped.

Behind him stood a pole of a man with a camera strung around his neck. Opal bent down to obscure her face when he raised his camera and snapped the photograph. When she stood back up, the smoke from his flash hung in the air. It wasn't until the men walked down the stairwell that Opal saw the woman standing on the platform above, appearing to have materialized where flash smoke disappeared.

The woman wasn't beautiful so much as she commanded the very idea of beauty: manicured hands, rouged lips, brows that had been plucked and shaped into perfect arches. Her hair was parted in the middle, pulled back on the sides by two barrettes. She wore a walking suit with two rows of buttons that reminded Opal of a soldier's jacket. Her skin was smooth, new, though not new. She wasn't young, so much as she was not old. Like Opal herself.

Bertie Tuttle.

Opal recognized her from the papers, too.

Dixie Ellison had reported that Tuttle's first wife died unexpectedly from influenza. But, then, just as quickly, Tuttle wed again, the daughter of an heiress. His mourning suit molted into a matrimonial costume. His first marriage was born of love, his second of aspiration.

Two years ago, when Albert Bremen, Bertie's father, passed away, he bequeathed Earthshine Soaps to his son-in-law. To Bertie, his only child and namesake, he left a sizable trust, accessible to her only after she bore an heir.

Dixie Ellison had declared Bertie a *wife of fortune and convenience*. And, yet, Dixie's column had described Bertie as barren. If Bertie's field was barren, Opal's was fertile, tilled, planted. She traced the arc of her stomach bracing against her maternity corset. Her belly was firm where it had once been soft; she could not help but touch it.

Bertie Tuttle descended the stairs slowly. Opal heard the padding of her boots on metal. When she finally came to stand on the factory floor, all the girls halted their work and gave her audience.

Even the factory dog greeted her. Nobody knew where Sudsy came from, only that he begged for scraps in the lunchroom. He was a cross between a Saint Bernard and something mangy, and someone had tied a small brandy barrel around his neck. Bertie bent to pet him. Even in bending she demonstrated good posture, her shoulders a perfect square. One of the girls apologetically pulled the dog by the collar.

"Oh, he's all right. I like an eager fellow," Bertie said, straightening, and everyone laughed.

"Hurry along, Mrs. Tuttle," her husband hollered from where he stood across the room, showing the newsman the soap-stamping machine that pressed the Earthshine mark onto each soap cake.

Bertie straightened and smoothed her skirt, then she scanned the girls standing on the factory floor. Their work slowed but did not stop completely. She let her eyes fall on Opal, then she tilted her head as though to ask: *Do I recognize you?* She walked to Opal's station and stood directly in front of her. "What a beautiful necklace," she said. "I've never seen a stone like that."

"Moonstone," said Opal.

She looked as though she might reach out to touch it, but then she stopped herself. "Striking. It catches the light. Like an opal," Bertie said.

There it was, her name in plain sight, like a box had been unlatched and a forbidden object tumbled out. Opal's knees felt weak for a moment, all water and no bone.

Madame de Fleur had explained the ancient Greeks named moonstone Aphroselene, after Aphrodite and Selene, the goddesses of love and the moon. She said the stone had the power to draw two people together under the correct celestial conditions. She said this as she fastened the jewelry around Opal's neck, a gift.

"Like the moon," Opal said to Bertie.

"Perhaps my great-grandfather should have named the soap Moonshine and bragged of its intoxicating quality," Bertie said, and here she reached out her finger and touched the stone.

After all that would happen—all that people accused her of—it would be this moment Opal held in her memory long after, Bertie Tuttle standing like a gasp of air on the factory floor, her finger delicately pressing the moonstone like it was a button on one of the factory machines. In the moments right before her death, Opal would think of the way Bertie's eyes connected with hers and how she saw in them something she recognized: a woman stuffed inside another woman, a human nesting doll.

Soon, the moment ended. Bertie moved along. Charles Tuttle posed for some photographs in front of the bricked furnace, in front of the giant conveyor motor that resembled a whiskey barrel, in front of the rubber pullies that stretched to the machines that hung tenuously from the rafters. Finally, Tuttle led the newspaper man toward the narrow back hallway and into the mixing room with the large vats the more senior girls stirred with paddles.

Bertie wove herself in that direction, strolling with her arms behind her back, like one does at a museum to convey she has no intention of touching. For seventy-five years the factory had belonged to her family, and had she been born a boy, the factory would have belonged to her, too, her destiny thwarted the instant the midwife checked between her legs.

Bertie stopped near one of the windows and tried to open it, but the glass had been painted shut. From where she stood, Opal knew she could see the entire basin. The city squeezed itself between the Ohio River and the hills that sat above it like a shelf. Porkopolis, the city had been nicknamed long ago. Cincinnati was famous for its hills, for its pigs, for its steamboats and carriage manufacturers and breweries. It was a thick-aired, industrious city, a welcoming one, full of merchants and immigrants, full of people with dreams of new lives. People like Opal herself.

"Ladies," Bertie said. She turned from the window to face the factory floor. She fanned herself with a gloved hand because the air was hot as summer, though it was only the first day of February. Fans overhead accomplished little but plowing heat from one side of the room to another. "My father considered himself a supporter of . . ." She trailed off. Something in her startled. She gazed to her left, to where a row of small boilers lined the wall.

That's when that sound entered Opal's field of awareness again. Tick. Tick. Tick. The metronome changed speed, increasing in tempo and volume, and she finally recognized what she was hearing: not a jammed machine or a pipe being repaired. No, a boiler on the verge of overheating.

The foreman recognized this, too. He sounded his buzzer. "Back," he yelled into his megaphone. "Everyone, back. Now!"

The explosion itself was small. Still, the force of it knocked Opal to the ground and dislodged the fan from the rafters until it hung by a single wire. She placed her hands protectively over her stomach. The machinery came to a sudden halt, and the factory was quiet for a moment, so quiet Opal could hear her own breathing.

Then, chaos.

Some women fled toward the exit door—the one that was usually left propped open because it locked from the outside—but it was shut. Next, the panicked pounding of fists on the windows, and when that didn't work, some began hurling soap cakes against the glass to break it. The fire grew teethy orange, then another small explosion. The foreman pleaded for calm before he and a group of machinists created an assembly line of water buckets. It took only a few minutes for the men to put out the fire.

After the flames were safely extinguished, Charles Tuttle ran onto the floor, followed by the newspaper man whose camera smoke did little to bring comfort to the scene.

"Darling, I thought you were behind me," Tuttle said to his wife. From the way he said *darling*, one would not suspect he was the kind of man capable of an affair like Dixie had been reporting, but some men are like that: the more outwardly amorous they appear, the more likely they are to be hiding poor behavior. Jagr had been that way, too, always touching Opal in public, always staking his claim. Opal leaned against her station to steady herself. She hugged her middle. She was okay.

Bertie sat on the floor, her back to the wall, her knees tucked up to her chin. Her husband held out his hand. She stood and dusted her skirt. "I'm fine," she said, and then to the newspaper man: "My father used to inspect the machinery himself. Weekly."

"Broken gauge, I suspect," the foreman said. "More bang than flash, luckily. I'll see to its repair." He cleared his throat.

"Does this happen frequently?" the newspaper man asked. He held his pencil to his notebook.

Tuttle took him by the elbow and directed him toward the exit. He nodded to the window that'd been shattered, introducing cool air to the factory for the first time in years. "Modern-day air-conditioning," he said. Then he slapped the newspaper man's back and ushered him out before any more photographs could be taken.

The foreman called for an early dismissal.

Shaken, Opal collected her lunch pail, and that's when she heard the whimpering. It was Betsy, the girl who normally sat two stations away. Her whole body was a tight tendril folded in on itself. She writhed on the ground, moaning.

Maria squatted next to her and helped her to sit. Betsy's breathing was ragged. A burn braised her arm.

"She needs a doctor!" Maria yelled.

"No—my husband would kill me," Betsy said. Like the rest of them, she probably couldn't afford one. She had dark hair cut bluntly across her forehead and the tips of her teeth were browned like cotton balls dipped in cod oil. Opal had heard a rumor that Betsy had once gotten pregnant by a soldier who'd fought in the Boxer Rebellion, but she'd never spoke of that child, and now she was newly married and pregnant.

She curled her body over her wound again. She whimpered, and Opal couldn't bear it, the sound of the girl in pain when she knew she could do something to help. From Jagr, Opal had gained some training: She could dry herbs and seeds, and decoct leaves to extract their oils. She could measure milk of licorice or baking soda on the balance scale and add it to the powders he'd compounded. On a few occasions, she assisted him with emergency procedures—farm accidents, hunting wounds—threading catgut sutures like shoelaces.

She found a mason jar and gathered some ash from one of the stoves. From a barrel she poured some lard, then added sawdust from the woodpile. Opal reached down her dress and unraveled the bandage from around her breasts, which released them with an ache. Then she knelt beside Betsy.

By now, the wound was white as bone and angry around the edges.

"I shouldn't have been standing so close," said Betsy. "I should have noticed."

"It's the boiler's fault," said Maria, who knelt behind Opal.

"It's Tuttle's fault," said another worker, and several others nodded in agreement.

Opal took Betsy's arm. She applied the poultice with a gentle touch, then she wrapped the bandage as she'd seen Jagr do: twice around the wound, then spiraling up and down the arm to secure it.

"Are you a nurse?" Betsy asked.

Opal shook her head.

"A midwife?" Maria asked.

"Then how'd you know what to do?" Betsy clutched her arm.

It was foolish of Opal to bring attention to herself like this. She couldn't very well tell Betsy the truth: her husband was a doctor, but now her husband was dead—murdered, that's what the papers had said. The headlines had read like a gauzy dream. *Husband not expected to live. Wife on the run.* When she'd read the articles, it was like reading about someone else completely. Someone dangerous. A woman gone mad. Authorities claimed to be seeking all leads.

Opal felt the eyes of the Earthshine Girls press upon her. She touched her stomach for a moment, but quickly pulled her hand away. *Cautiously alert.*

"Who are you anyway?" Maria asked. All the women turned toward Opal now. In their white uniforms they looked like something of a militia that might mobilize against her at any moment.

How could she explain she'd been an ordinary wife until she waded into the river and heard a voice? How could she tell them she was pregnant with a baby from the Other Side? How could they possibly understand all this when she didn't fully understand it herself?

"I'm just an Earthshine Girl," she managed. For a moment, she couldn't breathe. Then Betsy emitted a small, birdlike peep, and promptly passed out from the pain.

January 4, 1986

Interview with Jane Doe No. 2

By *The Cincinnati Inquisitor*

CI: What drew you to Earthshine Soap?

JANE DOE NO. 2: I swore by Earthshine Soap. There's nothing else like it, really. When it came out in the 1950s—the "new and improved" formula in that yellow canister with the girl's face—I was a kid. I loved their commercials, especially the one with the Earthshine Girl as that secretary who saves her boss from ring around the collar. She sings to the tune of that children's song. [Sings] *Ring around the collar, the dirt will make him holler. Earthshine. Earthshine. The clean you need.*

CI: Did you feel misled by those advertisements?

JANE DOE NO. 2: Looking back now, that commercial seems to be saying she needed to clean her boss's shirt so he wouldn't yell at her anymore. But I'm not one to be fooled by advertisements. Earthshine really worked. My goodness, I used to have to scour grime all day to get the same effect. And I used it on everything: in the bathrooms and kitchen, on wood and glass. I sprinkled it on my carpets. I added a quarter cup to every load of laundry, and it got out even the most hard-set stains. And my hands—they felt so soft after I used it. They say you can take a bath in it, but I never did. Earthshine really was some kind of magic.

CI: Now you sound like an advertisement.

JANE DOE NO. 2: [Sings] *The clean you need.* [Laughs.] I miss it. I do.

CI: But then something changed for you, correct?

JANE DOE NO. 2: Yes. I started to notice things—abnormalities, you could say. Pain. Mood swings. Increased appetite. My periods got longer and longer, but my cycle got shorter and shorter. And when it was my time of the month, I just felt so . . . pent-up. Frustrated. Like I might burst out of my skin. Like I was angry about something but I didn't know what. But then all that stopped, just like that [snaps fingers]. I'm not a young woman anymore, but I'm not old. I know the body changes. But I believe it was the soap. I used it for years. I used it on everything.

CI: Why didn't you come forward sooner?

JANE DOE NO. 2: [Pause.] Because for a long time, I didn't realize anything was wrong.

1986

Freshness, charm—the Enticement of Skin More Precious than Personality or Cleverness—do you seek it?

—PALMOLIVE SOAP

Stella had been beneath the ground a week now. Nobody heard her cries or the frantic banging from the casket six feet under.

I began to manifest Stella's stress in my own life. Taphephobia: the fear of being buried alive. At work, as I walked from the parking lot to the studio, my senses were assaulted by the flash of bulbs, news cameras, and boom mics pointed down in my direction. "The Earthshine Girl!" someone shouted. A circle began to form around me, so I turned backward, toward the stairs, but I snagged my heel. I tripped and nearly fell.

"Easy, there." He grabbed my elbow and pulled me up, then spun me around. John Dale Fox from Action 13 News. He had on a blazer over a turtleneck, the same outfit he wore when I'd met him six months ago during a gig my agent found for me hosting a fund drive. Now he handed me a business card, slipped between his two fingers. "Give me the first interview. Please. Can I call you?"

"Like last time?" I said.

"It won't be like last time, I promise," he said.

"I don't know anything about those women."

"You know what they're saying," he said. "*Alleging.*"

"Earthshine Girl!" someone yelled again now, and a woman emerged from the crowd. She was one of the handful of protesters I'd seen near the factory entrance in the mornings as I made my way to the studio—another bored housewife, I assumed, looking to attach herself to a cause. The woman wore braids and a yellow visor, the color of the Earthshine canister, even though it was early and the sun wasn't yet out. "Do you feel responsible at all?" She toted a camera—not a news camera but a personal camcorder, a bulky contraption strapped across her chest and connected to a box with coil wire.

I was a kid, I wanted to say, but then I saw a blur of white before I felt it: the pelt of the egg that slid down my coat and dripped onto my shoe.

Can you be buried alive without ever being put underground?

I hadn't heard from Wyatt in six days, the longest we'd gone without speaking.

I hadn't told him yet about how I'd seen a doctor again, for the bleeding that started a couple months ago, like a period without a period, more like a comma or an ellipsis. In the exam room, I'd shivered in my paper gown. Why are doctors' offices always so cold when they know we disrobe? The fluorescent lights flickered overhead. The doctor had an ink splotch birthmark on his face, and though I'd already filled out the office forms and narrated my symptoms to the attending nurse, the doctor read through my chart and asked, "How are you doing today?" and out of habit I responded, "Good! How are you?"

He sat on his stool and swiveled toward me. "But maybe you aren't so good."

"No," I admitted. "Maybe not."

He flipped through the pages on his clipboard, and he read to himself. "History of . . . uh-huh. I remember."

What a story my uterus could tell. It would explain how Wyatt and I tried for a family for years. How he switched from tighty-whities to boxers after reading an article in *Popular Science* hypothesizing that cooler balls lead to stronger sperm. How, soon, it was tests and shots and procedures and doctors telling us when to have sex, or when not to. Recovery periods and waiting periods and fertile periods, then monthly periods. Then nothing, followed by excitement, followed by something worse than nothing, a something that was not a baby, but a painful whooshing of blood that felt like a punishment for my attempts to have a baby in the first place.

The doctor called for a nurse, who entered then stood by the door, bored. He asked me to lie back. I put my feet up in the plastic stirrups. "Now let's hear your body talk," the doctor said.

"That's an Olivia Newton-John song," I said.

"What?"

"Scooch forward," the nurse instructed. "Till your bottom touches the end of the table."

The doctor pressed my abdomen, and I felt pressure, a stitchy pain, then the familiar warmth of blood as he slid his fingers inside me.

"Sorry," I said. He peeled off his gloves and dropped them in the biohazard bin, and then he scrubbed his hands so vigorously as to insult me.

After the first miscarriage, Wyatt had gone out to get lunch to save me the pain of seeing him cry. I knew this because when he arrived home his eyes were bloodshot, and he was holding a pastrami sandwich out like an offering. I couldn't eat it. I could see the pain in Wyatt's eyes, and yet a small part of me resented that, too, that pain of his that wanted equal recognition, his need to suddenly do something useful and the best he could do was pastrami. Besides, pregnant women are told to avoid lunch meat altogether for fear of trichinosis, so that sandwich seemed further insult.

Wyatt hadn't dealt with the blood. The blood that soaked through pads more quickly than I could change them, the clots reminding me of cherry jam that I would never eat again, blood-soaked tampons that looked like gruesome mice I held by the tail, the blood that made me feel like this was an injury from which I would never recover. I would never recover, but I'd also never speak of it, never again. Not to Wyatt and not to anyone else, not even when it happened a second time, then a third.

The doctor left. The lights dimmed. I was lying on my back, naked from the waist down. A technician pressed a wand to my stomach. The screen looked like a weather radar. The technician called for the nurse. They pointed and nodded. I watched their expressions, their eyes scrutinizing what was there, a body reduced to its most functional components.

Once, in my Stage Presence class, the teacher squirted his students in the face with water from spray bottles as he yelled insults at us. The goal was to remain unflinching. We were supposed to imagine ourselves a mountain and chant: *I am made of stone.* I can still imagine the needling spray on my forehead. The purpose of the exercise was to show how a good actor can divide her body from her mind, separate emotions from experience, and, in this way, open herself to the possibility of containing someone else.

I decided I would be stone. I would be Stella in that box beneath the ground.

When I got home, it was late. The moon sat fat in the sky. I could see it out my bathroom window as I stood practicing my lines in the mirror. "Can anyone hear me? I'm coming!" On *Stars and Shadows,* Vincent Glass proposed to Celeste, but then she'd caught the mysterious disease that Stella had ostensibly died from, only her cure didn't work because Bianca Dupont had swapped out the vial of medicine for something vague and sinister. Somehow, from beneath the ground, Stella knew all this. The script called for me to paw at the fabric lining of the casket while the camera cut to Bianca Dupont cackling.

In her last scene Stella managed to use her dagger-shaped necklace, a parting gift from the people of the island nation of Notelddim Trop, to break through the coffin and to begin digging her way up, up, up. I tried the line again, this time channeling Stella's desperation, her determination, too.

In the mirror I was framed by the shower curtain Wyatt had picked out—white with navy blue stripes. It looked vaguely nautical, and I never told him I didn't like it. Now, I imagined I was on a boat in choppy waters, adrift at sea with nobody to save me. "Can anyone hear me? I'm coming."

Melodrama is a legitimate technique in soap operas. Characters say exactly what they mean, and there's beauty in that, in speaking so directly. In real life, this rarely happens. I couldn't just call Wyatt up and say: *I'm confused about what we are to each other*. I couldn't just ask: *Should we fix this marriage or abandon it?*

Maybe I didn't want to know the answer.

In my bedroom, I dialed Wyatt's number. It rang three times before his answering machine picked up.

The last time I saw Wyatt we made love in his new apartment. I called it making love, but maybe it was just sex. To be honest, I'm not sure I know the difference. I imagine lovemaking means you're in love, and this wasn't quite that, more like we were staking claim to something we believed to be ours. Breaking up is a series of goodbyes, and sex just another farewell. He was using our old pie chest as a dresser. I could see bulbs of his rolled-up socks through the glass. He'd brought all his plants from home, the ones he kept in our sunroom, and now they were squeezed onto the ledge by the bay window. He used to feed his plants his hair clippings, saying the nitrogen and phosphorus acted as fertilizer, and I used to love that about him—that he never wasted a thing, not even his hair. I thought about what it felt like to have his mouth pressed against my own, and about desire, and about how petty sex can seem, in light of everything.

Now I stood in my bedroom and scrutinized my body in the

full-length mirror. At forty, my breasts sagged. I cupped them and pushed them up. I sucked in my stomach. I tried to imagine my body as a lover might. I had fine lines around my eyes, despite the mud masks and oils and serums I frequently applied. When my scenes called for close-ups, Elliot directed the cameraman to use a special filter to soften my image.

The moment I turned off the bedside lamp the phone rang. It was past eleven o'clock—too late for a casual call. "Wyatt?" I said when I picked up. Nothing at first, just some breathing.

"Halley . . ." Charlie's voice.

"Charlie. This is Nona," I said. "Wrong number."

"No, no," he said. His voice sounded thick, filmed with mucus. "It's Halley," he said. He cleared his throat.

"Is she okay?" I asked. I turned on the light. I'd promised her I'd stop by after work one day this week, but I hadn't yet.

"No," he said. "No, she's not."

"What is it?"

"Nona, she's gone."

"Gone where?" I asked. Halley had run away before, had turned up in all sorts of places: rehab, police stations, Reno, West Virginia. Once Charlie flew to Paris to retrieve her.

Charlie didn't say a word, just sat on the other end sniffling. That's when I knew.

"No," I said. "Are you serious?"

"Why would I—"

"Are you sure?"

"I'm sure."

"How?" It's the first question we ask in the face of death, as though the manner of death matters, as though we aren't all born marching toward our end. But my mind couldn't quite grasp what I was hearing. I wanted details, proof.

"Drugs," he said. "Pills. Booze, probably, too. She left a note. I'm still learning the details." We held the line quietly for thirty seconds or thirty minutes. The whole world felt small, like it could fit through the tiny holes in the phone receiver. Or maybe I was the one who felt small, already perceiving the cosmic shift in my world and my way of knowing it.

"I could have done more for her," he finally said. "She kept saying the comet was a sign, that everything was connected. She claimed Bertie had it out for her. She and Bertie never saw eye to eye—you know that. She had become more erratic, fanatical, but I never thought . . ." His voice cracked.

"Charlie," I said. I didn't know what else to say. I took a few breaths to control my emotions, like I'd been taught at the conservatory. *I am made of stone.* I tried to think of what you're supposed to say at times like these and how they're called *times like these.* I felt an ache in my rib cage, so I pretended I was in scene. *I am Stella.* What would she say, I asked myself, but then I felt stupid for even thinking that. Then I returned to myself. "You did a lot," I said to Charlie. The receiver was wet with my breath.

"Not enough." He sniffled. "She'd gotten worse. After that rehab stint in Paris, we thought she was better, but she got worse. Maybe it was my fault for not being there when she was young. Did she think I was a good father?"

"Of course, Charlie," I said. "Don't even ask that." But I was already asking myself: *Had I been a good friend?* If I'd stopped by when she'd asked me, we'd have sat on her couch together, and she'd have played an old record, and I'd have held her hand as she told me whatever she'd wanted to say. Halley always laughed when she cried because she felt stupid, so it was difficult to discern which emotion she was actually expressing.

We always make death about ourselves, don't we? We paralyze ourselves with what-ifs. What if I had gone to her apartment like I told her I would? She wanted to talk, but she refused to have a conversation on the phone. She claimed it wasn't safe, but Halley could be dramatic sometimes. We called her eccentric to explain away what we didn't want to see.

Once, she took me to a farm a few miles outside Cincinnati. *If you understand what I'm saying, Bessie, then blink!* The cow had dewy round eyes and a piece of cud hanging from her mouth. Halley was a vegetarian because she believed one day we'd be able to communicate with animals, and she'd written a song about it called "Cowgirl." Finally, the wind shifted, and the animal's lids closed against the cold. *Didn't I tell you?*

Halley saw things others didn't. That's who she was.

Was.

Halley was gone.

And she wasn't Stella. She couldn't come back from the dead. She couldn't suck water from a tree root, then slowly inch her way toward the light.

After I hung up with Charlie, I turned off the lamp and lay in my bed. I wanted to cry, but I couldn't. The tears wouldn't come. I thought of how, as a girl—before I was discovered—I wanted to be a ventriloquist. I'd seen the commercials for Tootsie Roll Fudge with Paul Winchell and his doll, named Jerry Mahoney. Paul was the comedian, but Jerry said all the best lines. My mother had asked me: *Have you ever seen a lady ventriloquist? You could be a teacher,* she said. *Or a nurse.* But I begged her for a doll like Jerry, and one day she relented and ordered me a *Boys' Life* booklet about ventriloquism.

The first step, according to the book, was to stare in the mirror, to smile while allowing your teeth to touch, to wiggle your tongue around in your mouth to get a feel for the space you can work with. Some sounds were easy to say through clenched teeth, but the trickier letters required deft substitutions, a *D* sound, for instance, in the place of a *B* sound, which, with practice, can trick the ear.

Doy. Doy. Doy. Boy. Boy. Boy.

I'd use my rag doll with a stitch of yarn for a mouth, but that missed the whole point. The trick was throwing the sound; while my mouth stayed shut, a puppet's mouth opened. Finally, my mother brought me home a dummy—a real one with a hinged jaw. She'd found it in the basement of a house she cleaned, and the woman said she'd planned to throw it away, so my mother could keep it. It didn't even bother me that the doll was someone else's trash. The paint on its face was chipped. I wrote my name along the spine. I called the doll Sal.

A girl who wants to throw her voice, to give it to Sal to deliver the best lines, strikes me as sad. Maybe we're always looking for someone who can say what we can't, what we're afraid to say. When I cleaned out my mom's old house after she'd died, I'd given Sal to Halley because she thought it was kitschy and she collected vintage things. For a while, she'd kept Sal on a shelf in her apartment and brought it down from time to time when I'd come over. We'd pass it back and forth between us, using the doll to admit our most private thoughts—secret longings or regrets. Our friendship had no room for judgment, but sometimes it was just easier to have someone else do the talking. If I had Sal again, I'd have the doll say this: *I let you down, Halley. I love you. I'm sorry.*

1910

Opal hugged her handbag to her body and slipped her fingers beneath the flap to check the contents. Inside, she grazed the edges of Jagr's formulary. It's not as though it would have disintegrated since she'd left her apartment. Still, she touched it carefully, like Eve must have first fingered that forbidden fruit. Jagr forbade her from handling his formulary, but now it seemed like the very thing that could set her free.

The sidewalks were slick from the flurries, and Opal hopped on the streetcar heading toward the market. When she'd first ridden the streetcar, the jerky mechanical brakes knocked her over, and she'd cried after that—that a simple ride could cause her such distress. She was learning to be alone in the world, to take care of herself. Now, she braced her legs and held tight to the strap above her, wrapping it around her wrist like a horse's rein. She thought of the stories Jagr had told her, of women who'd ridden on bare horsebacks to self-terminate pregnancies. Or of women who soaked in turpentine baths or used common household items like candles or curling irons.

Everywhere she still sensed Jagr. How to excise him from her mind? At cafés she'd study the menu, certain of what he'd choose. The bank teller had the same habit of licking the tip of his pen before dipping it into the inkpot. A stranger walked ahead of her on the sidewalk with the same long, loping strides. She feared the stranger would turn and it *would* be him, in the flesh, a ghost incarnate.

Impossible.

With her first paycheck, Opal had bought a new coat, a new dress, too, trimmed with black fringe and wide lapels that resembled the wings of a bat. *Widow's weeds,* the shop owner had called them. She wore these clothes now, swapped out for her uniform on her day off from the factory. The dark flowing fabric obscured her gravid form, made her appear, instead, like a woman who wrapped herself in her husband's absence. Invisible except for her sorrow. When she got off at her stop, a man tipped his hat toward her as though to say, *I'm sorry for your loss.*

Yet, in his absence she could think so much more clearly. Jagr's elixirs had muddied her mind. He'd always insisted she wear her hair drawn back, and sometimes he'd gather it in his hands and yank it when he had his way with her, pull it this way and that, as though her head were a planet meant to orbit him at will. She wore her hair short now; she'd cut it herself. When she caught a glimpse of her reflection in storefront glass, she hardly recognized the woman. Dare she admit she was beautiful? Some women grew more youthful when expecting, their features softening. But Opal's face was tight and angular, masculine if not for her otherwise feminine form, her large, rounded bosoms that ached as they were, pressed into her dress.

It was early yet, and the snow stopped, and Opal could hear the sounds of the city still waking: the café owners unlocking their gates, the rumbling of vendor carts, the streetcar squealing away in the distance. She, too, was waking. Unthawing, she liked to think. Reaching for spring. These days she found herself marveling at the golden outlines of the clouds or rubbing the fabric of her dress just for the pleasure of it. At night, she traced her body with her fingertips and lingered in the warmth of skin on skin, the possibility of it. Above her now, electrical lines crisscrossed like a cat's cradle. She stopped to buy a paper, and she admired the newsboy's hat, the color of marigolds gone brown. Then she walked on through Fountain Square.

The stone woman at the center of the fountain stood with her arms outstretched, water pouring from her hands. Her face was placid, on the verge of sadness, like she wished she could reveal something vital, like she reluctantly drained herself of water. The placard called her *The Genius of Water,* which suggested, at least, a certain self-awareness.

The reek of livestock and manure slid through the air as Opal reached Washington Park, and even that held a certain aliveness. Certain scents could trigger one of her episodes, but she did not hold her breath. *See?* she wanted to tell Jagr. She wasn't as helpless as he'd convinced her she was. *See? I'm taking in the world, and I'm fine. I'm just fine.*

At the entrance to the Court Street Market, notices directed farmers to the tunnels that ran beneath it, narrow pens that led the hogs toward the slaughterhouse. She made her way inside, through the crowd. Chickens hung one-legged from hooks. Sausages were strung from nails like holly. The stiffened trotters of quartered hogs pointed toward the ground. Opal hadn't the stomach for meat these days or the thought of cutting muscle with teeth. It amazed her how much the baby could make its preferences known, though she hadn't felt a quickening yet, not even when she stilled herself completely. Not even when she begged the baby for a sign, then felt foolish for doing so.

She continued on, past the stalls of cut flowers and spices and spooled fabric and wooden trinkets, until she found what she was looking for: a storefront on the other end of the market. The entry bell dinged as she opened the door.

Dowd's Drugs.

The pharmacy had a Grecian aesthetic. The counter that encircled the perimeter of the store was supported by large white columns, which reminded her of pictures she'd seen in a travel book. At the center of the pharmacy was another counter, lined with stools where Clara Dowd sat, taking stock in her ledger book.

Clara was a sparrow of a woman, somber clothing, soft, magnetic eyes, hair swept back as though by accident of both hairpin and wind. *She's more worried about the bottom line than the hemline,* Dixie Ellison had said of her. Well, the papers could be useful—give one a sense of things. Opal surveyed the cabinets filled with products: Dowd's Facial Cold Crème, Dowd's Tooth Powder, Dowd's Monthly Perfume.

"I understand you sell Swirling Spray," Opal said, leaning onto the counter. She felt for the formulary in her bag. Clara set down her pen. She looked toward the clock. It was half past eight. At that moment, a long-haired tabby cat jumped up on the counter and purred, and Opal let it nuzzle her hand.

"Canning!" Clara yelled toward the back. "Swirling Spray!" She pulled the cat down from the counter.

"Oh, I'm not looking to purchase any. I only saw the circular."

"Never mind, Canning!" she hollered. She resumed writing in her ledger book as Opal took a seat. "Swirling Spray's a useful product. An irrigation. Helps with uterine colic and nervous prostration, all sorts of feminine maladies."

"Maladies—that's why I'm here, in fact. I'm glad you mentioned it," Opal said. She set her handbag on the countertop. She unfastened the latch and took out the formulary.

Opal didn't know why she had taken Jagr's formulary. When she'd pulled it from his cabinet, it had fallen to the floor with a startling smack, and her whole body shot through with something electric. Her fingertips felt prickly. A body knows things before the brain can register what it might be. As she'd crouched down to pick up the gray notebook bound with twine, she understood it had value, even if she didn't know what that value might be. Now, out in the world, it could be worth something.

"I've a whole formulary of botanical medicines, American and foreign," Opal said. Just saying those words aloud felt wrong, information she should not have revealed. "I'm looking to sell them. Seventy-five formulas in all that treat everything from gastritis to consumption to—"

Clara held up her hand. "No need to go on. I'm not interested.

With everything the paper is saying about that comet, I have proposals coming out my ears. A cure for this. A remedy for that. Those scientists say the world is ending, and it's never been better for business." She walked to the back end of the store, swiped a finger along the tabletops to check for dust. Opal followed. Clara opened one of the cabinets and rearranged a few items on the shelf. She hollered again toward the back of the store: "Canning, please see to it that Mrs. Crandon's order is filled by nine sharp. She's sending her courier. Now," she said, turning back to Opal. "I do appreciate you thinking of me. But, as you can see, I am busy."

"Please," said Opal. She heard the desperate sound in her voice, and she hated it, but she *was* desperate, wasn't she? Her rent was due soon; her budget was tight; her weekly wages, which seemed sufficient at first, couldn't get her to France soon enough, even if she went without eating.

"Where did you get this formulary?" Clara asked. She studied her with suspicion.

"My husband . . . passed away." She'd never spoken this fact aloud, and now she wished she could take the words back, shove them back into her throat. She'd exposed herself so easily, and for what? For a silly book full of Jagr's scribbles.

Clara took note of Opal's dark clothing, and pity passed over her face. "I see." She leaned forward and softened her expression. "Why don't you leave your card with me. How does that sound? That's the Dowd way: We listen to every customer."

"I'm no customer," said Opal. Her voice cracked as she spoke, and she despised this weakness, her inability to contain herself.

Clara opened a cabinet and pulled down a small glass bottle sprayer. She set it on the counter. "Everyone is a potential customer, dear. Here, a complimentary sample."

"Swirling Spray?" Opal asked.

Clara shook her head. "Mourning perfume." She slid the bottle across the counter. "It helps with grief."

At home, Opal sprayed herself with the perfume. She smelled like grapefruit. She couldn't say she grieved, exactly, though she did feel something akin to grief. In her parlor she held the most recent letter from Madame de Fleur. By now, they'd developed a regular correspondence. Every time Opal had written the woman, she'd written back—but how slowly these envelopes traveled. Someday they should invent a telephone that spanned the ocean. Opal imagined the woman's voice traveling through the coils submerged in the dark of the sea.

She glided her fingers across the woman's handwriting, feeling the pen's indentations. Then she read as quickly as she could, devouring each line as though she'd been starved her whole life. And she had been, in a way:

Dearest Opal,

The scientists say Halley's Comet is already visible in some parts of the world. Can you see it there? They say when the Earth formed, gravity did not draw the comet to its center, that it orbits space, illuminated only by the sun. Do you know it emits no light of its own? You probably do, but I like the idea that an object in darkness can appear so illuminated by something else. That a ball of rock, from a distance, can look to be set on fire. In that way we can see the shape of it. We can know it.

I like to think we are scale models of the universe. I do not claim to be the sun. When I'm communing with the Other Side, I am myself, embodied by a self. Two people at once, two consciousnesses, two sets of desires, but only one body through which to experience it. This is my way of answering that question in your last letter. And your other questions: Did I really sense Oren that night? Do I really want you to come to France? Do I really know a man with a Spirit Machine? I'll answer now, and simply:

Yes.

I'm sure you read by now about that scientist, Camille Flammarion, who says the world will end May 19. He's French, you probably know. He says toxic gases from the comet's tail will impregnate the atmosphere and destroy the world as we know it. Snuff out life, he says. I don't believe in science. I trust my own senses. I think the comet will save us, not destroy us, in the end. And, anyway, I am not afraid of death.

—*M*

Opal thrilled at the woman's signature on the page, that *M*, the intimacy of it. An invitation, but to what? Beneath it, the woman had pressed her inky fingertip, the lines and whorls like a miniature galaxy. Opal fit her own fingerprint to the woman's. A universe. Then she lifted the paper to her nose. Even on top of her mourning perfume, she could smell cotton and musk.

For a moment, Opal thought she might die—and like *M* she was not afraid of death. She was not afraid at all.

1986

More Like Sisters! Be admired like your daughter for the radiant freshness of your skin.

—SWEETHEART TOILET SOAP

Halley believed in ghosts, but not the Holy One. Still, her funeral took place in a large church downtown. The chapel had vaulted ceilings and brass fixtures and pews, and I couldn't help but think how much Halley would hate it here, how ridiculous this all was.

I scanned the crowd for Wyatt, and I found him, seated an appropriate distance from the front. Of course he arrived early. I could just see him formulating some relationship-to-pew ratio in his head. He stood and hugged me, then we sat. He put his arm around my shoulder, and I nestled against him. He'd grown a beard, and he smelled like an aftershave I didn't recognize.

A large crucifix hung over the altar, with the muscular body of Jesus splayed out, the divot of his hip peeking above his loincloth, and I couldn't help thinking about Wyatt stepping out of the shower, a damp towel wrapped around his waist. What was wrong with me? I tried to think of something more appropriate, but I kept returning to how good it felt to be tucked into Wyatt's chest, how good it felt to be touched at all.

Van Morrison's "Into the Mystic" played over a speaker. Celeste Shadow—Samantha was her real name—paid her respects to Charlie. Halley never liked her, and out of loyalty, I didn't either. Now, the person in front of me began to sob. Wyatt squeezed my hand. Halley loved music, but I'd never known her to listen to Van Morrison. *Let your soul and spirit fly into the mystic.* I tried to conjure tears, but I still couldn't. I was worried I felt nothing—that I'd become numb to any feeling—but that wasn't quite it. I was thinking of all the people I knew who had died. My mom of cancer my first year at the conservatory. Wyatt's dad of a heart attack when we'd been married two years. Our baby who was born at twenty weeks, of *natural causes*. The baby was young enough to be called *still* and not *dead*. Halley was *still* now, too.

I recognized another Earthshine Girl in the pew diagonal from me. She looked like me, only younger. Same coffee-colored hair, same slope of the nose. Her name was Edith; she was the actress who'd replaced me in the commercials. In front of her was another replica of me, still younger. Janie. Round eyes, rounder cheeks than mine with dimples beneath each. She'd replaced Edith, once Edith began developing breasts.

In a row near the front, just behind Charlie, sat the current Earthshine Girl. I didn't know her name, though I'd recently passed her in the studio when production schedules overlapped, and she never acknowledged me or even seemed to know who I was. *You're me,* I always wanted to say to her. She had a gap between her teeth, freckles across the bridge of her nose—just like I had at that age. Now she wore a black ribbon tied in a bow atop her hair.

In front of me, a woman turned and whispered: "I see Vincent Glass! And Celeste Shadow!"

"Where's Bertie?" Wyatt whispered. I shrugged.

Bertie Tuttle's presence always announced itself by her security detail and, later in life, by her caretakers. It's rumored she'd received several death threats over the years, and security at the Tuttle mansion rivaled that of the White House: pats down upon arrival, cameras everywhere, a security guard scrutinizing television feeds of the mansion's hallways and entry points. *I have the right enemies,* she used to say proudly, which I understood to mean that any woman with power will eventually become a target in a world that wished she had none.

I raked my eyes across each pew, but she wasn't there.

This shouldn't have surprised me. Halley's relationship with Bertie had been strained for as long as I could remember. Once, on set when I was ten, we had hours to kill before call time, and Halley found me a robe and led me down the long hallway that connected the studio to the factory. She plucked a bobby pin from my hair.

"Hey!" I said. The hair and makeup lady always scolded me for messing with her art. Back then I didn't think hair could be art, but now I think anything can be, really.

"Shhh," she said, and she picked the lock and unlatched the door. Another series of hallways led us to the factory floor. We climbed some metal stairs and looked out. It seemed like a set from a sci-fi movie. Square steel contraptions burped and churned; conveyor belts zigzagged; the workers wore hairnets and masks and gloves and aprons. To my young eyes, they looked like menacing mad scientists.

"That's the machine that fills the canisters," Halley had said, pointing. The machine made a zapping sound, then a cylinder popped out onto a holding tray.

"Look," she said, pointing to a large machine that resembled a giant mixer, like the kind my mother kept on our counter because when she wasn't cleaning houses, she was baking pies and cakes to sell at church. When she was done mixing, she'd hand me a wire whisk and let me taste the batter, pretending to elicit my advice. *Need anything?* she'd ask. *More sugar,* I'd say. I always said that. At that moment, the giant machine bowl began to spin, and a tube carrying a white powder tilted to fill it. The whole factory burst into the scent of lavender. Halley held up her sleeve to her face, and I did the same.

"Smells awful," I said, "when you smell it all at once." My lungs felt dusty, the cage of my chest tightened. I understood now why the workers wore masks.

"Only she knows the formula."

"Your grandma?" I asked, but it felt strange to call Bertie anyone's grandma. She'd dined with Eleanor Roosevelt, sipped tea with Queen Elizabeth. She once took a flight with Amelia Earhart. There's a picture of it in *The Juggernaut*—the two of them behind the plane's propellers, holding them like oars. Sudsy sits at Bertie's feet.

"Locked in a safe in the basement," she said. "Right below the studio. Safe's as big as you. I've seen it myself." Halley gathered her hair in her hands and twisted it like a rag being wrung. "Now why would Bertie need a giant safe like that? I think something else is in there."

"Bodies?" I had asked.

"Secrets," she said.

Now the music in the chapel shifted to more formal, churchy sounds. The ceremony was beginning, and Bertie still hadn't arrived. By now, I knew she wouldn't. Everyone in the room grew quiet. Charlie sat in the front pew, joined on either side by his secretary and Mr. Longworth, the family lawyer. At seventy-six, Charlie still had a full head of hair, mostly gray, but with enough dark patches I could still remember what he looked like when I first met him.

Charlie didn't deliver a eulogy. What would he have said? That Halley was an addict? That she took her own life? Halley didn't have many obituary-worthy accomplishments—she never went to college or married or had children, though she had been arrested three times, and all three times Charlie was able to get the charges dropped. That was something. The minister offered vague and clichéd condolences. *She's free from suffering.*

Maybe good things can come from suffering. The whole point of life isn't to escape it but to use it, to turn it into something productive. There's a whole school of acting devoted to this. Buddhism, too.

After the service, Wyatt kissed my forehead and left. He promised he'd stop by after work. Every time we got together, he wanted to have sex, and I don't know why I was so agreeable, because afterward he left, and I felt worse.

There'd be no burial. In her note, Halley had requested her ashes be scattered in the French countryside. She said that's where she felt most at peace in her life, most herself, though she'd only been there twice. In the basement lobby, they'd set out a punch bowl and cookies on a banquet table. The floor was scuffed and the particleboard ceiling hung low, and I ate and drank my sadness until my tongue stung in punishment from all the sugar.

More sugar, I'd tell my mom again, if I could.

I gathered my coat from the rack, and Mr. Longworth spotted me from across the room. He held up a finger, motioning for me to wait.

"I was hoping to catch you," he said. "We need to talk."

Recently, Mr. Longworth had contacted me at the behest of Charlie about my marriage. He'd wanted to discuss marital property and a Case Management Plan. When I explained Wyatt and I were just taking a break, he warned me I needed to get out in front of it.

Now Mr. Longworth was wearing a suit with a pink handkerchief tucked into his breast pocket. He had a Tom Selleck mustache but not a Tom Selleck face. All lawyers look a little smug, and he was no exception. He jangled his keys. "Halley left something for you."

"For me?"

"For you."

"What?"

"I don't know," he said. "She had only three hundred and fifty dollars in her bank account though, so don't expect to be retiring anytime soon." He knocked back his punch. His mustache was wet. "I'll be in touch."

I waited long enough to say goodbye to Charlie, then I left. The winter wind chilled me as I walked to my car, up a hill so steep that it allowed me a perspective of the church where Halley's body still lay, of downtown in the distance. The city looked beautiful in the winter, like the backdrop of a movie: brick buildings and red church spires and the concrete dome of Union Terminal, which resembled a giant table clock. Art deco, I remembered my mother calling it, which I used to think was someone's name. The building was designed to honor the machine age—a sideways funnel, as the designers had conceived, a modern marvel—the largest half dome in the Western Hemisphere. It used to be a railroad station, but now investors were trying to turn it into a mall.

I unlocked my car, and I climbed in, and I closed the door. As an actress, I've been trained to contain my emotions, to conserve them for the necessary scenes. I turned off the stereo and snapped on my belt and pulled down the visor to look at myself in the mirror. I stared into my own tired eyes, as though it were a stone-face contest and I was daring this other woman to blink first. Then I smacked my cheek, hard. The sensation needled my skin, like the ice water I splashed on my face each morning. The woman in the mirror blinked. Finally, I allowed myself to cry.

Halley had left me something.

THAT HALLEY HAD A SAFE-DEPOSIT box struck me as odd, from the moment Mr. Longworth had called me with instructions. She didn't believe in institutions; she had a general distrust of authority. She despised cops and most any worker in a uniform, even the UPS guys. Once, she was kicked off a plane for accusing the flight attendant of putting nitrous oxide in the oxygen masks. Now, weeks after Christmas, the artificial tree was being removed from the lobby of First Star Bank, replaced with a toy telescope and a strand of twinkling lights. Someone had made a cardboard cutout of a comet, but it looked more a like a sperm descending upon an egg.

The woman who met me wasn't a banker but a secretary of some sort. Horsey face. Wool suit. I followed her to the vault room. Inside, there were no windows, only rows of metal boxes with keyholes for mouths.

The quiet made me uncomfortable. "Can you believe this weather?" I asked.

"Hopefully the groundhog sees his shadow this year," she said.

She pulled the rectangular box from the wall and led me through a door to an adjacent room with a single table, jarring fluorescent lights, a mirror on the wall. It looked like the kind of interview room you'd see in one of those cops-and-robbers shows. I'd once played a perp on one, and the director had told me to imagine the glass of the two-way mirror was like the mirror in *Snow White*. It revealed internal truths, our flaws, our fears.

The woman set down the box in the middle of the table. "I'll give you some privacy," she said.

When she left, I ran my hands along the smooth edges. Though Halley was part of the richest family in town, she had little herself, her family doling out her allowance like she was a child. Her apartment was spare: orange Aztec rug, plants everywhere, knickknacks from her travels, things like geodes and sand art.

When I lifted the lid of the box, I saw the manila envelope. I recognized Halley's handwriting on the outside. The contents felt heavy. *For you, Nona,* she'd written. I took a few stabilizing breaths. *I am made of stone.*

Life, unlike television, doesn't rely on tight camera angles, close-ups, or musical scores that draw emphasis to our plot points and tell us: Pay attention! We can only recognize important moments in hindsight, when we can finally freeze the screen in our memories and say that—there—was the moment that shifted the course of my entire life.

I broke the seal with my finger and opened the envelope.

Inside, the gray cover was stiff with age. I carefully pulled it out, unsure of what I was holding. An old notebook, bound with twine. The paper had yellowed and was crumbling at the edges. I unbound it.

The pages were lined blue, and the writing was small and neat and tight, from a time when people still cared about penmanship. The ink had faded with time. I thought it was a cookbook at first, except for the numbers that had been scratched out and recalculated, small math equations at the edges. Each page contained a list in compact rows. I recognized some words: turmeric and rosehip and cloves. Other names, like burdock and yarrow, sounded like cities out west. Formula no. 16 for appendicitis. Formula no. 28 for summer colds. Formula no. 37 for sterility. Formula no. 44 for *unusual episodes.*

When I turned to the final marked page, the photograph fell out, like Halley had been using it as a bookmark.

A photo of us.

In it, I still had the plump skin of my youth, a glow I didn't recognize. For a joke one Halloween, years after I was let go, I dressed up as the Earthshine Girl from that commercial where she's getting married. Halley had found a near-replica white dress, the kind that laced up with ribbon. I still had that dress at home, in a box in the basement.

Halley's costume was made of cardboard and Hula Hoops. She had her artist friend paint a rendering of the package. She's supposed to be a canister of Earthshine Soap. In the photo, we're holding both hands, like we're about to take vows. Wyatt had been with us that night, and some guy named Jerry or Jimmy that Halley was dating; you could see the back of his head in the photo, the little bull's-eye of a bald spot. Wyatt and I had been dating a couple of years at that point, but all you can see is his elbow and a swath of flannel he wore that night, saying he was Paul Bunyan. I felt homesick for that time.

I am made of stone. I am made of stone.

I saw a shadow pass behind the mirror. A minute later someone knocked on the door. The bank worker poked her head inside.

"A few more minutes," I said. She disappeared.

I flipped the photo over, thinking Halley may have written something there, but nothing. I examined the page the photo had held. The handwriting was looser and loopy, different from the rest of the pages.

At the top, no formula number or designation, only a name: Comet Pills.

Comet Pills sounded like something out of *The Twilight Zone.* I imagined a capsule with a tiny ball of light inside my intestines, like a Dexatrim, only brighter. Beneath the row of ingredients was a jumble of numbers and letters, equations I didn't understand.

I held the page up, closer to the ceiling light. Near the bottom edge, her name had made an impression deep enough I could feel the pen's grooves. The *O* and *D* were dramatically scrawled, and the cross of the *t* expanded the length of her name, like a strikethrough made in anger.

Opal Doucet.

I ran my fingers across the name, then I put the photo back in the book and the book back in the envelope.

Just a notebook, I told myself. Nothing sentimental, except Halley wanted me to have it. She loved antiquing and finding little treasures at garage sales and flea markets. Old hats and postcards; mannequin parts and books with funny titles; clocks and figurines. Last year for my birthday, she gave me salt and pepper shakers shaped like a Dutch man and woman that, if set together, appeared to be kissing. Halley believed she was saving these old objects, granting them second lives.

The bank worker led me out. She commented on the weather again, how Punxsutawney Phil would be brought to the White House to visit Reagan. She must have sensed my distraction. She'd probably seen this scene before: a grieving individual, a locked box. She held the door open with her body and said: "You never know what people find valuable, or what secrets they might leave behind." Looking back, it was the way she said it, the flinty sideways glance she gave me as she held the door open as I brushed past her, my purse now heavy with that notebook.

I kept my eye on my rearview mirror as I circled my way out of the parking garage, my headlights bouncing in slick puddles. It took me several moments to notice the dark sedan behind me, the kind with tinted windows to disguise important people, the kind the Tuttles hire. The car followed me to the highway, and in and out of traffic, and when I signaled to get off at my exit, that car signaled, too.

I thought about what an acting teacher had said about channeling anxiety into performative power. He told us to press our fingers together, to feel the pressure pulse on the tips. Many of my classmates went on to perform on the stages of New York or the screens of Hollywood, but I got married and stayed in Ohio, a word shaped like a tractor, if you look at it.

It's hard to be taken seriously as an artist in the middle of the country, an area more into the price of corn than aesthetics, an area where everyone is constantly apologizing. Have you ever been grocery shopping in the Midwest? It's a chorus of "opes" and "pardon me's" sung by people pushing carts full of ranch dressing and ground beef. It took me years to get through the grocery store without once uttering "I'm sorry" for the simple act of taking up space.

After the conservatory, my agent had suggested I box up all my old photos and tapes from my Earthshine days. She said I was acting the same part in all my auditions, suggested I "display my range" so I don't seem "trapped in the role." Agents are like therapists. They help you self-actualize, for a commission. Wyatt dragged the boxes of memorabilia to the basement. Afterward, he unwrapped a Klondike Bar for me because sugar was his way of being gentle.

My agent was right. Soon, I found better roles, no blockbuster hits, but gigs hosting pageants and bit parts on sit-coms, since my contract prohibited me from doing mass-market commercials. I landed a guest spot on *WKRP in Cincinnati*, the one time it was shot locally and not in a Hollywood studio. In that episode, Les Nessman wanted to compete with news helicopters, but all he could afford was a biplane, and I played the part of the copilot. I handed Les Nessman a clipboard. "All systems ready." That was my only line. I was listed as a "special guest."

My agent lobbied to keep my recurring role on *Stars and Shadows*, and I did medical informational videos for things like deviated septum surgery. *Do I still look like me?* I asked in one, my nose bound up in surgical tape.

Now I squeezed the steering wheel. I'd never filmed a chase scene. That car zigzagged behind me, in and out of traffic. I'd read too many scripts. I'd seen too many movies. Wyatt and I watched *Vanishing Point* in the theater on one of our first dates, and this wasn't quite that. Besides, nobody was behind me when I pulled into my driveway.

When I got out of the car, I noticed the mess. At first I assumed the toilet papering had been done by harmless teen vandals, but then I saw the sign hammered into my lawn. Heavy cardboard. Metal spikes. Yellow paint. Thick strokes.

EARTHSHINE BITCH, it read.

1910

After the boiler explosion, the factory had closed for two days and all the machines inspected and declared in good working condition. Now, however, the Earthshine Girls startled at every unfamiliar click or clang or hiss. Perhaps that's the reason Opal jolted when Maria shouted her name. The very utterance of it seemed dangerous.

"Opal Doucet—"

Maria pronounced her name like it was French. *Do-say,* she said, an invitation to speak, not *do-sit,* how Jagr said it, a command to find a chair. She had spotted Opal's full name on the foreman's clipboard.

"Opal Doucet," she said again, loud enough for others to hear. Earthshine Girls always spoke above the noise, and sometimes they found themselves shouting, even outside during breaks. "Can you hear me? I'm talking to you."

"Shh. Quiet down," Opal said. She leaned over her station, the crate beside her nearly full. She folded paper over the rectangle of soap, flipped it, and dabbed the ends with wax. Behind her, a machine worker banged on pipes, doing maintenance on the boilers. She didn't like the disruption of her work, the impact it'd have on her numbers. Workers who exceeded their quota received an extra dollar at the end of the month, and Opal was counting on it. She lifted another cake of soap from the table and dug her fingernail into it. She wrapped the soap, pleased that this tiny dent would make its way into someone's home, a secret sign of her existence. "I'll cover for you, if that's what you want."

"Not that—something else," Maria said.

Maria's cap rested far enough back on her head to reveal her dark hair and the powder she'd not rubbed in all the way. Strung around her neck on a simple chain was a silver ring, wide as a quarter, the accessory popular among the girls who'd lost their husbands.

"Then what?"

Maria's lips parted, and she stood there for a moment, on the verge of speaking. She twirled a cake of Earthshine, her hand moving like one of those mechanical trinkets Opal had seen at the shops near the river. "I know your secret," Maria said.

Opal didn't speak. Her whole body tightened. She eyed the exit. The machine workers' blowtorches sounded like wind.

"Did you hear me? I said I know your secret."

"I'm not deaf, you know."

The late afternoon light came in through the window slantwise and golden. Opal set down her work and began tidying her station. Her whole body vibrated, but she didn't make a sound. She stacked the papers. She capped the sealing wax. She swiped crumbles of yellow powder to the floor to be swept.

Your secret. She was dizzy with anticipation. Maria must have seen those papers. Her mouth felt dry, her tongue a thick swollen weight. She couldn't be sent back to Gallipolis as a criminal. And what would they do about the baby? *Her* baby.

"I've always thought there was something a little off about you. No offense. You don't talk much, eat your lunch alone, always rubbing that necklace of yours. Sometimes I seen you looking into the distance, your lips moving like you're talking to someone who ain't there. And when you helped Betsy, sitting on the floor there with her burn . . . I noticed . . . I figured it out."

Opal felt far away from her body, like her head was a balloon that'd floated up to the ceiling, and now she could observe herself down below. An *unusual episode.* In her apron and cap, she appeared indistinguishable from the other girls busy at their stations. But she'd always felt such distance between herself and others. Such difference.

Maybe Maria knew about Jagr. Or maybe Opal's uniform shift, tied high on her waist, hadn't obscured her middle well enough. How stupid of her to think she could fool anyone. She could walk out right now and leave. It was close enough to the end of the day that she wouldn't raise suspicions. She still had free will. She still had choices, hadn't she? She could go home and pack her things and still have time to take the evening train. But what good would free will do her then? She needed a job. She needed the money if she wanted to make it to France.

Maria stacked two crates and sat atop, her legs tucked beneath her. "My cousin in St. Louis, she told me about this doctor," she said. "He can see sickness inside people, just by touching them. My cousin's friend, she saw him once. She'd been lame all her life. He told her she had copper in her liver, or something, but he cleared her up. The spirits taught him. They tell him what to do. She walks better now. I thought it was all flimflam when my cousin told me." She rested her index finger inside that ring around her neck, as though it were a lever that might detach her head from her body.

"You've lost your husband," Opal said, trying to deflect the conversation, to appear casual despite her galloping nerves.

"Everyone knows that," Maria said. Her lips bent upward in a sad sort of way, compelled to smile, even though the occasion did not call for one, the habit of women trained from birth to be pleasant.

"There is such a thing as Mourning Spray," Opal began to say. "It smells like—"

"You're a spook—" Maria said.

"—grapefruit."

Now the wave of factory sounds receded. A pocket of quiet held the two of them.

"That's how you helped Betsy, isn't it? I've heard of people like you, but I've never met one," Maria finally said. "A spiritualist."

It took a moment for the word to take root in Opal's mind, then a lightness. She exhaled. She hadn't even realized she'd been holding her breath, but now she no longer felt dizzy. Not an *unusual episode* after all. Relief spread through her in the form of hunger. Her stomach growled. This was the secret Maria knew. Not about Jagr. Not about the baby.

A spiritualist.

She felt the urge to move wildly, but she didn't. She remained very still. In her mind, she already began composing her next letter to Madame de Fleur. *Maria sees it in me, too—this gift you say I have.* And didn't she have it? Hadn't she heard that voice? Hadn't she touched the Other Side? The baby was proof.

Madame de Fleur had told her that all bodies contained maps to the deepest reservoir of their souls. The body knows what our souls cannot speak. Opal remembered when Madame de Fleur pressed her forehead against Opal's, only that small table separating them. *Can you sense his presence?* the woman asked. With her forehead pressed against Madame de Fleur's she did sense *something*.

"I've been unwell," Maria continued, whispering. "But he says nothing is wrong with me."

"Who?"

"My doctor. I . . ." Maria started to say, then: "Oh, this is silly. I'm silly. You must think I'm a fool. It's just . . . at night, I can't sleep and my chest feels tight, like someone's sitting on me. I can't breathe, and when that happens, my heart starts pounding, and I want to escape, only I don't know to where because I am already home with my children. And I feel so helpless, so out of control, and . . ." Here she leaned in closer. Opal could feel the quickness of her breath. "When I wake up in the morning, I feel . . . I feel dread. I don't know how else to describe it, and I don't know what it is I'm dreading. I have plenty of good things in my life. Children, a job. I can feed them plenty. I know I should be grateful."

"Did your doctor tell you that?"

"And it's not just me. The others—Betsy, Gilly, Ruth—they've all said the same, like it's contagious or something. Mildred's family sent her away to Marietta to see a doctor who specializes in ennui. Can you believe it? A doctor who specializes in that?" She tapped her skull, as though pointing to something inside. Ennui, perhaps. "Maybe it's the comet," she said. "The paper said it can cause all types of unusual disturbances."

Opal had read in the papers that the comet had been blamed for avalanches, windstorms, hurricanes, even rheumatoid arthritis and migraine headaches from changes in barometric pressure. "I don't believe it," Opal said.

"You don't believe in science?" Maria asked. She stood and began organizing her workstation. She kept a small paintbrush in her apron pocket, and now she dusted the surface of the table with it.

"I think the comet will save us."

Maria asked how, but Opal didn't know.

When Maria finished dusting her own work surface, she helped Opal clear her own. "So— Are you like him? That doctor in St. Louis? The spiritualist?"

Save her, she'd heard a voice say that night in the river. She hadn't been able to tell if it was a man's or a woman's—but it was as clear as if she'd lifted a telephone receiver to her ear, as clear as when Alexander Graham Bell said those famous first words ever spoken with electricity: "Mr. Watson, Come here. I want to see you." A desire disguised as a command. A telephone requires two people to hold the line, but only one to speak.

"Yes," Opal said. "I am a spiritualist."

There, she'd named it.

The foreman's buzzer signaled the end of the shift. Opal brought her attention back to her station. It was noisy, hot. Maria stood to gather her things. The floor manager collected their crates and made some tick marks on a clipboard. Their numbers.

Only after the floor manager left did Maria speak again. "I'm not asking for anything free. I'll pay you for a cure."

Just last spring Jagr let Opal accompany him in the woods, collecting plants he'd place in his specimen cabinet. He knew how to evaluate each plant for the potential fructification; he knew which to cut with shears and which to dig out. He dug up the roots of a shrub and balanced it so gingerly, she thought it might be an injured bird. She'd never known him to be that gentle. Opal herself could recognize by sight many medicinal species: black haw, red clover, fringe tree, wild geranium, bloodroot. She knew which plants were useful for the flower, the root, or the seed. She'd seen sick people empty their pockets for one of Jagr's cures. He'd been a very good doctor.

"Tomorrow," Opal said. "At lunch. We'll sit. We'll have a little séance."

As she headed for home, Opal thought of a girl she once found on her porch, back in Gallipolis, when Jagr was away on a call. Her hair was red, and she couldn't have been older than sixteen, and Opal recognized her as one of her husband's patients who, like Opal, had been brought to him to cure her of her shame. The girl said nothing at first, just pointed. "Look," she said.

Opal turned in the direction the girl was facing. The barn would need painting in the spring. In the fields behind it, the wheat bent their heads. Jagr would be home soon. "Do you hurt?" Opal had asked. "Are you ill?"

"Look how lovely the moon is tonight. How I wish I could hold it in my hands."

Opal looked up to the sky and longed to see the beauty. The moon was a moon. When had Opal lost her sense of wonder? The stars once made her breathless. She could measure the vast expanse between them with her thumb and finger, capturing the distance of millions of miles with her very own hand.

"I need more medicine," the girl said, growing somber. She clutched her stomach, and when she caught Opal's arm to brace herself, Opal smelled something sweet and musty, like a wound.

When Jagr arrived home, the girl was sitting by the fire, mesmerized. The flames aimed upward, spindly fingers. Jagr pressed her abdomen. He checked her pulse. "The pain medicine. She's had too much of it," Jagr explained.

"Please. It's the only thing that helps," the girl said. "Without it, I'd . . . I'll do anything. I'll—" But Opal had cut her off before she could offer something she'd regret. Jagr sent the girl away. He discarded some pills in the compost bucket that he expected Opal to dump behind the woodshed. The formula needed reworking.

Afterward, Opal had opened the lid of the compost bucket. She allowed her fingers to sink past the peels of potatoes and rinds of squash, to the pills at the bottom of the container. She placed one on her tongue. She walked to the sink and ladled water into her mouth. And then she swallowed. An hour later, she looked up to the sky. The stars were staccato beats of light. The moon was a round, fat face grinning behind the trees. It wasn't a man at all. She stepped out on her front porch and studied the space between the stars. She thought of how these same stars held the memories of all life on the planet—that anyone who'd ever existed had seen this exact canopy overhead. Some of them were already dead. A pang of grief hit her, but it felt like ecstasy. Her longing became a kind of pleasure.

She's had too much of it, Jagr had said. But Opal thought: *I haven't had enough.*

THE LUNCHROOM WHERE OPAL AND Maria met the next day was a converted closet, narrow and windowless, only large enough to accommodate two long tables and some chairs. To access it, one must cross through the women's washroom, so the lunchroom was considered a private space, safe from the foreman and machinists who took their meals upstairs. Even so, most of the Earthshine Girls preferred eating their lunches near the benches out back, even in the winter, seeking a reprieve from the factory's heat.

Maria sat in the corner. Opal pulled out the chair across from her. At the other table three women leaned into one another, with an open newspaper among them.

At first Opal and Maria said nothing to each other. Maria's lunch pail sat on the table, untouched. Opal's stomach grumbled against her will, the baby begging for food.

The other women in the cafeteria folded up their paper, laughing; then they stood and left.

When they were alone, Opal reached for Maria's hand. The woman drew back. Light from the mantel lamp bounced on Maria's face. Opal hated electrical lights, how they hummed, how they assaulted her senses, making her eyeballs throb. She preferred the natural glow of fire, how it illuminated some things and cast shadows on others. How it demanded stillness in a world intent on constant motion. Maria lowered her eyes.

Human minds are trained to resist the unfamiliar, that's what Madame de Fleur had told her. But with time, one can grow accustomed to that which appears, at first, unnatural. It's a matter of gradients, the incremental arriving at a place of familiarity where doubters become devotees.

Opal now took Maria's hand. This time, she allowed it. How awkward to hold her hand, but how comfortable, too. How miraculous that human hands fit together by design, little pawed puzzles. Opal had not touched another person since she'd left Gallipolis, unless she counted the accidental brushing against shoulders at the market, which, she was loath to admit, provided her a pleasure so deep she felt ashamed.

Maria's hands were warm, dry like her own. She studied the texture of Maria's fingernails, the color of her palms, the visibility of blood vessels just beneath her skin—the way she'd seen Jagr do hundreds of times with his patients. Now, she clasped Maria's wrist and noted her pulse, how quickly she breathed, and the scent of her breath; she studied how frequently Maria blinked and whether her eyes looked glossy or her skin malnourished. Clairvoyance is, first, a study in observation.

"It's a bit like telephoning," Opal explained, how Madame de Fleur had explained it, the first time they sat together, the first time they held hands.

"And you are the operator?"

"I am the telephone box."

Opal allowed her body to relax, to simply be. Now, across from Maria, she hummed and felt the vibrations spread from her lips, down her body and out through her limbs. She blanked her mind. She thought of Madame de Fleur, the arch of her neck, the lines of her jaw—*I am myself, embodied by a self. Two people at once, two consciousnesses, two sets of desires, but only one body through which to experience it.* When Madame de Fleur sat in séance, she spoke in a deeper register than her natural voice. Her lips formed a shape that, if traced by her finger, would be a perfect O. In that moment, Opal felt something—a tug at her mind, like a piece of thread that snagged on a knot. The room warmed and cooled in equal measure. "Someone's come through," Opal said. She pitched her voice deeper now; she made a circle of her lips.

Maria gasped. How simple it all was, really. Opal imagined a body climbing into her own, limb by limb, like her skin was a suit someone else could pull on. She contained. She was contained.

She listened for a voice, but all she could hear was a distant sound, a radio out of tune—static and a noise drowned out behind it.

Opal asked for a description of Maria's ailments. Maria again explained how she felt exhausted and she couldn't breathe and sometimes she felt like the walls of the factory, or her house, were closing in on her—and not just in her mind. When this happened, a kind of terror overcame her, like she needed to escape or like she was going to die, even if she knew she wouldn't. And what was worse? The dying or the feeling like she might? As she explained this, she looked like she might cry, but instead she smiled. "The problem is, nobody believes me, but look." She pulled back to reveal that her hands were shaking.

How many times had Opal tried to explain to Jagr what she felt, but he would never listen to her, instead wanting to characterize the experiences of her own body. *You're overtired,* he might say, for instance, if ever she dared to cry. Feelings were a symptom, not a disease. *Feelings,* he'd said, *cannot make you sick.*

"Do you know what's wrong with me? Can you fix it?" Maria's eyes were wet with anticipation and worry. "I have children. They have no one else. I can't be this way. I don't want to be."

Opal bit the inside of her cheek until she could taste blood. She had never been comfortable asking for what she needed. But now she had this baby, and she needed to get to France before she was born. Opal used that deeper voice as a mediator: "Fifty cents for a cure."

Maria nodded. Opal thought of how long she must stand on the floor to make a single dollar, how many crates of soap she'd need to fill. The women each had something the other wanted, and each was willing to make the trade.

That night, at home in the rooms she rented from a man who spoke mostly German, Opal removed Jagr's formulary from the cabinet where she kept it. She pressed it at its crease. How different the notebook looked here, in this city, in this light, his formulas written in his cramped, neat style. Jagr believed in precision and science, and so entire pages had been erased and rewritten with a meticulous hand.

There, in her small kitchen, by the light of two candles, she studied Jagr's formulary like her mother had once studied the Bible. Each formula was numbered and beneath the number he'd listed its uses. Insomnia. Fatigue. Heart disease. Nervousness. Sadness. Menstrual problems. Gout. Hysteria. Pain. The pages were annotated, describing his processes, his experiments, his mistakes. Formulas had been worked and reworked, each calculation neatly transcribed by his hand. He'd marked beneath each formula with his initials, so small it could have been a drip of ink.

She turned to the formula for *emotional disorders.* Hysteria, Jagr once said, is a social disease. He'd once treated an entire family of sisters—eight in total—who all suffered convulsions, but he could find nothing medically wrong with them. Jagr believed the mere suggestion of illness was enough to bring on symptoms in another. And symptoms are not always evidence of disease. Jagr had prescribed each convulsing sister two capsules a day. Soon after, their symptoms disappeared.

But what did Jagr know of emotional symptoms?

Opal began with Jagr's formula but then added to it the ingredients she'd known to work in such cases, ingredients she herself took for pain or unusual episodes, though minus the narcotics. She made a list: milk of licorice and common nettle. Motherwort and skullcap. Black cohosh and valerian root. Lavender and lemon balm. In the morning, she visited the medical botanist on Court Street. She scoured the fields just outside the city for familiar shrubs. And later, in her small kitchen, she filled pots and set them to boil. When she was done, she turned to a blank page in the formulary and recorded the ingredients, the measurements, her process.

A few days later, at her station on the floor of the Earthshine Factory, she interrupted her working rhythm—fold, flip, tuck—to pass the pills to Maria. She'd stored them in a scrubbed sardine tin. Maria pocketed them in her apron, then dropped a handful of coins into Opal's lunch pail.

"What do you call them?" Maria asked, opening the tin. She sniffed tentatively.

Opal hadn't considered naming the medicine until this very moment. Jagr had only ever used numbers to designate his cures. Now, she thought of Swirling Spray and Mourning Spray. She thought of the comet—Halley's Comet—named after the man who, knowing he'd not live to see it, first theorized this celestial object would return again, then again. She thought of Madame de Fleur's most recent letter: *I think the comet will save us, not destroy us, in the end.* It was the *in the end* that now seemed hopeful to Opal, the unspoken *in the beginning* behind it, the idea that something must be destroyed to be saved.

WOMEN HAVE A MODE OF distributing private information without newspapers or switchboards or telegrams. Mouth to ear, the old way. The girls at the Earthshine factory began whispering about Opal as they walked by her station to distribute empty crates or replenish her stacks of overwrap.

"What do they call you?" one girl had asked. Her name was Amanda Mahooney. She was young with plump skin, unmarred by age, and she sat a few rows back.

"They?"

"The other girls. When you sit with them. You know, your spiritualist name, like a stage name or something. Something with a little mystique." She didn't seem to be skeptical of Opal, but she was certainly no believer.

Of course she thought of *M* in this moment, of Madame de Fleur. She'd wondered if the *M* stood for Madame—or if it was her first initial. Mary, Martha, Maggie, Mabel. None of these seemed to fit.

"Madame Doucet," Opal said to Amanda. She pronounced it like Maria had—Do-Say. It sounded French.

Madame Doucet.

She sat with Betsy, next, in the lunchroom. As they conversed, Betsy flattened her bangs against her forehead. The burn on her arm had left a white scar that resembled a bicycle, two large circles connected by a bridge. She was pregnant after less than a year of marriage. Her stomach pushed against the fabric of her uniform dress like a small round of bread concealed in a sack. She twisted the bottom of her apron as she described how at night she cried, sobbed so hard it was like she was expelling something from her body. The sobbing and the darkness provided some sort of relief. On occasion her husband would wake and ask her what was wrong, and Betsy would tell him she was just so happy, so excited to become a mother, but it'd all been a lie. *I've been pregnant once before,* she whispered. *A soldier.*

Victoria felt on edge, nervous all the time. Ruth's anger manifested as an appetite, and she'd gained ten pounds the past six months alone, stuffing herself with any sugary treat she could find. Gilly sometimes experienced lethargy so deep, so penetrating she couldn't make it to work, and the foreman had given her a final warning. She said she'd lie there in her bed, her limbs heavy as tree branches, and a tree can't very well go to work. Pearl described herself as alternating between crushing anxiety and intense joy. Up and down and up and down. Some days she wanted to crawl out of her skin from terror. Other days she felt she might explode from the beauty of the world. She was exhausted by it. "I have nobody to talk to about this. Nobody to tell me if it's normal or not."

"And when did your symptoms start?" Opal asked. It was that deeper voice that asked it.

"Last year. Not long after I started working here."

"Have you reported it to the foreman?" Opal asked.

And to that, Pearl doubled forward and laughed and laughed.

There was an intimacy to it all—the holding of hands, the whispering, the way their voices fused as they hummed. In the cave-like lunchroom, they could speak candidly, say things one might not say aloud otherwise, tell the stories as though observing some oddity or curiosity apart from themselves. Back at their stations on the factory floor, the Earthshine Girls resumed their distance. Later, Opal would pass them the cure.

In the kitchen of her rented apartment, Opal opened a window and set a pot to boil. The tenant upstairs had complained of the smell, and her landlord had given her a warning. Three more and she'd be evicted. Opal hadn't a Bunsen burner or beakers or a pill press, so she made do with her stove and a casserole and some glassware. Steam from the boiling pans dampened her skin. When the concoction thickened, she strained it and let it cool. She'd been tinkering with the formula to improve upon it. An eighth of a gram more this. A fourth of a gram less that. Jagr's formulas continually evolved. Good medicine, he'd said, requires persistence and humility. Precision meets failure. Adjust accordingly. While she waited, she made the necessary notations in the formulary. Then, at the top of the page she wrote it out—not a number, like Jagr had assigned each formulation—but a name: Comet Pills.

January 15, 1986

Interview with Jane Doe No. 4

By *The Cincinnati Inquisitor*

CI: Describe your experience with Earthshine Soap.

JANE DOE NO. 4: I took to cleaning with Earthshine the way an alcoholic takes to drink. Not with a passion, but with a need. I thought I loved Earthshine Soap, but it wasn't love. My knees would dig into the linoleum. My arms would ache from working circles. My body hurt, but it felt good in a way, you know. All my friends complimented me on my apartment. *I should hire you!* they'd joke.

CI: Would you say the soap changed your life in any way?

JANE DOE NO. 4: The more I cleaned, the more I felt I needed to clean. Like a dopamine hit, only the high didn't last. Toilets. Sinks. Counters. Baseboards. I couldn't stand dirt. I scrubbed the damn walls. It was an addiction. I used to have dreams, aspirations. I used to think I'd be like Christa McAuliffe, that teacher going into space, you know? I used to think I'd be like the Earthshine Girl. She was adored by everyone. And I thought if I just made all the right choices—if I was good, and kept tidy, and worked hard, my life would click into place. But it never did.

As I got older, I started to have . . . urges. I'd think unclean thoughts. And whenever that happened, I bathed in Earthshine Soap, just like the Earthshine Girl does in that one commercial, the one where her dog jumps in the tub. I began to feel such emptiness, such melancholy. I was proud of my apartment, of the way I kept it. But I felt . . . I *believed* the only way to feel better was to hurt myself. And so I would [hurt myself].

CI: And what would you do?

JANE DOE NO. 4: [Silence]

CI: How do you know it was the soap?

JANE DOE NO. 4: What else could it be?

1986

> Another love-match shipwrecked . . .
> on the dangerous reef of half-truths
> about feminine hygiene.
>
> —LYSOL

We always look back to previous generations with smug self-satisfaction, because *we* know better. In 1910, we say now, it was ridiculous to think the poisonous tail of the comet would suffocate the Earth. Back then, experts—scientists, some of them—convinced themselves that the noxious gas—cyanogen—from the comet's tail would cause instant death to all who breathed it. The gas in the tail, as it turned out, was too diffuse to do harm. Follow the science, that's what we say today, as though science is static, as though science itself isn't limited by perspective.

Two weeks after Halley's funeral, I met Charlie for lunch. His secretary, Carol, made us a reservation at the Riverview, a revolving restaurant atop a hotel tower in Covington, Kentucky, just across the river from Cincinnati. I took the elevator to the top floor. The restaurant was a circular galley, and it rotated on a central axis—not quickly enough to make you sick; it wasn't an amusement ride.

Charlie stood when he saw me. Behind him was a view of the Ohio River, metal bridges that connected its two shores, high-rises that would look stumpy if compared to a larger city but from the Riverview appeared majestic. A barge floated up the river, and I remembered a field trip I'd taken to the public landing as a child. There they'd staged an old steamboat so we could see where passengers slept on the old Cincinnati Line, the one that sailed to the confluence of the Mississippi until it reached the Louisiana coast.

Charlie kissed my cheek, then hugged me tight, held me for a moment longer than I expected. He'd lost weight since I'd seen him last. He pulled back, then studied me, paused like he was trying to find the right words. "Let's sit," he said, finally.

We studied the menu in silence. We ordered coffee. By the time the saucers were set on the table, the steam rising from the cups in cursive shapes, Charlie spoke again.

"I've been going through her things," he said. A pause, like a swell of water between us. "I found some photos of the two of you. I'll have Carol send them."

"I'd like that," I said.

Charlie nodded. He took a deep breath. "I think I'll have the soup," he said.

Out the window, an American flag atop the Carew Tower whipped in the wind. Bertie had paid the city an undisclosed amount for permission to use the building in the opening and closing credits of *Stars and Shadows*.

Charlie stirred sugar into his coffee. His spoon tinked against the porcelain. "I've been to her apartment," he said. "To gather a few personal effects. Things I wanted to keep."

"That's good."

"I saw where it happened," he said. "Where they found her."

Charlie could read the questions in my eyes, but I didn't want to ask too much. What did the details matter anyway, now that she was gone?

The truth was, I didn't want to imagine Halley's last moments. Instead, I thought of what Stella might say. She's the kind of person who uses the words *lovely* and *darling* and *terrific* and *wretched.* She'd say *difficult,* not *hard.* "That must have been difficult," I said. "To see."

"Her couch," he said. I pictured that couch in my mind. Purple velvet. Button-tufted back. Rolled arms. Halley said it reminded her of where Guinevere might have shagged Sir Lancelot while her husband wasn't looking.

Charlie drew circles around the lip of his coffee mug. "There's nothing sadder than staring into the closet of someone who died, seeing the clothes they used to wear. What do you do with it all?"

My coffee mug had cooled to the touch. "Goodwill?" I was trying to be strong for Charlie. What good would my grief do him? I lifted my coffee and held it there. I didn't take a sip.

"I kept that sweater she always wore. You know, the gray afghan-looking thing. My goodness, I thought it was ugly."

"She looked like a sheep herder in it," I said. "I told her so." We laughed.

The waitress returned, and we both ordered soup. The scenery behind Charlie had changed. I could see the baseball stadium across the river, the old one shaped like a slide tray. Once, Halley took me to a Reds game. She wasn't a fan of baseball, but her family had box seats, and that night fans were invited to the field to run the bases. We were drunk by the ninth inning, and when we climbed down to the field, it was just me and Halley and a bunch of small kids. I tried to back out, but she pulled me along the diamond, gleefully jumping two feet on each base, our feet kicking up dust until we slid into home. When we stood, she pointed up: We made it on the Jumbotron.

"How are you doing?" I asked. I picked up my napkin and spread it on my lap. "Really. We hardly spoke at her service. You were surrounded."

"The people who come out of the woodwork," he said. "Some of them see grief as a prize. They want a piece of it. Not knowing her, they want a piece of it." He took a sip of his coffee, then pushed it aside.

"I'm sure everyone is just trying to help. How's Bertie taking it?" I asked.

"She fired Halley. Threatened to cut her off completely."

"Why?" Halley hadn't told me. I'd assumed she'd done something stupid again. I thought of Halley's words the last night I saw her: *You don't know Bertie Tuttle.*

Bertie had always been good to me. Not maternal, but aspirational. She put me through the conservatory after my mother died. She invited me to off-Broadway performances at Music Hall where she had her own box. Bertie once used her connections to get me a small part on a movie out west, but the producer had quit before filming began, and that was the end of my big screen career.

My own mother didn't understand art or see the use for it. She never turned on the TV except for the news and *I Love Lucy,* which she'd watch while doing puzzles. She never went to a museum or a show. Never read books except the Bible on Sundays. She met Bertie only a few times, and each time my worlds awkwardly collided. I didn't know which me to be.

"That's just my mother," Charlie said. "She means well, but she can be exacting. She has rigid expectations and demands loyalty. She's not an easy woman. Halley had told her—oh, what does it matter?" He paused and looked like he was blinking dirt from his eyes. He picked up a sugar packet and played with it. "I just keep asking myself why Halley would do it. I keep imagining her there on her couch. The television was on. She was wearing a coat—did you know that? A coat and a hat, like she was going somewhere. I keep thinking about the last thing she saw before her eyes closed. What was she thinking? Did she hesitate? Why didn't she just ask for help? I would have helped her." He stopped spinning the sugar packet in his hands. "I'm sorry," he said.

"Don't be," I said.

Sitting across from her father, I felt heavy with shame. Halley *had* asked for help. She'd wanted to talk to me, said it was important, that it couldn't wait. Halley had driven me to auditions and brought flowers to my shows and drunk wine with me when Wyatt left, and held my hand as we ran those bases, laughing as we wiped away red dirt that had kicked up onto our legs. And in the end, she left something for me. Only I didn't know what. I didn't know why.

As if reading my mind, Charlie asked: "I heard she left you something. What was it?"

Sometimes I look back on my life like that bonus material you can find on a movie's DVD, where the director's voice is transposed over the film, explaining all the directorial decisions. I can almost hear myself speaking as I recall this, wondering how the story might have changed if I'd told Charlie about what I found in the safe-deposit box. We'd have discussed it. Charlie may have reminded me that Halley was an addict, and he had no idea how Halley got the notebook—a family heirloom. He'd admit he did once show her the safe in the basement of the Earthshine Factory because she'd been so curious about it and she begged him and he couldn't say no. I'd have told him none of it made sense, and he'd have made a lighthearted joke about family secrets kept locked in a vault, and we'd have eaten our soup and enjoyed it.

But I didn't answer him. Behind him, I could see a line of women making their way toward us. A few of them held posterboards colored with markers and paint, like bad elementary school projects, and a waiter tried to intervene to stop them, but they pushed past him to our table. "Charlie . . ." I tried to warn him.

"Did she happen to—" he was saying, but by then the women had formed a barrier around us. I felt the heat of their breath before I could make out their words.

"Our bodies, our soap!" one of them shouted. She wore braids and a sun visor. I recognized her from the group that had confronted me outside the studio. She held a camcorder, which, at present, was aimed directly at Charlie.

Charlie set down his spoon and dabbed his mouth with his napkin. He pushed out his chair. "It's been like this," he whispered to me. "Just ignore it. They'll go away."

"When Earthshine Soap came out, birthrates plummeted," the woman yelled. "Dramatically. That's science. That's a fact."

"Get that camera out of his face," I said.

"Every woman I know who's used Earthshine says they've felt—"

"He's grieving his daughter. Show some decency," I said.

"Oh, look. The *Earthshine Bitch* coming to his defense. That's rich," another woman shouted. She wore red glasses like Sally Jessy Raphael. "*We're* grieving. Where's *our* decency? Where's our decency? Where's our decency? Where's our decency?" The women around her tried to pick up the chant, but it didn't take.

The restaurant manager came over. "I'm so sorry, Mr. Tuttle," he said. "I'm not sure how they got in." Now two security guards approached.

"You're going to arrest us?" said the woman with glasses. "Arrest him! Arrest both of them. Do you even know what's in Earthshine? Poison. Read the papers. Read what all those women say. Not just me!"

"Let's go," said Charlie. He took my hand and pulled me up, out of my chair.

"I want to ask you something," I said to Charlie once we were inside the safe square of the elevator.

"They're not dangerous women," he said. "Just misguided. Their lives disappointed them. They want someone to blame. The PR firm says it's best to ignore them. Eventually they'll go away." He took out a handkerchief and began blotting his forehead.

"Who is Opal Doucet?" I asked.

He folded his handkerchief into a square and placed it back in his pocket. He pulled a loose thread from his sleeve. "A Jane Doe?"

"No. Someone else."

"Give me a clue."

"Her name is the clue," I said.

The elevator dinged, and we stepped out into the quiet lobby. A car waited in the covered driveway, the cold turning its exhaust into a chemical fog. Charlie hugged me again. "I'll have Carol set up another lunch—somewhere we can talk privately. And don't forget," he said, "that event at the observatory. My mother is speaking. They say if the skies are clear, we may be able to see the comet. Carol sent out the invitations. Please. It'd mean so much to have you there. And bring Wyatt."

"Of course," I said.

He stepped toward the car and then, like in so many dramatic scenes, he stopped, paused, turned around. "Opal Doucet," he said. He tapped his lips. "One of the women who died in the factory fire. That's it."

Later that day, I went there, back to the factory to see for myself. I touched the bronze plate affixed to the wall near the front of the entrance. It's supposed to be a historical marker, but Halley used to call it a gravestone. The plaque commemorated the date the Earthshine Factory was nearly destroyed by a fire: May 19, 1910. I studied the list of the Earthshine workers who died there until I found her name.

Opal Doucet. I ran my finger along the raised bronze letters, feeling each curve and line, like I had on the page of that notebook. Of course I'd seen her name before. Right here.

The fixtures in our lives become the static, unexamined facts of it. A pie chest used to sit against the wall in my kitchen. I used to eat dinner every night at this table, across from my husband. I was a friend. I was an actress. I was a wife.

But even facts can come undone.

1910

Opal waited to see if the woman might go away. She didn't dare move, not even to peer through the peephole. When the woman knocked a third time, Opal relented. There Bertie Tuttle stood, umbrella aloft, a gasp of yellow against the morning gray. Her expression was pleasantly inscrutable. She wore honeysuckle perfume, like the coming of spring.

It was only the first of March. Rain bore down, making Opal feel lightheaded, far away from her body. When she felt this way, Jagr would give her a tonic to ensure the weather didn't trigger an unusual episode. "Bottom to the top," he'd say, tipping her glass until she nearly choked on the liquid. Now, she reminded herself to breathe.

"I found your address in your employment file. I hope you don't mind," Bertie said. Behind her, a bright yellow Franklin with gleaming chrome attracted the attention of neighborhood children. She motioned to the driver, and he pulled away, up the street and around the corner, out of sight.

"Mrs. Tuttle," Opal said. "How unexpected." She tried to focus, to anticipate why Charles Tuttle's wife would be here, at her home. It couldn't be good. Hadn't she always been taught to never bring attention to herself? Isn't that why her mother brought her to Jagr in the first place?

Bertie extended her hand to be shaken. Her nails were manicured, filed to a point. How could she manage the most basic tasks with nails so long? Then she remembered: domestics.

"Please, Bertie."

Bertie. Informal. Familiar. Not the way she'd imagine the woman might speak to her help. Her voice held a musical quality—years of enunciation training from the finishing school she'd attended in New England. She remembered how when she saw Bertie a month ago, the woman had walked right up to her and touched her necklace, as though they were already intimate.

Opal motioned Bertie inside.

Opal's rented rooms were shotgun style, no hallways. The door opened directly into the front parlor, and Opal gestured toward the chair near the window. Bertie set her umbrella in the stand. She registered the table, the muslin window coverings, the unlit hearth, the wallpaper the color of weak tea. She removed her coat and unpinned her hat, then, looking about for a place to hang them, finally handed the items to Opal.

"My husband would be in a fit of pique if he knew I was here," she said. "I don't need to be the further subject of gossip in the *Inquisitor.* Dixie Ellison, the classic quidnunc, now really. She'd twist any story into a sordid tale, make it about the depravity of human nature, the undoing of mankind." She stopped and turned toward Opal. This was a woman accustomed to an audience, but now she recognized the two women were finally alone. She softened some more. "Well, you know what I mean, I'm sure, since she's recently made you a subject of her writing."

Opal did know. Two days ago, at the beginning of her shift, the Earthshine Girls had crowded around her station. Betsy produced the newspaper and spread it out. "You're famous, Madame Doucet," she said. "I bet they'll want your picture."

Her picture in the paper was the last thing she wanted.

Now Bertie produced a cutout of Dixie About Town, as though

evidence of a crime she'd committed. "I've come to talk to you about this." She set the paper square on the table between them.

> *An Earthshine Girl who goes by Madame Doucet claims to be a medical spiritualist who can divine ethereal cures from "the other side" and is treating the Earthshine Factory Girls for a variety of mystery ailments with Comet Pills. Such quackery, as has been seen in other cities, makes a mockery of Christianity and modern science alike. Pity the girl ensnared by such fleecing.*

Opal's eyes fell on her name. The words "Madame Doucet" looked foreign to her, like the name of an actress on a playbill after you've come to know the character she played onstage. "I need my job. Really, I do. I was only trying to help the women. Tell your husband—"

"My husband is not the reason I'm here." Bertie removed her gloves and set them on the table. They looked ghostly, satin white and still molded in the shape of her hands. "Trusting you'll keep my confidence, I won't have to bring my husband into this at all. In fact, I prefer it that way." Her words contained a threat, though she delivered them conspiratorially. She took a seat, adjusted herself, and said: "I've come, myself, for a cure."

Rain pitter-pattered on the roof. A barge horn sounded in the distance. Opal wondered if this was a test of some sort, and what she must say to pass it. Bertie was a woman of means; what help could she possibly need from someone like her?

"You're unwell?" Opal asked finally. "Like the others?" Betsy had missed three days of work last week, but when she returned her complexion was dewy with what the other girls called a pregnancy glow.

"The others," Bertie said. "I don't want to talk about the others. That's the problem with doctors. They're always comparing me to someone else."

"I don't claim to be a doctor," Opal said. Though she had helped, hadn't she? The Earthshine Girls reported their ailments had subsided. The Comet Pills brought them relief—euphoria, even. Pearl's moods had evened out. Ruth lost a few pounds. Gilly reported she'd never felt more energetic in her life. At her station, Maria looked radiant. She'd hold a bar of soap aloft before wrapping it—"Don't you love how it just fits so perfectly in your hand?" she'd say. Maria couldn't imagine why she'd ever felt so glum. She asked for a refill of Comet Pills; all the girls did.

A clap of thunder in the distance, unusual for this time of year. The news blamed anything on the comet: temperamental weather, electrical fires, the stock market, influenza.

"You must understand, I've never been to . . . one of . . . *you* before," Bertie said.

She was uncomfortable saying *spiritualist* or *psychic,* or *medium,* or *spook.* She was too bent on propriety; she wouldn't utter those words any more than she'd utter aloud the term for a man's reproductive anatomy. A *congress limb,* she might declare it, if pressed. She sat back in her chair and held her head at a tilt, as though the world appeared crooked and she intended to right it.

Bertie continued: "Dixie Ellison calls me a wife of fortune and convenience, though whose fortune? And whose convenience?" She pressed her fingertips together as she spoke. "It's my family's company, though you'd think I'm the one who married him for money if you read the papers. It's all so embarrassing, especially since I have no control over it." She took in a long breath and exhaled like she was extinguishing a candle. "I've seen all the doctors. I even went to supposed experts in New England, and yet nobody can seem to answer the simplest question, the only question I want answered."

Opal understood. Her fortune, her inheritance, at the mercy of her reproductive organs. "Sterility," Opal said, and Bertie looked in receipt of an insult, shocked.

"So I'm told."

Opal had seen plenty of sad-eyed women who'd visited Jagr when nature didn't take its course. The causes were varied: anemia, overeating, tight girdles, too much reading, a faulty condition of the uterus, an unbalanced lifestyle, a husband's frequent visits to prostitutes that left his poor wife with disease. Jagr had told Opal stories of "secret insemination" or other procedures performed under anesthesia, but he treated sterility with only botanical remedies.

That was the irony: Her husband could remedy sterility—or he could render it, like he had with her. He viewed each patient as a series of symptoms seeking relief, as a problem to be solved. He was a good doctor. His cures did not discriminate.

"My husband doesn't read the gossip column," Bertie said, and here she stopped speaking and her eyelids fluttered, just enough to register that *she did*, and so she knew what Dixie had written about her husband and his mistress. "I'll make sure he doesn't see this article. I'll make sure there are no repercussions if he does see it." Bertie folded the newspaper clipping in half, then in half again, then she tucked it into her pocketbook. She straightened her posture.

Then her eyes narrowed. She wasn't looking at Opal so much as she was looking through her, as though her gaze were an X-ray machine that could detect the bone of her existence. Opal resisted the urge to move, to give away her nerves.

Opal settled herself at the table and leaned back against the chair. Recently, a pain had lodged itself beneath her rib cage and it wouldn't relent unless she stretched herself backward. Her body was not her body, but something shifting and taking new shape.

"A little amusement, if nothing else," Bertie said, lightening. "What, are the ghosts here?" She laughed, and sound returned to the room: the pigeon roosting outside the window. The rain like a scurry of animals against the glass. "We could all use some amusement, couldn't we? Those scientists say the world will end with that comet, that's all you hear about. It gives me the morbs. I don't want to think about endings."

"Then let's think about beginnings," Opal said.

A few minutes later, Opal struck a match. She and Bertie joined hands. Their toes touched beneath the table. The room sparked with anticipation. She asked Bertie to count with her to three, then Opal let go and pounded the table with her fist. She sensed the tingling at her feet that rose up through her bones. A warmth. The slowing of her heart. A stillness and excitement. A kind of fear. A kind of ecstasy. As she spoke, her whole body felt buoyant, like she was floating on water. She listened.

Bertie closed her eyes, and Opal studied her respiration, counting her breaths. She made note of her nails and her coloring, and her pulse, which could be felt by extending her finger to graze her wrist.

"Think of the good I could provide for a baby," Bertie said as the two women began to hum. "Think of all the good I could do with my inheritance." Bertie squeezed Opal's hand, and for a moment the world contained only possibility.

1986

Lovely, appealing skin attracts men,
just as honeysuckle attracts bees.

—LUX TOILET SOAP

Technique can be taught: elocution, stage presence, articulation, posture. It's not just skill that captivates an audience. Real stars affect a celestial presence—of the sky, of the heavens—more God than human. Someone who can't be touched.

I was not a star.

At the studio, Elliot pulled me aside. "You see next week's script?" he asked.

Another Jane Doe had come forward, and now there was talk that the lawsuit could turn into a class action. I'd watched her interview with John Dale Fox on the local news. Her voice had been altered, her body shadowed. Since she'd spoken out, she said she'd been receiving death threats. Her phone rang in the middle of the night. Cars honked past her house, and in the morning, she'd find garbage tossed into her yard. She believed coming forward had ruined her life.

"You're doing it, Nona. You're killing it in these coffin scenes," Elliot said. "Our ratings are up. They want more of you."

"Gotta scratch my way out of that ground first," I said.

"Today," he said.

The backdrop of the stage was a Gothic cemetery, the kind with gates and marble monuments, trees draped with Spanish moss. Vincent Glass paced the stage in his tuxedo, his hand tucked into his cummerbund, rehearsing his lines. The wardrobe assistant came by and made a few adjustments to my collar, then the makeup girl smudged my cheeks with charcoal and mud.

"Lights. Roll sound," Elliot said.

I took my place beside a mound of dirt that had been dumped on the stage. The scene involved a close-up, then the popping of my hand above the dirt, but the camera angles were tricky. Elliot instructed me to reach through the dirt and upward to achieve the effect. Vincent Glass, who'd been at my graveside contemplating his love for Celeste, who was dying, would see my hand and grasp it.

"Action!" Elliot yelled. The clapperboard. The close-up. My neck twisted; I rested against the dirt, and it was cold on my skin. I dug, dug, dug with my dagger necklace, with my hands, my fingers, all of me.

I pushed my hand through the dirt, like I was being birthed a single body part at a time. My fingers writhed—undead, unstill. I lived in my character's head for a moment, but then my mind spiraled. I thought of the latest Jane Doe, her silhouette filmed behind that green screen. When John Dale asked her if she regretted coming forward, she didn't respond. She sat in silence for a full five seconds, which in television is an eternity. I thought of Halley sitting alone in her coat. I imagined her clapping a handful of pills to her mouth, then swigging some vodka and swallowing. I thought of my baby, my still baby, how when they brought the baby to me, it had been wrapped in a white blanket with footprints on it. The nurse asked me if I wanted to hold her, and I shook my head, didn't even say *no*, and Wyatt looked away from me, out the window. The most dramatic scenes have no lines.

Art is not held at time's mercy, not like our own lives. Art is time, keenly felt. Stella had been underground for several TV weeks, but only a few days of her own life. I blinked dirt from Stella's eyes, and when I did, the whole world appeared magnified. Since Halley died, I hadn't been sleeping. Last night I managed only two hours. I blinked at the ceiling, replaying an imagined conversation in my mind, over and over, as though I could will it to alter reality.

We need to talk.

Let's talk then. I'm listening. I'm here.

So much of acting is stillness, waiting for a moment to arise, then moving toward it without hesitation. I held the scene until I felt Vincent Glass's hand pulling me to the surface, until he said, "Good gracious, she's alive," and I cried real tears and the actor who played Vincent cradled me until Elliot yelled, "Cut. Cut. Perfect. Cut."

THE NEXT MORNING, I STOPPED at Dowd's Drugs to pick up the prescription my doctor called in, birth control pills to help regulate my bleeding, ironic, given the years I'd spent trying to conceive.

Dowd's was a local pharmacy, not one of those national chains. The place was vintage, a portal to a different time. Inside, a large onyx counter sold old-timey sodas for a dollar, and if you wanted to stay there to drink it, they'd put it in a beveled green soda glass. You could sit at one of the stools and pretend you're in *It's a Wonderful Life.*

I never cared for that movie title, by the way. I think it's a lie. Too often we're willing to live with scarcity, to accept smallness in our lives, to feast on crumbs and pretend we're full. In the movie, George dreamed of seeing the world, but he never did see it. He never would, probably.

The pharmacist, Gary, nodded when he saw me. He was a nice guy, a cross between a hippie and Santa Claus, which is to say he had long white hair and a beard he kept well-trimmed, and he never stared at my breasts. And, like Santa, he knew all my secrets.

Gary himself compounded the fertility medication I'd taken. From Gary, I ordered pregnancy tests by the dozens and basal thermometers and ovulation kits and estrogen patches. Gary knew I'd gotten pregnant because he'd filled prescriptions for pills to help with morning sickness and for prenatal vitamins so big he cut them in half.

He'd counted Klonopin after I lost the baby. It was supposed to help me sleep, but instead I hallucinated that the baby had come home with us. I slept in the nursery, and that's where Wyatt found me, curled up in the glider next to an empty crib. I switched to Valium. Gary didn't say *I'm sorry for your loss* or *everything happens for a reason.* Instead, he stapled my receipt to the bag and reminded me to take the medicine with food. There was comfort in that.

Gary had bagged my prescription by the time I approached the counter.

He rang me up, and we did our exchange.

"Have you ever heard of Comet Pills?" I asked, putting away my billfold.

He laughed like I was playing a prank.

"I don't even know what I'm asking," I said. I shoved my wallet back in my purse.

Gary leaned forward and rested his elbows on the counter. He wore a wedding ring that he now twisted on his knuckle. "When Halley's Comet was here last time, people believed the gas in the comet's tail would eradicate *all of mankind.*" He rubbed his beard. "Back then, anyone could bottle anything, slap on a label saying it cured this, prevented that. Snake oil salesmen—the world was full of them. There are laws to regulate drugs now, though. The Sherley Amendment. Thank goodness. Now everything is tested."

"And then the comet came and went," I said. A bell rang, and someone entered the store.

"Someone will be right with you," Gary yelled. He turned to

me. "Came and went. Dowd's still has the old inventory books dating back to the 1880s. And Comet Pills, the ones sold at Dowd's anyway, didn't have anything to do with the comet."

I heard someone order a milkshake, and the blender whirred to life.

"So the pills—what did they do?" I asked.

Gary laughed. "Mood enhancers. Happy Pills. All I really know is that they sold well, according to the ledger, and then one day—poof—they disappeared. No more sales recorded. Guess everyone got happy. Inventory gone like that," he said, snapping his fingers.

The most recent Jane Doe to come forward was a housekeeper, like my mother. She said years of using Earthshine had led to low libido and depression so bad she couldn't get out of bed for days. She thought of ending her own life. She'd fantasize about how she'd do it, but then she thought of her kids, or she thought of her husband having to explain it to them. Her kids would never recover, and—she didn't want to be the cause of that kind of trauma, or to be a ghost that haunted them their entire lives. When I'd read the article, I thought of my own mom. I never considered that she might have held secret fantasies of any kind. Her hands wrinkled prematurely, and she rubbed them each night with cold cream, explaining hands are the first place where a woman shows her age.

Someone waited behind me in line now—an old woman with a headscarf tied beneath her chin. She stood with the help of a walker. She could have been Bertie's age. I wondered if she were alive the last time Halley's Comet came around. I wondered if she'd ever taken a Comet Pill. She smiled at me. She looked happy enough.

The bell on the front door dinged. The front register worker yelled out, "Welcome to Dowd's!" A stocky man in a suit stepped inside. He wore dark glasses he didn't remove. His hair was buzzed on the sides, and the front came to a point, which could have either been menacing or a sign that, like most men, he didn't know how to use hair gel.

To act well, one must have instincts. Acting comes not from our mouths but our guts. That's what so many aspiring actors get wrong.

I felt this man's presence in the core of me. I knew in an instant what the man was looking for: not aspirin or hair gel, of that I was certain.

"Thanks," I said to Gary, then quickly cut past the old woman and down the first aid aisle, past gauze and bandages and ointments meant for burns. But the man headed down a different aisle, cut over, and caught up to me. He blocked the door. Then, he handed me an envelope.

"You've been served," he said, then he pushed open the door and disappeared.

I opened the envelope right there, inside the pharmacy. A form letter with a fill-in-the-blank answer set. On a blank line someone had written my name: Nona Dixon, and on another blank line someone had written my description: Original Earthshine Girl.

A deposition summons for the Earthshine lawsuit. I'd been called as a witness.

1910

Opal viewed her life across some great misty field, always walking toward it but never quite reaching the other side. Just when she'd managed to save some money, her bills were due. Five and a half dollars a week didn't go very far in the city, even with the money she brought in from her cures. Sure, she could stretch a dollar. The bakery sold day-old bread for a penny. She found complimentary coffee in the lobby of the grand Hotel Sinton, where the monied people stayed. Nobody seemed to mind when she took the elevator to the residential floors and borrowed toiletries from the cart of the cleaning staff. Her work dress gave her a kind of invisibility in such spaces. Most assumed she was the help.

She measured her time by the letters to and from Madame de Fleur. She read and reread each one like her mother used to read the Bible at night by the hearth, searching, looking for answers. Madame de Fleur wrote poetically about ideas and the universe. The woman's private life was exotic, unknown, while her own felt trivial and small. All Opal could think to write about was her literal life, how she felt with the baby inside her. Tired. Big. Embodied. She told Madame de Fleur of the Earthshine Girls and their illnesses and how she sat with them in séance in the lunchroom and how she prescribed them Comet Pills, which improved their spirits. *When I sit with those workers,*

I can see you, in my mind, on that platform, in that tent. I can sense your presence. But you say you're not the sun. If we are scale models of the universe, what is the center? How can we know it? Right now, it feels as though this baby is the whole of me, as though someone might point to my middle and say: that's Opal right there. But I existed before her, didn't I? I'll exist after, too. I used to believe in science, but science cannot explain that night or why this baby has come to be, even if I understand how. You'd tell me some mysteries must remain so, that certainty robs the world of possibility. But I want to know: What are the possibilities? Can the Spirit Machine tell me that? Can you?

She stared at the words on the page, which seemed to arise from her hand, independent of her mind, like the automatic writing Madame de Fleur had told her about. She felt flushed after writing. Naked. Exposed. Relieved.

At the factory, Opal packaged the soap. Her ankles swelled from standing. Her ears rang from all the noise. At least once a shift, an Earthshine Girl passed her a note. She was sad or tired or angry or alone. She couldn't sleep or couldn't eat or couldn't think, her head in a permanent fog. And during lunch, in the cramped lunchroom, Opal held her hands and felt her pulse and watched her breathing and listened to her describe her symptoms she'd be too embarrassed to describe anywhere else.

One evening, as she was leaving work, a young woman approached her on the sidewalk. "Madame Doucet?" she asked. Opal no longer startled at the sound of her name. At the factory, it'd become something of a refrain from the other girls seeking cures. *Madame Doucet, Madame Doucet, Madame Doucet,* like a frantic melody.

The girl was wearing a too-big overcoat, which gave her the appearance of a child, though she was probably at least sixteen. Opal didn't recognize the girl, not from the factory, not from anywhere else. She wasn't wearing a uniform, and she didn't dress like a domestic. "Who's asking?" Opal asked. Still, she must be careful.

"Me. I'm asking," she said. The girl pushed up her sleeves and whispered: "I need a cure."

Opal stopped walking. "Who sent you?"

The girl looked confused. "Everyone knows about you and your Comet Pills, Madame Doucet."

In the evenings, she wrote to Madame de Fleur. She told her about the girl. She explained how strangers now waited for her outside the factory. They'd heard about Comet Pills from their sisters or mothers or cousins or daughters. At night, after her shifts, she labored in her kitchen, boiling and grinding and filling the capsules, her windows wide open to ease the smell. To work she'd begun carrying extra tins, stuffed inside her apron so the metal rattled each time she bent down to set another crate to the floor to be counted. She was saving more than she was spending now—she hoped to leave for France by May Day, well before the baby's arrival.

Opal sent letters to the woman more frequently than she could possibly expect replies. *I'm afraid they'll learn how ordinary I am, how just two months ago I scraped my husband's work boots and scrubbed his drawers and made soap from wood ash and cooking grease because he didn't believe in buying manufactured goods. I'm a woman who once boiled eggs and pickled beets, and maybe I still am, but I don't feel ordinary feelings. I don't think ordinary thoughts.* She dropped the envelopes in the morning post. Lately it seemed like the events of her life only truly happened once she had sent the letter off, that it was the writing that made it real, that Opal existed only to tell her story to someone else.

Had it been only seven months ago since she'd met Madame de Fleur? Back in Gallipolis, Opal had watched the assemblage of strangers descend upon the fairgrounds, their wagons loaded and covered, long poles sticking from beneath the cloth. It took a full day for the tents to be erected, the white fabric billowing in the wind like a thing come alive.

The circus.

She'd wanted to go, but Jagr forbade her, said it wouldn't be good for her condition, but then Jagr had been called away for the month to Wheeling for business. Normally she obeyed her husband's wishes; she'd been trained to please him. Yet she felt pulled toward the fairgrounds, toward the music and cannon booms she could hear those first few nights when she stood in her yard, emptying the washtub. With her husband gone, Opal made her way to the giant circus tent, the white canvas like slack skin.

Inside, a woman dangled from a piece of silk, another stood atop a horse. She saw a fire-eater, a sword swallower, and an armless man, lying on the ground and juggling balls with the soles of his feet. As a girl, she'd read *Alice's Adventures in Wonderland,* and she marveled at how falling into a dark hole led to someplace spacious and colorful and strange. Now here she was, Alice herself.

And then, as though she'd been destined to arrive there all her life, Opal stood before the threshold to another tent. She smelled burning sage. A thin thread of smoke plumed through the doorway like a curled finger beckoning her. She read the sign: MADAME DE FLEUR: SÉANCES AND SPIRIT HAPPENINGS.

Opal pulled back the heavy curtain and stepped inside. The woman on the stage sat quietly in a chair. She wore a dark flowing frock and a white medallion that shone like the moon. The room was awash in red from the pendant lights. She looked at Opal with startled eyes, as though their eyeballs were magnetized, as though she was seeing something in Opal that Opal couldn't see herself.

"You have awoken the spirits," Madame de Fleur said.

The tent was cramped with spectators who now all turned toward Opal. For a brief moment, she worried she might be recognized by someone who'd report the sighting to Jagr. But, then, wouldn't they have to admit to attending a séance, too?

Madame de Fleur's hands were bound with rope. Still, a steady knocking came from somewhere in the room, and nobody could locate the source. The sound, like the clopping of hooves, originated from above and below at once, from the woman herself. A man in the front clasped his hands, begging to contact his son who'd succumbed to scarlet fever.

"Step forward," she instructed him. Her voice was low and even and velvety and soft, like a warm blanket thrown over the world. It held an accent so imperceptible Opal may have imagined it. "He stands in front of you. There." She lifted her bound wrists to point. "Young boy. Delicate features. White hair. Reach out."

"I don't see him," the man said. "Walter? Are you there? Tell me you're here. Give me a sign."

At that moment, all the lights extinguished at once, and a few people screamed, and the audience sat in total darkness until they heard the strike of a match from the stage manager and Madame de Fleur again became illuminated, her hands now unbound.

Later, outside, Opal watched a woman walk a tightrope that'd been strung from two poles. The performer wore a fur-lined skirt, a half-bodice dress that pushed up her breasts like two loaves of bread. She carried a parasol, and when she dramatically tipped from side to side, on the cusp of a fall, she'd hold the parasol high and right herself.

Across the way, Madame de Fleur emerged from her tent and scanned the crowd until she found what she was searching for. She walked toward Opal.

Up close, Madame de Fleur appeared older than Opal. Creases around her eyes lent her a softness, an Old World knowingness. A curl had escaped her bun and clung to her neck. Opal smelled dampness on her skin, and something cottony and musky and floral at once. Perfume.

"You've lost someone," she said.

"We've all lost someone," Opal said.

"You wear it like a cloak. Your grief."

"Who then?" Opal challenged. She crossed her arms. How stretched her grief for Oren had become, like the dough she made for braided holiday breads. Her grief had morphed into bread, something she fed upon on special occasions. She waited for the woman to speak.

"Tomorrow," the woman said. "Sit with me, and I will tell you. Come by, before the show."

At home, Opal studied herself in the mirror. Her eyes were caves, sunken. Soft lines waved across her forehead. Her skin dulled, even in the light. How different she looked from the woman she imagined herself to be—the woman she used to be. She'd once been described as beautiful. Now, she stared at herself, unblinking, half believing the woman in the mirror might speak. And what would she say? She pulled the pins from her hair, and it fell to her shoulders in a mess that she then brushed and brushed until her arms grew tired. *You've lost someone,* the woman had said.

Oren. It'd been so long since she'd allowed herself to really remember him. Opal had liked how his name required her to make a circle of her lips, as one does when whistling, like Oren had been doing the first time she saw him walking across the Malarkeys' field. A wooden box rested on his shoulder. He stopped midstride when he spotted her. "Hello, kid," he said. Something struck Opal as so peculiar about the way he called her kid, as though he were addressing someone else. She looked behind her. "It's dangerous to look up today," he said. He hitched his thumb toward the sky. He wasn't wearing gloves, and his hands were red and cracked from the cold.

Immediately she drew her eyes to the ground. The fields beneath her feet were fallow. The Malarkeys had a daughter just a little older than Opal, and rumor was she'd killed her father's crops by bleeding too much between the legs, until one day the bleeding stopped and she ran off with a millworker. Opal had been fascinated with the story, with the idea of a life beyond town, and a girl who could leave and never come back.

"I'll look where I want," Opal had said.

"Burn your eyes out, unless you have one of these." He patted his box, and for the first time Opal studied it: a sawed-out circle at the bottom, a square of tin affixed to one end with a hole drilled through it. The inside of the box had been painted white. A solar eclipse, he explained. The moon would align itself between the Earth and the sun, blotting out the light, turning day to night.

"Totality." He said the word like a line of poetry. "Seven minutes of it."

"A few minutes doesn't feel very total to me," Opal had said.

"When the moon lines up just right—that's when you can look directly at the sun with your naked eye." He blushed when he said the word *naked.* He patted his box. "Like staring into the eye of God."

He demonstrated how he'd put the box over his head, and then use the tin to attract the sun and project the eclipse onto the other end. "But you have to be faced away from the sun. That's the trick. That's what most people don't know—that to observe it, you have to look away from it. But then, if you're lucky . . ."

"Totality," Opal said. Her body warmed.

Opal would later learn that Oren saw dark spots in his vision from staring at the sun through a telescope. The sky held all his dreams. He'd lived up the road at that hospital for a time, until he'd been cured of the seizures that'd plagued him since he was a child. Now he worked as a farmhand. Months later, after they'd been together, on a blanket thrown between a row of cornstalks, his face lit up as he pointed out constellations. He made her stand, naked still, and she thought he was going to explain the sky to her again—there the North Star, the Big Dipper, Orion's Belt—but he didn't this time. He wrapped the blanket around her shoulders, and they swayed together, dancing.

Standing there in the Malarkeys' field, she felt breathless from the cold. Woozy. She didn't know why she removed her hat and let this stranger place the box over her head. The wood scraped her forehead going on, and the weight of it pitched her forward so that Oren had to catch her by the shoulders. They took turns with their heads in that box, studying the sun—the closest star, but not the biggest, he explained. How intimate to put that box over her head and breathe in the air where Oren's breath still floated. Intoxicating.

THE NEXT EVENING, OPAL FOUND Madame de Fleur sitting on a cot in the small room behind the stage. She buried her face in her hands when Opal sat across from her, and at first, Opal thought she'd misunderstood the woman's invitation. She shifted in discomfort, then rose to leave, but at that moment, Madame de Fleur slid a small wooden crate between them. She lit a candle. Opal sat again, and the woman reached for her hands.

The woman's hands were impossibly soft. Warm. Her long fingers slid through Opal's own like a puzzle box, now complete.

"It's like telephoning," the woman had said.

"I can call someone up?" Opal said, too quickly. She'd revealed her nerves, and, besides, she'd rarely used a telephone, and when she did, it was Jagr's voice on the other end telling her he'd been called away for work or to the hospital to see a patient who'd taken ill.

"Everything lost returns," the woman said. "The fundamental rule of our lives." She spoke softly, her voice nearly a whisper, so Opal had to lean forward, strain to hear.

Opal could not speak, her own voice a solid object lodged inside her throat. She tried to imagine Oren standing in this room. She should leave—what would Jagr say if he found out?—but the woman now gripped her hand tighter, as though she'd overheard Opal's thought.

Together, the women sat in the darkness. The candlelight bounced off the fabric of the tent; shadows curled and arched. Opal breathed quickly, or maybe she'd forgotten to breathe. She had to keep reminding herself to pull the air through her lungs. Madame de Fleur began to hum, and Opal felt the vibrations where their skin touched.

After a few moments the woman said: "He's come through."

"Who?" Opal challenged. Even if she wanted to leave, she feared her legs would not listen. Her body seemed to be revolting. Outside she heard the circus goers gasp, then applaud. The night was only beginning.

"Hello, kid," the woman said.

Opal's vision expanded, then tunneled, until it was like she was looking through a keyhole at the woman.

"Hello, kid," the woman said again, softer now, and so quiet Opal leaned even farther forward. She remembered when Oren was sick, just before he passed, she'd visited him. *Hello, kid.* He could only speak in a whisper, like his voice was the first part of him to cross over.

Now Madame de Fleur pressed her forehead to Opal's. "Can you sense his presence?" she asked. Opal could hear the woman's breath; she could feel each dewy exhale. A warmth enveloped her, a familiar energy. That's how she'd describe it: energy. Like she could light a room with it.

"Oren?" Opal said. She hadn't spoken his name out loud in years, and to speak it now brought him there. She could feel it. Madame de Fleur squeezed her hand in acknowledgment; Opal squeezed back. How could she ever describe the truth of that first moment? The depth of it? She didn't care what she'd heard of spooks and spiritualists, what she understood then—what she felt—was as real as anything she'd ever experienced.

"Yes," Madame de Fleur said. "It is me."

Now they both stood, their hands still clasped, their foreheads still touching. The women moved together. Madame de Fleur seemed to lead and follow at once. Outside, Opal heard the boom of a cannon, then the band started up. Inside, the women swayed. They were dancing.

The next day, Jagr had called to say he'd been delayed another ten days, and that evening, Opal waited for Madame de Fleur after her show. Outside her tent, she didn't know what to expect from the woman. That night, and the week that followed, they walked through Mound Hill Cemetery, so close together they brushed arms, then shoulders, then hips, and Opal felt suddenly aware of her body, how tensely she held it. The cemetery appeared more beautiful at night. Pebbled paths wound past rows of gravestones. Madame de Fleur stopped to read the names and trace her fingers along the carvings, those dates and dashes the sad summaries of their lives. One night, they came upon it—Oren's grave, a rectangle of sandstone already tarnished at the edges.

Opal hadn't been here in years. She stooped to pick a mum from a patch that grew at her feet and placed the flower on his grave. Madame de Fleur laughed, not meanly, but even so, Opal felt foolish, like she'd broken a rule she hadn't known existed.

She must have looked hurt, because the woman draped her arm across Opal's shoulder and told her there's no comfort to be found in stone. The dead don't want for flowers and condolences.

"Then what?" Opal had asked.

"My dear, those on the Other Side crave what we all do: contact. Touch."

Afterward, they lay on the sloping bank of the river, making a blanket of the grass. They looked for shooting stars, meteor showers from the comet still months away, but they found only bright, stationary light.

"What is it you want from this life?" Madame de Fleur had asked her.

Nobody had ever asked her that. She hadn't known she could have desires of her own. She ran her fingers through the grass beside her, as though she were searching for something. The summer air was bathwater. In Madame de Fleur's presence, she felt submerged.

She'd told the woman the stories she'd tucked away—about the person she was before now, a different self altogether. The stories were so old, they arrived like lies upon her lips, but as she spoke they hardened into truth: how she carried Oren's baby, how her mother had taken her to see a doctor who would soon become her husband, how her husband forced her to take medicines, perpetually worried about her weakened state. Wanting, for her, had never proven useful.

"Sometimes the smallest decisions paralyze me," Opal admitted. "I stand in front of the icebox, and stare into it. Rump roast and potatoes or beans and salted pork? I can't even decide. Isn't that ridiculous?"

"I asked you what you want from life—not for dinner," Madame de Fleur said.

"My point is, how can I even know that answer, if I can't choose between rump roast or salted pork. Which do you prefer?" Opal asked.

"I don't want to influence you either way," Madame de Fleur said, smiling.

She belted her arm around Opal's waist and held her there in a way that didn't ask for anything more than closeness. "When we're like this—I can feel what you two shared. He wants so badly to get through to you." They stayed like that for a while, then Madame de Fleur turned, until she was flat on her back staring up at the sky. She drew her arms behind her head.

Opal did the same—she studied the sky and felt diminutive beneath it. She searched the sky for a little trail of light. When the comet arrived, the circus would be long gone. Madame de Fleur would be long gone, too, and Opal's world would shrink. So small again. So ordinary. Sometimes she imagined her life like a winding path through the dark. She could see lantern light up ahead, but she didn't know how to reach it. She could barely make out her own feet.

Opal rolled onto her stomach. Her body inched closer to the woman. She studied Madame de Fleur's eyes, which looked like pools of ink in the moonlight.

"I want him to get through to me," she said.

"So, there, you can choose," Madame de Fleur said, then she quieted. "Listening is a choice. Shhh." Opal heard insects and a train whistle in the distance, but nothing else. She had lived to be older than Oren ever was, and it made her sad to think of him so pristine, so young, so untouched by time. She considered what kind of man he might have grown to be. Would he have been so tender with her still? Accepting of the woman she'd become?

Madame de Fleur propped herself up with her elbow. Her dress fell away from her shoulder, and Opal followed the slope of her neck. Her heart thumped everywhere inside her at once. In the distance, the town's lamplights flickered like fireflies. If she tried, she could find her house. It was late.

Opal touched the woman's lips and felt the waves of her breath. Then, the woman caught Opal's hand and pressed it to the bone of her chest. She could feel the thudding. "Is that what you want from this life? Oren?" Opal hadn't known what she wanted until that very moment when she faced it. The moon tucked behind a cloud. The world around them fell away.

She wasn't surprised when Madame de Fleur kissed her. Or was it she who leaned in first? They drew to each other, all at once; they magnetized. It felt different from kissing a man. Madame de Fleur's lips were soft and her breath was light and she smelled of cottony perfume. She grazed Opal's neck with her fingertips, encoding a message onto her skin. Opal breathed it in, all of it, the presence and the memory of it, the pleasure of it, the exhilaration of it, until Madame de Fleur pulled away.

Then the world returned again, unchanged. Cicadas chirped in the distance. Neither woman spoke.

"Now, for a swim," Madame de Fleur finally said. She stood. She removed her shoes, then her shirtwaist, then her belt, then her skirt. Her slip fell away like skin; her body limned with light. Opal had never seen another grown woman naked before, and she studied Madame de Fleur with curiosity. The hair between her legs was trimmed. Her hips drew wide and round. Her breasts were shaped like bells, fuller at the bottom.

As a final act, she removed her moonstone necklace and bent to fasten it around Opal, telling Opal the powers of the stone—that it could draw two people together, if the celestial conditions were right. Opal hadn't known what she meant by that. Still, the moonstone offered cool relief against Opal's skin. Even in the night it appeared to glow.

Then the woman walked toward the water until she was a shadowy figure at the bank of the river, until she jumped in headfirst and disappeared.

Opal again studied the stars above her and considered how this same sky spread over the entire world. She listened to the sounds of the night. Owls. Crickets. Coyotes howling in the distance. The night teemed with life one missed when sleeping. She watched a barge move down the river in the distance, its flatbed carrying a pyramid-shaped mound of coal. The first Europeans to settle Ohio were French and, upon initial sight of the Ohio River, had called it La Belle Rivière. She always felt an instinctive pull to its water. As a girl, she used to wade into its shallow edges or swim across the bank at its narrowest point, paddling until she touched the shores of West Virginia, which felt like a different world to her altogether, even though it had the same shaggy trees, the same mossy rocks, the same waves that lapped at her feet as she looked back toward the other side.

After a few moments, the woman still hadn't come up for air, and now Opal hurried to the bank, calling her name, worried she had snagged herself on a tree root or hit her head on a rock. She pulled off her shoes and her stockings and her skirt, and waded into the water to her knees. "Madame de Fleur?" she yelled. "Are you there?" She drew her hands beneath the surface of the water, feeling for her. Reaching. The moon popped out from behind the clouds. She spun in a circle until she was dizzy and breathless, until finally the woman's head breached the surface, her hair clinging to her face.

Madame de Fleur gulped air and laughed.

"I thought you were dead!" Opal said, and when she spoke, a frantic sadness passed over her body, like the woman was already gone from her life.

"I plan to live forever," Madame de Fleur said. She smoothed her wet hair and water dripped over the bony ridges of her shoulder.

Years later, when she'd remember this moment, Opal would swear that time had slowed, that the world around them ceased to exist. Time cracked and expanded and contracted. There was no time. Only the two of them in space. The woman waded closer to Opal, and Opal to her, and they drew together, aligned until they fell backward, their lips and hips touching, their bodies pressed tight so it was impossible to tell where one woman ended and the other began. In that timeless space of free fall, before they landed on the bank, Opal knew. She *knew*. What she'd lost had returned to her.

The next day, Jagr, too, had returned, earlier than expected. In Wheeling he'd learned of some new medical advancements. He'd brought home with him some herbs. He busied Opal with chores. He'd asked her to separate the stems from the leaves. He'd instructed her to grind the seeds to powder with the mortar and pestle. He told her to weigh milk of licorice on the balance scale and add it to the pill press as he took notes in his formulary. When he caught her crying, he said she was not acting like herself. An unusual episode, he'd determined, and he'd forced her to drink that elixir, bottom to top, and she was thankful, in a way, because then he would not touch her.

Finally, a few days later, he was called away to check on a patient. Opal stood on the hill above the fairgrounds, where for more than a month the circus tents had billowed like a breathing, living thing. Before she even crested the hill, before she allowed her gaze to affix itself below, to the brown grass of the field that held the memory of posts and stakes, before she discovered the note Madame de Fleur had left for her—attached by a peg to the small square shed that once served as the admission booth—she knew. Again she knew. Madame de Fleur was gone.

She pulled the note from the post and read it. One sentence: *I prefer rump roast.*

Beneath it, her forwarding address. France. An ocean away.

The world shrank, until the sky and the ground formed a little box around her. For a moment, everything went silent.

1986

Husbands grow cool when wives grow careless . . .

—LIFEBUOY SOAP

Like Rome, Cincinnati is called the City of Seven Hills, but I know there are more than that. Wyatt and I bought our first house together atop one, in Mount Lookout, an area so named because of the old observatory located there, its property line backing up to ours. Beyond the fence, the rounded dome rose like a giant breast through the bare trees in the winter. When we first moved in, I asked Wyatt why men always design things to look like boobs, and he reminded me that men never use the word *boob,* not ever, and so we made a joke of it, called it the Boobatory, which wasn't funny at all, except to us, because marriage is an excuse for stupid jokes.

It was winter, and the trees could hold no secrets, and I stood in my driveway with a bag of groceries. Have you ever seen a bag of groceries on TV or in the movies that didn't have a baguette poking out? My bag contained no bread. It was filled with sugar and wine.

"Nona Dixon," Mr. Longworth said. He climbed the hill that

was my driveway. "I was in the neighborhood. Let me help with that."

"Oh," I said. "Where's your car?"

"Parked down the street," he said. "That's an odd question."

"You startled me is all."

He took my bag of groceries. Mr. Longworth's teeth were perfectly straight and appeared too big for his mouth. They reminded me of windup teeth that chattered when wound and set on a table. "I heard you and Charlie were heckled at lunch. Things are heating up."

"I've noticed," I said. Outside the factory, the protest had grown. Now news trucks were permanently lined along the drive. Now women filled the sidewalks and lingered in the parking lot, throwing Earthshine products—tampons and toilet paper and toothpaste—at anyone who appeared to be a worker. Police officers had to be stationed near the gate to ensure nobody blocked the entrance.

"It's a marketing nightmare for sure." He walked to my door with me and waited while I fumbled with the key. Inside, my house was a mess. Dishes stacked in the sink. Unopened mail cluttered the counter. Shoes in the middle of the room where I'd suddenly decided to step out of them. I'd become the kind of person who used the clothes dryer as a dresser drawer.

Mr. Longworth set down the bag on the counter, next to several weeks' worth of unopened mail. "Working much?"

"Just *Stars and Shadows* right now."

"That's right. My wife's been wanting Celeste and Victor to reunite for a decade."

"Vincent."

"Right. Vincent. Say, Nona. I stopped by because I wanted to talk to you about something." He smiled that denture-y smile. I've never met a lawyer I trusted. I think some part of you must be broken if you choose to go into corporate law. "I—" He paused. He began withdrawing items from the bag: ice cream, Tab, banana taffy, discounted Lambrusco.

"I can do that," I said.

"Yes. Sorry," he said. "Habit. Happy wife, happy life." He turned and leaned against the counter. "I want to remind you of the confidentiality agreement you signed with Earthshine. It was part of your severance contract, I'm sure you remember. Confidentiality, in perpetuity." In perpetuity. Such a lawyerly phrase. So eternal. So vaguely threatening. "I know you've been summoned as a witness," he said.

"I was going to tell you."

"I already know." He held up his hands. It was a deposition, not a trial, he explained. Information gathering. Fishing. "Their case must be really weak if they're calling *you*."

"Thanks?"

"You know what I mean. Not even sworn testimony. No courtroom. No judge. But . . ." he said, "you can't talk about Earthshine Soap. At all. Not there. Not anywhere. Not to anyone. Look," he continued. "It's especially important now, with all those women coming forward. Everyone wants in on it, you know? That's how these things go. Social contagion. Like the Salem witch trials. The consequences would be dire."

"They hung the witches," I said. I picked up my stack of mail and nervously sorted through it. There, in a large, heavy envelope decorated with stars, was the invitation to Bertie's event at the observatory, just like Charlie had told me. I held it up. "Going?"

"Are you listening to me?" Mr. Longworth said. "We can't have anything getting out. Not a word. I'm serious now. We'll rehearse what you'll say, you and me. I'll have my secretary make an appointment for next week. The Tuttles are counting on you, Nona, to be on our side."

That night at the country club, Halley had said something similar to Charlie: *I thought you'd be on my side.* I only now remembered it.

"The shareholders are counting on you, too, of course," he said.

"I don't even know anything," I said, and that was true. I didn't know anything specific, not really. Not yet. I only had what you'd call a gut feeling, and I didn't trust my gut or my feelings. I spotted

Halley's envelope on the kitchen table, and I felt protective of it. Of her. I was on Halley's side, I wanted to say to Gene Longworth, but I didn't. Instead, I turned my attention to the invitation in my hands: gold embossed lettering on cream card stock thick enough to cut a stick of butter. Her intertwined initials at the top of the page. *BBT.* Bertie Bremen Tuttle. *The Tale of the Comet with Bertie Tuttle. January 28. The Cincinnati Observatory.*

"Her last public event, they say," he said.

Bertie planned to share her own memories of the 1910 comet: How they said the world would end. How the media drummed up fear to sell papers. How the Earthshine fire was set the night the Earth passed through the tail of the comet, a pivotal moment that altered the course of both her family and her business.

"You'd think the comet was coming just for her bon voyage. You won't need a designated driver, at least." He pointed out the window to the Boobatory rising above the tree line. "Let me ask you something. Halley—what was in her safe-deposit box?"

Truth is a natural state. It's our bodies, in moments of discomfort, that condition us to lie. My own body was reacting to Gene Longworth standing so close in a confined space. My stomach tightened. "Nothing," I said. "Why?" I could hear the way my words came out, sharp edged, the way I sounded when Wyatt accused me of nagging.

"Nona, you surprise me. The Tuttles are your friends. Think of all they've done for you. You should be grateful."

"I'm sorry," I said. "I'm no good with grief. It was personal. A photo. Sentimental stuff. We were close."

"I know. It must be hard," he said. He hung his head for a moment, then popped up again. "You wouldn't mind if I took a look then?"

It grew quiet, and I heard the clock ticking on the wall. Had it been a scene in a movie, the director would have focused on the sound, on the way the ticking amplified the tension between us. *Tick. Tick. Tick.* A bloated pause. I wasn't sure what to do. On my kitchen table, I could see that old ledger book atop the fruit bowl filled with wooden apples that looked so lifelike that Wyatt once chipped his tooth when he tried to take a bite out of one. I walked over, grabbed the photo from between the pages, and turned, hoping he wouldn't see from where I'd pulled it.

Halley didn't trust lawyers either.

"Here," I said. "This." I handed over the Halloween photo: me as the aged-out, soon-to-be-wedded Earthshine Girl, Halley as a canister of soap.

"Heh. Technically, this is a violation of contract, the unauthorized representation of the Earthshine Girl's likeness," he said.

"Maybe that's why she locked it up."

He studied it, then gave me a sideways scowl. My body buzzed, but not in a good way. "I'm joking," he said. "Sort of. And the other contents, the other sentimental stuff—"

"Look—it's late," I said. "I need to find it. And if you want to know the truth . . ." I leaned in, lowered my voice. "I'm . . . having some feminine troubles. Aunt Flo. Horrible cramps." I wrapped my arms around my waist. "I think I need a heating pad and some Pamprin."

Mr. Longworth straightened. Nothing makes a man more nervous than the kind of blood that comes from between a woman's legs. Let him have his gangster movies. Let him hunt and sling carcasses atop his car, take them home and butcher them into tenderloins for supper, but even hint at menstrual blood, and he'll squirm.

"If now's not a good time," he said. He dug into his pocket and dangled his car keys from his thumb. "We can talk again soon. My secretary will call you in a few days. Remember what I said, okay? Nobody. It's tempting to step into the spotlight, but trust me, this is not the kind of fame you want."

"Of course not."

"Good girl, Nona."

Good girl, indeed.

THAT NIGHT THE PHONE RANG, late, and when I answered, the voice on the other end sounded metallic and staticky, like an airline pilot reporting the altitude over the plane's intercom. "Is this the Earthshine Girl?"

"Who is this?" I asked. Breathing. Nothing.

The caller hung up. I lifted my window shades. The toilet paper still swayed from the trees, and in the moonlight it looked beautiful, like the billowed sails of a ship. I tried not to imagine my life as a horror movie. It could have been anyone—the protesters who'd vandalized my yard or a prank call from a neighborhood kid.

I tried to go back to reading my script. Stella was to be taken to Port Middleton Memorial, where her aunt is dying. Celeste needed a blood transfusion to save her—and Stella was her last hope, the perfect match, but she was severely dehydrated and weak and needed a course of IVs and antibiotics.

The phone rang again, and I ignored it this time, but then I heard the unmistakable beeping from Wyatt's fax machine in the basement.

I tugged on the pull chain to illuminate the basement stairs. I held on to the rail. Once, I played the role of a middle-aged woman whose laundry machine was haunted, and the final scene was a close-up of her feet descending the stairs. The director—a young guy in his twenties—had wanted to film that scene with me barefoot because he thought it tapped closer to the intimate core of the character and her motivations. "She's raw," he said. He described everything as "raw." I tried to tell him that no woman I knew would go barefoot in an unfinished basement with concrete floors.

My slippers touched the landing. Wyatt's new apartment was too small for a home office. He'd left behind his desk and word processor, his executive leather chair with steel studs. Propped against the lamp was a picture of us, from a trip we took to the Grand Canyon to celebrate our five-year anniversary. In that photo, I stood in front of him, his arms wrapped around me like a cardigan tied at the sleeves. Behind us the giant striped craters extend beyond the frame.

I ripped the paper off the fax. I stared at the words.

Does your husband know?

The words seemed to magnify, right there on the paper. My eyes zoomed in. I could see each pixel of ink. If a director were blocking this scene, she'd probably advise I do something external to dramatize my internal dilemma. The outside reflects the inside. *Scene work,* they call it. I tore at the paper in the fax machine until it was a mess on the floor. I switched off the power button. I crumpled that message in my fist.

Does your husband know?

Before the separation, I had cheated on Wyatt.

I had cheated on Wyatt, and somebody knew.

I wouldn't quite call this cheating an affair because it involved no romance, just a couch in a green room and another time, another couch. The jokes about the casting couch—I know them well. Couch sex is rarely comfortable. There's little give for the knees. I'm embarrassed, not because I find couch sex embarrassing but because I find the person with whom I had sex embarrassing.

John Dale Fox. Anchor. Action 13 News.

All my life, I had been a good girl, a rule follower, as obedient as a show dog. If I checked out at the grocery store's express lane, I made sure I didn't have a single item over ten, and I did, in fact, count duplicates of the same item. I made dinner every night that included a starch, a meat, and a vegetable—that perfect trifecta before carbohydrates became criminal. I studied my scripts, memorized my lines, even for table readings that didn't require it.

Back then, I thought the affair was necessary. I'd have blamed Wyatt, and all the ways he'd made me resent him. I'd have blamed the distance between us or the miscarriages or the fact he communicated more with his coworkers than he did with me, sitting in the basement until late, until after I'd already gone to bed. He was nicer to them, too. I'd have pointed out how when Wyatt got home from work, he'd recline in the living room watching the news, waiting for me to start dinner. And I envied that, really, I did. His stillness, his patience in the face of hunger.

I did Wyatt's laundry, and I folded his clothes. I vacuumed and dusted and got on my hands and knees scrubbing toilets and tubs and linoleum and baseboards, as my mother had taught me. I did the grocery shopping. I planned our meals. I emptied the refrigerator of leftovers, scraping out moldy food from Tupperwares. In the kitchen, he feigned incompetence. When he unloaded the dishwasher, he'd asked where each item belonged. He had a regular nine-to-five job. He made more money, I'd reasoned. I'm better at these things. It's easier for me. Only, it wasn't just that. From the start, I'd wanted to please him, and I made a habit of this pleasing. We both got used to it.

"Do you like it?" I'd ask during dinner, trying to coax gratitude for the meal I'd cooked.

"Yes," he'd reply.

"Do you think it's good?" I'd asked, still fishing. I felt pathetic, but I wanted his approval. *Good girl, Nona.*

"I already said yes," Wyatt had said. "It's just a casserole." He took another bite.

I dropped another little stone into my resentment jar. Plink, plink.

Yes, I would have claimed I cheated because of my overflowing resentment jar, and Wyatt's dinner plate that, instead of clearing, he'd push forward on the table like some poker hand he was playing. I'd make a game of it, too—leave the dishes on the table to see who would clear them first. I lost every time, because after twelve hours I couldn't take it anymore, the smear of day-old tomato sauce on plates or the crumbs that formed constellations on the table. I might have said that Wyatt didn't respect domestic work, but the truth was he didn't see domestic work because I'd made it invisible to him.

And whose fault was that?

That night, I'd made a casserole called Johnny Marzetti—people from Ohio love to name casseroles after men—and the cheese stuck to his plate like abstract art. A single noodle and meat crumble rested on his fork as though he'd grown full midbite and suddenly stopped.

"Your plate," I said to him.

Wyatt's head was inside the refrigerator, looking for something sweet. He was wearing a pair of socks with holes in them, the ones I'd put in the dust-rag bin at least a dozen times before he rescued them because he still thought they had some use.

"I got it," he said.

"Good," I said.

"Go," he said, and he pulled down a bowl for ice cream, knowing I was trying to lose weight because my agent kept telling me the camera adds ten pounds, which I finally took to be the veiled suggestion that I was fat.

Baby weight without a baby.

I went upstairs to do a workout video. I had Jane Fonda's on VHS. In it, she wore a chevron leotard, purple tights, and leg warmers. Behind her, in the background, was a shirtless man slicked with baby oil. I watched from my floor. I lay on my back, my legs extended up over my head, reaching back for the floor behind me. "Oh, that feels so good," Jane Fonda was saying on the screen, but I didn't think so. Not good at all. Since I'd lost the baby, nothing felt right inside me. I heard the hum of the dishwasher from the kitchen beneath me. I stretched back. "Oh, that feels so good," Jane Fonda was saying again.

After my workout, I went to the kitchen for a drink. Wyatt had cleared the table of the plates and utensils, and, yes, the dishwasher was running. But he hadn't put the spices back in the rack, and all the pots and pans were still dirty on the stovetop. The counter was a battlefield of crumbs. Napkins were twisted like dead soldiers.

"You said you'd do the dishes!" I yelled into the family room.

"I did."

"But—" A dirty spoon was on the countertop, the colander was in the sink. A few dry noodles that missed the pot insulted me further. Something in me shifted, a gear I didn't know existed. Anger, still contained. "You did the dishes we *ate* on. The plates. You didn't even put the leftovers away." I still wonder who Johnny Marzetti is; probably the husband of the woman who'd made the meal.

"Oh," he said.

"Oh? Oh?" I said.

"Okay, okay. Who cares? Calm down."

I growled. I'm sure I growled. "Don't turn me into a nag, Wyatt. You won't like it."

"Too late," he said.

Plinkplinkplinkplink. My resentment jar overfloweth.

For so long, we had tried for a family—would that have saved us, a tiny human tether? But I gave birth to a *still* baby, not a moving one. Why not use the real word for the thing: dead.

My milk came in after that. Nobody had told me I'd have full boobs that sagged and ached. Boobs, Wyatt. Breasts sounds so clinical and tits too crude. Just say boobs. It's not that difficult. And couldn't he at least do the dishes? *All* of them? Including the pots and pans? Including the casserole dish that I assembled from ingredients I procured from the store that I loaded into my car and drove home and put away? My time matters, too. Do you think I want nothing else but to serve you? I am not your mother—not *anyone's* mother. That's what I was thinking. Couldn't he, at the very least, do the damn dishes?

Obviously, this wasn't just about the dishes.

Wyatt's ice cream bowl sat in the sink, filled with water and dairy flotsam. He claimed he was "soaking" it. A warmth overtook me. I removed my sweatband, and I spun slowly in a circle, trying to see the world through Wyatt's eyes. The reserves of Wyatt's mind were never occupied with grocery lists and almost-empty detergent bottles, with dirty baseboards or dusty lampshades, or weight loss, or basal temperatures and monthly cycles and breast pads and guilt. I was an actress, not a cleaning lady, not like my mother. I refused to live a small life. I was the Earthshine Girl. I was Stella. I had spent four years at the conservatory. I could put myself in the mindset of another character. I could be anyone I wanted.

I heard Wyatt laughing in the family room. He was watching *Night Court.* The theme song played. *It's a hostile work environment.* I put the dirty pot in the sink, filled it with sudsy water. *My marriage* was a hostile work environment. *My marriage* had made me small. That's how I felt in that moment as I scrubbed the dried noodles off the stovetop with a sponge, and when they wouldn't give, I used my fingernail to pry them free. My fingernail chipped. I had just gotten a manicure because the next day I was hosting the Christmas in July Fund Drive at Action 13 News. Sure, not art, exactly, but it paid well. I examined my chipped nail, the sharp edges. Something wild unleashed inside me. That's the moment I decided on it, the affair. I didn't know with whom yet. I didn't know how. But I knew it was necessary. I believed it was the only way.

So, yes, I cheated on Wyatt. Sleeping with someone else did not make me bigger or more worthy of my anger. That second time, when John Dale sat up and pulled on his pants, then slapped my thigh, saying *atta girl,* all I wanted was Wyatt. Wyatt unwrapping Klondike Bars, Wyatt cutting his entire plate of food for efficiency, Wyatt pressing a bag of frozen peas to my butt after those fertility shots, Wyatt warming my side of the bed with his body before I slipped under the covers. Because that's what marriage is, an accumulation of minor details that resemble something like love.

But now in the basement, I unplugged the fax machine. I turned off the basement lights, then the kitchen lights, and then my bedroom lights. I crawled into bed, and it was cold there by myself. I wished I could talk to Halley about this. I wondered what she'd say. I remember when I confessed the affair to her. I'd taken down Sal and had the doll mouth the words: *I cheated on Wyatt.* She didn't judge me or console me. She told me I'd been conditioned to believe sex was freedom, and it is, and it isn't. I tried to think of who could have sent that note. Who could have known? I thought of the Jane Doe who'd said her life had been ruined by coming forward. *Does your husband know?* I turned my pillow vertically, and I clung to it like a body. I never wanted Wyatt more than I did in that moment when the threat of losing him forever became clear.

1910

Opal's front door wouldn't budge. She *had* been three days late with her rent, and on top of that the neighbors now twice complained of the unpleasant odors wafting up from her kitchen whenever she'd made a batch of pills. The landlord had given her a second warning, but hadn't he promised three?

Opal gave another hipped push, and finally the door relented. It hadn't been locked, only jammed by the thick envelope dropped through the mail slot that somehow managed to wedge itself underneath.

The envelope was square. Heavy. Wax sealed and stamped. High-quality card stock. Neat penmanship—not Madame de Fleur's. She tore it open.

The writing was upright and small, as though the writer was intent on conserving paper and ink. A gold embossing bordered the edges. Opal read by the waning light of the window.

> *I'm writing for the sake of business and in such cases, I think it's best to speak plainly. I understand you have been prescribing and dispensing, through your own means, medicines that have proven surprisingly effectual. Comet Pills. Come see me again. I have a business proposition. I believe we could form a lucrative and mutually beneficial partnership.*
>
> —*Clara Dowd*

Opal set down the letter and, finally, her handbag and lunch. The audacity of the woman, after turning her away with nothing more than a sample of Mourning Spray. But, still, something inside Opal stirred at the very idea that someone had come to *her* with a business proposition. Imagine that, when just months ago she was wringing out Jagr's underdrawers. A business partnership. Who was she to believe herself capable of such a thing? How dare she even think it possible?

But then there was the baby, growing inside her despite the impossibility of it, the miracle of it. She waited for a quickening, a tick, a sign. Everything lost returns, Madame de Fleur had told her, like the comet that now traced its path toward Earth, like Oren, like the baby, like the woman herself.

THE BELL DINGED WHEN OPAL closed the pharmacy door behind her. She silenced it with her fingers. Her handbag was heavy with the weight of the formulary, with the samples she'd brought with her. Clara Dowd led her to the back office, a windowless room with chairs and a desk, papers stacked to leaning.

Clara spoke first. "I'll tell you up front, I don't believe spiritualism. Or any ism for that matter. Give me something specific. Give me something useful. A body doesn't care for isms either. Give it results. Changes. Relief of symptoms." The woman sat behind her desk. Her sleeves were rolled like a washwoman's.

Opal had seen plenty of positive changes in many of the Earthshine Girls, she told Clara. The foreman announced that fewer girls missed days this month than any other month all last year; their numbers were up. A fifty-cent bonus was added to their weekly paycheck.

But, still, new girls sat with her in the lunchroom. Nervousness. Low libido. High libido. Anger. Frustration. Rage. Crying, often, so much, all the time. Hopelessness. Helplessness. Desire. Terror. Exhaustion, but not just physical. They spoke in hushed voices like they were confessing a secret they'd long held in, as though the confessing itself was some sort of relief.

"Odd that all those Earthshine Girls have *illnesses,* don't you think?" Clara said. "Factory work is hard on a body and mind. Not everyone is fit for it." Her cat jumped up on her desk and some papers fluttered to the floor. Clara lifted the cat and pinned it beneath her arm, a feline clutch.

"If you called me here to discuss working conditions," Opal said, "I can tell you it's no shirtwaist factory. Better than that, but only by a margin." The story had been all over the papers. The Shirtwaist Strike, the Uprising of 20,000, the papers called it. A few months ago, those women garment workers had gone on strike, citing horrendous working conditions. Locked exit doors. No washroom. Unbearable heat.

"Well, then. We'll get right to it. I want your brand."

Opal thought of the goats Jagr once kept, the gamy stink of their flesh when he'd branded their flanks.

"Comet Pills—" Clara said. "Did you come up with the brand name yourself? I've read in other cities hucksters are selling pills and elixirs that purport to save people from the toxic gas in the tail of Halley's Comet. Can you believe that? Capitalizing on fear."

"I don't believe what I read in the papers," Opal said.

"You and I are alike then, except . . ." Clara leaned forward, elbows to her desk. "I do believe you have a product that's helpful for those feminine maladies about which most women dare not speak. I've heard the stories from my customers. Euphoria—that's how they describe it. Like morphine without the troubling side effects. No sleepiness or lethargy. In fact, quite the opposite. One woman I spoke with described it as a little capsule of happiness. Do you know how many inquiries I've already received?" She paused for a moment, then answered the question herself: "Many."

Dowd's had the means to bring medicines to the masses, Clara explained. She pitched the terms of the agreement: pricing, commissions, stocking fees, initial order size. Opal would provide the product, and Dowd's would take care of marketing and sales. In thirty days, Opal would receive her initial commission, the standard agreement Clara made with all her vendors to ensure all up-front costs were covered and enough time to run some ads in the circulars.

"Four hundred dollars," Clara said.

Opal tried to look unsurprised, to look like a *businesswoman.* It'd take at least a year of working in the factory to save that much. She couldn't even calculate how many boxes of soap she'd have to pack or how many women's hands she'd have to hold in the dimness of the lunchroom. "And you couldn't do eight hundred?" Her voice pitched deeper as she asked it.

"The most I could do is five," Clara said. "Five and a half. Not a penny more."

Clara produced a contract, and they both signed it. Opal withdrew the samples from her handbag. Clara held the open tin and tentatively sniffed it. Then she pulled out one pill and touched the tip of her tongue to it.

"No more selling onesie, twosies," Clara said. "Think volume. Think scale. Think of the women you'll be helping."

OPAL HAD BEEN TAUGHT NEVER to think about money. Jagr would have preferred her to believe it didn't exist, that he was the center of all transactions. He hid his tinderbox. He never let her handle cash, instead setting up accounts in town that he settled himself once Opal had gone shopping. Now, it was all she could think about. Money. Money. Money.

She counted the tins of pills as she made them—fifty, sixty, seventy, two hundred. Counting eased her nerves and occupied her mind. She bent over the stove, the steam letting off such an odor she wrapped a handkerchief over her face and resembled a bandit, like Jesse James, who was killed for a $10,000 reward.

Opal counted the days until the Dowd commission was paid: twenty-nine. Twenty-eight. Twenty-seven. At work, she counted the crates she filled in a day: seventeen, nineteen. She counted the hands she held in the lunchroom: eight, ten, twelve.

She preferred to be in motion, and on her day off, she went walking. Down near the public landing she watched the children scrambling up and down the bank like little crabs. Across the river, a railroad followed the Kentucky shore. So much of her time had been spent indoors. Now, when she looked out into the distance, her vision blurred, unaccustomed to such stretches. She blinked and watched the people around her, moving about. Men in wool suits carried attachés; a woman strolled with a package tucked beneath her arm; a group of sternmen rolled a cart up a boat ramp. And beyond them, the steamboats, both majestic and utilitarian. Something in Opal always stirred at the sight of a steamboat, with its sturdy stacks and stern wheels that implied motion, reminding her that all rivers flow to the ocean, drawn to the current of a larger body.

"Excuse me, lady," said a voice, startling her. "You got a match?"

The boy was no older than six. He was missing his front teeth, and he wore a newsboy's hat, though he wasn't selling anything, just standing before her with a stubby cigar.

"Aren't you a little young for that?" she asked. He looked like an old man in his hat, with his face scrunched up from the morning's brightness.

"The world's ending anyway, lady. That comet's going to destroy us all. Boom!" Here he crashed his fists together to imitate an explosion.

She told him she didn't have a match and that the world wasn't ending, and then he turned and ran away, his strides short, his pants falling from lack of a belt, so he had to hold them up with his fist.

Comet Frenzy, the papers called it. Talk of it was everywhere. Newspaper astronomers blamed the unusually warm spring on Halley's. Dixie Ellison reported the comet was responsible for the rise in heart attacks in the elderly. The tailor down the street advertised a Comet Sale—"Buy a suit you'll want to wear for eternity." That French scientist Flammarion predicted the possible extinction of humankind, and the papers reported he was himself taken by spiritism;

he believed in telepathy, that ghosts were nothing more than spirit recordings that a person left behind and that these recordings could be played if one could access a spirit phonograph.

She wondered if a spirit phonograph were much like a Spirit Machine. She tried to imagine what a Spirit Machine might look like: nodes and wires extending from a box. She considered her baby was neither here nor on the Other Side, not dead but not yet born, somewhere in between the worlds, somewhere dark, waiting in the house of Opal's body.

Opal walked farther down the path, toward the man who sold bratwurst. She felt most comfortable in motion these days. A string of uncooked meat hung like a rosary from a metal hook on the side of his cart, and fire poked above a barrel fitted with a grate. A gust of wind bent the fire, and the flames lifted higher. Opal started. The fire had a nose, a mouth, a face; she swore it. She rubbed her eyes. She was tired. At night, she couldn't sleep. Her stomach made her uncomfortable. Her legs would cramp so badly, she'd wake up howling.

The vendor reached for a poker to turn the meat. The fire rose higher, and Opal made out a neck now, shoulders, sinuous stretches of orange shaped into arms. "Nothing to be 'fraid of, ma'am. Just a little grease from the bratwurst."

She stepped back. For a moment, she felt faint. Her condition, she thought.

"You okay, ma'am?"

She was *fine. Fine.* She was better than fine. In twenty-four days she'd have five hundred and fifty dollars from Dowd's. In twenty-five days, she'd board the *Ephemera.* What a name for a steamship. She'd already begun to think of her current life as something to be discarded after use. A house to be razed. When she arrived in France, she might look back at who she had been across the ocean and realize it was the necessary passage to where her life had been leading her all along.

"I'll take one," she said. "With sauerkraut."

Suddenly she was ravenous. Some days, she felt she could eat and eat and eat and still not be sated. The baby hadn't kicked yet, but she did demand food, the hungry girl. "Make that two," she said. Some days, she'd fill herself with cheese and bread and butter and eggs and salted pork she purchased at the market, and she'd crave more and more still. Insatiable. Opal liked expanding, taking up space. Though she hadn't felt the baby move, her girth had been its own reward. As she ate her bratwurst, she stood in front of the public posting board. She wiped her fingers on her cloak.

Before she even lifted up the posting from its tack so she could read it, she saw the photograph. The image hewed her in two. She was this Opal and that Opal. Two women. One body. She dropped what remained of her bratwurst, suddenly sick.

She plucked the paper from the post to examine it closer. The photograph had been taken on her wedding day. She was seventeen and dressed in her mother's light blue gown with a stain at the hem. Her face was so plump, so youthful, she could hardly recognize herself. Her expression held bewilderment and sadness. Even so, she could admit she'd been a beautiful bride.

Wanted, Runaway Wife. Opal Doucet has left my bed and board, stolen from me, and behaved dangerously and unlawfully. I will not pay a cent she may contract on my account, unless she is returned to me, along with my goods. Reward $100.

Her husband's name was printed beneath.

Jagr.

Her vision tunneled. She could see nothing but the sign, his name, her picture. The papers had said Jagr was not expected to survive, that his funeral was planned, that his wife had poisoned him. Murdered him.

But the papers had been wrong.

The so-called poison was a combination of medicines: the capsules he prescribed for insomnia, the pain powders he gave to patients who'd suffered injuries, and the elixir—that special elixir—Opal took for her unusual episodes.

On the evening of her wedding, Jagr had given her a glass of water mixed with laudanum. "To relax you," Jagr had said. "Prevent your headaches from . . ." He didn't finish his sentence. She stood against the wall of this strange house where she was now to live, the same house where her mother had brought her after Oren's death when it became clear that the physical symptoms of her bereavement—loss of appetite, exhaustion—were something else.

The doctor had been kind enough then; when she'd cried, he tucked a strand of hair behind her ear. "Pain," Jagr whispered, "is a sign that it's working."

Her mother believed she'd been ruined for marriage—but Jagr said he could cure anyone. Opal had been beautiful then. Compliant in her grief. A year later, they'd been married.

"Drink it," her new husband said on the night of their wedding, holding out the laudanum, and Opal did as he instructed because her doctor was her husband now. He nodded as Opal tipped the glass back. By now she knew he preferred agreeable patients. The liquid was bitter on her tongue.

It didn't take long for a feeling of lightness to hit her, as though she could lift right from her toes into the air and hover there. The laudanum. Jagr's lips were shiny, wet. Warm. She inhaled and calm washed through her, extending out to her fingertips. Jagr may have led her by the hand, or she may have floated. Either way, her dress was soon on the bedroom floor, a discarded skin. He sat on the bed, fully clothed, watching her as she undressed.

She disrobed slowly, a button at a time. She didn't love him, but something in her wanted to please him. She wanted to be good, believing goodness could cure her. But of what?

Did she think of Oren that night, how it should have been him, there atop her? Did she call him to mind with longing and regret, or think of the time they lay together in the cornfield, the grass scratching at her knees? She did not. She thought only of herself and her pleasure. But who was this indulgent self? The drugs had separated her body from her mind. Her only thought was how cool the air felt on her neck, how the lantern was surrounded by halos of sparkling light. She felt the weight of sinking into a mattress and the warmth of his body and the darkness.

The laudanum had been Jagr's greatest kindness. And that drink she offered him the night she ran away had been hers, for she could have done it another way. Instead, he took the glass from her, then rattled it. The ice tinked. He tipped back a sip, and his mustache remained wet. *Drink it faster,* Opal willed him. *Drink it all.* She hadn't much time.

"Would you like one more?" she asked when the glass was still half full.

He took another sip. Then another.

The night Opal ran away, she'd made a rump roast, but they would not eat it. Instead, she would gather the money from Jagr's tinderbox. Instead, she'd board the sunrise train for Baltimore. From there, she'd buy a steerage ticket aboard the *Ephemera.* Then: France.

Madame de Fleur had described her house in a letter—stone with two chimneys, a rounded brown door, a garden with fleurs-de-lis and hydrangeas that reminded her of a pompadour. In the letter, she'd told Opal about spirit photographers and spirit telegraphs and spirit typewriters and self-appearing slates; she'd told her about mesmerists, about ectoplasm exteriorized from the spiritualist's body, and about ghostly fingerprints that appeared as impressions in putty. Some mediums could pass messages from the dead through automatic writing. Others could play trumpets or guitars through mental clairvoyance alone. In France, the medium Eva C. would manifest light between her palms—*like she's holding the whole world between her two hands.*

That night Opal drugged him, medicated him—poisoned him, the newspapers said, but she hadn't meant for him to die—she prepared the fire, stacked logs on kindling. She made him a second drink, dissolving in the liquid, again, the contents of medicines she'd stolen from his office. The key to the cabinet was on the shelf, beneath the table bell where he kept it. The table bell was used to summon Opal for this chore or that. He considered her weak only when he needed her to be.

When Opal handed Jagr his second glass, his eyelids were already droopy, his voice sounding as though he'd stuffed marbles in his mouth. He'd thrown his hat on the rug, and it landed upside down. She could see a ring of dirt inside. "Are you okay?" Opal said.

"The light. It's . . . My eyes are tired," he said, then closed one eye completely and knocked back another gulp.

"Maybe something's coming on. Rest." She helped him down the hallway to their bedroom and removed his boots. She had only meant the drugs to put him to sleep.

Afterward, she crept into his office and opened the cabinet where he kept his tinderbox. She unlatched it and lifted the lid.

There, at the bottom, where she'd expected to find a thick wad of bills, lay just a single dollar and some coins. She dumped the box over to be sure it wasn't hidden in a recessed compartment or stuck beneath the lid. Nothing.

But what could she do? Her plan had already been set in motion. When he awoke, he'd know what she had done.

Later, in the darkness, Opal's husband lay heaped on their bed making noises like an injured whippoorwill. She stood before the bed and watched his labored breathing. He neither blinked his eyes, nor focused them. She'd washed his hat, and now she placed it upturned on his chest where, when he opened his eyes, he would see it was spotless.

She recalled that train ride out of Gallipolis, how the empty seat beside her rattled, how when the conductor came around to collect tickets, he looked at the seat and said, *Traveling alone? Yes,* she'd said. *Alone,* but she was not alone. Her breasts ached. Her stomach cramped and bloated. She watched trees tick by outside her window.

Now, by the riverwalk, the photograph of herself its own kind of haunting, she was alarmed by the idea that Jagr lurked among the crowd. He didn't know about the baby. She'd be punished for leaving him. She'd be forced to—

She looked behind her, to the facades of buildings that stood facing the river, to the rickshaw ticket booth where one could purchase fares. She scanned the carriages lined up to take arriving passengers to their destinations and the stacks of pallets that were being unloaded from the steamers. A man with Jagr's hands held a piece of timber. A messenger boy on his bike stooped with Jagr's shoulders. A bag boy whistled, and it sounded like Jagr's. There was the vendor selling grilled meats. The fire rose up again from his barrel. Yes, Opal saw it: eyes and a face and body, tilted forward, Jagr himself.

WANTED, RUNAWAY WIFE. REWARD $100.

Opal folded the paper and stuffed it in her pocketbook.

At home, she leaned over the basin of the sink and splashed her face with water. When she righted herself, she felt it. *Finally* she felt it. A swift kick in her stomach—a flutter really—then, again, two more quick movements. How to explain this moment? How brief but profound it seemed. The baby had spoken, finally—just to her, in a language only she could understand, a secret only she knew, an otherworldly whisper. Could the baby hear her, too? Soon, the life inside her would cross over to *this* side, to *this* life. She was the threshold between the two worlds, the very space where the crossing occurred.

Opal reached up to her highest cabinet, where she kept her own medicines. When her hand touched the vial, the baby moved again. Now, she filled her glass from the faucet. She balanced the pill on her tongue. She'd leave the day the money came in. The very moment the cash touched her hands. She let the pill roll to the back of her tongue, then she lifted her glass.

Opal dressed for bed. The lights spangled. Her mind relaxed.

Darkness washed in waves around her. She drew a hot bath. She scrubbed her skin with the Earthshine Soap she'd taken from work. She rested her neck on the lip of the tub and listened to the coal barges moving up and down the river, their thin, low horns moaning on behalf of the world.

January 21, 1986

Interview with Jane Doe No. 12

By *The Cincinnati Inquisitor*

CI: Describe your experience with Earthshine Soap.

JANE DOE NO. 12: The weekends smelled like lavender. Saturdays, I scrubbed the kitchen and bathrooms with Earthshine while my husband watched baseball on TV with the baby and my other kids played in the basement. I could only clean on weekends because the rest of the week I worked a regular nine-to-five, and when I got home it was time to get supper on the table or help the kids with homework. I never had time to myself. I'd lock myself in the bathroom and cry, and if someone knocked I'd say I was disinfecting the linoleum, which I was. That was true.

My insides hurt, but all my doctors told me nothing was wrong. Pain in my stomach, in my pelvis, in my back. Sometimes I couldn't breathe from the pain, and I couldn't cook or eat or take the children to the park. My periods never returned after nursing my third child. I'd wake lethargic in the morning and count on my fingers the hours till bedtime. The doctors said it was all in my head.

CI: What happened?

JANE DOE NO. 12: We hired someone to help around the house. She had this gentle, wide smile, but I could sense it in her, this loneliness, too. One day, she was rehanging the living room curtains, and I asked her—Do you ever feel just, like, there's something wrong with you, but you don't even know how to describe it? And you wouldn't know what to do about it, even if you could?

L--- said yes. She told me she suspected the soap. She told me she'd once stopped using it for a while, and she felt better, but the people she worked for complained that the sinks weren't white enough, the floors weren't shiny, so she switched back. She didn't want to live like this.

Nothing felt real. She started to cry, and I did, too, and we just held each other right there in that living room, the curtains still down, right there for the neighbors to see. I didn't care. It felt so good to hold her. To be held. That is when I knew my whole life had been a lie.

CI: And you believe Earthshine Soap is responsible?

JANE DOE NO. 12: I know it is.

1986

Out of the shadows and into the light of new loveliness!

—CAMAY SOAP

It was early still, and dark. I turned my radio off and sat in the quiet of the studio parking lot waiting for call time. I studied the factory, lit up even at night, the smokestack that read BREMEN, Bertie's maiden name. At the Earthshine Grand Re-Opening Ceremony I had stood next to Bertie in that dress she bought me. My mother watched from the crowd. She was thin and square-shouldered in that same beige coat she wore for every occasion.

When I was younger, I'd read in my science textbook about spontaneous combustion. A man was dining with a woman at an Italian restaurant, and midbite he simply combusted. "Talk About a Hot Date," read the title of that section, and I remember how terrified I'd been, how my mother set a fire extinguisher next to my bed, just so I could get some sleep. Only now do I consider that fire extinguisher could have been more for her than for me, a way of saving herself if I burst into flames.

Does your husband know?

What would my mother think of me now?

Someone knocked on my window, and I jumped. "Get away," I yelled. "I have Mace." I had taken a self-defense class at the local YWCA. I'd learned to use my voice, to "yell and tell," my instructor explained, to make myself out as a difficult target.

"It's just me, Nona. Jesus."

The glass squeaked as I rolled the window down. The car was old, but Wyatt claimed the engine would run forever.

"Hello, gorgeous," he said. John Dale Fox. The collar of his coat flipped up. His hair was slicked back. Makeup caked his skin. "I heard they might make you a regular."

"Was it you?" I asked.

"Maybe. Depends. Was it good?"

"Spooking me into giving you an interview? Threatening me? A fax? Really? And then you just happen to show up here? It won't work." I was overtired. I had slept only ninety minutes. Maybe I'd hallucinated the whole thing. *Does your husband know?*

"Really, I have no—"

"And does *she* know? Your wife?" I asked. Halley once swore all you needed to do to bed a man was touch his thigh to signal interest, like Hitchcock's strangers tapping shoes on a train. The first night it happened, John Dale stopped by the green room to check on me after the fund drive ended. I acted first. I touched his thigh. *My closest friends call me J.D.*, he'd said, and moments later we were kissing. Men are not that difficult.

"I could tell her," I said.

"Cliché, don't you think?" he asked. "The wounded mistress."

"'Call me J.D. Only my closest friends call me J.D.,'" I said.

"My close friends do call me J.D. I mean, look, it's like this: When a guy goes out to a bar, do you think he's looking for the most attractive woman he can find? No. He's looking for the most attractive *flawed* woman. The hottest woman will be a pain in the ass; she can afford to be choosy. It's the hot chicks with flaws who are the real prize. I think it's game theory, or something."

"So I'm a hot chick *with a flaw*?" I was seething, but at the same time I wondered what my flaw was—what weakness John Dale might have perceived in me. I thought the whole thing had been my idea. I touched his thigh! Exhaust trailed from my car's tailpipe, and I could hear what Wyatt would say about atmospheric pollution. He was principled, the kind of man who'd never cheat. Other cars were pulling into the parking lot now. Their headlights washed over John Dale. He had a mole on his cheek, colored taupe from foundation.

"What I'm saying is this: Flaws aren't inherently bad. They're ratings gold. Viewers love to believe they hold the power of forgiveness. It's the story of redemption. Look at Noah's Ark."

"Suddenly you're quoting scripture?"

"Did you see the last *Inquisitor*? Twenty Jane Does now. A huge class-action lawsuit is coming. I mean, holy shit, Nona. You were the Earthshine Girl. You need to speak out. Defend these women or something."

"It *was* you."

"At least acknowledge them. That's all they want. The Tuttles own this town. The Jane Does just want to know you're on their side."

"Look at you, the moral mayor. Reverend J.D. himself."

"The Tuttles won't talk. Bertie Tuttle is ancient. She'll be dead before this thing goes to trial, and now her granddaughter swallowed a bottle of—"

"Halley," I said. I felt sick. I heard car doors slamming, footsteps on concrete. The sky was lightening into an overcast morning, and already the protesters were beginning to line up. I could make out their yellow visors and the rectangular shapes of their signs. "They're grieving."

"Even the media wouldn't stoop that low," John Dale said. "But it's not a good look for the family. Now those women are blaming the Earthshine Girl. They're coming for *you*, Nona." I could see Halley's handwriting. *For you, Nona.* I wondered when she'd written it. For how long had she kept her own plans a secret?

"I don't know anything," I said, and even though I didn't, not really, the words sat heavy inside me, like a lie. I knew Halley well enough to know she didn't trust Bertie Tuttle. I knew Halley well enough to know she'd felt what she left me was important, especially if she'd kept it in a safe-deposit box.

"A detail. Something that seemed off. You've got to know something. You've been friends with the family for years."

"Bertie's hardy. She might outlive us all."

"That interview—come on. Let's do it. You and me. Who can deny our on-air chemistry?" He opened my car door, then stepped aside.

The first evening we slept together—I hate calling it that because we didn't sleep; sleep requires greater intimacy than what we did—we'd cohosted the WLAX Action 13 News annual Christmas in July Fund Drive to support the local children's hospital. My agent encouraged me to do it, said it'd be good for my *recognition value.* They had me wear elf ears, a curved hat, and a shiny sequined vest with a Christmas tree on it. In the final segment, the director asked me to hold a five-month-old baby—not a patient, but the infant daughter of the meteorologist. They thought the shot would be tender and authentic.

When John Dale set the baby in my arms, the baby's demeanor shifted. By which I mean, the child screamed. The entire live segment. The entire time I held her. To deliver my lines, I had to raise my voice, which made me sound angry. The baby, in her fit of temper, tugged off one of my felt ears. I was elfish Van Gogh.

"I'm going to be late," I said.

"So it's a maybe?" John Dale said. "Look, I'm sorry. I'm an asshole. That was your flaw—you couldn't see it."

"You never even called me," I said.

"You wanted me to?"

"No. Hell no. My husband can't find out. He can't. Do you understand me?"

"I thought he'd left you already."

"We're taking a break. That's all. Just for a little bit. How do you even know that?"

"Word on the street."

"A real investigative reporter."

We were quiet for a moment. A group of women now headed for the studio door—extras who played the Port Middleton nursing staff.

"This is big, Nona. Bigger than you. Bigger than us," John Dale said. "Think about it. You can redeem yourself. A redemption story is the greatest kind of story there is."

He leaned against my car as I stepped out and passed him. I felt nothing when our bodies brushed, two objects in time and space.

THE DOCTOR'S OFFICE AGAIN. FLUORESCENT lights. Plastic diorama of a uterus that looked like a bull's head. Pamphlets about menopause. A jar of oversize wooden tongue depressor things that were not for depressing tongues. I sat on the exam table, fully dressed. The doctor came in, same inky birthmark. His mood was jovial; he walked on his toes.

From his body language, I expected good news. He whistled and bounced. He flipped a light switch with his elbow, and a wall-mounted box illuminated. Then he placed a film up against it. "Here," he said. "And here. And here." The film looked like the deep ocean. I tried to make out a fish. "Tumors," he said. I sucked in my breath, but he held up a palm like he was taking an oath. "Calm it. Not cancer."

I exhaled. Still, I felt dizzy. "That's good," I said. "Right?"

"Good? No, I wouldn't call it good. No tumors at all would be good."

"Then what?"

The tumors were the size of kiwi fruits, he told me, and I thought of the week-by-week pregnancy book I'd read, how every stage of the baby's life is compared to a fruit or vegetable. Why think of the uterus as containing food at all? It leads one to believe the mother will eat whatever's inside.

The tumors had a name that sounded astral, like something you'd find in outer space. But this wasn't outer space we were talking about. This was my body. This was me.

"There is some good news," he said. "A hysterectomy. The science has advanced. We'll take the whole thing out. Three days in the hospital. Six-week recovery. Boom."

"No boom," I said. "No boom." The back of my knees stuck to the pleather exam table. The doctor turned off the box light, and the picture of my uterus went dark. "What are my other options?" I asked.

The doctor spun on his stool, then pushed himself up. Small tufts of hair poked above the V-neck of his scrubs. "This is a relatively common procedure for women like you."

"Like me?"

I touched my stomach protectively, as though the doctor would attempt to yank my insides from me right then and there. I imagined the scene, the two of us in some anatomical tug-of-war.

"Middle-aged," he added.

Middle-aged. That's what my agent had called me, Elliot, too—middle-aged. The term is never not an insult.

I drove home in silence. I tried to consider the bright side: no more periods, that monthly window of socially condoned rage. No more bleeding, no more cramps. No tampons or pads cluttering my bathroom cabinets. More storage space for other products. Nair! Mustache bleach! Those bendy curlers they advertise on commercials. No more obsessively looking at the calendar. Women were bound by time in a way men never would be. In fact, no calendar at all. Time would expand, or collapse. What did it matter? I'd never have a child, and so my time would be my own.

And, then, I heard it again, for the third time: What I thought was a baby's wail in my head, filling the space so loudly I took my hands off the steering wheel to cover my ears. *Waa. Waa.*

I was tired. I needed sleep.

I thought of what that nurse had said to me as they began the procedure to extract my *still* baby: "Tummy's still flat." She was saying it as a compliment, I know, but it felt like an insult. I'd never know what I'd look like with a melon-round belly unless I played a pregnant woman, and I'd never been cast as one so I could only figure I didn't look the part.

When I was pregnant, I only ever looked bloated, like I'd eaten a diet of bacon and beans. Still, Wyatt would see me pulling up from the store and wave me in. "I'll get the groceries," he'd say. He'd kiss me on my temple and lift the bag from me because he didn't think I should carry heavy things, and I wanted to ask him: *Well, how'd you think I got the bags in the car?* But I wouldn't say that, because the gesture was intended to be sweet, and half of marriage is learning the right moments to keep your mouth shut.

After our child was born—or unborn, not born, stillborn, dead—Wyatt and I stopped talking. Maybe we figured we'd talk about it later, when it didn't hurt so much, or maybe it never stopped hurting, or maybe I felt guilty, so guilty, responsible somehow.

I don't believe in coincidences, really I don't. Or maybe I do—maybe I do believe in signs, like Halley did, because it means I can hand myself over to the universe. I can stop worrying about whether the choices I've made were the right ones. There's a freedom to that. I walked into my house; I hit power on the TV. *Stars and Shadows* was on. Vincent stood at Celeste's hospital bed. A nurse was covering her with a sheet. Bianca Dupont was comforting him. They were about to kiss, then it cut to commercial, and there she was on the TV in my living room: the Earthshine Girl.

The Earthshine Girl had a gap between her teeth, like I once had. She was submerged in a sudsy bath, her hair cascading past her shoulders, covering her chest. Her hand hung over the lip of the tub; in it, she held an Earthshine canister.

It's strange to look at someone who so resembles you. It makes you feel an odd sense of proprietary longing, of protection, of nostalgia, too. It makes you think about yourself—of the past and your own childhood, of your mother and the shape of her hands and how they held you once as a baby. It makes you think of the whole of it, the cycle of life. The casting director was good. The girl looked just like me. The Earthshine Girl could have been my child.

But she wasn't.

There's power in creation, isn't there? If I could create a baby, I could do anything. But I couldn't do anything. I could do nothing. A sense of unfairness hit me—cosmic unfairness, you might call it—that a casting director could keep spawning Earthshine Girls in my image, when I could not spawn any living thing myself.

I thought of how in the hospital, the nurse asked if I wanted to hold the baby, but I shook my head. Wyatt looked away; he wouldn't meet my eyes, and that cut me in half. I could see his face in profile, a mix of pity and disdain. In the years since then, I've questioned that moment, my decision. It'd been the only chance to see my true likeness, and I'd refused.

We never spoke of it again. Back then, one didn't talk about that sort of thing, and isn't that the whole problem? That we're asked to keep quiet on the subject? That we do?

It's so hard to look back on memories without polluting them with hindsight. I turned off the TV. A pair of Wyatt's jeans were slung across the chair in my bedroom. I reached for them, letting the legs unfurl, and I pressed the fabric to me. I remembered a story I'd once heard about a ceramicist who was overcome with grief from the unexpected loss of her husband. After she buried him, she sat among his things, and that's when she noticed the days-old indentation in his bean bag chair from where his body once rested. She made an impression of it and cast the impression in metallic clay. Then she set about making an entire installment wherein her husband's shape was carved out of everyday objects: a bed, a couch, an office chair. The woman would fold herself into the hollow that was once her husband, claiming that those were the moments she felt closest to him.

Sitting in our bedroom, I felt grief akin to what that ceramicist must have felt, a longing to be held again. I'm not sure it was even about Wyatt, but I ached for him, his physical presence, the familiarity of his body. The freckles on his shoulders. The divots above his hips. The long muscles of his calves. The way his stubble scratched my cheeks in the morning, and he called it natural exfoliation. We are all bodies. We crave other bodies because it roots us to our own experience and reminds us we exist. I wanted to be touched—isn't it ridiculous to admit that? That in this moment when I felt grief, all I could think about was desire? That's the thing with grief—it takes no material form, so we project it onto any object we can find.

Soon, I went searching for an object. I foraged beneath the kitchen sink for the Earthshine canister. The holes on the top resembled the ones in the telephone receiver, only larger. I turned the Earthshine in my hands, spun the familiar label with an illustration of my young face. I must have looked at that picture at least a million times in my life. The familiar becomes invisible. That's how we can hurt the people closest to us. We stop seeing them in detail. EARTHSHINE SOAP was written in bold block letters, underscored by a fading line. I studied it closer. Then I saw it, on the package, clearer than anything I'd ever witnessed in my life: the streak beneath those words, brighter at one end and broadening at the other, not just a design but the tail of a comet.

I remembered when I was still the Earthshine Girl and Halley led me on that tour of the factory, past the burping machines and conveyor belts and workers, to a dusty old storage area where they kept memorabilia: old soap-stirring paddles and white uniform dresses and vintage posters and wooden crates packed with cakes of soap that crumbled if you picked them up.

"Treasures," Halley said, because she loved old things. At the back of the room, against the wall, leaned weatherworn pieces of the old sign that used to be nestled in the hills of Mount Adams, near downtown. I used to be able to read it from the road below—EARTHSHINE—as though announcing the name of the city itself. It reminded me of the HOLLYWOOD sign in Los Angeles that I'd first seen when Bertie Tuttle took me there to watch her star dedicated on the Walk of Fame. I stood next to her in costume. It'd been my first time away from home.

Halley stretched her hands above her head, trying to gauge the height of each wooden letter. Up close, the paint was rough like alligator skin. I touched it, and she told me not to because of lead. "I want that *H*," she said. "Wouldn't that be fun? Hang it on my wall?"

"Do you live in a mansion?" I asked.

"Bertie does."

"I'll take the *N*," I said. The letters were at least twenty feet tall, and one would never fit through the door of the small house where I lived. "What does it even mean, *Earthshine*?" I asked.

It was an astrological term for when sunlight reflects off the Earth's surface and illuminates the dark underside of the moon. Poets call it the new moon in the old moon's arms, or moonglow, or the ashen moon, or the Da Vinci glow after Leonardo, who first explained the phenomenon. But poets aim for emotion, not accuracy. To them, something is always like something, defined by what it isn't, so it's hard to grasp what they really mean, even if they claim to simplify complexities. Halley was a poet in her own way, I guess. "When the sun talks to the moon through the Earth," Halley said, "you know, like Sal? That's earthshine."

"Why name a soap for that?" I asked.

Halley thought for a moment, then she erected her posture, put a fist to her chest, and affected the voice of a radio announcer: "Earthshine Soap. So effective you'll see parts of yourself you didn't know existed."

Staring at that canister, I could see myself clearly now.

I must have stood up at some point. I must have thought about the Jane Does and Halley and that notebook. Perhaps I unbound the twine and flipped through the pages, then stopped to study the handwriting on that final page. The *C* in Comet Pills had little curlicues, and Opal Doucet had drawn a square around the words, boxing them in. I must have collected the canisters of Earthshine Soap from my house. One in the bathroom. One in the linen closet. One atop the dryer in the basement.

You don't recall a memory—a memory recalls you. This is what I remember now, all these years later: standing in the garage in Wyatt's jeans, the Earthshine creating a plume of dust when I threw it in the trash. I was bleeding still, heavily. I could feel it between my legs.

1910

The photograph of Reginald Goodman resembled a turtle: large body, small head. His hair was parted in the middle and waxed, and he wore round spectacles at the tip of his nose. Goodman owned Goodman's Beard Wax out of Pittsburgh, and now, according to the papers, he was buying Earthshine Soaps.

The news came as no surprise—they'd all heard the rumors.

"Do you think we'll be out of work?" asked Maria.

"Maybe they'll spare us. We're cheap labor. The machine workers get paid twice as much for the same hours. And all because they have a little wee between their legs," Betsy said.

"To think that one's wages are determined by your privates," Maria said.

At that moment, the foreman descended the stairs from his platform. He rarely came down to the floor unless there was a mechanical issue or an injured girl. He stopped in front of Opal's station. "Follow me," he said.

It'd been a week since she'd plucked Jagr's poster from that board. How quickly he had tracked her down. Why is one always surprised by endings when that's what we're marching toward all along?

She considered her options. She could run, but she wouldn't get far. The foreman would call for the help of the machinists, who would quickly overpower her. She could pretend to pass out or call "Fire!" or fight with her fists, but what good would that do her? To call a woman the weaker of the beasts was simply an observation of muscle mass.

Opal followed the foreman up the metal stairs and past his platform. From this vantage point, the floor of the factory looked different, smaller and more massive at once. She could see all the girls toiling below. Up this high, she could see right out the window to the cityscape, to Union Terminal in the distance, the train station that resembled a giant table clock.

What would she say when she saw Jagr? *I'm sorry* wouldn't quite cover it. She hadn't meant to hurt him as she had. She'd miscalculated the strength of his drugs. She thought of all she'd have to do for him, all he'd make her do. Maybe it'd be no different from the life she'd led with him before—always having to apologize for the ways she'd failed his expectations, always getting out in front of these apologies by trying to please him in the first place.

As she followed the foreman, she considered how she'd describe this moment to Madame de Fleur. What details would she remember? The stubble on the back of the foreman's neck. The cracks along the walls shaped like veins, as though the factory were a living, breathing thing. She wanted to ask her if those on the Other Side always knew the ending. She wanted to ask if those on the Other Side were ever wrong. Did they long for anything other than what they desired in life? How could they be so certain without their bodies to guide them? Could they love without a body? Were they freer that way?

The foreman led her down a narrow corridor, past the room where she could see the machine operators taking a break. Their lunchroom had windows and electrical lights, a water jug, an icebox to keep their lunches cool. Finally, he led her into yet another room with green carpet, a large oak table.

At the far end of the table sat, not Jagr, but Bertie Tuttle.

Relief washed over Opal with such intensity, she felt as high as she did on laudanum. She might very well float out of her shoes.

The foreman shut the door behind him. Bertie motioned for Opal to sit. On the wall hung a portrait of Bertie's father. He resembled something of a walrus with his mustache and his hair parted in the middle.

"Your cure worked," Bertie said. She had read milk was the key to a healthy pregnancy. She sipped some now from a pint bottle.

"Thank the spirits," Opal said.

"I'm not thanking anyone. Not yet anyway." Bertie emptied her pint, then looked like she might vomit. She bent forward and pulled a newspaper from the handbag at her feet. "And now I need something else from you," she said.

"Morning sickness?" Opal asked.

Bertie shook her head.

"*Beard* wax," she huffed. "It's my father's factory. Once the baby arrives, Charles won't need to sell. I can finance him. He can do whatever he wants." She explained that Charles believed there wasn't enough money in soap anymore, not enough *value.* Too many competitors. Too little profit for too domestic a product. He had bigger dreams—electronic appliances, plastics, pharmaceuticals—and that was the problem, his ambitions. She'd told him she was pregnant. She begged him to keep the news private until she was further along, and still, he moved forward with the sale of the factory, despite the promise of the baby. "I don't think he believes me," she said.

"That you're pregnant?"

"That it will take. That it won't be like . . ." She paused and seemed to look directly at that portrait of her father. "Like the last few times."

"I'm sorry," said Opal.

"I don't want your pity," she snapped, then softened. "It all feels so silly, to be sad for something I never even had. I don't even know that *sadness* is the right word."

Opal understood what she meant.

"I know he has a mistress," Bertie said. "A desperate working girl from what I hear," she added, "as though it isn't humiliating enough."

The girl is not at fault, Opal wanted to say, but did not. Because she knew Amanda Mahooney, who was desperate, but not in the way Bertie assumed.

Just last week, Amanda had sat with Opal in the lunchroom when the other girls had left. Her fingers were slender, but her nails were bitten to the stubs. "He says he loves me, but . . . He says . . ."

"Heartache?" Opal asked, trying to understand.

"I've gotten myself into some trouble," Amanda said. She looked downward, scrutinizing the table, and Opal realized what she'd come for. A cure for her shame.

"You don't have to explain."

"You probably think I'm a terrible person." She chewed her lip as though she'd wanted to eat herself up, bit by bit, devour herself completely.

"Brave to admit what you want. That's a difficult thing to do, wouldn't you say?"

Amanda nodded gratefully. "Will it hurt?" she asked.

"It will," Opal said. "At first. But then you'll feel much better."

"Because I won't be in pain?"

"Because you won't be afraid."

A few days later, when the other Earthshine workers stood in the coatroom, dressing to go home, Amanda's coat hung abandoned on the hook.

"He probably sent for her again," Betsy said.

"Who?" the newest girl asked—but the rest of them already knew. Amanda Mahooney was the woman Dixie described as *trim and salacious.*

"Charles Tuttle, you dummy. Amanda's the employee of the year."

But there, in that green-carpeted room, Opal didn't share all that. What good would it have done to turn Bertie against poor Amanda Mahooney? She wasn't to blame. Bertie adjusted her gloves, pulling them up at the fingertips, then down at the wrists, and then she made a fist, as though she'd caught a mosquito in her grip.

"I need to ask you for another favor," Bertie said.

"A love potion?"

Here, Bertie laughed so heartily she nearly lost her breath. She loosed herself from her perfect posture and doubled over. When she regained her composure, tears wetted her cheeks. Opal hadn't known Bertie could release herself like that, and it made her more fond of the woman. "I haven't laughed like that in a while. It feels good, you know?" She heaved a breath. She removed her gloves and wiped her tears with them. Then she pushed the newspaper forward. "I need you to talk to the other Earthshine Girls. It's my father's factory, you know. It means something to me."

Opal must have looked confused.

"Organize them, whatever you want to call it. Like these women at the shirtwaist factory in New York." She now pointed to the article about the Shirtwaist Strike. After eleven weeks, the strikers finally negotiated an ending to the ordeal. In the photograph in the paper, the women linked arms. They looked flushed and victorious, but their tight, straight smiles revealed anger simmering still. "Convince them to strike," Bertie said. "They'll listen to you."

Opal's silence forced Bertie to continue. "They will fire every single one of you Earthshine Girls, you know. Old Goodman plans to bring in his own workers. He's moving them here from Pittsburgh. From his beard wax factory. Beard wax," she scoffed.

Bertie stood and faced the portrait of her father. She touched the canvas tenderly, as though smoothing his hair. "My father introduced us," Bertie explained. "At the time, the prospect of marrying Charles seemed promising. He can be surprisingly sentimental. A portrait of his first wife hung on his wall. It still does. He's afraid removing it would betray the woman, and I'm not jealous. I told Charles, at the very start, I do not want to be a common wife. Let me work with you, I told him, like I worked with my father. I wrote some of my father's advertisements, you know. But I think it's different when it's your wife. Some men claim to want an equal until they realize the logistics of it."

Something about facing that portrait allowed Bertie a moment of such candor. She seemed to notice this and turned her back to the painting. "Queen City's Soap. It's not contested. Pure and clean, your dirt's arrested," she recited.

"That was you?" Opal said. "That rhyme always stuck in my head. You have a knack for jingles."

"Charles calls it a hobby."

"Why do you want the factory so badly?" Opal said. "You've seen it yourself. The heat. The noise. The machinery is ancient. Just last week one of the girls nearly cut off her finger on the slicing machine when a bolt loosened. And the workers, half of them are sick."

"Sick from work." Bertie laughed. "Now you sound like Dixie Ellison."

Last week Betsy had come to see her in the lunchroom. *I feel strange,* she'd said. While they sat together, Opal felt the woman's driving pulse. *Is it the baby?* Opal had asked. Betsy shrugged; her cheeks had rounded out, her belly, too. *For a moment, I was standing there, and I didn't feel real,* Betsy said. *Lightheaded?* Opal asked. Betsy nodded, then shaded her eyes and squinted, like it was too bright in the dim room. Opal helped her to sit. *You're real, see?* Then she pinched the skin at the base of Betsy's palm, but the woman did not flinch. Afterward, she'd given Betsy some more Comet Pills, and she didn't charge her the customary fifty cents.

"My father was a great defender of the women's cause," Bertie said. "He believed what women needed most was to work. Industry. That's the great equalizer."

But Opal had worked all her life, hadn't she? Even before she'd made a single dollar of her own. She had spent hours of her life toiling in the kitchen making goulash or mincemeat pie. How she loathed cooking and scouring the pans afterward; how her stomach pitched at the flotsam that rose to the top of the dishwater that Opal had to skim off with a strainer so she wouldn't clog the sink.

"And yet you want us to walk off the job? It makes no sense."

"Just temporarily. Just until I can prove this pregnancy will take, until I'm further along. Charles can't sell a soap factory on strike. Nobody would want to be associated with it. Poor publicity, angry women, all that, not to mention what it could do to the brand. The newspapers would be all over it. Front-page material."

Opal couldn't risk her picture in the paper again—not with Jagr looking for her now. "They won't do it," Opal said. "They need their jobs. We all do."

"Think about it: You girls could improve your position. A calculated risk. Look at these women in New York. They negotiated higher wages. Nearly double!"

"And better work conditions," Opal added. "No exploding boilers or unbolted machines."

"Now," said Bertie, as thought they had settled the matter. "You have my word. If you convince the girls to strike, afterward, I'll inspect every square inch of this place, and make improvements, even if I have to do it with my own two hands." Bertie pinned her hat and readied to leave. "From the start I suspected you were different. Ambitious." She offered an approving look, then picked up her bag. "We could help each other," she said. "What is it you *really* want?"

That question again. Opal stood now and straightened her apron. Wasn't this just another way of asking: *Who are you? And what are you willing to do to become her?* Wasn't Bertie just daring her to say it out loud? And what if she did?

I want the Dowd money, she might have said. But that wasn't quite right. *I want to go to France,* she could have said. Or, *I want to save this baby*. Or, *I want a different life*. Or, *I want what I want. I want to be able to want.* Now that was closer to the truth, but she couldn't quite put it to words. Plus, the women weren't intimate enough for that kind of conversation.

"I want a space of my own," Opal said. "A place to work. Spirit work." In a single week, the Dowd order had already doubled. She hadn't the space. Her kitchen was cluttered with glass dishes and bowls and botanicals strung from twine with clothespins to dry. The pots were at a constant boil, decocting roots and herbs. And recently, her landlord had given her that final warning. Her rented rooms reeked of sulfur and soured wine and something pungent and medicinal. The neighbors had complained again. The scent of it kept even her awake at night, her baby enhancing all her senses.

Bertie suggested the old testing laboratories at the Earthshine Factory. She knew the building's layout—and a better, more private way in, she'd explained. She led Opal outside into the sunlight, then across the street to a stout annex building where they stored maintenance supplies. Bertie took Opal down a set of stairs and through the old tunnel so they wouldn't be seen, lagering tunnels that once served to cool beer when the factory was a brewery, before her family owned it. *Beer caves,* she'd called them. The beer cave was chilly, with brick archways tall enough for transporting casks. Two lamps were plenty to illuminate the way. Old barrels were stacked along the sides, like forgotten trunks in the hold of a ship.

They arrived at the base of a slat-wood staircase. Upstairs, Opal found herself in a square room where she'd never been, a separate entrance from the one she used, all the way on the other side of the factory. A memorabilia room of some sort. A small sign, a replica of one that hung over the city, bore the company name: EARTHSHINE SOAP. Advertisements lined the walls. Women in kitchens. Women in aprons. Women in sudsy bathtubs with long-handled brushes. SO CLEAN, one read, against an illustration of a woman radiating beams of light from her skin, HE'LL SEE YOU FROM MILES AWAY.

"That sounds like an advertisement for a telescope," Opal said.

Soon they arrived at their destination, and Bertie turned on the light; a naked bulb hung from a wire, which now illuminated the laboratory. Light reflected orange on the glass beakers, glass bowls, glass measures of varying sizes. In the back, three large vats looked like giant metal mixing bowls, paddles and all. Opal spun in slow circles. She took quick inventory of the shelves: Reduction pans. Bunsen burners. Balance scale. A pill press. Mortar and pestle. Small tins and overwrap. String. Clamps. Pipettes. "And your husband won't mind?" Opal asked.

The corners of Bertie's mouth tucked, just slightly. Sudsy had found them, and now he licked her hand that she held out toward him to be kissed. "I've asked him to stay away from the factory for the time being. Charles can do that much for me."

"I see."

"There's no need for it, really. He has a foreman, managers, all that. Besides, if he's so ambitious, he should focus on publicity. The look of things. We haven't told anyone yet about the baby, but when the world finds out, what will it look like? *A working girl.*"

THE LUNCHROOM HAD NEVER ACCOMMODATED so many Earthshine Girls at once. A body occupied every chair, every space against the wall. Some made seats of the tables.

So many bodies heated the room. Opal wished for water; she was endlessly thirsty. She lit the candles she'd brought from home. She adjusted herself in her chair. The small of her back ached from all the standing. The baby tired her easily, but she couldn't sleep. She couldn't get comfortable.

She closed her eyes and remembered watching Madame de Fleur in her tent at the circus. Once she sat silent for a full ten minutes, so long that people began leaving, suspecting she'd fallen asleep. The stage manager tapped her shoulder, and Madame de Fleur woke with a banshee howl. She howled so long and with such a feral force that many in the audience covered their ears. Some left. Opal moved closer to the woman and felt vibrations rattle her insides, like she was standing in front of a train.

"Why are we here?" Betsy now shouted. She nervously smoothed her bangs.

At that moment, a rapping sound. The room collectively inhaled, exhaled. Then, silence. Opal stretched out her foot until she could feel the string she'd affixed to the bottom of the table, the weight of the apple holding it taut. Two knockings, the thump of the apple bouncing against the wall.

Opal began to hum. The rapping continued, louder, so Opal lifted her voice. "He communes with me directly. One knock means yes, two means no. Ask of him what you wish." Opal positioned her leg just so.

"Are you a ghost?" Maria asked. *Knock.*

"Are you real?" Amanda shouted toward the ceiling. *Knock.*

"Are you of this world?" *Knock knock.*

"Were you ever alive?" *Knock.*

"Do any of us know who you are?" *Knock.*

"Are you my mother?" Betsy said. She covered her eyes, as though she didn't wish to know the answer. *Knock. Knock.* "Thank goodness," she replied, and everyone laughed.

"Then who?" No knocking now, only silence.

"Now I'd like for everyone to join hands," Opal commanded. "Please, hurry." The women quickly outstretched their arms and formed a large circle that spanned the room. Some women closed their eyes. Opal thought of the Shirtwaist Strike again, of the workers in their coats overlaid with sashes. PICKET LADIES TAILORS STRIKERS. They linked arms like a human chain. Look at all they had gained!

The Earthshine workers held the room in silence. Their eyes were closed, and Opal imagined them sleeping, for what is sleep but daily surrender, the hope you'll get back all you let go. She relaxed her body. She imagined her skin unbuttoning, like a corset, until she could breathe more freely. She tried to remember the sound of Madame de Fleur's voice, her habit of clicking her tongue. She clicked her tongue now, too. Her baby seemed to respond to this, offering her a firm kick.

Opal let go of the hands she was holding and leaned in toward the flickering flame. Wax pooled on the tablecloth. She dabbed it and felt it harden around her fingertip.

"Someone else has come through," she said. "Bremen's the name. Albert Bremen." Bertie's father.

Some women gasped. A young girl stood and ran out of the room.

"What does he want?" asked Maria.

Opal took a breath and steadied herself. People believe what they choose to believe. "I want to help you." Opal's voice held now a German accent, harsh with sharp edges. She thought of her landlord, how he spoke to her in chipped English while his young son ran figure eights through his legs, counting *eins, zwei, drei.* "I've watched the conditions under which you labor. You stand all day, from morning till evening, few breaks, and even those all too short. The machine noise is horrendous. The heat from the broilers unbearable. Penalties for arriving late. Penalties for relieving your bladder. Lined up like cattle. I've watched it all. And for a pittance, I'm afraid. You have become victims of my own ideas," Bremen's voice said.

The room pressed with silence. Nobody spoke.

"But I need to work," said Betsy now. Her dress sleeves were pushed up. The scar on her arm had faded completely. "I need to put food on the table." She bounced her leg.

"We're not complaining," said Maria. "Tell him we're not complainers."

Bremen's voice continued. "Strengthen your bodies by strengthening your position."

"What do you mean?" someone asked.

"A cure?" asked Maria.

"More hours?" asked Betsy.

The Earthshine Factory didn't have 20,000 workers, but it had five hundred Earthshine Girls. She knew the ways they struggled to make ends meet, and the demands that met them when they arrived home. Some of them packed only buttered bread for their lunches. Some of their shoulders were marked with milk stains from their babies, burped. "Better conditions. Higher wages. Job security."

"A strike?" asked Maria.

"Like those textile workers in New York? My cousin was there! She was one of them!" said Gilly.

"My daddy was a miner," said another girl.

"A strike?" asked Pearl and Victoria, both at once.

"A strike?" asked Amanda Mahooney. "We can't—"

"A strike!" Opal said, now standing, her index finger aloft like a preacher at the high point of his sermon. Her body vibrated. The voice receded. The veil lifted. She stood now with the women.

FOUR DAYS LATER, AT WHAT should have been the start of their shift, the Earthshine Girls stood on the steps to the factory, blocking the entrance. Maria held a megaphone. Betsy's back was pressed against the main door, her wrist chained to the lock. From across the way, a commotion. Pearl led the others in a single-file march to mark the strike line. By noon, already a small crowd had gathered to watch. The machinists found the whole event amusing at first. Newspapermen took notes. A group of young boys tossed stones in their direction.

The Earthshine Girls wore picket sashes over their uniforms that they'd hastily made from felt and flour sacks. Gilly had brought an American flag. Pearl and the other girls carried signs. OUR BODIES, OUR SOAP, one read. Opal traced the picket line, back and forth. She scanned the crowd for Jagr. When a newspaperman held a camera in their direction, she shielded her face with her sign. Chanting with the women left her breathless. The baby slowed her gait.

The papers would first describe the strike as a small gathering of upset women. They would explain how the comet made them act in atypical ways. It'd been widely reported that even domesticated dogs were behaving unusually, much as they do before an earthquake. The papers described the comet as a nucleus and enveloping body, with a tail of varying configurations in the shapes of swords and scimitars. But what was in that nucleus still remained a mystery to scientists and astronomers, some of whom believed that the comet contained the very matter that created our solar system billions of years ago, primitive compounds. Primordial elements. Stardust. The very stuff and essence of life. The very thing Opal held inside her at this moment, the very thing Madame de Fleur had given back to her.

Later, at home, Opal reread Madame de Fleur's most recent letter.

Dearest Opal,

I could see the moon in the sky today, all day that sliver of white against the blue, and I wondered if you could see it, too. I love when the moon makes itself known in the daytime, this orb we associate with night. It has nothing to do with darkness, except that's when we tend to look for it. The world wants what is easy. You may want that, too. You want me to list for you the possibilities. The comet is two months away. The world could end. Or it may not. Your husband may find you, or he may not. All outcomes will be hard on us.

I was delighted with all your good news: the Comet Pills, the contract. When I read that you felt the baby move, I placed my hand to my own stomach and imagined it was you. I believe this baby has come for a reason. The Spirit Machine can tell us more. You seem to believe I hold the answers, but I cannot promise you the future. I do not know it. Like you, I can only convey what I feel: I worry you will not make it here, but that does not mean I do not want you to come.

—M

Opal didn't know how to explain the effect of her letters except to say the words patched a hole in her heart, but also bore a hole in it. She found herself wondering what the woman looked like tired or sleeping, or upon waking when one is most tender, most herself. She wanted to cook her a rump roast and watch her eat it—though she couldn't say why that idea thrilled her so. She had never cooked for Oren. She wanted to look for the moon in the daytime and point; she wanted the woman's eyes to follow her arm up to her fingertip up to the sky. She wanted the thrill of the woman's voice, saying, *Yes! Yes! I see it, too.*

How long until Jagr tracked her down? Days? Weeks?

Opal clutched the paper to her chest now. She tried to imagine it: The Spirit Machine would give her the answers and then—

Her *bébé* would wade in the Seine, not the murky Ohio. Her girl would walk down the Avenue des Champs-Élysées, that street named for the Greek afterlife that promised eternal bliss. In France, they'd eat pain au chocolat for breakfast every morning, if she liked. She'd wear lip rouge in bright red, like she'd seen in the magazines. She'd open her own apothecary. She'd hang a sign: COMET PILLS AND OTHER CURES. Recently she'd bought a book of French sayings. *Vouloir c'est pouvoir.*

To want is to be able to.

1986

Don't let them whisper behind your back!

—LIFEBUOY HEALTH SOAP

If only I could bottle the zeitgeist of 1986. We believed we could be anyone. We could do anything. A child could find Halley's Comet in the sky by fashioning a wire coat hanger into a star frame. One could build a homemade STEBLICOM box from power magnifiers and two seven-watt night-lights, and this contraption could give amateur comet-watchers access well beyond that of even the most advanced scientists of 1910. NASA planned to send the *Challenger* shuttle to space to take pictures of the comet, and an ordinary schoolteacher was among the crew. That's how much more advanced we were: We could photograph the comet. We could blast high school teachers into space.

I'd called my agent, and she was able to track down numbers for Edith and Janie, the other Earthshine Girls. "Don't do anything stupid," she said, and I promised her I wouldn't.

Edith and Janie agreed to meet me at Eden Park, in the gazebo usually reserved for prom photos and horny teens. Edith arrived right on time, carrying a cardboard take-out tray with three coffees. Her hair was pulled back into a ponytail. She walked toward me, heel to toe, the way I'd been trained to do.

When I was seventeen and Edith eight or nine, she visited the Earthshine studio. She had watched the shoot from the recording box. I saw her and asked the wardrobe assistant who she was. "She's nobody."

"Is she an actress?" I asked.

"Just practice your lines."

I couldn't focus. I was cold, and I said so. My nipples had grown hard, becoming little jagged tips poking the fabric of my slip. "Oh, geez," said the wardrobe assistant. "Someone get me some Band-Aids!" She pulled down my costume and taped the Band-Aids over my nipples. Even then I was being conditioned to hand over my body, to make it pleasing for others. I watched Edith watch me. The wardrobe assistant pulled up my dress and fastened it. "Don't move or I'll stick you," she said as she worked to repin my dress.

The girl in the booth held no expression—no smile, no frown. She sat so still, so restrained, so motionless, I knew she must be an actress. I didn't know who she was, but I suspected. My growing body was becoming a nuisance on set, my widening hips, my rounding breasts. The production assistant set up a single space heater and pointed it in my direction.

"Take one," the director yelled. "Roll camera. Roll sound . . ."

The Earthshine Girl stood at an altar decorated with artificial flowers that smelled skunky. She wore that wedding dress that laced up the back. Her hair was done up in a bun with a little loose curl hanging down each side, and I remember how looking through the veil reminded me of looking through fog: I could see, but only enough to take one step at a time. I didn't realize this would be the last commercial I'd ever film.

"I'm about to make the biggest commitment of my life!" I'd said *commitment* in four syllables—I still hadn't taken elocution classes.

The camera panned to my hands. I wasn't holding a bouquet, but a canister of soap. I whispered: "I'll say 'I do' to Earthshine Soap. An indispensable part of every union." I was instructed to wink, and I remembered how I had to do the winking shot in several takes until the director yelled: "You don't have something in your damn eye!"

Everyone on set had laughed—but not Edith. Her hands were pressed against the glass of the recording booth. That's the moment I figured out who she was and why she was there. That's the moment I knew I'd no longer be the Earthshine Girl. I saw myself on the recording screen, and I saw Edith in the booth, and for a single moment I thought I understood something profound about acting, about life, about how a camera captures you, locks you in space and time, and then you're stuck, trapped as someone else forever.

"Morning," I said to Edith now. I didn't resent her—not anymore, though for a long time I had, watching her do those commercials after my contract was terminated, knowing she had taken my place. Over the years, I'd bumped into her a few times at auditions, and it was like running into someone with whom I shared an ex: We were friendly and awkward, at once, with the knowing of what we shared. Now, she handed me a coffee still capped with steam, even though I didn't really want it, feeling already hyped from my diet pills.

Halley had never mentioned being close with Edith, but I knew they'd spent a lot of time together. That was her job: chaperone to the Earthshine Girl. They'd traveled together to conventions. Once, they flew to Germany for the opening of a new overseas factory. Halley brought me back a souvenir: a coffee mug that read I DON'T GIVE A SCHNITZEL.

"She always talked about you in a way that made me feel I could never fill your shoes," Edith said.

"Sorry. I mean, thanks," I said. Grief is awkward. Nobody ever knows what to say. I wondered if Halley had told Edith about the time we snuck into Celeste Shadow's dressing room and combed her wig with fish oil, or the time Halley gave me my first sip of alcohol, vodka mixed with Hawaiian Punch, that I drank in the studio parking lot between takes.

We waited for Janie.

Janie stopped acting after her short stint as the Earthshine Girl. She married young and had kids. "CEO of my household," she said when she arrived. "Just until they're in school." She was wearing gray sweatpants, moccasins that may have been slippers. On her shoulder hung an oversize bag, the kind all moms carry. She swigged her coffee. "What's with the reunion?"

"The Jane Does . . ." I started.

"No. No. Mr. Longworth would have a total cow," Janie said.

"You said this was about Halley," Edith said.

"It is. I've been called as a witness at that deposition."

"What's that have to do with us?" Janie said.

We'd all signed that confidentiality agreement with Earthshine. Mr. Longworth had laid out consequences for breaking the terms of our contract—*dire ones*—legal action and fines, among other things. None of us could afford that. That's what legal action really meant to us—the threat of someone with money taking all of ours. The whole legal profession is based on that model. The more you have, the easier it is to take.

"Did you see yesterday's *Inquisitor*?" I asked.

Earthshine had put out a page-length ad in response to the now class-action lawsuit, a letter signed by Charlie himself. I assumed it was written by his PR firm, since it used phrases like "soap family" and "household cleanliness journey."

"I saw it," Janie said. "That stupid photo of a baby holding the soap?"

"What does Halley have to do with the deposition?" Edith asked.

"I need to testify," I said. "I need to tell them what I know."

"That's child abuse, to let a baby play with cleanser like that," Janie said.

"I still can't believe she's gone," Edith said. She leaned against the railing of the gazebo. "Like that. I heard she was wearing her coat."

"How do you know that?" I asked.

Edith shrugged. "What made her want to do it?"

We all got quiet. Janie took the final gulp of her coffee, then crushed the cup and put it in her giant purse.

"Addiction," I finally said. The simplest answer, but not the whole one.

"Don't you think we'd know if we were addicted to Earthshine, like they're saying?" Janie said. "Don't you think we'd experience the 'adverse health consequences' they talk about on the news?"

"Maybe it doesn't affect everyone the same," Edith said.

"She left me something," I said.

"Halley?" Edith said, now curious. "What?"

"I don't know," I said. "An old book of formulas."

"*The* formula?" Edith asked. She looked like she was trying to solve a complicated math equation in her head, all *x*s and *y*s. "The one Bertie kept in the safe?"

A group of teenagers with cigarettes walked into the gazebo; then, noticing us, walked back out, trailing thin wisps of smoke behind them.

"No," I said. "I don't think so. Medicines, I think."

"For what?" she asked.

I hesitated for a moment. "All sorts of things. Gout. Indigestion. Depression. And . . . one for Comet Pills."

As I said it out loud, I felt foolish. Comet Pills sounded as fanciful as pixie powder or star dust. Camille Flammarion, the scientist who theorized Halley's could end the world in 1910, was also an author of science fiction. In his book *Omega* a comet threatens to destroy the Earth.

"Comet Pills?" Janie asked.

"Did Halley ever mention the name Opal Doucet to you?" I asked.

"That friend of Halley's who visited her on the set? I think she was her drug dealer," Janie said.

"No—not her," I said. "She was a massage therapist."

"The woman who died in the factory fire," Edith said. "One of them, anyway."

"Yes," I said. "But did Halley say anything else?"

Janie rooted around in her bag and produced some ChapStick. She smeared it on her lips. "Why don't you just ask Old Man Tuttle these questions," Janie said. "You were always his favorite."

"He's grieving," I said. "Did she say anything? Anything at all? This could be important. She left me a notebook—and I know it's related to the Jane Does. To everything they're saying. I'm beginning to feel . . . I think . . . there really is something in the soap. Something addictive or mind-altering or . . . I don't know. Look, it's *my* face on the package."

"It's our faces, too," Edith said.

I had to admit, we did all look alike. Same brown eyes. Same hair we described as "coffee-colored" to add a layer of exoticism to brunette. When I looked at them, I imagined I was looking in a reverse time-lapse mirror. The unforgiving slack of my skin now tightened. The lines around my eyes disappeared.

"I have three kids," said Janie. "I use Earthshine every day, and I'm not exactly infertile. The opposite." She checked her watch. "Didn't you ever want kids?"

"You can't ask those kinds of questions," Edith said.

"No," I lied.

"Why not?" Janie asked.

"They'd get in the way," I said.

"Of what?"

"My art."

"You mean when you were an extra on *WKRP*? Or when you pulled lotto balls from that suction machine?"

I bristled. Janie stared at me, unapologetically. Now, I can see she was defending herself—her right to give up her career for her kids. Her life, she was saying, was important, too. But in the moment, I'll admit, I wanted to slug her face.

"Gene Longworth would murder you for talking at that deposition," Janie said.

"I know," I said.

Edith began to whisper something, but right then a man walked into the gazebo. He was dressed in a baja, like he'd just walked off some California beach. "Hey, Earthshine Girls," he said. He pulled a camera from beneath his baja, and the flash made a sound like a bug zapper. In the photo, Janie hoists her ChapStick midair; Edith leans forward like she's blowing out candles. And me? My eyes are wide with surprise, with the words Edith had whispered to me: *Madame Doucet. They called her a witch. She could talk to the dead and divine cures from the Other Side. But she killed people with her cures, they said.*

BY MORNING, OUR PICTURE WAS in the *Tempo of the Times,* and Mr. Longworth left three messages on my machine. *We need to talk,* he said. *Now. Call me.* His voice held the patronizing tone of an angry father considering consequences.

I poured my coffee, then picked up my kitchen phone and dialed Edith. I wrapped and rewrapped the phone cord around my finger. *She killed people with her cures,* she'd whispered, coming in so close that her lip brushed my ear. *They called her a witch.* I thought of Samantha from *Bewitched,* the Wicked Witch of the West, *The Witches of Eastwick.* Some good. Some bad. And now *Madame* Doucet. What kind was she?

In drama, a single detail can reveal the whole of a person—sharp particularity, one of my conservatory professors called it—and I thought of Opal's signature in that old notebook, the dramatic loops, the *t* crossed in anger. What had led her to that rage?

You don't know Bertie Tuttle, Halley said the last night I saw her.

I didn't know Opal Doucet either.

But I knew Halley. She'd left me that notebook—a message from beyond—because she wanted me to see the name Opal Doucet. She wanted me to know her, this witch. She had marked the page with our photograph. I sensed that learning about one woman would help me understand the other. I took the last sip of my coffee, and there at the bottom of the schnitzel mug Halley had once given me I saw my own reflection, a tiny, ghostly, glistening version of me.

The phone rang and rang. Edith didn't answer.

So much of how we behave in life comes from movies and television, from roles other people have played. Maybe I'd seen too many old episodes of *Dragnet.* I took the white pages down from the pantry shelf where we kept it. I opened it like a sacred tome. I know I'd seen this scene before in a movie. The camera cuts to a close-up of the telephone directory, of a finger scanning down a column of tiny print.

Doucet. Two listings.

I lifted the receiver. Our kitchen phone was an old rotary. I watched the dial spin. I heard the smooth trilling of the call, like birds. Wyatt used to love to watch the birds each morning. He kept the *Peterson Field Guide to Birds of North America* on our back porch. So attentive when he chose to be.

Two more rings, then an operator's voice: *This number has been disconnected.*

Who did I think I was, Magnum P.I.? My resolve began to falter, but then I thought of the Earthshine Girl, me, wearing a slip, a mud mask. Me wearing that wedding dress. I thought of me, the Earthshine Girl, as that plumber dressed in white overalls, my hair curved under my cap. I was a lady plumber—that was the whole joke.

"If she's a plumber, wouldn't she be *fixing* the sink? Unclogging the sink? Repairing the sink?" I remember Linda Gibbons, my roommate from the conservatory, asking. "Didn't it feel dirty?"

"Soap?" I had said, and the other girls laughed, even though I hadn't meant to be funny. The lady plumber secretly embodied their fears: They didn't want to be women trying to make it in a man's world.

I thought of the Earthshine Girl, me, as a nurse, as a secretary, as a Native American—*Use Earthshine in every teepee*—me, as a cook, a teacher, a wife, a mother, me, the Earthshine Girl who held a canister of soap toward the camera with two hands, pleading with women to buy it.

Cradling that phone, I was thinking of all the ways the Earthshine

Girl had been crafted to be good, obliging, pleasing, deferential, only secretly clever. I *was* the Earthshine Girl. I'd been trained to neglect my own needs, and that wasn't virtue. That wasn't talent. It was fear.

I willed myself to be brave for Halley.

The next call rang five times, and just when I was about to hang up, a woman's voice answered. "Hello?"

I briefly remembered something I'd read, about how Thomas Edison was the one who encouraged the etiquette of saying *hello* when answering the phone. How else to address the unknown but to acknowledge it? Edison was deaf, and he claimed his deafness allowed him to tune out meaningless sound and focus. He considered his deafness a gift.

"Hello?" I said.

The woman on the other end was old. Her voice was scratchy, like she'd just woken up. I could hear *Wheel of Fortune* in the background, and I apologized for interrupting, but I was doing a bit of research, trying to track someone down, and I wondered if she had any relation to someone named Opal Doucet.

I listened to the woman's breathing, heavy, like a smoker's, the whimsical pinging of letters illuminating on the TV.

"You a Doucet, honey?" She pronounced it like "Do Sit."

"No," I said.

"What's that clicking noise?" she said.

"I didn't hear it," I said.

"Maybe my hearing aids. I hate these old things. Too bad you're not a Doucet. I thought you was kin. Everyone's all but dead and in the ground."

"No relation. It's part of a . . . history project," I said.

"A history project, you say. Well, I'm my daddy's only daughter. Now my father was just as charismatic and loving as can be. Real gentle. Nothing like my husband—ex-husband. Though now he's dead, too."

"Oh, gosh," I said. "I'm sorry."

"Which part, honey?" I heard an unmistakable flick of a lighter, then a deep inhale.

"All of it," I said.

"Well, you know how it can be. In the beginning someone can seem one way, and then . . ." Her voice pitched higher. "Maybe if we all remained strangers we'd be better off. Nice and polite to one another."

"So no Opal Do-sit?" I tried to pronounce the name as she had, but as my tongue tapped the roof of my mouth, it sounded too harsh.

"There's that click again," she said. I'd heard it, too, this time. Like the quick clack of a keyboard.

"Maybe a bad connection?" I offered. "Someone else pick up the line?"

"I live alone, honey. Ain't you been listening?"

"Sorry," I said.

"Quit saying sorry, honey. *Sorry*'s a bad habit. Only say it when you mean it. Anyhow, let's see: Besides my daddy I had an uncle named Jagr Doucet. Didn't know him too well. Tall and gangly fellow. Big bushy eyebrows. Doctor of some sort." Another inhale. Another click click, but she made no mention of it, so perhaps she was just playing with her lighter. I heard rustling, like she was pulling apart a bag of chips, then the crunching to confirm it. "He was from Gallipolis. Up the river. That's where my daddy's from. You ever been there?"

"No," I said. My attention drifted to the white pages again. I ran my index finger down the column for a name I may have missed.

"Not much there—except that insane asylum. Guess they don't call them that now. I never know how to say things right no more. My niece tells me that. Tells me I'm offending somebody, but I'm just saying it like I know."

"So you do have relatives," I said.

"Just my niece. My brother's kid. He's dead, too. Anyhow, my father said it was haunted, that hospital. He should know because his brother sometimes worked there. When I was a girl, though, I saw people sitting out on the lawn, and they didn't look sick to me. Just bored. Just sitting there outside while those attendants watched them."

"Is he alive still?"

"My father?"

"Your uncle."

"Uncle Jagr? Goodness no, honey. Died close to . . ." I could imagine her counting on her fingers. "Close to twenty years ago, I'd say, '67 or '68. That was the last time I was back in Gallipolis, for his funeral. They buried him next to his first wife. Opal Doucet. So there's that name for your history project." I found my pen and started taking notes. "Uncle Jagr had some giant monument, and she had this tiny little marker right beside it. I remember thinking that was kind of funny but also sad. Didn't have much occasion to return again. Life does that, you know, has a way of creeping up on you till one day you wake up and you're an old woman who barely recognizes her own self. I've got whiskers, honey. They pop out of nowhere, and I begged my friend Dorrie that when I die, please come over and pluck them out before the funeral. Say, what do you look like?" she asked.

I described myself: brown eyes. Little gap between my teeth. Freckled nose. Hair in two braids.

"You sound like a little girl," she said. Click click. The line was bugged, or I'd seen too many movies. I was Nona Dixon, not Columbo. "Anyway, don't know much about Opal. It's Do-Sit—that's all I can tell you. Like putting your fanny in the seat of a chair."

I ended the call and set the phone back on the cradle. I opened that gray notebook again and ran my fingers over the ink's indentations. I turned the pages, carefully. The paper was stiff and crumbly at the edges. I paused when I came to Formula no. 37, for sterility. Chasteberry. Maca. Indian ginseng. *Cyperus rotundus.* Primrose oil. I wondered why my own doctors couldn't have helped me more, why modern medicine couldn't fix a woman when men can walk on the moon. Then, I noticed it there, at the bottom corner of the page, the initials so small I took them for an inkblot. JD. I turned the pages and saw them again and again. JD. JD. JD.

Not J.D. Fox, anchor, Action 13 News.

No, Jagr Doucet. Opal's husband.

It was like trying to piece together a puzzle without knowing what the puzzle looked like. When my mother did puzzles, her strategy was to begin with the border pieces to give it shape. I began with what I knew: Opal Doucet had written in her husband's notebook a recipe for mood-altering drugs—Happy Pills, my pharmacist Gary had called them. Edith claimed Opal had killed people with her cures, but they were her husband's cures, mostly. She'd died in the fire, her body taken back to Gallipolis to be buried. Anecdotal evidence, Wyatt might call it, because he lived by the numbers on his spreadsheets. He believed in facts. But feelings are facts lodged in the body before the brain can resolve their meaning.

In that moment, here's what I felt, without any proof: Bertie kept the notebook with these formulas locked up in her safe with the Earthshine recipe, and Halley stole it because she believed it was all connected, the lawsuit, the Jane Does, me. *You don't know Bertie Tuttle.*

If that was true, I didn't know myself. Where would I be without her? *Who* would I be? She discovered me all those years ago, handpicked me from thousands of other girls. She saw it in me, something special. That's what I always believed. That's what I *convinced* myself to believe. "It's her," she'd said, and with those words I began to travel forward on the path she'd paved. I began to orbit her world.

Her world.

I didn't want to see it.

I recalled a story I'd read, about a man who recovered his sight after nearly thirty years of blindness. This man had functioned just fine in the dark, had even become an abstract artist of some renown. He eventually married. One summer evening as he sat on his back porch with his wife, he sensed a shadow cast lengthwise near his feet. Soon, the shadow turned to a fog. By the time he went to bed, he could see blurry images of items he held in front of him: a cup, a toothbrush, his slippers, simple things he hadn't seen since he was a boy. The world came into sharp focus. His sight had miraculously returned.

It should have been a happy story, to see things you couldn't once see—but it wasn't. The man wore sunglasses indoors. Too much looking made him tired. He was overstimulated. Anxious. His paintings did not look like they had in his head, which led to a total creative block. Darkness had given him the freedom to imagine; his vision had come at a cost. "This is not the life I thought I was living," the man said.

All these years later, I finally understood how the blind man felt, how when he looked around his own living room he wanted to cry because suddenly he did not recognize anything. I sat at my kitchen table and felt the weight of my empty house. A couple of years ago we'd repainted the kitchen, and now I could see the outline of the pie chest we'd been too lazy to move at the time. I rested my cheek on the sticky surface of the table. My eyes were level with that notebook, that ledger, whatever it was. I ran my thumb along the spine. I remembered what became of that man who didn't want to see.

He'd gouged his eyes out.

IN STELLA I FOUND COURAGE, and in turn, I projected my own emotions into her character. I became someone else. Some might call this necessary dissociation, but in theater we call it the Strasberg method. Ratings were up for *Stars and Shadows*. Stella now recovered at Port Middleton Memorial. The trauma she'd suffered underground induced amnesia, and she didn't recognize Vincent or Bianca or Celeste, who now wavered on the cusp of death. Vincent had been tricked into falling in love with Bianca Dupont. The script called for Stella, with her natural antibodies to the mystery illness, to regain her memory and save her aunt. Drama. Chaos. A last-minute blood transfusion. A doctor who looked like Adonis in scrubs. The gift of life.

The security guard waved as I passed the booth on my way to the set in the morning. "Hi, Stella!" he said, as usual.

"Hi, Mr. Security Guard," I said. This was our shtick. I knew his name was Mike.

Inside the production assistant—a new girl—blocked the door. "I can't let you in," she said. "Sorry."

"Nona Dixon," I said.

My name wasn't on the call list. She checked her clipboard and checked it again. She was wearing denim overalls with an oversize sweater underneath that made her seem both large and small at once.

"I play Stella." The curtness of my voice surprised me.

"Oh, I know who you are," she said. Despite her mass of clothing, I could tell she was young, an intern, the kind of girl who might have been an RA in her college dorm and believed this small power extended to the wider world. A bureaucrat in training.

"Let me talk to Elliot," I said.

"Look, Mrs. Dixon," she said. "All I can tell you is you're not on the call sheet. If you're not on the call sheet, I can't let you in." I hated her for it, for doing her job.

"Just tell him I'm here," I said.

"I always wanted to be an Earthshine Girl," she said.

"Everyone did."

"Must be embarrassing now, with what all those women out there are saying." Indeed, on the way into the studio this morning, the crowd numbered in the hundreds. When a group of women noticed me pull up, they began yelling my name, calling me a traitor—and worse. One of them carried a cardboard cut-out image of me with devil horns. The EARTHSHINE BITCH. A police officer escorted me from my car.

"Look, there's some mistake. Please," I said, then hated myself for saying it, hated the way the corners of her mouth curled inward in the slightest recognition of her power.

"I like your sweater," I added, so she'd know I was trying to be nice.

"Thanks," she said. "I suppose I can go ask once more."

"Yes. Yes, please. Would you do that?"

"Do you think it's poisoned?" Her voice softened. "I use it all the time. Used to."

I didn't know how to answer. What could I say? Halley had left me a book of medical formulas and Opal Doucet was a witch who dabbled in pharmaceuticals, and now my doctor wanted my uterus, and Mr. Longworth left threatening messages on my machine, and my yard was littered with toilet paper and signs, and I was afraid my phone line was bugged, and someone out there knew about John Dale, and I was terrified Wyatt would find out? That seemed like a lot to drop on her at once.

"You'll be fine," I assured her. Everyone was still learning about class-action lawsuits, about how they can accumulate. The tobacco lawsuit hadn't happened yet, and certainly that was given more national coverage because it impacted not just women. "Everyone uses it," I said.

I thought of the images my doctor had shown me, of my womb, of the masses on it that looked like blackened, shriveled fruits. I'd relented and scheduled my surgery for late spring, telling myself I could always reschedule. What were my options—bleed forever? I don't know why, but the thought of losing an organ—*that* organ—made me feel like I'd be less of a woman. I realize how stupid that sounds now. How naïve. As much as I didn't want to be controlled by my body, here I was arguing for my own limitations. Or, maybe—maybe I believed a miracle might occur before then, shaped like a baby, like Mary and her immaculate conception, without all the religion. Women are supposed to want these things. But then again, an angel ordered Mary to have that child.

I waited while the intern disappeared between the folds in a cloth partition. Behind it, someone was doing a sound check. *One. Two. Three. Check. One. Two. Three. Check.* The hammering of the set designers could have been the baseline of a rock song.

The production assistant came back a few minutes later. "They decided to go in a different direction," she said.

"Stella just dug herself out of a freakin' grave!" I said. "She's saving Celeste's life with that blood transfusion. Even after Celeste's amnesia made her who forget who Stella was!"

"Stella didn't make it," the girl said. "She was just too weak."

"Did you tell him I'm here?"

"You're not on the list," she said. With a pencil, she made imaginary marks on her clipboard to avoid looking at me.

On my way home, I passed a new billboard for *Stars and Shadows.* Celeste Shadow indeed had recovered and now stood in a white sequined gown, her hands fisted on her hips. Apparently, her memory had returned—only a temporary forgetting. Bianca Dupont finally produced that vial of cure, her gift to Vincent. And now Celeste Shadow and Vincent Glass were *finally* getting married after more than a decade apart, live and televised, an event so anticipated the producers bought prime-time hours.

When I passed that billboard, I thought of Bertie's biography, *The Juggernaut.* It describes Bertie's marketing genius, her ability to spin tragedy into company growth. She revived Earthshine Soap years after that fire. She put up that placard to honor the Earthshine workers, even though they'd been accused of burning the factory down. The company finally took responsibility for the strike, and this admission earned them public trust. They wanted to rewrite history. *The Soap for Women.* The first commercial aired during *Stars and Shadows,* perhaps Bertie's boldest marketing tool.

On the billboard next to Celeste stood Vincent in a tux. Behind them, in black-and-white, was a still shot of me, taken from the original funeral scene, my eyes shut, my hands folded, my dagger necklace an unused weapon. Soon, Celeste would call for my cremation and, together with Vincent, on the eve of their wedding, would visit the incinerator and watch my body burn.

Do you know what rage feels like to me? Like hunger no diet pill can stave off. Like hunger that's been building for years, a muted pain suddenly recognizable. You want to devour everything in sight. At home, I pulled my framed diploma from the conservatory off the wall and tossed it. I dumped the boxes of Earthshine memorabilia on my living room floor and trampled old VHS cassettes with my feet. I located all my old headshots and shredded them, one by one, until they were paper confetti. The last glossy photo to meet the shredder was taken when I was pregnant that first time—and my expression was softly victorious. When anyone learned I was pregnant, they'd say *your hair is amazing!*

My hair had been amazing. It was lush and thick. I conditioned it weekly with margarine and egg whites. I used only silk pillowcases. Now it was ruined, overpermed and damaged from chemicals.

I found Wyatt's grooming kit beneath the bathroom sink. I lifted those heavy shears from the case. I held tendrils of my hair and snipped, one at a time, and the strands spilled onto the floor.

Cutting my hair seemed to release something in me. I felt a lifting, a lightening, a coolness. I felt how Stella must have felt as she broke through to the surface of the earth, how she could finally breathe. Snip, an *S* for Stella on the floor.

I set down the scissors.

I ran my hand through my roughly chopped hair—uneven, asymmetrical, like Cyndi Lauper's, only worse. What would Wyatt think? Then I hated myself for even having that thought, because I shouldn't care what he thinks. But I did. I did still care.

For our honeymoon, Wyatt had suggested Miami because he wanted to take a tour of the Everglades. I didn't mind. When he was off doing this, I pinned my hair up as I floated on a raft in the pool, smelling of coconut oil and chlorine. Beads of water pilled on my skin like little balls of mercury. In 1973, when we got married, crisping yourself like a Cornish hen was very on trend. As a Midwesterner, I measured the success of a vacation by the depth of my tan.

That evening, Wyatt arrived back at our room with two daiquiris from the downstairs bar. Hibiscus blossoms floated atop the glasses. Wyatt set them next to the bed where I lay, reading through a script my agent had sent me.

He didn't wear a beard back then, and he had a small dimple on his chin, and I touched the divot because it was mine to touch. Wyatt pulled up the back of my shirt and kissed me along the burn lines where the edge of my bathing suit touched my skin. His lips only made the sunburn feel warmer, I wanted to tell him, but I also didn't want him to stop. I didn't know how to speak my desires back then. I was still young, still learning about my body. The internet as we know it didn't exist yet; I couldn't just look things up. Back then we learned by doing, and you know, I think it's better that way.

I reached for my daiquiri on the hotel nightstand and took a sip. The alcohol warmed my body even more. My sunburn felt more burny. "Did you find the fountain of youth?" I asked.

"That's in St. Augustine."

"Same state," I said.

"Other side."

Back then there was such a thing as flirtation, a purposeful withholding. It created tension, the good kind, the anticipation of pleasure.

I peeled off his shirt and noticed a scratch on his side where he'd been jabbed by some palmetto branches. I kissed it. He was still wearing his jeans, and he crawled beneath the sheets with me. You're looking for something sexy here, but you won't get it. That's the thing with flirtation—it's its own kind of pleasure. We fell asleep. We woke up. By morning, Wyatt was covered in poison ivy.

I caught it, too, from the oils left on his clothes. For the rest of our honeymoon, we were rendered helpless. It hurt to move. We didn't mind—we had the rest of our lives, didn't we? The future spooled out before us. Hope is a kind of love or a willful naivety. Either way, we believed the best parts of our lives were yet to come. We took turns going to the bar downstairs and ordering daiquiris and food to bring back to the room. I'd rub calamine lotion on his rash, and he'd rub it on mine. I desired Wyatt, yes, but I cared for Wyatt. I helped him button his shirt because his fingers were too swollen.

When we married, I was young, and I still foolishly believed I was like George in *It's a Wonderful Life*. I could lasso the moon, if I wanted.

But George never did lasso the moon, did he? He buys a fixer-upper, finds himself with too many kids, and nearly loses his family business to shoddy bookkeeping by a drunken uncle. He wanted to see the world, but he never did. His most heroic act is giving up his dreams.

When did it all go wrong?

If they make the movie of my life, what scene would they highlight? What's the inciting incident? The rising tension? The dramatic moment that represents the whole of things? That's what kills me: I'd once been so optimistic, and so very, very wrong.

I thought of our first kiss, the same night he came to see me play Audrey in *As You Like It*. It was my first lead role at the conservatory, my first time stepping onstage as someone other than the Earthshine Girl.

Do you wish, then, that the gods had made me poetical? That's Audrey's best line. The audience cackled when I delivered it because she's euphemizing her lust. She's a hedonist, ruled by desire. Onstage, I wore a dress with a corset that amplified my cleavage, and I held a leash attached to a goat we'd rented from a petting zoo.

After the show, we'd gone back to Halley's place. We sat on her purple couch. "'Do you wish, then, that the gods had made me poetical?'" I said to Wyatt. Even then I was playing a part, borrowing lines. We locked eyes and leaned in slowly, so very slowly, like we were measuring the distance between us in molecules, marking each one because we knew once our lips met, our lives would never be the same.

A movie moment.

"WHAT HAPPENED?" WYATT SAID THE next day when I opened the door with that ridiculous haircut. He'd come over to pick up some things: his mail, his racquetball goggles, some snow boots I'd never seen him wear. He rang the doorbell instead of using the key. "Your hair is . . . uh . . ." His face drooped with concern.

"They wrote me off," I said. "Stella—she died for good." I must have looked feral with my mess of hair, my eyes wild. I was wearing his jeans, and they sat low on my waist.

"She always comes back," he said.

"Not this time." He reached for my hair and ran his fingers through it, studying it like a problem to be solved. "It's awful, I know."

Wyatt led me to the bathroom and put a towel over my shoulders. He had me sit on the edge of the tub. From his grooming kit he withdrew the razor, and he swapped out the attachment and clicked a piece of plastic into place. He turned it on. I felt the buzzing in my head and down through my arms to my chest. All that buzzing reminded me of those 1950s fat-jiggling machines, the ones that promised weight loss without the work. I watched my hair fall to the ground in clumps.

"Fresh start," Wyatt said.

I ran my hand over my head—so soft. Softer than Prell shampoo could ever make it. Not coarse from hairspray or gels or chemical perms. More like the pelt of an animal.

In the mirror, I was surprised at the image of myself: my neck, which looked sleeker than ever before, the boxy angle of my jawline, the contours of my face, which appeared so different without the counterpoint of hair. My face looked brighter, despite the signs of age that had settled into my skin: the quotation marks at the sides of my eyes, the parentheses around my mouth, as though everything I said was an aside.

"Fresh start," I said.

He removed the towel from my shoulders and brushed the hair from my neck. He'd thought to plug the tub so the drain wouldn't clog, and I loved this part of him, his foresight, his practicality. He found an old bread bag and began collecting my hair in it.

"How are your plants?" I asked. The room blurred from my tears. I didn't want to cry. Wyatt put his arm around me, then pulled me into him, and let me cry there, in the hollow of his chest, a place that felt warm and dark and familiar.

I wanted to tell him how sorry I was, not for the affair he didn't even know about—not yet—but for all of it, for our lives not leading where we thought they would take us. For not being me in real life. For being a cliché. Melodramatic. Made for TV. I'd saved the authentic parts of myself for the camera. My real life is where I'd done the performing.

Nobody ever tells you that at some point in a marriage, you may start to loathe the person you've become. Nobody ever tells you that you imagine car wrecks and downed planes and sunken ships with your spouse on board, and what shocks you isn't these fantasies but your reaction to them. You aren't always sad.

But sometimes you are.

Wyatt kissed the top of my head, and I felt the distance in that kiss. He used to like to tell the story of how we met: late summer, my classmate's Labor Day cookout. We all jumped into the pool with our clothes on after a few too many gin and tonics. I don't know what had happened to us. Falling in love is like jumping into that pool; it's exhilarating. Intoxicating. You feel so alive. But then you have to climb back to the real world, and the air is cold, and your clothes are heavy with water, and there's a lot more effort to that, to the climbing out.

"Good thing you have a symmetrical head," Wyatt said.

They killed off Stella, but Stella, she always came back. She fashioned weapons out of jewelry. She filled her belly with earthworms. She sucked moisture from roots. She could hoist herself up through rock and mud. Like Opal Doucet, she could dig herself out of any grave.

1910

Bertie had been right: The Earthshine strike stopped the sale of the factory. But it did not stop Charles Tuttle. A week later he stood on Opal's stoop.

He wore a dark suit and a fedora, and he smelled of cologne. He held a strange-looking box. Opal studied it more closely. A wooden bell box. Atop it were two bronze call bells, and Opal couldn't help but think that all objects designed by men resembled breasts.

Standing behind Tuttle were two others, whom Tuttle now introduced: an alderman named Arnold Jenkins and Colonel Davis Bloodworth, a medical doctor and a veteran of the Spanish-American War.

She tried to put it all together: the men, the bell box. Jenkins wore a camera on a strap around his neck and produced an official-looking document from his suit pocket. "We understand it was you who encouraged the Earthshine Girls to strike," he said. "This is my district."

Suddenly she understood. She took the paper, and the whole world stilled. In eighteen days she'd receive the Dowd money. Now she imagined herself wearing the uniform of a workhouse inmate: shabby shift, gray apron, a skirt made of material that would chafe—punishing women even sartorially. She wondered if Bertie knew where her husband was right now, and, if so, if she'd tried to stop him. Why hadn't Opal been warned?

She pleaded with Tuttle. "Gentlemen, you're mistaken. Albert Bremen spoke to them. Not me."

"Hogwash," said Tuttle.

"If Bremen delivered the message, then we'd like to speak to him," said Jenkins. "Directly. You can do that, yes?" He stepped up to the landing. Opal took a step back into the doorway.

"We're simply here to observe," Colonel Bloodworth said. "I assure you that's our only goal this evening." He had a scar beneath his eye from an old injury. It resembled the track a tear might take, and as such made him appear tender from the start.

Within minutes they all sat in Opal's parlor. They brought two chairs from her kitchen. She took her time extinguishing the fire by heaping ashes on the flames. She drew the window shades. She'd done this before, she told herself. She tried to take deep breaths to calm herself, but still she felt lightheadedness coming on.

Colonel Bloodworth watched her as she withdrew candles from the sideboard. She felt the pressure of his gaze, like his eyeballs were an instrument he was using to measure her. While the other men busied themselves taking off their coats, he removed a small journal and a pencil from his pocket and jotted some notes.

Opal lit the candle at the center of the table, the smoke from the extinguished match curlicuing away from the burnt tip. The room smelled of musk and shaving cream, of sweat and gasoline. Of men. Jenkins slumped a bit forward on his chair, tapping his foot. His lips were pursed, not unlike a kiss, but a pained one.

"Ready?" she said. She tried to affect calm. She smiled at Jenkins to set him at ease, and he ceased his foot tapping. Tuttle scowled.

Despite the candlelight, the room was dark, and shadows bounded off the wall in sinister shapes: a scythe, a bone, a revolver. Colonel Bloodworth's gaze pressed upon her again; she could sense he was the kind of skeptic who badly wanted to believe. He took out his journal and made another note.

She asked the men to join hands.

She closed her eyes. She began to hum, and she instructed the men to hum along with her. When their voices were finally in unison—like a quartet—that's when she felt it, the presence, descend upon her like an inviting fog.

"Someone's come through," she said. She held Jenkins's hand on one side and the Colonel's on the other. She tightened her grip. "The old man is exhausted. We take something of our former lives to the Other Side, you know, and he's in a weakened state. Unwell."

"We've come to ask him a few simple questions," said Tuttle. His voice was full of air and condescension, like he was talking to a pretty bank teller whom he didn't trust to count the bills.

More silence. Thirty seconds passed, then thirty more. She felt a headache coming on. She remembered that Ida McKinley took up knitting to distract herself from her condition, darning thousands of socks to give away to charities, but Opal loathed the dull repetition required of needles and yarn.

Without letting go of the men's hands, she pressed her forehead to the table. The pressure gave her some relief. Once Madame de Fleur thrashed upon the floor in what looked like an epileptic fit so violent, someone called for a doctor. *It takes so much out of me,* she said later from her cot as Opal pressed cool rags to her forehead. She liked imagining a life where she could care for the woman.

In her parlor, Opal rocked her forehead against the cold relief of the table. She began to moan, and the noise released something in her, not headache pain, but some unexpressed feeling. The Colonel touched her between her shoulder blades. He may have been checking for a pulse or a sign of medical distress, but she let his hand rest there because she longed for touch, even this kind.

After a few moments, she jerked upright and said, "Charles Tuttle, how dare you?"

A German accent. Albert Bremen.

In the candlelight, Tuttle's mouth looked cavernous, his teeth stalactites. It was Colonel Bloodworth who spoke first. His voice was a glass of water. Cool. Refreshing. "Please forgive the interruption," he said. "And the hour. Where are you now?"

"What does it matter where he is?" said Tuttle.

"I'm trying to establish a record of fact," Bloodworth replied.

Opal waited for someone else to speak.

"Personality can extend beyond the body. In theory," Bloodworth said. The candlelight reflected in his eyes; it amplified the contours of his scar. He was a man who'd known loss, who'd felt it deeply.

"Please, Mr. Bremen," said Jenkins. "Can you tell us why? Why have you instructed the Earthshine Girls to strike?"

"This is preposterous," Tuttle said.

"The laws of business," Bremen's voice said, "differ from the laws of humanity."

"And you still consider yourself human," asked Bloodworth, "on the Other Side?"

"For the love of God, what does it matter if he considers himself human?" said Tuttle. "Tell us something we don't know—something to prove yourself already. Otherwise we'll know this is gas!"

Opal pressed her forehead to the table again and grew quiet. Her head throbbed now. Jagr had warned her about the strains of pregnancy. He was a good doctor. She shouldn't have doubted that.

Jagr and his measly reward. $100. She would not go back to him. Never. She refused to even imagine it.

"My daughter," said Opal in Bremen's voice. "Bertie. She's expecting. A surprise to you both, yes? Congratulations." Everyone turned toward Tuttle to register the dismay on his face. "An heir at last."

Silence.

"Is this true?" Jenkins asked.

"Impossible," said Tuttle.

"So it's not true?" the Colonel said.

"Lucky guess. Any married woman—"

"Swore you to secrecy. Didn't want her name in the paper again. Didn't want to jinx it, did she?" asked Bremen. "Didn't want to see all those pitiful looks like when the earlier pregnancies didn't take. We have papers over here, you know. *The Expired Times.* News so old it's news again."

Colonel Bloodworth laughed, and Opal was encouraged by the sound of it.

"Rubbish. All women gossip," said Tuttle. "Why, Bertie was just—"

"She drinks milk all day to fortify the child," Bremen said. "You've had to double your dairy deliveries. Perhaps you should keep a cow in your drawing room, next to that portrait of your first wife you insist on keeping hung there."

Now nobody laughed. Nobody said anything—not Opal, not Tuttle, not the other men. Opal could hear the city noises outside her window: Horns. Hooves. Shouting. The domestics returning home for supper after a day of work.

"It's true then," said Bloodworth, finally. "The spirit has told us something only you could know. You've said so yourself." He made a note in his journal, then tucked it back into his pocket.

Tuttle now pulled a box up from the floor—the one he'd arrived with. "This," he said. Between the bells was a piston and crown that, when pushed, caused the bells to simultaneously ring. Tuttle demonstrated now. "You want to clear your name, yes? I'm talking to you directly, Ms. Doucet. You want to prove you did not incite a riot?"

"A strike," Opal said.

Tuttle set the contraption on the table.

"You want to prove you can talk to ghosts? The test is simple. You'll channel a spirit to ring this bell," Jenkins explained.

"Telepathically," Tuttle said.

Jenkins, who brought with him some baling twine, now stood, then began trussing her arms and legs to her chair, ensuring she could not reach the box.

"Gentlemen, is this necessary?" Opal asked. Perspiration slicked her underarms, the back of her neck. She was forced to sit at an angle that cramped her ribs. "I am not a physical medium."

The twine, intended for hay or kindling, dug into her skin when she moved, so she tried her best to remain still, unfazed. When Madame de Fleur performed, her hands were often tied, and somehow she'd always found a way to unbind herself. Opal wriggled her wrists.

"One of my workers reports she heard rapping in the cafeteria as you led a séance. Do you not consider that a physical feat?" Tuttle asked.

She assumed the worker in question was Amanda Mahooney. After all she'd done to help the girl—but Opal didn't have the luxury of wounded feelings at present.

"Just one ring of the bell," said Jenkins. "One tiny ding-ding. Now that can't be difficult for a woman of your abilities, especially considering the circumstances. See, it's easy." He tapped the bell.

Opal was testing the restraints, wiggling her wrists to see if she could free her hand, but it was no use. Already, she began imagining different constraints, prison—or worse. "How do I know the bell is not rigged?" Opal asked. "Perhaps it's mechanically unsound or has been intentionally jammed or . . ."

Ding. Ding. Tuttle rang the bell, again and again. It sounded like an unanswered telephone. "Would you like to ring it yourself?" he asked. "Just to familiarize yourself with how it works?" She stretched her finger and Tuttle brought the box to her bound hands. Ding. Ding.

Silence settled in the room. Opal couldn't move. She made fists. She could feel heat radiating from them. The room grew too hot, and she felt a tingling sensation in her feet that crept its way up her body. The restraints were tight. Her midsection felt like it'd been hollowed out and building mud set inside to fill the hole. She couldn't think for a moment, could only feel the hardness of the chair press into her hind quarters, could only feel the burning from the twine digging into her wrists. She closed her eyes to focus, and she tried to imagine the bell, what it looked like, what it sounded like. Imagination is the first step toward freedom. She thought of Jagr—of the table bell he kept near his desk that he'd ring—that excruciating ding, ding—when he wished for his midday meal.

"Shame on you, Tuttle," Opal said after some time, for she couldn't just sit there. She needed to do something. Her voice was Bremen's again. "Destroying three generations of my family's work. Selling the factory? And for what? Your silly ambition?"

"Ring the bell and we're done," said Jenkins.

Now, Opal looked straight at Colonel Bloodworth, who looked back at her, unflinching. They locked eyes—a standoff, a gentle deadlock, as though one were daring the other to look away first. A subtle movement of his neck told her he'd swallowed.

"Enough of this chatter," said Tuttle. "The bell."

"If you're so interested in bells, go to church."

Jenkins stifled a laugh. Even the Colonel looked amused. "The lady's getting clever," Tuttle said. "I give her that."

Opal stared at the box, at the bells atop it. The silence pressed into her ears; she could hear a thumping. Her stomach rumbled. Her baby kicked—surely a sign of some sort. She tried to shift in her seat, but could not. How willingly these men would hand her over to Jagr, if they knew.

She couldn't have that—not when she was so close. These days, Opal spent almost every evening in the laboratory compounding powders and filling capsules, then delivering crates of her cures to Dowd's Drugs to be shelved, sold, and taken by women across the city. Jagr believed a cure often resided in the mere act of doing something curative. A placebo. Once, during the Spanish-American War, soldiers were injected with saline when medics ran out of morphine, and the saline eased their pain.

In just a few weeks she'd have enough money to leave for France, and this evening would collapse onto paper, into a story she'd write about to Madame de Fleur. They may even laugh about it, eventually. But how to get to the other side of this moment so she could look back on it in amused hindsight?

She closed her eyes again and tried to imagine herself pushing the lever, tried to hear the sound of the bell in her mind. She remembered what Madame de Fleur had told her: Listening is a choice. She dinged the bell over and over in her imagination, tried to conjure the way the tip of her finger had felt on the piston when Tuttle had brought the bell to her hands, but nothing, no sound in the room except the quick breaths of the men waiting.

"Well?" Tuttle said after some moments of silence. "Are we quite finished? Do we have enough to charge the woman, Jenkins?" All eyes were on Opal, who tried to affect dignity, bound there to her chair. The pressure squeezed her head. Her condition. Now, her whole body acted against her will. Her body's weight rocked the chair. Thump, thump, thump, like the clopping noise she'd heard that first night she'd watched Madame de Fleur perform. Now she felt far away from herself again, able to observe herself from the outside. She could see her hands bound with twine, her body shaking. Outside her body, she couldn't register fear. No, instead a calmness overtook her. Her mind focused. She noticed a subtle movement from across the table—she'd grown accustomed to observing shifts in the dark. She began to hum loudly, buzz like a bee, like a swarm of bees intent on seeking exit.

Colonel Bloodworth leaned forward, just slightly. He brought his hand up from beneath the table, and he reached out for the bell box.

The other men didn't notice because at that moment Bremen came through again, growling through Opal's stiff mouth, shaking the chair so mightily now that Opal thought she might very well tip over and crash to the floor. "Charles, you rotten egg. You cockroach. You pin-headed pig. You were nothing without me. Without my daughter. Not a penny to your name, you ungrateful bilker. You embarrass me, all of you. She's only a woman," Bremen said.

At that moment, the Colonel's finger fell down upon the bell in a smooth, quick flick. Before the rest of the committee could turn, he'd withdrawn his hand to his lap. Now, they were looking at the bell box, which still seemed to vibrate, even though the sound had dislodged itself and faded to silence.

"She did it," Jenkins whispered.

Tuttle stood, grabbed his hat, and marched out, forgetting his overcoat. The other men stood slowly, muttering among themselves. Bloodworth picked up Tuttle's coat from the back of the chair.

As they were walking out the door, Jenkins turned to face her, lifted his instrument to eye level. Before she realized what he was doing, she heard the whirr and the snap. The smell of flash powder, then a burst of light, bright as an exploding star.

Photography seemed to her a bit like dark magic: her image was now contained to Jenkins's camera, but it'd emerge again, another self, uncontrolled, even by her. She'd read that when inventors first dabbled in the field of photography, they could easily capture an image. It came down to the simple science of lenses and light. The biggest challenge to the field of photography was permanence, getting the image to remain on photographic paper without fading. This had more to do with chemistry—the correct compound of chemicals.

Opal herself felt chemically altered, unsteady. She recalled the evening as though through intoxication, how she so often felt on Jagr's tonics and elixirs. And what of the Colonel and his tear-shaped scar? What of the tap of his index finger that had rung that bell? The men had left the bell box behind. She rang the bell freely now. Ding. Ding.

She didn't need clairvoyance to know this: The relationship between men and women was always transactional. The Colonel would call on her again.

January 23, 1986

Interview with Jane Doe No. 27

By *The Cincinnati Inquisitor*

CI: How often did you use Earthshine Soap?

JANE DOE NO. 27: Almost every single day for sixteen years. When I was a kid, I wanted to be the Earthshine Girl. She was so funny in those ads. I liked the lady plumber one the best where she wore those overalls.

CI: And how would you say the soap affected your life?

JANE DOE NO. 27: I loved the soap. Worked great. Smelled great. You could use it on anything. They called it "The Soap for Women," but maybe I wasn't woman enough.

CI: Why do you say that?

JANE DOE NO. 27: I don't know. I guess I just always felt different than others, set apart in the things I liked, the way I dressed. As a kid, I was a tomboy. I didn't want to be a plumber, but I liked working with my hands. I liked overalls, too. [Laughs] I grew out of that, then. I guess you could say I grew into my body. Breasts. Hips. Curves. You can't very well be a tomboy like that. I got married like I was supposed to do. But I was plagued with miscarriages. Seven. I never made it past eighteen weeks. I hate the word *miscarry*, like I'm the one doing it wrong, like I'm the one at fault. It wasn't me. I didn't carry anything wrong. It was the soap.

CI: Did your doctor tell you that?

JANE DOE NO. 27: My doctor didn't tell me anything.

1986

Queen of the laundry.

—JAS. S. KIRK & CO. SOAP MAKERS

Once you play a role, that character becomes part of you, that character is you, a you who is multiplied, like light through a prism. In this way, I don't agree with my old acting professors. You don't lose yourself—not at all. Instead, you expand, you multiply, you become only possibility. I was the Earthshine Girl and Stella. I was a Christmas fund drive host and Audrey and a deviated septum patient and Les Nessman's copilot. I was a daughter. I was a woman whose laundry machine was haunted. I was Wyatt's wife. I was a cheater. I was Halley's friend.

But if I stripped myself of all my titles, all the roles I played, what would remain of me? Who would I be? My acting teachers and directors had spoken of channeling the essence of a character, but what was the essence of me? That was the real question. If I were a character playing Nona Dixon, I'd have to ask: What did I want? What was I willing to do to get it? An audience won't root for a passive character.

The deposition was a week away. What did I want? I wanted the truth, I could say. That'd be true enough, given the vantage point of time. But in the moment, I didn't know what I wanted. I only knew what I felt in my body: a tightness like invisible hands were gripping my shoulders. A fist in my stomach. An aching at my jaw where I'd been clenching my teeth. My therapist has since told me that one must listen to her body, ask: What is my body telling me? What is the message from my deepest self?

My deepest self seemed to be saying this: fuck it.

The three-hour drive to Gallipolis took me four because of snow. I followed the Ohio River, its murky brown water a familiar marker until the road gave way to large houses, a tiny downtown still decorated for Christmas.

Gallipolis had a population of three thousand—the kind of town that was friendly but suspicious of outsiders. An old woman wearing a Sherpa hat stopped me almost as soon as I arrived. "You lost?" she asked.

"Maybe," I said. I had that old gray journal in my car, but now I hardly thought it could be of use. "I'm looking for someone," I said.

"Who, dear?"

"She's not alive."

"A ghost?" the woman said. She laughed, and when she did another woman—a younger one—appeared.

"Come on, Mom," she said. "Let's get back." She hooked her arm into her mother's elbow. "I'm sorry," she said to me.

"Don't be," I said. Then: "Not a ghost. Just a gravestone, maybe. Someone who was buried here."

"Mound Hill," she said. "Just east of town. That's where we all go, eventually."

Mound Hill was a sloping plot of land along the river with a maze of grave markers. I could see Gallipolis down the river, in the distance, just a scattering of houses tucked into the hillside.

The snow had stopped and all but melted. The heels of my boots sank into the soft earth. I walked through the cemetery until the grave markers looked darker and greener from moss. I read the dates marked on the gravestones. How odd it is to mark the range of time one lived, as though the hyphen summarizes the blur of events between birth and death. The little dash contains our whole lives. The woman on the phone said Jagr Doucet was buried next to his first wife. I wondered what kind of name Jagr was; it reminded me of the Jägermeister that Halley and I used to drink in bars when we were young. It tasted like black licorice.

As I turned down another row, I spotted it. A plot with an obelisk like a rocket ship pointing upward. A giant phallus. I thought of the shuttle that'd be heading into space soon, of the comet only weeks away, how all the answers to life seemed to be contained in the sky. I looked up. No sun, no clouds—just a low-hanging expanse of gray. A concrete sky.

I removed my gloves and touched the letters that spelled out Jagr's name. The stone was cold, damp from the weather. The monument faced the Ohio River. I remembered from our field trips to the public landing in elementary school that the first settlers of Ohio rode flatboats down the river, filled with supplies. The river flowed southwesterly. If I dropped a coin into the water here, it'd drift all the way back to Cincinnati.

I didn't see a smaller marker—not like the woman on the phone had described. I got down on all fours and rooted around in the grass until I felt something hard. I dug through denser dirt than the kind Stella was buried beneath. Finally, I unearthed a white square stone, the etched name now dark with grime: Opal Doucet.

Who was Opal Doucet?

I still didn't know. Just a name written on a block of stone. A name written on a plaque in front of an old factory and also in an old notebook. Looking up, I could see the river's strong currents carrying branches downstream. The last time the river froze over was nine years ago, 1977. Back then the news warned of gas and food shortages because barges couldn't travel. The river was solid and lumpy; the water had iced midwave. After another heavy snow, Halley and I crossed the river on foot into Kentucky, slipping the whole way, clinging to each other because of the cold, laughing. "We're walking on water!" Halley yelled. "We're walking on water!" I yelled, too, because it seemed like we'd performed a miracle, standing on that river. We felt unbound by the laws of nature. Free. Wyatt got mad afterward. *You could have died,* he said. I was younger then. I didn't think much about death.

I wiped the dirt from the grave marker. I traced the *O* in *Opal,* over and over, making little loops with my finger. With each loop, I tallied what I knew of the woman: She died in the Earthshine factory fire. She had written a formula for Comet Pills. Her pills made people happy. She was a witch. She killed people with her cures. She could talk to the dead. Bertie knew her, somehow, had kept her book of medicines locked in the safe with the soap formula. But why? What did this have to do with the Jane Does? Or with Halley? Or with me? That's what I needed to find out.

I sat six feet above her bones. By now, they'd turned to dust. I thought about Halley as an urn of ash. She requested her ashes to be scattered in France, and I wondered if the Tuttles would honor that wish, after the deposition, once they'd found out what Halley had left me.

I sat back on my heels and examined the stone. Stamped beneath the name Opal Doucet were the years she lived and died, that hyphen of her life adjoining her birth and death. I looked at the numbers. I rubbed the stone again with my coat to be certain I was reading it correctly: Not the year of the fire, 1910, the last time Halley's Comet could be seen, but later, much later.

1939. The year Halley was born.

CARL JUNG SAID LIFE DOESN'T really begin until you turn forty—that everything up until then is research.

Research.

The storefront of the five-and-ten appeared small, but the inside opened to high ceilings, the shelves stacked taller than I could reach, with a hodgepodge of items in no immediately perceivable order. Kitchen strainers and candy and cabinet hardware. Dish towels and electrical tape and WD-40 and Christmas ornaments and little plastic toys, green soldiers, like the ones Wyatt still had somewhere in one of his boxes in our basement.

"Can I help you?" The woman had a pretty face, though she wore too much makeup. Her name tag read: ROXANNE.

"Maybe," I said.

"Not from around here, are you."

I shook my head. "How'd you know?"

"Your hair," said Roxanne. "Only freaks and sick people have hair like that, but you don't look sick. Are you sick?"

"No," I said.

"You know, I wore a wig when I was Miss Gallipolis in 1967. You're in the presence of a beauty queen."

"Oh. That's neat," I said, but the moment I spoke the word, it felt wrong, insulting, like when people said it was neat I was an actress.

"You don't have to call me your highness. Royal majesty will do," Roxanne said, then turned down an aisle and started straightening a mess of sorted-through winter hats.

I followed her, watched for a few minutes as she tidied the shelves, then explained I was doing some research. Her bangs fell over her eyes, and she moved them by blowing one strong poof of air upward. "I thought you might know something, seeing that you're Miss Gallipolis and all," I said.

I explained to her I was looking for information about a woman who used to live here—a long time ago, but maybe she still had family in the area. "Opal Doucet," I said. At first I pronounced it "Do-Say," but then I corrected myself.

"She's dead, I'm sorry to tell you."

"I know that," I said. "I just visited her grave. Puny, compared to her husband's."

"I wouldn't be too keen on buying a fancy headstone either if someone tried to poison me."

"Jagr?"

"You knew him?"

I shook my head. Roxanne waved me on through the store, and we went back to the register, where she took a drink from a giant Styrofoam cup.

"Well, everyone around here knew him. Richest man in town, anyway—you saw his big penis monument. A doctor who worked at the old hospital. You probably passed it on the way in, big sandstone towers. Not open anymore, obviously. Well, his wife up and used his own medicine on him. Put some poison in his drink and watched him gulp it down." She slurped her drink. "He got sick as a dog. Almost died. Then she ran away."

"To Cincinnati," I said.

"You know the story, then? People think there's some answer in big city life."

"Most people think it's small."

"I don't know the whole thing—just bits and pieces I put together or heard over the years, but gossip's the best way to get to the truth of the matter, don't you think? Apparently, she got into some trouble down there. Took up with some other man. Her brain wasn't right. Too many narcotics rotted it, made her hear voices and all. She was some kind of druggie. That's why her husband brought her back and had her committed to that loony bin hospital where he worked." She took out a compact and adjusted her hair. "Now you're looking at me all funny. What?"

I was trying to make sense of it. A poisoning. An affair. Voices. Drugs. It sounded like an episode of *Stars and Shadows.*

"It's just, Opal Doucet's name is on a memorial plaque, right in front of the Earthshine factory." I thought of that plaque now and of the day of the Grand Re-Opening Ceremony when Bertie bought me that dress, yellow, the same shade as the Earthshine canister.

"Well, I don't know anything about that," she said, then: "The Soap for Women! Can you believe what they're saying about it now? Not that I trust all those Jane Doe people. Just want attention, don't you think?"

On my way out of town, I pulled my car over to that old hospital. Nothing remained of it except three sandstone towers, like ancient ruins. An arched door at the bottom and two squares for windows at the top had been filled in with mortar. Now, nobody could get in or out. I stood there for a while, surveying the turret. It looked like a witch's hat, a ledge where the brim would be.

I can't say I felt a sense of déjà vu, but I felt *something*. A warmth in my chest. Wind in my hair. Exhilaration. Relief. Looking back, I wish I could say this was the moment I knew what Halley had set me on a path to discover, but it wasn't. I *believed* Opal Doucet had been connected to what happened to the Jane Does, and to me. I *felt* Bertie was complicit.

But I didn't *know* it.

So often women doubt what they know because of their way of knowing it. Since elementary school I'd been trained to think only facts mattered. That's what those lawyers at the deposition wanted from me. Information. Not how I felt, but what I knew.

I needed to speak with Charlie. There could be a simple explanation. A factual error. I remembered pictures I'd seen of Bertie in *The Juggernaut*. In one, she's standing at the Tuttle Foundling Hospital, distributing packages to a group of new mothers, each holding a bundled infant. In another, she's standing on the picket line of the Earthshine Strike in solidarity with the workers.

Halfway home, I pulled over to a telephone booth, got out, and dialed Charlie. Carol, his secretary, picked up. "He's not taking calls," she said.

"It's Nona," I said. The inside of the booth had been tagged with graffiti. *What did they take from you?* someone had written on the glass in marker. Beneath it someone else had written: *Twenty-five cents.*

"I know who it is," Carol said. "It's just, the girls—the Jane Does—the protesters . . . That article in the *Inquisitor* . . . Mr. Longworth instructed Charlie to talk to nobody. Not without his clearance first."

"But . . ."

"Not even you, Nona. Sorry." Silence on her end. Some shuffling of papers. I thought she was about to hang up, but then she spoke again, quietly. "Mr. Longworth's been trying to reach you about that deposition next week."

"I know," I said.

"He's pulled some strings. He found some loophole. You don't have to testify anymore. What a relief, I'm sure—but you didn't hear it from me, okay? He wanted to tell you himself."

I didn't respond, just pressed the phone to my ear. Outside, cars whizzed by on the road. From inside the phone booth, they sounded like horseflies.

"Nona?"

I hung up.

I held the receiver and listened to the hum of the dial tone until the busy signal jarred me to my senses. *What did they take from you?* I read, then I swear it, I heard that sound in my head again, that *waa waa,* like a car horn or a signal or a voice still too far away to understand.

1910

The Colonel called on Opal by post. His handwriting was neat, with broad, confident strokes. No named was signed, but no name was necessary for Opal to understand who the sender was. *I apologize for the way you were treated. And, now, I request your services. I'll send my driver at quarter to ten tomorrow morning. It's a matter of some urgency. Please.*

It was the *please* in his note that intrigued her. The hint of desperation.

Right on time, an automobile pulled up, a black Model T with a shiny, thin frame. The driver was young, pink-faced, with a nose that looked like it'd been fashioned with clay and then flattened. She didn't recognize the man—a domestic, she assumed, from the way he dressed, thick work boots and a tailored work coat. He offered her a hand to step up into the car.

They drove away from the city, up the giant hill of Sycamore Street, passing the EARTHSHINE sign as they picked up speed and made their way out of town. She drew her hood over her head. Jagr could be anywhere.

"Where are we going?" Opal shouted over the wind. That was the problem with automobiles, so loud it was difficult to hold a conversation. Opal preferred carriages, the rhythmic clopping of horse hooves, though the papers said it'd be only a matter of time before all horses were retired to the rural areas.

"Up the Swing Line. Indian Hill. The Colonel prefers a bucolic setting. For his work."

She coughed, inhaling dirt. Perhaps he wished to discredit her. And yet, she remembered the tenderness in his eyes. The delicate manner in which he held his hand to his chest. The way he'd reached out and, with a peck of his slender finger, saved Opal. What must she pay for it?

The road soon gave way to a winding country lane paved in gravel. Woods on either side opened to wide swaths of fields. Though they'd been driving for only half an hour, she felt far from the city. She spotted a farm in the distance and large patches of grass still browned from the winter.

A few moments later, the driver turned down a lane marked only by a stone fence. They passed a stable and a carriage house, a maple tree just beginning to bud. Then they came to a stop in front of a stately manor.

The foyer opened into a square room with a hearth, a fire already blazing, a woman's portrait hanging above it. The room was lit by gas lamps, for electrical lights were a thing of the city, and he had chosen a quieter life. The walls were made entirely of beadboard; stuffed birds hung about, their heads small, their eyes dark and dull, their short thick wings stretched as though about to take flight. Set about the room were several contraptions, metal boxes with wires and nodes attached to circular leather bands, shaped and sized proportional to the human skull. Colonel Bloodworth was a medical doctor whose phrenology experiments had gained him some notoriety, according to the papers. These must be his tools, sturdy when she picked them up. They'd feel heavy, no doubt, attached to her.

"Hello," a man's voice said, and she stilled herself when she heard it. "Thank you for coming."

Please *and* thank you.

There stood Colonel Bloodworth in the flesh, his beard well-trimmed, his hair coiffed, his scar white and feathery in the light. She surveyed the room again, the portrait of the woman on the wall. His late wife.

"You see, I study the human body," Colonel Bloodworth said. He stood near the hearth; his cheeks were pink. "But I also study the human mind—how the two are connected." Now they were sitting. He had brought her a cup of tea and a biscuit and offered to hang her coat on the rack in the corner. Opal refused, worried he'd see her gravid form. "There's so little we know of this connection. And yet, this modern world of ours pushes us forward, to the brink of new discoveries. X-rays, telegraphs, radioactivity, electricity—look around at our transforming lives. Only a decade ago we were living crudely, in the dark ages."

"Thank you for this little history lesson," she said. She held her hands over her teacup, balanced on her lap. The steam dampened her fingers. She focused on that, the pleasure of it.

"I'm sorry. Pierre Curie. You know him?"

"Not personally."

"Pierre Curie, the famed scientist. He studied all the most modern advancements," he said, though he explained he'd died the most old-fashioned way, by stepping in front of a horse-drawn carriage. He believed the spirit realm was the key to unlocking unknown energies that held answers to the scientific realm—the human realm. "And I agree," he said. "If one can tap into the mind of the dead, one can potentially unlock some fundamental aspect of the human mind that isn't limited to the physical brain. The mind without a body—the essence of consciousness, as it were."

"So you believe cadavers will tell you something," said Opal. She was suddenly alert to her senses being filled: the air pressing against her skin, the mossy smell of the wood near the fireplace, the snapping of logs.

He sat back. "Is this too much for you to take in at once?"

"You assume me to be delicate," Opal said. She swallowed the last of her tea and set the cup down on the table beside her. She felt her innards warming, her blood pulsing in places other than her heart. This was a symptom of her pregnancy, she had to assume, this flowing of blood, this electrical sensation, this desire to touch and be touched. At home, nude in her bed, she'd run her hands over the hill of her stomach, her breasts, between her legs where it was wet.

"Very well, then. I want to show you something," the Colonel said. She followed him past the hearth room with the stuffed birds and portrait of his wife, past the fire with its low burning crackle. He led her to a door, recessed behind a bookshelf, hidden so well that Opal had not noticed it.

Opal knew it was his laboratory before he lit the lamps to illuminate the room. She knew it from the coolness of it, from the astringent smell of formaldehyde that burned her eyes. As the room was lit to a glow, she did not recognize what she was looking at, lined in large jars along the farthest wall.

The jars reminded her of the pickled vegetables she once stored in the cellar. These, however, contained something large and putty-colored with ridges like the markings of river worms.

"The human mind," he said.

She touched the outside of one of the jars gently, like she may startle what was floating inside.

"You say you are not delicate," he said.

She picked up the jar and was surprised by the weight of it. Then she felt the urge to vomit.

"This is the essence of human life," the Colonel said, taking the jar from Opal and setting it back down. "It may unsettle some, but the brain houses the human mind and personality. What lives here during one's life, if I'm correct, can survive on the astral plane."

"The Other Side," Opal murmured. She moved along the table and picked up another jar. The brain contained the same folds, the same deep crease down the center of it, the same weight—three pounds, according to the Colonel. "Do you know who they were in life?"

"I have record of their names, occupations, cause of death. This one, right here," he said, picking up the smallest jar among them. "Wallace Quinn. A farmer. Influenza."

"What about this one?" she asked, pointing to another, the largest jar. "Who is he?"

"She. Margaret Beard. Mother of five. Consumption."

Opal lifted the jar and held it close to her face, peering into the liquid. The contents looked not too dissimilar from the pickled pig's brains she often saw at the market, and this thought made her queasy.

He took the jar from her once again and set it gently on the table. Clearly, he thought tenderly of its contents. "Structurally, at least, it seems to be an unsexed organ. Dr. Harvey Cushing—an Ohio man as well—has made a career of stimulating the brains of patients with epilepsy, meningitis, or injury, to locate which parts of the brain are responsible for what. Someday we'll know for sure. Science is moving along at a rapid pace. In a decade hence we'll understand it completely."

But what would that change?

She imagined her own brain, which she'd never see. Would he someday point to the organ and say, *This was Opal*? And what was *this*? Who was *this*?

The Colonel drummed his fingers on his cabinet. "An impressive performance the other night. You convinced some of us," he said.

"Only some?"

"Some men are suspicious of the spirit realm," he said. "It makes them feel impotent, small, so they look for ways to overcompensate, to display strength. That's what the bell was all about. Not about you—but about them."

"I should say thank you."

"They don't understand how it works."

She observed the shape of his face, the cut of his shoulders, broad and square. He was a man that Oren would never grow to be.

They returned to the hearth room, and Opal took a seat.

The Colonel moved behind her chair. She was aware of his hands so near to her shoulders. He struggled to find the right words. He cleared his throat. Nervousness. "There is someone I wish to reach, someone I've been trying to reach for the better part of a decade," he said.

A log snapped on the hearth. "Shouldn't you consult the committee?"

"This is a personal matter," the Colonel said.

"This person you wish to reach, she's a woman, is she not? A relation."

"Yes," he said. He cleared his throat again and moved to stand by the fire. "Technology will soon allow us to communicate with those who've crossed over."

"Make a spirit incarnate. Capture it forever," she said. "Like a photograph." She wondered if he already knew about the Spirit Machine.

"Exactly," he said. He flicked his eyes toward the portrait above the hearth, then steadied his gaze on Opal. Perhaps that was the pull she felt toward him, the recognition of his grief that dwelled inside him like a living being.

"Your wife," Opal said.

"Hazel." He said her name like a sigh. She'd died in childbirth and took with her their child. What a tragic way to succumb, while pushing life into the world, as though one's whole purpose is to flower, then fruit, then die.

Opal faced the man. He held his palm to his chest, then he touched his scar. What would Opal's life have been like, had Oren lived? Would they have married? Would he have danced with her still? On the riverbank, when they'd finally dried off, Madame de Fleur had lain in the grass, her skin a pale lake, a body of water beside the shore. Now when Opal conjured Oren she conjured the woman, that lake, the dark.

Opal envied Hazel in this moment, Hazel whose portrait still hung above the hearth, whose very name made the Colonel's eyes dewy.

The best the Colonel could produce for Opal was a small chess table and a kerosene lamp. When they sat across from each other, their knees bumped, and Opal felt warmth at all her contact points. She tried to ignore the unusual nervousness she felt. She asked him to draw the shades and extinguish the fire and hold her hands. The room cooled.

He closed his eyes. She closed hers. If all relationships are transactional, she must transact. One gives. One receives. She'd done this with Jagr before—anticipate his needs so she wouldn't be asked for it. In this way, she could pretend she gave herself freely.

The Colonel gripped her hands as though she might slip away. Sitting there, Opal imagined herself someone else. A different marriage. A different life. She thought of Jagr and Oren and the baby and Madame de Fleur and all that had transpired since she'd run away. She was tired. She longed for a resting place, and maybe that made her weak. Maybe that made her a woman.

She opened her eyes to watch the light flickering on the Colonel's face. His eyelids were shiny; a swoop of hair draped his forehead. His jaw pulsed, and when she closed her eyes again, she felt a calmness wash over her. She thought of the way Madame de Fleur would hold her around the waist, a human belt.

What would it feel like to be Hazel? How might this man protect her? How tempting to relieve herself of her own existence for just a while, to let Hazel's consciousness settle into her mind? She felt a body steal into her own. His wife.

It was easier to be someone else, anyhow. Freeing. Relieved of self, she had no inhibitions. She could do anything. Be anyone. She squeezed the Colonel's hand. Her voice was high, clenched, melodic, a song restrained. "Darling," she said. "At last."

The Colonel gave no sign of surprise and, yet, no immediate signs of delight. He'd been fooled before. "If this is you, dear Hazel, straightaway, tell me, what pet name did I call you?"

Nobody wants to be played a fool. But desire hides in plain sight, in the details of one's life, in where one places her gaze, what she notices. Opal surveyed the curiosities placed about the room, the metal contraptions, birdcages, the smoking hearth, the portrait above it. Hazel's head was small, like the bird, but not in an ugly way. She wore a feathered boa around her neck, and now Opal studied the stuffed birds hanging about the room like trophies, or like reminders, or . . . or like a memorial. The birds were grouse. The Colonel was looking at one now. She recognized the bird's small head and feathered feet, a bit like the common chicken, but more dignified.

"Grouse. You called me Hazel Grouse." The Colonel's hand squeezed tighter. "You spotted one—"

"—the same year I met you."

His face relaxed, and he looked not so much at Opal as through her. Before he could say anything else, Opal stretched her body across the tiny chess table and touched his scar. He did not recoil, though something in him did startle. Her belly grazed the table. She pressed her lips against his, and they were warm. Until the day she died she'd remember this kiss, how the warmth held the memory of something familiar and distant. A woman can want so many things at once, but she has only one body. She clung to him. He let her kiss him until his body eased and, finally, he kissed her back.

Soon, they were upstairs, in a bedroom. He pressed against her bare chest. Hazel moaned louder than Opal ever had, always keeping her own pleasure to a stifle. She didn't know who she was then, lying there, tangled in his limbs, her impulse to pull him closer and closer, despite the obstacle of her stomach. Though it was dark, she didn't hide her body, nor did she feel the crush of the Colonel's weight, which he carried in his arms, braced against the mattress. The Colonel was gentle, intertwining his fingers with hers, as though, together, they were praying. And, like a prayer, too, he sank into her while whispering her name, over and over, an incantation: Hazel. Hazel. Hazel.

January 26, 1986

Interview with Jane Doe No. 33

By *The Cincinnati Inquisitor*

CI: When did you first start using Earthshine Soap?

JANE DOE NO. 33: In 1978, after I got married. I'd seen the commercials, the one where the Earthshine Girl is wearing pearls and that glittery dress and she's sitting at a table in some fancy restaurant, and her husband, who's just off camera, arrives with a single rose and sets it on the table between them. He compliments her soft hands and says he loves her and she turns to the camera and says: *Should I tell him he's in love with the soap?*

After we got married, my husband expected more of me, different things than before. I found myself not wanting to be . . . touched in that way. I thought it was just me. I thought maybe the Earthshine Girl was on to something. I bought the soap, and I washed our bedsheets in it. I loved the smell of it. Lavender. I polished our silverware we'd gotten as a wedding gift. I scrubbed coffee stains out of my husband's favorite mug. I soaked the yellowed pits of his undershirts in it until they were white again. Earthshine worked wonders. I even bathed in it, because it was gentle enough for that—it said so right on the canister. It said it was "The Soap for Women."

CI: How did your life change after using Earthshine?

JANE DOE NO. 33: Our apartment was spotless. At first my marriage improved. We were . . . very friendly with each other for a while in the bedroom. But after a while, I was doubling over in pain each month. It was like a cactus was growing inside me. The period flu. Three days became four, then five, then sometimes half the month, menses so heavy my doctor suggested a diet of red meat for the iron loss. A year in, our family asked: What, no grandchildren?

The worst part was the staining. Our sheets, my undergarments. I had to use towels on the couch. I could no longer leave my apartment for more than a few hours, or if I did I had to bring a change of clothes. I'll never forget my husband's look one day I came home from the grocery store with red saturated through the fabric of my skirt. I felt like Carrie from that movie. My husband looked at me as though I were some horrifying aberration. [Pause.] There's nothing like Earthshine for stains.

CI: So you continued to use it?

JANE DOE NO. 33: No, I stopped buying it. I lived with the bloodstains. Everywhere I sat. Everywhere I lay. My clothes. My couch. My car. My marriage lasted two more years. My doctor told me I'd never have a child.

1986

A skin you love to touch.

—JOHN H. WOODBURY'S FACIAL SOAP

As I pulled onto my street after my drive back from Gallipolis, an unfamiliar silver car idled near my house. Through the windshield, I could make out the driver wearing a baseball cap and sunglasses, a large coat zipped up to the neck. The driver honked at me, and I honked back, just laid on my horn with all my might.

The vehicle's reverse lights flashed, and it backed up to my mailbox. At first I thought they were trapping me in my driveway. Maybe I'd be kidnapped, worse. *Never let them take you to a second location,* I recalled from my YMCA self-defense class, because a woman moving through the world must always be primed to the threat of sexual violence.

Finally, the driver's side window lowered. Edith sat behind the wheel. I heard the thunk of my mailbox as she opened and closed it, stuffing something inside.

"For fuck's sake," she said, before speeding away. I watched her taillights shrink to red dots in the distance.

The hinge moaned as I pulled down the lid. Tucked in the back, a manila envelope that'd been folded: *For you, Edith.*

Jealousy rose up in me as I recognized Halley's handwriting. For a moment, I resented Edith, just like I used to when she'd taken over as the Earthshine Girl. Then I felt stupid. I had no claims on Halley. I knew this. Love requires space; it's not a constraint but a means to freedom. I loved Halley. I did. Of course she'd spent time with Edith. Of course they'd become friends. Of course she'd given someone else a way to discover the truth. How wise of her to do so, because she knew me—she loved me, too.

I opened the envelope and peered inside. A stack of envelopes. Letters, of some sort, addressed to Opal Doucet. The return address was stamped France. I pulled one out, and that's when it dropped to the ground, the necklace. A simple silver chain, tarnished from age. From it hung a stone, translucent white. It seemed to glow in the dark.

Inside, I sat at my kitchen table. One by one, I read those letters, more than twenty of them written over eight months, starting in 1909. I felt like a voyeur, like I was reading something I shouldn't, a confession, even if nothing was directly confessed. Each was addressed to Opal, written by a woman named Madame de Fleur. M, she sometimes called herself. She wrote directly and indirectly at once. I'll admit, like a poem, I didn't understand them, but I could sense what they meant. I could *feel* it. I could glean enough to know why Halley had given the letters to Edith.

Opal Doucet had been pregnant. Pregnant. I don't know why this news came as such a surprise, as though Opal couldn't have done bad deeds while carrying a child. Procreation doesn't make one morally superior. I read about how Opal Doucet had heard a voice, and about a Spirit Machine that could provide some answers, and about the cures she was making for the other Earthshine workers who complained of *emotional disorders*. The woman had been expecting Opal in France, but Opal had been delayed. Madame de Fleur wrote of mystics and scientists, of the sun and the universe and of our lives as scale models of such. She wrote of Halley's Comet, how three wise men followed it. She said she wasn't afraid of death. Her final letter was dated April 22, 1910. I read from it:

> *You say I speak in riddles, but now the occasion calls for directness: A spiritualist cannot be held responsible for the messages received from the Other Side. This would be akin to smashing the telephone box for bad news spoken through its lines. You were trying to help those women with your power of mediumship. I believe this, truly. It's clear to me, from your description, however, that your cures have unintended consequences. I am sorry for the sad circumstances of those women's deaths and that you've been put at the center of it. The Witch of Walnut Street! What an unfortunate insult. And, yet, I'll tell you what I suspect you already know: This may be an instance of a cure being worse than the disease.*

I folded the letter and stacked it along with the others. At the cellular level, I felt changed, different. Joseph Campbell would call this the "dark night of the soul." It's a necessary part of the Hero's Journey. In the movie of my life, the director might have me stare into a mirror, searching for someone recognizable. Was I going crazy? Isn't that funny—that I'd finally found some tangible proof, and I only questioned myself? But the thing about the dark night of the soul, I'd learned at the conservatory, is that it leads to light. To revelation. To change.

Marriage gives us a witness to all the moments of our lives, even the dull ones—a built-in audience. Friends can provide this, too, of course, but Halley was gone. I called who I so often called in urgent moments—the person I'd relied upon to ground me: Wyatt.

Years ago, Wyatt occasionally answered the phone imitating the sound of ringing, and he perfected this trilling because that's what Wyatt did, he applied himself. He'd fooled me many times when I called him, and I'd sit on the line, waiting for him to pick up, only to realize he was already there. But now the ringing was just ringing. No answer at all.

Upstairs, I found a business card tucked into my underwear drawer, and I dialed the number.

"My favorite elf," John Dale said when he answered.

"Let it go," I said. Click-click. I could hear it so clearly now. I was walking around my house with my cordless phone squeezed between my ear and shoulder. I couldn't stay. My phone had been bugged. I sensed I was being watched. I began to stuff a bag with clothes, with a toothbrush, with underwear, with Wyatt's jeans.

"Anger is sexy."

"Not now." My Earthshine dress was crumpled on my living room floor. I picked it up and shoved it in my bag. I don't know why. Some things we do by instinct. "I'll do the interview," I said.

"Really? Great." He grew serious.

"I can't talk now," I said. "They're listening."

"Come here," he said.

"Your wife."

"She's visiting her sister in Louisville." Click. Click.

I sat on the line, thinking.

"We have a guest room," he said. "I'd never compromise my sources. Code of ethics. I'll make you coffee in the morning. We don't even have to speak until the interview. I'll give you my address."

"Don't say it out loud," I said. "I remember."

THE LIGHTING CREW AT WLAX readied the set for our interview. John Dale Fox had arranged it. He sat across from me in a director's chair. He'd done as he promised—made up a bed for me in the guest room, had coffee waiting in the morning; he left before I woke. Now he wore a tie, uncharacteristic for him, which signaled to me he thought this interview might get national air. His hair was parted above his left eye and combed to the side, and he looked like a little boy before church on Easter morning.

Behind him, I could see the line of televisions with the broadcast feed. Today the *Challenger* was going into space, taking with it a crew of astronauts and a civilian teacher and a camera to study the comet. The national news was covering it, not the local networks. I was glad my interview would be taped, not live. I thought of the time I said West Vagina instead of West Virginia when I was hosting the Reds' Opening Day Baseball Parade, and the producer had to cut to commercial. I was never offered live work again.

"Are you sure you want to do this?" he said. We were sitting in director's chairs across from each other.

"With you?" I said.

"Be nice." He was holding a yellow legal pad with questions written on it.

"I don't *want* to do this at all," I said, softening.

A makeup girl came over and applied some cake makeup to my face. It felt tight on my skin like glue, dried. "Do you want a wig?" she asked me.

"No," I said.

"New stylist?" asked John Dale. I shot him a look and he turned serious again. "What will you do if they come after you? When," he corrected. He arched his back, stretching in his chair.

"I haven't thought that far."

"After all the Tuttles have done for you," he said. "For your career."

"Whose side are you on?" Tonight was Bertie's final public talk at the observatory. *The Tale of the Comet.* I never responded to her invitation.

"Yours—but you can't get past those facts. They discovered you. Bertie Tuttle made you who you are."

I thought of my own mother, of how when she'd bought me that *Boys' Life* booklet on ventriloquism, she'd given me her old hand mirror so I could watch myself practice. She helped me repaint Sal. She oiled his jaw so it wouldn't squeak. It never occurred to me until later that maybe I was her own life presented back to her. A second chance. With Sal, I could say anything I wanted. Things she could never dare.

"Their lawyer—what's his name—Gene Longworth. The guy has rocks in his stomach. He swallows people whole."

Behind him, I noticed the producer standing by the live feed. He shushed everyone and turned up the volume. On the television, we watched a live clip of young teens in an auditorium. They were somewhere in New Hampshire, from the school where the teacher on the shuttle worked. Christa McAuliffe taught social studies, and she had won a contest that would shoot her two hundred thousand miles away from her husband and two kids. The space shuttle *Challenger* would carry her and the crew and the SPARTAN satellite to study the spectra of Halley's Comet before its perihelion. Meanwhile, I had been bound by gravity, by the boundaries of my own choosing.

On the screen, the kids realized they were being filmed, and they waved to the camera, braces flashing on their teeth. The difference between ordinary people and celebrities is that celebrities never wave.

"Twenty seconds," the personality from the national affiliate said. He began counting down. "Nineteen, eighteen . . ." John Dale adjusted his tie. "You'll be okay," he said. "What you're doing is important. I mean it. This story . . . We're talking millions of women, if not more. You'll be on the right side of history."

"Fourteen, thirteen, twelve . . ." the announcer counted.

"You'll be famous. A household name," he said.

"On a household product," I said. "That's how I'll be remembered." I turned again to watch the screens.

"Why not just go to the cops with this?"

"The Tuttles own this town. You know that," I said. "You've said so yourself. I'm afraid that if I—"

On the screens behind John Dale, smoke was bursting from the booster nozzles of the *Challenger*. Once the shuttle launched, the satellite would travel for several more days to reach the comet. Space travel is slower than you think. We pinch our fingers together to measure the stars, but, up there, the distance is vast. The comet would be visible to the naked eye from Earth, and that's what's truly astonishing about comets and eclipses and stars: We can see that light from millions of miles away while we often can't see what's right in front of us.

"Four, three, two . . ." I shifted to get a better view of the television.

One.

You already know what happened next. But at the time, I wasn't sure what I was seeing. The grip crew stopped what they were doing and turned toward the televisions. John Dale's mouth gaped. The producer covered his eyes and peeked through his fingers. On the screen was a streaming ball of fire—not a comet, but something else. An explosion, then a cloud in the shape of a caterpillar. I watched the cloud transforming into white limbs against a blue sky, then drifting down the screen toward the earth. The makeup girl gasped. She dropped a hand mirror, and it shattered.

Then, silence. Pure silence. Most of us don't know the sound of pure silence because we're conditioned to the constant hum of electricity. Our brain adapts easily to background noise to shut it out. Sound is perception. Memory is perception, too.

In my memory, the televisions were muted. I remember the stiff quiet of the room, the smoke and shrapnel that streamed down from the sky. I thought of the kids on the television, the students of Christa McAuliffe, the teacher inside the shuttle. I remembered how, on the day we moved into our house, Wyatt and I placed an egg on the hardwood to test the evenness of the floors, and the egg rolled and cracked against the wall. I don't know why that memory came to me at that moment, probably because the children on the screen had been oblivious to what was going to happen next, how something so jubilant can be ruined in an instant.

John Dale jumped up and changed the channel to a different network. Did he think the news would be different somehow? That this was a trick of the camera? There it was again, on a loop, the same footage from a different station and a different angle: The explosion and the branching cloud. Another channel. Another clip. I know seven astronauts were aboard, but I kept thinking about the teacher. The civilian. The footage made it seem like she'd be caught for an eternity in this moment, trapped between below and beyond, looping forever.

John Dale was the first to speak. He stood and unclipped his microphone. "I'm sorry, Nona, but . . ."

"I know," I said.

"I've got to get on the ground," he said. "Interviews, reactions. Call around and find local connections." He was making a mental list.

John Dale walked me to my car. He hugged me and he smelled like Old Spice and he whispered, "Soon. I promise." His body felt like a body. He kissed my forehead. I looked up to the sky, where the shuttle had exploded. Of course I couldn't see it, even if it was the same sky above us. I tried to picture her, that teacher in space, how she packed her son's stuffed animal frog among her things, how nervous she must have felt upon liftoff, how she'd never felt weightless, not even for a moment.

I DROVE AROUND FOR A while after that. I drove past my agent's office, decorated in flamingos and palmettos. I drove past Wyatt's new apartment building. I looked up to his window, and I imagined him inside, in one of those soft, gray T-shirts he loved to wear. I drove past the lunch spot where I used to meet Halley. I'd ordered inside-out egg rolls, but Halley called it what it really was: a cabbage salad. I drove past the gym where I spent so many hours on a treadmill—how odd it seems to jog in place, never getting anywhere. I drove past the hospital where I stayed those horrible nights a couple years back, and then past the house where I grew up. Someone had torn out my mother's rose garden and replaced it with a shed.

And then, finally, I drove to my own house. It'd been vandalized again. Toilet paper swung from the trees in graceful loops. Someone had strung caution tape from one porch lantern to the other. It looked like a crime scene. Maybe it was. Domestic crimes had been committed, crimes of the heart. *Oh, don't be melodramatic,* I could hear my agent say. *Save it for Stella.* But Stella was dead.

I turned off my car when I noticed Wyatt sitting on our front porch. As I approached him, I could tell he'd been crying. His nose was rosy. The rims of his eyes were pink. I didn't care if tragedy had brought us together, if we'd always tell the story of how the day the *Challenger* exploded was the day we realized something about the impermanence of life. We'd try to fix what we'd broken.

"It's so terrible," I said. "Awful." He stood, and I reached for him. My arms slid around his waist, but he pushed me away.

"John Dale?" he said.

"What?"

He handed me the paper. "*Tempo of the Times,*" he said flatly.

I shuffled the pages until I found what Wyatt wanted me to see. A full-page spread. A series of photos. An accompanying article. John Dale and I were caught mid-embrace. You can see my open car door in the background, the fuzz of my steering wheel cover, a curved blur of white. In the photo, John Dale's mouth is to my ear, and my eyes are looking up, not at John Dale but toward the sky. It looks like I'm laughing, but I'm not. I wasn't.

Beneath that photo were others, the quick shutter clicking of the photographer: me, walking into his house last night. John Dale, carrying my bag. Me, looking back over my shoulder before I step inside. The article called it an affair. Not a tryst or a one-night stand or a movement of bodies in space and time, or a kind of revenge against my own life, the anguish of it, which is exactly what it was. I'm not excusing it. Beneath the article was a still from the set of the Christmas in July Fund Drive. There I was as that elf, holding the screaming baby. How unnaturally I was holding that child. Her neck bent back, unsupported. No wonder she was crying.

"Wyatt—"

"Stop."

"It's not what you think," I said.

Wyatt turned to go inside the house, and I followed him.

"You didn't sleep with him?"

A pause.

"You don't understand." I covered my face. I tried to think of what to say. I closed my eyes and opened them again. "I tried to call you. You didn't answer. You never answer. You never talk to me. I went there to—"

"Oh, I know why you went there."

"Halley left me something. It's about Earthshine. It's connected to the Jane Does, to the lawsuit. This is bigger than us." I used John Dale's words.

Wyatt walked to the refrigerator and looked inside, then slammed it closed.

"There was a woman named Opal Doucet. She was medicating these women with Comet Pills, but they had these terrible effects, and she was pregnant, and she was trying to get to France. I read all these letters from her friend or—or I don't know what they were to each other. But Opal didn't die in the Earthshine fire—it's not at all like Bertie said."

"John Dale Fox." He was still on that. He still felt rage, which, looking back, was a good sign. Rage contains love, I think, the pain of something you want being taken from you. I felt rage, too. "I mean, look at him. He looks like Wham! in a suit. And you look . . ."

"Like what?" I said.

Let me dispense this advice: Never ask a question you do not want the answer to.

"Desperate. Really fucking desperate. Clinging to your last shred of fame. Riding the wave of a third-rate soap character. Pretending like those stupid commercials were the best thing that ever happened to you, like you're something to the Tuttles other than marketing material. They have to be nice to you, Nona. Your face is on the fucking package. Stella is dead, and now you're nothing. You've aged out. Middle-aged. You're done. Next."

In fifteen seconds, all my fears articulated. Maybe that's the difficulty with marriage in the first place. You must hand yourself over, armorless, knowing your vulnerabilities might be weaponized against you at any point. It's a long-term struggle not to say the meanest things we could possibly say in order to protect ourselves and our pain. I could have said plenty to Wyatt in this moment. About him. About how this wasn't the life I wanted, about how I was desperate, but not in the ways he imagined.

I dug into my handbag for that gray notebook Halley had left me. It was a formulary—a list of drugs and their ingredients—I know that now.

"They call them 'showmances,' right? So you don't come out looking slutty?" He opened and closed the cabinets, looking for something, though I didn't know what.

Wyatt's neck beat with his pulse. His nostrils flared, and it occurred to me how rarely I'd ever seen him angry, how rarely I'd ever seen him yell or cry or react with anything other than perfectly measured breathing. I tried to imagine how I looked to him, standing there with that old formulary, holding it out like it was the answer to all our problems.

"Get out," he said. "I pay the mortgage. This is my house." He was pointing toward the door as if I didn't know where it was. "I don't even know you anymore. Look at you. That hair. A walking midlife crisis. You look ridiculous."

"Maybe you just don't like me."

"Maybe I don't."

We locked eyes and stood there in the living room until Wyatt kicked the coffee table and it landed on its side. I could see the ring mark from where he'd once set a glass down without a coaster. *Who cares?* he'd said at the time. I did, that's who. I cared, and didn't it matter what I cared about?

"I want a divorce," he said.

The word *divorce* comes from a Latin root that means "to divert, to change direction." But I had already changed direction. I was moving toward the door.

1910

Opal could hear the chanting from Liberty Street. *Our bodies, our soap.*

She'd overslept, and now she walked as quickly as her legs would take her. She wore her cloak with the hood drawn over her head, despite the warm temperatures. One day, Jagr would appear, like a monument in front of her. Stone. Solid. The kind in a children's book that came to life. Her eyes were steadied upon the sidewalk, cragged with cracks the shape of lightning bolts. When she heard a rumbling, she suspected thunder, but instead, it was a group of boys who pulled each other on a wooden go-cart. She followed them all the way to the factory.

When she crossed the street, she saw them, the Earthshine Girls, on the steps of the factory, but they weren't alone. Others had joined the strikers now, holding up signs like advertisements, like proof of their righteousness. The Women's Christian Temperance Union. The local chapter of the Women's Trade Union League. The National Woman Suffrage Association. Some women stood in uniforms, others in dresses and jackets. OUR EMPLOYERS HAVE WEALTH; WE HAVE THE POWER OF REPRODUCTION, one picket sign read, and at that moment Opal felt a fleeting sense of her own magnitude, with her child growing like a miracle inside her. If she could create a life—this life—what else could she create? What else might she do? She was growing; she was multiplying. In just two weeks she'd receive the Dowd money, and then she'd cross the Atlantic Ocean and leave all this behind. The waters would be vast and blue and open, just like the sky. She imagined herself leaning out over the rail, water misting her face, and it'd feel a little bit like flying. Would she think of these women then? Of this life she willed into existence?

Would she think of her evening with the Colonel, how they'd fallen asleep holding hands, and how, in the first light of the morning, he called her Hazel Grouse, and she'd answered to that name? Later, he insisted on driving her home himself, and by the time they reached the city limits, she'd noticed in him a hard-to-place aloofness she might have mistaken for guilt or regret.

A group of newspapermen moved toward the front of the crowd, toward Gilly, whose limbs stretched out like a starfish. Betsy and Maria worked quickly to wrap a thick chain link around her middle, up and under then over her shoulders. In seconds, she was fastened to the door.

"Nobody goes in until our demands are met," Maria shouted through the megaphone. However, Opal knew another way in, down through the old beer caves and up through the memorabilia room—the way Bertie had shown her.

Betsy noticed Opal standing near the empty planters by the curb, and waved her over to join them. Betsy smelled of cigarettes. She handed her picket sign over to Opal, then held her rounded belly, as pregnant women do, like it was a ball that may drop and bounce away.

"How's the baby?" Opal asked. She rested the sign over her shoulder. Together, they began to walk the picket line.

Betsy laughed. "The world's ending and you ask about the baby," she said.

"You believe all that?" asked Opal.

"Why wouldn't I? I read about it every day in the papers."

In the papers, historians noted that the comet in the year 1066 signaled the overthrow of King Harold II by William the Conqueror, while the 1456 apparition marked the Siege of Belgrade. Some scientists theorized that with each orbit, Halley's became smaller in mass and would someday either split in two or be expelled from the universe.

Where does one go when expelled from the universe? And can one return? Can a machine make it so? Look at all the machines that had failed: the factory boilers, the soap plodder. At least once a week the conveyor belt ran off its track and jammed. Just two years ago, Orville Wright's airship fell from the sky, and he was gravely injured. His passenger died.

Betsy stopped walking for a moment, so Opal stopped, too. "We can stand here all day and scream as loud as we want, but it's like screaming in the dark to stop the morning from coming. The sun will rise either way." The day was gray but bright, and a light patch in the clouds revealed the sun's efforts. Betsy looked toward the sky. "It's up there, somewhere, isn't it? Halley's. Makes one feel so small and useless. I think, what kind of world is this for a baby anyway, especially if she's a girl. Nothing's ever going to change." She held her middle and bounced on her toes, as though she was lulling the baby to sleep in the bassinet of her womb.

Opal refused to believe that nothing could change. Look at her own life; she'd transformed it in just a matter of months when before she'd have thought it impossible. "Why are you here?" Opal asked. "If you think nothing will change?"

"I'm supposed to want these things," she said. A wagon pulled forward, and another group of women got out to join the crowd. They wore white dresses, large-brimmed hats that looked more appropriate for the Kentucky Derby.

Across the way, Maria shouted through her megaphone. *Our bodies, our soap.* Betsy bumped Opal playfully with her shoulder, and Opal picked up her pace.

At the edge of the picketers stood Amanda Mahooney. Amanda

twirled a ring on a chain she wore around her neck, a new ring with a bright green emerald, rumored to be a gift from Charles Tuttle. Who knew the man had such a tender heart? He'd read poetry to her. Keats. *Can death be sleep when life is but a dream?* She'd recited the line to the other girls, doing her best to convince everyone of his humanity, despite his unwillingness to meet their demands. She stood on her toes, scanning the crowd, as if expecting someone. And there he was, Tuttle himself, materializing in a tan suit. He removed his top hat. He motioned for Maria to hand over the megaphone, and, reluctantly, she did.

"Ladies," Tuttle boomed, and then he adjusted his volume so he wouldn't appear to be yelling. "Let's be reasonable."

"It's too late, Mr. Tuttle." Maria looked more vibrant than Opal had ever seen her. Her skin glowed; she pulled her shoulders back, square, stiff. The Earthshine Girls stood behind her like mutinous foot soldiers in their white uniforms.

Now another man pushed his way forward. He stood not quite to Tuttle's shoulder and resembled something of a German schnauzer. Tuttle's lawyer. He raised his camera to eye level, and Opal covered her face. "I'm only documenting, ladies," he said. The camera hissed as he wound it. "Now," he said, hanging it around his neck and removing a small notebook from his pocket. "You claim your work conditions are unsafe and dangerous. Let's address that first, shall we? It's hot, I understand. Perhaps we can bring in more fans." The Earthshine Girls began shouting again, and the man took out a handkerchief and wiped his brow.

"Girls, girls," Tuttle said. "Please. Listen. We've given you jobs. We've given you independent wages. Some factories wouldn't even hire you. Have you heard the floor manager complain? Or the machine operators? No. You get paid for women's work. At the end of the day, you go home to your husbands and children, to your families who need you."

"Get to your point!" Maria yelled.

"I'm willing to raise your weekly wages. Fifty cents," he said. Silence, at first. The women didn't know how to react, so they looked toward one another. None of the picketers spoke. The lawyer zapped his camera a few more times. Betsy saluted him with her middle finger.

From somewhere within the crowd of women, someone hurled a bar of soap toward the men. They ducked to avoid it. Then, all at once, more women began hurling cakes in their direction.

"My girls, my girls!" Tuttle said, still hunched in a protective position.

"We are not your girls," Maria yelled, then the crowd picked up on it, chanting in unison. *We are not your Earthshine Girls. We are not your Earthshine Girls.*

The women didn't stop. The men raised their hands over their heads to protect themselves, and Tuttle lifted the megaphone one last time. His voice was not unkind, almost marveling: "Leave it to a woman to make a weapon out of soap!"

THE FOLLOWING WEEK, BETSY WAS not at the picket line, and by lunchtime came the news. Her baby had come early. She'd given birth to it in the bathtub of her apartment; the baby never cried.

"They said it looked like a potato with fingers and toes," Maria said, because she'd talked to Betsy's cousin. Betsy bled out in the tub, right there with her baby. By the time her husband found her, she was unconscious.

Laid out on the bed were her Earthshine dress and apron. Inside the pocket the police found a tin of Comet Pills. She died at the hospital a few hours later. She'd lost too much blood.

The picket line came to a stop. Nobody chanted. Nobody held their signs. A newspaper man asked if the strike was over, or if they'd agreed to Tuttle's new terms, and Maria told him the women were on hiatus from the strike, but she didn't elaborate. In front of the factory, the mood was somber. Gilly wept. Pearl's legs grew weak and fell out from under her. Maria did her best to console the other women. Everyone set down their signs and sat on the pavement.

Opal had heard sad thoughts could impact a baby, and, if so, what were its chances of survival now? She'd been drinking milk and taking supplements, but now she felt she couldn't trust her body. She couldn't trust herself. Maybe her baby would also come too early, and, if so, who could she call for help? She thought about the times she'd sat with Betsy in the lunchroom and held her hands and felt her pulse and checked her respiratory rate and the color of her nailbeds and the texture of her hair and the whites of her eyes and the tone of her skin, and, still, she'd missed the most important part.

Maria crouched next to Opal on the pavement. At first, Opal thought Maria was about to embrace her, console her as she'd consoled the others.

"Can you . . ." Maria started to say, but she couldn't finish her sentence. She began to choke up, so she sat back on the heels of her boots. She removed her cap, which left an indent on the skin of her forehead, an invisible crown. There was something saintly about Maria, ethereal, this woman in white. "Can you reach her? Can you commune with her yet, there on the Other Side?"

"Betsy?" Opal asked. The mention of her name now brought Maria to tears.

"I just thought maybe . . ."

As the woman cried, Opal considered maybe Jagr had been right. Maybe she *was* sick. She could have said: *I ran away from my husband. I stole his formulary. He was a doctor who taught me just enough to be useful. Just enough to be dangerous, too.* Jagr used to work and rework a formula, sometimes altering it by only an eighth of a milligram, intent on precision. His formulary was record of that. He believed in science and certainty. But how could anyone be certain a cure was no worse than the disease? Look at her unusual episodes and the drugs Jagr made her take that left her dull and woozy. How could she believe in science at all when she carried this baby from the Other Side, conceived that night by the river. *I don't believe in science,* Madame de Fleur had told her, *I trust my own senses.*

"She would have to want to come through," Opal said. A wave of nausea passed through her. Strong emotions always manifested as physical sensations, which were easier to label, treat. What does sadness look like beneath a microscope? What are the symptoms of regret?

"It's this damn place," Maria said. She pulled at the hem of her skirt like she intended to rip it apart. Anger, if examined closely, is grief in disguise.

"We could take Tuttle's raise and stop this foolishness," Opal said. "That's a victory, isn't it? We'd be making almost as much as the machinists. Betsy would be thrilled."

"You're right. We've gotten something. We haven't lost, not completely—"

At that moment, a group of newsmen began moving toward the factory entrance, toward the door where Betsy had once allowed herself to be chained. The women followed. Opal could taste the powder of cameras as she got close. Then a jolt of surprise when she saw her: Bertie Tuttle pressed her back to the door of the factory. Her ankles were crossed, and her arms were raised. The mood seemed to lighten, and Gilly and Pearl and the others picked up their signs again and began walking circles. Opal tried to make eye contact with Bertie—but she wouldn't look in her direction. She was formal, inscrutable. Two Earthshine Girls made quick work of the chains until Bertie was fastened in place, half-crucified on the door of the factory. Then the Earthshine Girls began cheering. The mood turned jubilant, suddenly. Joyous. Everyone chanted now, except Bertie. Her lips never moved.

DIXIE ELLISON GATHERED PLENTY OF new material for the evening edition of the paper. She lamented how a good society woman like Bertie could become so readily duped, so influenceable, so easily won over to the cause. She then declared Betsy a *victim of the foulest sin,* further proof that *women do not have the appropriate constitution to work out-*

side the home. Dixie did not say—perhaps she didn't know—that Betsy often left her lunch uneaten or fed it to the pigeons that gathered near the benches outside. The other girls assumed it was symptoms of her pregnancy, the morning sickness that everyone knew could occur at any time of day.

Instead, Dixie concluded, *I believe this Earthshine girl's fate, and that of her child, was driven to its most unfortunate conclusion by the Comet Pills found in her possession. The city must eradicate all intoxicants. Nothing is more tragic than the death of a young woman and her unborn child.*

But what about the life of one?

What would Dixie say about how Maria picked up extra shifts to feed her children she left at home alone, under the care of her oldest child who was only eight, or how after her work at the factory she moonlighted as a seamstress to make ends meet? How would Dixie report Gilly's lethargy, how when she arrived home from her shift, she had to make dinner for her husband and tend to him as though she herself hadn't a job? If women really were the weaker of the sexes, why must they do all the tending, all the ceaseless, payless work? It made no sense. What would Dixie's spin be on Victoria's nervousness or Pearl's anxiety or Ruth's weight gain because the only joy she found was in sugar, and one must take her pleasure where she can find it?

And, yet, Opal could not help but worry that Dixie was at least partially right—that what happened to Betsy was an unintended side effect of the Comet Pills she'd taken. Recently, Maria confided in her that she hadn't had her weekly visitor in two months, nothing too unusual given the way she overworked herself.

"Could you be pregnant?" Opal asked.

"Not unless I'm the Virgin Mary," Maria replied.

Gilly, too, recently pulled Opal aside asked her if she had anything for the pain she often felt searing through her middle like she was being branded on the inside by the soap stamping machine.

Opal had written to Madame de Fleur about all this, and when she wrote back, Opal memorized her words. Madame de Fleur's letters usually communicated nothing and everything at once—but this one had been different. It almost pained her to read it.

That scientist, Flammarion, he's retracted his words about the end of the world. He says he was only theorizing one possibility, not predicting an outcome. The probability that the world will end by the comet's gases is small, but still, I worry about endings. They're always disappointing. Life is a moral hazard. Survival often relies on self-delusion. A woman must never apologize for what she wants or for what she must do to protect herself. I've found if you have to ask yourself a question that begins with "Is it possible . . ." the answer is usually yes.

You say I speak in riddles, but now the occasion calls for directness: A spiritualist cannot be held responsible for the messages received from the Other Side. This would be akin to smashing the telephone box for bad news spoken through its lines. You were trying to help those women with your power of mediumship. I believe this, truly. It's clear to me, from your description, however, that your cures have unintended consequences. I am sorry for the sad circumstances of those women's deaths and that you've been put at the center of them. The Witch of Walnut Street! What an unfortunate insult. And, yet, I'll tell you what I suspect you already know: This may be an instance of a cure being worse than the disease.

While you're not responsible for the messages from the Other Side, you are responsible for yourself. A spirit cannot compel one to act; the spiritist behaves according to her own will and desires. I say this with great risk; it may change everything.

We believe what's necessary for our survival. We can convince ourselves of anything. But do not convince yourself you have no power of self-determination. What damage might that do to the field of spiritualism, or to people like us? I want you to come to France, always, but not like this.

—M

That night, she dreamed of Madame de Fleur. In the dream, she'd placed her head on a railroad track as a train could be heard rumbling ever closer. Opal held the woman's head, felt the dampness of her hair. "They're looking for you," Madame de Fleur warned. "They're almost here."

"What should I do? Tell me," Opal pleaded.

Madame de Fleur said nothing. She folded her hands over her heart like she'd been laid in a casket.

"Should I run?" Opal asked in the dream. The train grew closer and closer. The sound of the whistle pierced her ears, then all grew quiet, and she could hear Madame de Fleur's rattly breath.

"Go!" she snapped.

"Go where?" Opal asked.

"Save her."

And then the train was there, on top of them.

FIRST DO NO HARM HAD been an oath Jagr repeated, his reason for being exacting about his formulas. Opal had harmed. She'd made a mistake, not once, not twice. She'd made several mistakes. She mustn't blame anyone but herself. Dixie Ellison now reported more mysterious deaths of women who'd taken Comet Pills. Gossip, perhaps, but she couldn't be sure.

If only Madame de Fluer had told her what to do. Or that voice. *Save her,* it'd said, leaving no further instructions. In moments of weakness, she longed for someone to be the boss of her. There had been some comfort in that with Jagr.

Yet, look at how capable she'd proven herself to be. Look at all she'd accomplished, alone. M had been right: She still had the power of self-determination. And this is how she'd use it: She'd refuse to fill another order of Comet Pills.

At Dowd's, however, she discovered every last tin of Comet Pills had already been pulled from the shelves.

Clara explained the Tuttle's lawyer had payed a visit. He was looking out for the interest of his client, especially after what Dixie Ellison had written. "You know how lawyers can be—nobody wants litigation, and certainly not me," explained Clara. She went quiet for a moment. "He's bought me out of the contract. Took all the stock with him—just loaded it up in his automobile—and, honestly, I'm not sure what they plan to do. Possibly destroy it." She arranged and rearranged some bottles in the cabinet, then made a few pencil markings in her ledger book. "It's only business. Nothing personal. I don't believe that nonsense in the paper. Sometimes nature just takes its course," she said. "But people want to place blame so they feel safer from the whims of their own mortality."

Opal struggled to understand. "What about my commission? From what's already been sold?"

"Didn't you read the terms of the contract?"

Now she felt foolish. She thought of how much it had cost to produce all those pills—money she'd invested with the guarantee of a larger return. The cost of doing business, she supposed, and perhaps she shouldn't wish to benefit at all from the Comet Pills. The money felt tainted now—plus what would Madame de Fleur think of her?

"If Charles Tuttle cared so much about his Earthshine Girls," she started to say, "then why wouldn't he just—"

"That's the odd part," Clara interrupted. "The lawyer wasn't sent by Mr. Tuttle. He was sent by Mrs. Tuttle."

Mrs. Tuttle. Bertie.

Opal didn't feel betrayal, exactly, since they hadn't a relationship to betray. But, still, she had trusted the woman.

And now her own life was reduced to a formula: time over money. She didn't have enough of either. It costs both to create a new self, which is why more women couldn't do it. But medicines weren't her only capital. First and foremost, she was a spiritualist.

Resourceful.

"SHE'S COME THROUGH AGAIN," OPAL told the Colonel when he'd opened his door. She wasn't sure what to expect of him since they'd been intimate. He hadn't called for her again, yet now he invited her in.

The portrait of Hazel above the hearth had been rendered cartoonishly. Her head was small and tilted upward. A ring glinted on her finger. Her lips were parted. The portrait artist had caught her on the verge of speaking.

Like Bertie, Hazel Bloodworth was born into wealth. According to the Colonel, she showed early musical promise and aspired to become a pianist. Her parents sent her to the Conservatory of Paris for proper training. There, she met the Colonel. She married, conceived, then died in childbirth. A woman with talent and ambition is still, first, a woman.

Opal asked the Colonel to play something of hers, and he set the needle to the phonograph. They held hands and listened to Hazel's piano arrangement from a performance in England. Not long ago, capturing such sound would have been impossible to imagine. Once, when a circus came to Gallipolis, the ringmaster brought a small phonograph into the tent and played a recording of a dog barking. The audience thought it'd been a trick, that a dog had been obscured with sheets, or perhaps a cage had been hidden beneath a recessed door. What once seemed impossible was now commonplace. Opal tried to imagine Hazel's fingers on the piano keys, and she tapped her own fingers against the flesh of the Colonel's hand. When the arrangement ended, he reset the needle. The world was changing quickly, but not quickly enough.

The two didn't speak. After the song played for a second time, the Colonel led her to the settee. Perhaps women are a mystery to men because they're hidden beneath so many layers of clothing. He removed her boots. He unbuttoned her dress and untied her slip. He unfastened her pregnancy corset, loosened the stiff plates that held her stomach in place until she felt the release.

Then he studied her stomach with such tenderness, she thought he might cry. He traced its arc with his thumb. He put his ear to her belly button and tapped her side, listening. Then, he guided her to lie down on her side.

Now, she became Hazel. She watched him undress. There was a

coolness to him. The patch of hair on his chest resembled a thumbprint. He stood in profile to hide the scar beneath his eye, and this amused Opal, that he'd hide a simple scar while undressing, as though that old wound was more private than his manhood.

Soon they were face-to-face. The tips of their noses touched, and they laughed. Jagr used to mount her like a farm animal until she'd knock her head against the wall. Oren had . . . what had Oren been like in these intimate moments? The details had faded with time, and all that was left was a nostalgia for something she could hardly remember, except when she'd been with Madame de Fleur. Had she really believed Oren had come through? And what did it matter? It was the woman she'd touched. The woman she still wanted to touch. Now, she touched the Colonel's scar. She pulled him close and had the sense she could not pull him close enough.

"I want—" she said, but then he'd pressed his warm lips upon hers.

After the act, the Colonel traced the curve of her stomach, the pop of her belly button, the way, perhaps, he'd done to Hazel the last time they had been together.

He drew his finger along her shoulder. She twisted her body. It was dusk, when the gray sky held on to the light. He searched her eyes. His skin was warm. She felt momentarily safe here against him, like nothing could go wrong, like nobody could find her.

But they would find her.

She tried to think of what Hazel might say. She considered how she might have told him of her pregnancy the first time: excitement blushing her cheeks, sheepish with the knowledge that part of him had planted itself in her. They'd speak in euphemisms. She might have told him to ready the chimney for the stork, and the Colonel might have tenderly whispered *Hazel Stork* into her ear. But Opal knew that storks were carnivores that ate small mammals like mice and shrews. No baby would be safe with one.

Likely, Hazel had been afraid, for maybe she had known friends, cousins, acquaintances who had died as they pushed a baby into this world, whose lives had been a threshold of a different sort.

"I'm afraid," Opal said. She hadn't used that word before—*afraid*—but she was saying it now, and she couldn't unsay it. It was out there, like a ball she'd kicked into the sky, and now she was waiting for it to fall.

He began to dress, pulling one trouser leg on at a time. Now his back was to her, and she felt silly for saying anything, silly for thinking this man could help. They were playacting. She hadn't convinced him yet. He could not love apart from Hazel—for that would be like asking a fish to swim with no water. The water contains the fish, but gives it freedom, too. That's the irony of the bond.

She thought again about what life might be like in France. About the Spirit Machine, about totality—how, to look at the sun during an eclipse, you had to first obscure it completely.

"We could go somewhere," Opal said. Soon, the baby would make it impossible to travel. "Before the baby comes—before it's too late. Like last time."

The Colonel stood. "What do you know about last time?" he asked. Now all his movements slowed: the tucking of his shirt, the buttoning of his trousers.

"You lost the most precious thing in the world to you," she said. She pulled her dress from the floor and covered her chest, suddenly aware of her nakedness. "We could go to Europe. They have the best doctors there. In France, they understand people like us."

"Like *us*?" the Colonel asked, and she knew she'd pushed too far.

"There's a machine. A Spirit Machine. I know someone who can make a spirit incarnate. It can give you answers. That's what you've been searching for, isn't it? That's what you want."

The Colonel glanced up at the portrait of his wife. He finished tying his boots. He put on his hat. "I'll have my driver take you home," he said, and she knew she had lost him.

NOW SHE MADE HER WAY through the beer caves in the dark, using her fingertips on the rough edges of the wall to guide her.

Inside, she lumbered up the stairs of the factory. Her legs felt heavy with her own weight, and she stood breathless on the foreman's platform overlooking the empty floor. A metal cart by the entry contained trays of perfect yellow rectangles. The door to one of the boilers had been left ajar. Nobody had bothered to sweep beneath the cutting machine, and soap shavings gathered there like dust. From outside came the chanting of protesters, the sounds of sirens in the distance.

To say she always wanted a baby would be untrue. The reality of it startled her: wailing, soiled diapers, a body that clung to hers, wanting for her milk like she was a farm beast.

She'd been doubted so much in her life; she doubted herself. She considered the freedom she'd have without a baby. How could she hope to make it to France, pregnant and alone, when she could barely manage the weight of her own body up the stairs of the factory?

Inside the laboratory, she lit a lamp. The formulary was cracked open, beakers still half full of water, powder in the mixer, tins labeled, empty capsules, cracked.

She lifted the notebook and scanned her finger down the page where she'd written out the formula for her Comet Pills. She'd only wanted to help, to do something more meaningful than washing laundry or wrapping soap. She had only one life, and she was tired of waiting for it to begin. So often she'd almost gotten what she wanted, but only *almost.* She wished she could be someone else. Somewhere else. Not just France, but a different time altogether. A distant future where a woman like her had more choices.

At the bottom of the page she hadn't initialed her name in tiny letters, like Jagr had done. Now she picked up an ink pen, and she signed it roughly, crossing the *t* with such force she nearly ripped the page. Her signature felt like a confession. There, now everyone would know what she'd done.

She flipped the pages of the notebook, and then she found it, the formula that had cured so many women of their shame, like she had been cured of hers all those years ago. She hadn't been given a choice back then, about the baby or her shame. She'd been told what to do, and she did it. Jagr assured her she could never again conceive.

Save her, that voice had said. Instructed. Ordered. She was sick of being told what to do. Wouldn't this baby shrink her world again, its insistence on her milk, its cries to be held? Maybe Jagr had been right: She was unwell, unfit to be a mother. Now she only wanted to save herself, and what was wrong with that? She took off her necklace and tucked it inside the formulary, with the letters from Madame de Fleur she'd kept there. *A woman must never apologize for what she wants or for what she must do to protect herself.*

Until she'd met the woman, she hadn't considered what she wanted. There in the grass by the river, time had condensed, but space had, too. She existed in another dimension where she'd collapsed into herself. Or maybe she'd expanded. If this was the Other Side, how she longed for it. Was she touching herself or the woman or Oren? Whose hands had reached for whose hips, whose mouth had covered whose lips? Her whole body had arched, like she might very well levitate.

But it wasn't just their bodies.

Now her thoughts were foggy. Exhaustion settled in her ankles, which felt fat and swollen. It's a curse of the living to tote around a body. How freeing it would be to live apart from one.

She gathered the bowls and the Bunsen burners. From her apron pocket she withdrew the herbs she'd brought from home, left over from when she'd formulated this very same cure for Amanda Mahooney. She lit a match, but as she set it to the igniter, the match extinguished. She lit another and another and another still, but each flame shrank until it was nothing but a hiss of smoke, as though invisible lips had extinguished it. The baby kicked inside her, and Opal felt a pang not dissimilar to hunger except stronger and deeper. It didn't hurt so much as compel her to move, to stretch her back and take a deep breath. But she couldn't manage to take in much air; her girl was suffocating her.

1986

Soap is a weapon of war as well as a tool of peace . . . Use it wisely and use it well.

—PROCTER & GAMBLE

The Mercantile Library was a private membership library, and the Tuttles were donors, and when I had once told Charlie how the library felt like a place out of time, how I loved the iron and mahogany and slant-topped desks, he bought me a membership I'd never used, not even once, until that day in early February I decided I needed to read firsthand about the fire that claimed those Earthshine women.

Why did I go to that library? I wish I could say it was my quest for truth. I wish I could say I was high-minded enough to have already realized that we all lived in the same world, all of us, and what happens to one of us happens to everyone. I want to say I already believed in sisterhood and feminism and righteous rage. But we can only first see through the lens of our own lives. Ever since I opened Halley's safe-deposit box, my whole life upended, my body wrecked, my career destroyed, my marriage imploded. By this point, things had gotten a little personal.

Bertie Tuttle once gave a keynote lecture at the library, and Charlie brought me as his plus one because he never seemed to date anyone—a *confirmed bachelor,* some said. After her talk we sipped wine and ate finger foods brought to us on trays, things like speared mushrooms and cantaloupe wrapped in translucent meat. A pianist had been hired to play old swing standards, and the room brimmed with people who'd paid $300 a ticket to admire Bertie up close, to tell their friends they'd met her in the flesh, this juggernaut.

Now, I took an elevator up to the eleventh floor. The library was bathed in natural light. A small placard boasted the names of the individuals who'd lectured there: Ralph Waldo Emerson and Herman Melville and William Thackeray. The air was tinged with formality, similar to a church. I thought that's what I felt when I stood in the reading room: the sanctity of the library. Of knowledge. Of institutions. Of history. The lights flickered. I sensed something strange, a presence, someone watching me from a distance.

But the room was empty, save the librarian and a man reading in a wingback chair near one of the windows. I crept up to the librarian's desk, the wood creaking beneath my feet, past the alabaster busts of dead men. I lowered my voice, asking to be directed to the archives for the *Cincinnati Inquisitor.*

The librarian was an older woman with short, dark hair that may have once been ginger. A mole above her lip resembled a tiny button. "How far back?" she asked me.

"Around 1910," I said.

"Ah," the librarian said. "More comet research. I've set those boxes aside. I think every middle school teacher in the city has assigned some sort of Halley-related project. It's fun to consider, isn't it, what life was like back then?"

"No, not the comet," I said. "The Earthshine factory fire."

"Oh?" said the woman. This seemed to please her, something more esoteric. She smiled, then led me across the room, past a statue depicting a woman draped in a Greek-style dress, one finger pressed to her lips. *Silence* was the statue's name, and when I neared her, I felt it again, that presence. She stood in bare feet, her other hand clutching a rolled-up scroll, her gown clinging to her breasts. I stopped in front of her, and the librarian did, too, and we both admired *Silence* for a moment. Her face held both admonishment and secrecy. She seemed to say both *don't speak* and *don't tell* at once, and her name suggested both a command and a state of being. It only occurs to me now that she's every woman I've ever known, cast in white.

"She had a sister, you know," the librarian said.

"The statue?"

"The New York Mercantile Library once owned the pair. *Truth* and *Silence.*"

"Where is she now?" I asked.

"Lost, I believe."

She led me to the opposite side of the room to a table that reminded me of the cold-read table at the studio. Oval. Wood. Ringed by straight-backed chairs. I counted the stack of the labeled banker's boxes, then made note of the ones on the floor.

"No microfiche?" I asked.

The woman shook her head. "We're a small staff, but maybe I can help," she said. "The Earthshine fire *and* the strike?"

I lifted the lid off a box and smelled the must of old paper. The word *strike* reminded me of a match being struck, and in that moment I felt like one, hot. Perhaps I was feverish. In my head, that sound, the one I'd been hearing for weeks, had become more consistent, like tinnitus. The *waa-waaing*. The librarian was talking but I could barely hear her above the noise.

"Sure," I said. "That's fine."

"Start there. You'll want this box," the librarian said, pointing. "There was a great column back then. Dixie About Town. Dixie Ellison—gossip queen, a real curmudgeon. A gossip column, but useful in its own way. Not quite *Tempo of the Times.*" She hesitated. "Don't

I know you from somewhere? You look so familiar." She studied me like a book she wasn't sure where to file on the shelf.

I ran my hands over my head, felt the individual prickles of hair. "I don't know," I said.

"Hmm . . ." she said, as though considering it. And then she left me to the box.

I opened the lid and rooted through the papers. I must have gone through a dozen papers that way, just opening and closing them, reading the front-page headlines, but I saw nothing I didn't already know: Charles Tuttle had intended to sell the Earthshine factory, but the workers had gone on strike, which prevented the sale. They'd demanded higher wages, better working conditions. They claimed the old factory was a dangerous work environment, old equipment, stifling heat. They'd argued they'd been underpaid. I piled the papers haphazardly on the table, until I reached the bottom of that first box.

Nothing.

What was I doing here anyway? What did I think I'd find? If they ever make a movie of my life, they'd cut this scene, because archival research doesn't raise anyone's pulse except an academic's, and I didn't own a single blazer with elbow patches. I thought the newspaper would have facts, a definitive answer to questions I may not have even known to ask.

What happened the night of the fire?

I read through the headlines in one box, then another. When my legs grew stiff, I stood at the window. I could see a small stretch of the river in the distance and people walking on the sidewalks below. Parked across the street sat a black sedan with tinted windows, the same type of luxury car the Tuttles had in their fleet. I knew the interior to be soft and leathery. I had to assume I was being watched.

Sitting down at the table again, I thought of what Roxanne had said, that gossip was the best way to get to the truth of a matter. *Useful in its own way,* the librarian had told me of that gossip column. What had she meant by that?

I heaved another box to the table, one I'd already gone through, then sorted through the stack. This time I turned to the last page of the *Inquisitor,* to Dixie About Town, a two-inch-by-two-inch column bordered with a thick, black line that set it off from the rest of the page.

Halfway through the box, I stumbled upon her name, and I felt relief and excitement, like I'd recognized an old friend in a crowd.

> *Madame Doucet, the Witch of Walnut Street, shall be put to a public test of her supposed ability to commune with the Other Side, this on decree of Mayor Louis Schwab who, at my urging, has vowed to rid our city of intoxicants. Should she fail this test, she may be arrested and incarcerated for a variety of crimes, including knowingly providing drugs to women, which have produced deleterious effects and precipitated several deaths of women across this city. This on the word of several of my sources. Should she not show, I've heard, from various sources, a warrant will be put out for her arrest. Tickets available in advance. May 18. Location and time forthcoming as arrangements are still being made.*

A trial, I considered. If she hadn't died in the fire, perhaps she'd been arrested. She failed the test—or maybe she didn't show. Maybe she'd tried to run away again. I wanted answers. The librarian sat at her desk, typing. The man in the wingback chair had set down his magazine and picked up a book. I could see *Silence* in profile, her finger to her lips. I wondered where her sister was—or how you lose a statue. Then, I studied the words there in print. Mystery ailments. Side effects. How could I not think of those Jane Does in this moment, of those interviews I'd read?

Beneath the article, at last, a photograph.

Opal Doucet's mouth was a perfect O, her angular face looked familiar, a celebrity I couldn't place. She wore a black lace dress with a high neck. Her eyes looked frenzied, despite the poor photographic quality. Something struck me as familiar in the angular shape of Opal's face, the way her eyes smarted, the squared-off chin, the nose that sloped like the bust of a Roman soldier.

Some years ago a bystander took a picture of me dining at an outdoor café where slick black grackles were begging for scraps of food. I tossed my bread crust to one, but the camera caught me midthrow. In the frozen frame, printed in *Tempo of the Times,* my arm is pitched forward. My jaw clenched. The bread crust looked like a weapon of assault, and I resembled Lyssa, goddess of fury. Photographs separate the moment from context, time from space, which is how they can lie.

While a director could use lighting and music and a montage of images to set the tone, I only have words, and sometimes words fail us. Isn't that what art is about? Saying what can't be said, knowing we'll never be able to say it right, though we keep trying anyway? Art is optimism in action. The news won't give us that.

Now my fingertips were inky with newsprint. I considered that the ink was seventy-six years old, about Charlie's age, born the night of the fire. The fire—that's what I was looking for, I reminded myself. The Earthshine fire. Bertie had told that story in *The Juggernaut*: The factory was burning. Everyone was looking toward the sky in anticipation. Some thought it was the end of the world, but for Charlie, it was just the beginning. The chaos caused Bertie's water to break—an early labor. She was dragged away from the fire. Before midnight, Charlie was born.

Someone tapped my shoulder. The librarian stood in front of me, holding a stack of books. Her dress was cinched at the waist, and she wore glasses, and she resembled Katharine Hepburn in *Desk Set,* that movie about a librarian named Bunny who falls in love with the computer guy who's come to automate her job. Critics say Hepburn's Bunny had too strong a personality. Now the librarian in front of me smirked.

"I know where I know you," she said.

"Oh?"

"You died. Poor Stella," she said, but I could tell she wasn't being serious.

"You don't strike me as a fan of the show."

"The billboards are everywhere. The commercials, too. A prime-time wedding in a few days. That's very exciting," she says.

"Brought to you by Earthshine."

"And you on the canister."

"Not me," I said quickly. "I sold my likeness. It was theirs to keep."

"Oh? You're someone new now? Someone who's interested in history?"

I didn't respond, just went back to sorting through the papers in front of me.

"Do you believe them? Those Jane Does?" she asked. "Because . . ." Here she took off her glasses and folded them, and she didn't look a librarian any longer, just a regular woman. "Because, I've wondered about it myself. And everything I've read, all the interviews I've seen . . . I know a lot of women like that, with stories. And I . . . when I've used the soap, I felt—I know this will sound crazy—an overwhelming sense of . . . I don't know. Maybe *ennui* isn't the right word."

"I don't know," I said, harsher than I intended.

"Maybe I just don't like cleaning." She put her glasses back on. "Anyway, I found a few more *Inquisitor*s," she said. "All the comet frenzy. Everyone wants to know about the last time, when they thought the world would end. It was on the Xerox machine," she said. She placed the paper on the table in front of me.

I stood again and stretched my arms. Below, that black sedan still idled, its flashing blinkers keeping time. I knew my answering machine would be full of messages from Gene Longworth. I wondered if Carol had told Charlie I'd called. What would I say to him when he finally reached out to me?

The fire.

I imagined what it'd be like to be burned alive—quicker than being buried alive and more painful. But what difference does it make? We die, anyway, then become organic matter or stardust or rocks.

Stella died of oxygen deprivation.

Cancer claimed my mother.

Halley, she took pills. But despite taking her own life, despite her own suffering, she saved me. She saved others. She gave me purpose. She gave them proof. But I'm ahead of myself.

The fire.

On the front page was a photograph of the burning factory. The fire drew attention to the shapes of the building, square windows, high slanted roof, large rectangular door. It was almost like looking at film negatives. Dark appeared light. The factory glowed. I knew what that article would tell me—the story I'd heard hundreds of times—and it did. I saw the names of the workers who died in the fire, the same women listed on that plaque.

I studied those names, let my eyes slowly drift over each one as though to say to their ghosts: I'll remember you. I sat at that table in the Mercantile Library, and I closed my eyes, and I placed my palms face down and pressed them against the smooth grain. I practiced the breathing technique I'd been taught, up through my toes, out through my head. I tried to imagine Opal Doucet. My lips became a circle. My eyes widened, like in that picture of her.

Then, I heard it again, so clearly this time. That warble of noises, that preverbal cry I'd been hearing. Some people will call me crazy, but crazy doesn't mean I'm not right. I felt something in that room, a haunting.

If this were a movie, the director would cut to my hands as they turned to Dixie About Town and I read the headline: "Earthshine Workers Strike a Match; Several Perish."

Though I've made no uncertain claims about my feelings on the place of women in the workplace, I pray the souls of the Earthshine Girls rest in peace until delivered to their Maker. Before she could be taken into custody for her involvement in starting the fire, Madame Doucet displayed the pre-telling signs of childbirth, and thus she was escorted by Mrs. Charles Tuttle, with the assistance of others, into a police wagon. May God save that child's soul.

My mind trained on Madame Doucet, on her pregnancy. She'd gone into labor, that night of the fire. Bertie was with her. But Bertie had gone into labor that night, too—that's what I'd read in *The Juggernaut.* That's what Bertie told me herself.

What I'm about to tell you is the truth, all of it: As I thought about Opal Doucet, there at that table, my legs weakened. My ankles felt swollen and fat with water. My body was heavy. My forehead felt tight. I thought I felt a kick inside me, then a cramp worse than any I'd ever experienced. I felt like I was in labor, like all the pressures of gravity, the forces that keep us tied to the earth, had come to focus in my core. My entire body seized. The pain terrified me, sitting there in that library. I thought I might be dying.

But I didn't die.

I opened my eyes—mine, Nona's—and the sensation was gone.

Some things are unexplainable, and this was one of them. I can't tell you how I knew, only that I knew. For a moment, I wasn't reading about Opal Doucet or thinking about Opal Doucet. I *was* Opal Doucet.

My therapist once told me it didn't really matter if an experience is real or not real. Real or not real is the wrong question to ask. One can get stuck because there is no answer. We live in multiple realities. Instead ask: Knowing this, how do I proceed? How can I keep moving forward?

I steadied my breath. I was okay, I told myself. I was tired. Overstressed. My eyes darted around the room. The librarian click-clacked on her typewriter. Newspapers spread out before me; I could smell them. The man in the wingback chair was now asleep.

Maybe Halley had been right—maybe the factory was haunted by those women. But Opal Doucet didn't haunt the factory; she haunted me. She'd gone into labor the night of the fire, not Bertie Tuttle. I touched my abdomen, the flatness of it. The emptiness. I'd never have a child of my own—but for a moment too brief to be counted, I felt it, that baby alive inside me, that baby heading for the light.

What happened to the baby?

Outside, dusk was falling. I'd read enough to make the connections. Bertie knew Opal Doucet. She'd been with her the night of the fire. It was Opal Doucet who'd gone into labor that night. It was Opal Doucet who'd given birth.

You don't know Bertie Tuttle.

I admit it—I didn't.

We always do this, don't we? We berate our younger selves for not knowing what we should have known, for not seeing things with the same clarity as our future selves. How could we have been so foolish? If only we'd done something *different.* We look back and regret decisions we didn't make, actions we didn't take, a life that could have been lived. But by the time we realize this, it's too late. A midlife crisis. A midlife chasm. A division of selves.

In that moment, I felt cheated. Used. The anger came easily. The hard part was grief. Mourning the *idea* of something but not the thing itself. Would I have been happier, then, in a life without Bertie Tuttle? Would I have become someone else?

Real or not real?

There are no answers.

Rage thumped at my fingertips. I had the sudden urge to move my body, like I might spontaneously combust if I didn't.

Halley had been right: I didn't know Bertie Tuttle.

But now I blamed her for what happened to me—for what happened to all of us. I was angry and full of grief, yes, but I was something else: I was willing to act.

There's nothing more dangerous than a woman with nothing to lose.

1910

The Tuttle estate smelled of oranges and floor wax. Opal's boots squeaked as she walked. Charles Tuttle had been called away to Pittsburgh for a meeting with Reginald Goodman, who'd come back to the table, according to the *Inquisitor*. Since Betsy's death, the strike had failed to gain momentum. Some girls were urging Maria to accept Tuttle's new terms and end the strike completely. Despite Bertie Tuttle's sensational appearance at the picket line, even the papers were beginning to lose interest in the story.

From the foyer, Opal could see into the drawing room: a conversation settee, a piano, a metal stand that held a potted plant with tendrils long enough to reach the floor. A portrait of a young woman hung on the wall: Tuttle's first wife.

The house girl offered to take Opal's coat, but she refused. The two of them had ridden over together, in the back of Bertie's Franklin, the girl insisting that Bertie needed to speak with her, but she wouldn't say why.

The house girl pointed her up the stairwell. Inside Bertie's bedroom, the shades were drawn. The radiators hummed. The fireplace burned to embers. Atop her bed rested Bertie at a peculiar angle, a rag to her forehead. Even in the dark, she looked pale.

Opal approached the bedside and realized why Bertie lay strangely.

A bedpan was beneath her; her back was twisted in pain. Opal understood now why Bertie had called for her.

"No magic pill for this?" Bertie said. She inhaled deeply and let out a rush of breath. When she moved, Opal could see dark spots on the rags under her.

Opal sat next to her. She didn't know what to say. "I'm sorry" seemed hardly enough. She understood. She thought of when she'd lost her own baby those dozen years ago. The spark inside her extinguished; a living thing was now dead. Some might suspect she grieved after that, but she did not. Inside her grew something else in place of what she had lost. "How long has this gone on?" Opal asked.

"Long enough."

"You should call a doctor," Opal said.

In the dark, Opal studied the shape of Bertie's mouth, the way her whole face looked squeezed. "I was a fool to think . . ." Her voice caught. "I did what I could, didn't I? But that's the trouble. It's never enough."

"It's not your fault," Opal said, but the words fell flat. Charles would eventually sell the factory, and Bertie was right: With no child to tether them together, he'd leave her. She thought of Amanda Mahooney and that ring with a gemstone the color of sea glass.

"I sent my lawyer to Dowd's."

"I know," Opal said.

A wave of pain passed through Bertie, but then she recovered herself. "I was trying to protect you. You've made something special—they'll just try to take it away from you. That's what they do. That's what they always do. Dixie Ellison's a powerful woman, you know. She has connections. But you and I, we could work together. We could build something. A partnership."

Perhaps the woman had been protecting her all along, looking out for her interests. A partner. A *real* partner. "The formula needs reworking," Opal started to explain. "I've miscalculated something.

Bertie continued as though she hadn't heard Opal. "Dowd's could hardly keep it on the shelves. Think of the women you're helping—of the women you've already saved. You don't need Dowd's. We can create our own brand—our own business. I have the resources, but first, I need your help." Her tone changed. She shifted uncomfortably on the bed. On her table was a call bell, but she didn't ring it. "Please. I'm willing to pay. Whatever the cost."

Now Opal leaned closer. She smelled Bertie's perfume, and that undid her, the thought of a woman suffering so much yet still dabbing herself with oil.

Opal understood pain, but she was no magician. No doctor, either.

"I need *something* to give to Charles. Before he sells it—before he can go through—"

Opal knew what she was asking before she finished the sentence. Men have weapons, hands strong enough to squeeze the breath out of another, should they choose. Without weapons or strong hands, a woman must find other means.

"You don't know what you're saying," Opal said.

"I know exactly what I'm saying," Bertie said. "Charles will take everything from me. I'll have nothing."

Imagination is the first step toward freedom. In the laboratory, she had let herself imagine a life without her baby, then a feeling rose up in her chest that she tried to suppress because this was the life she'd chosen for herself when she'd handed Jagr that drink. She couldn't do it—she couldn't swallow the capsule. *Save her,* that voice had said.

But a partnership. They could save each other.

For a time after, Opal would ponder this moment with a series of agonizing questions. What if she'd helped Bertie Tuttle poison her husband? Would it have ended differently? She'd considered her options for a moment. She knew there were simple methods. Cyanide. Morphine. A toxic cocktail drawn from Jagr's formulary.

"Do you know what it's like to want something so badly? To see it so clearly, but to be unable to grasp it?" Bertie asked.

"Yes," Opal whispered. "I do."

"I'll give you anything you want. Beyond my allowance, I don't have access to money, but I do have means. I do have standing and influence. What do you want more than anything?" Bertie began to cry.

Opal froze, stiff through the middle, her arms stiff, too. She was turning into stone, she believed, right there at the edge of Bertie's bed. She couldn't move her hands or her feet. She'd seen paralysis come on suddenly in Jagr's stroke patients, and for a flash of a moment, terror washed over her. Someone might have to carry her away, stiffened like a dead thing after rigor mortis set in.

What possessed Opal in this moment? Madame de Fleur? Another voice? She would think of it again and again. She felt tingling throughout her body, deadened limbs awakening. The body knows things before the brain can register what that might be. A primal instinct. She still had choices. She'd had them all along.

Then: The awkwardness of her fingers. The give of her fabric as she unbuttoned her blouse. The clock struck a new hour and chimed three times, and Opal took this as a sign. Every woman must divide herself into three parts, like those three gifts from the three wise men.

Root.

Flower.

Seed.

Darkness provides for certain allowances. That's why séances take place at night. What happens there, in the dark, remains unprovable. It was afternoon, but the windows were shuttered. Bertie watched as Opal unfastened each button on her blouse. Opal watched Bertie watch her. She felt powerful in this moment, but nervous, too. One button. Two. Three. Bit by bit she came undone. Her shirt went slack. She undid the stays on her maternity corset. She loosened it.

There it was, her secret, for Bertie to see: her belly, low and round, a half-moon of smooth, hard flesh. Bertie didn't appear to know what she was observing aside from exposed skin. Her first reaction was to turn away. Then she looked back, her eyes startled wide. There was something grotesque about it: Opal's round belly, like skin stretched over a smooth boulder. She reached for Bertie's hand and pressed it to her stomach. Her confused expression told Opal she'd done well hiding her form.

Bertie's hand unmoored Opal from some invisible anchor. A touch she hadn't known she'd wanted. Warmth from the contact point spread over her body, until she was set aglow, until her feet and hands buzzed with anticipation and relief. She waited for Bertie to speak.

"Whose?"

"Yours."

That voice had said *Save her*—and she was doing that, wasn't she? The voice hadn't said how. Opal imagined her girl in the bassinet in Bertie's room. She imagined her daughter drinking from bottles held by Bertie's nurse, her girl in white bloomers, a white shirt, a white cap. White everything, for the rich never got dirty and so did not have to dress for the possibility. Wouldn't this be a better life than the one Opal could provide?

This is what she told herself—what she'd continue to tell herself.

"When?"

"Two months."

When it was time to give birth, they'd travel to Bertie's country home in New Richmond, twenty miles outside of the city. Charles would never know the truth. The house girl would help. Domestics can be counted on for such confidential affairs. And then, France.

Soon the details would be sorted out, plans made, agreements uttered, futures imagined. But for now, Bertie slid off the bed and knelt before Opal's belly. She held it like a globe, like the whole wide world fit in her hands. Bertie kissed her bare skin. She kissed it again and again.

1986

Silent . . . speaking hands . . . be sure they
say nice things about you—always.

—IVORY SOAP

A big story lasts seven days in a news cycle before viewers tire of it and producers move along. Seven astronauts had died, a dozen more Jane Does had come forward, and now, a week later, Celeste and Vincent were getting married.

And I was getting unmarried. *Divorced.* Why did the word have to be so ugly? I thought of other words with *-vor* sounds, like carnivore. Maybe my marriage had eaten me alive.

Celeste's wedding dress probably cost $30,000. I thought of Stella, dead. Stella as ash, like Halley. I thought of my wedding to Wyatt, how when I walked down the aisle my world tunneled until it was just the two of us in that room, younger, thinner, our futures spooled out to eternity. His face held wonder and astonishment, like that blind man seeing for the first time.

When had he stopped looking at me like that?

After the ceremony and reception and dancing, we retreated to the hotel room. We drank champagne and ate chocolate-covered cherries room service had left us. *Let me slip into something more comfortable,* I'd said, a line I'd heard in a movie, but Wyatt stopped me: *Wait,* he'd said. *One more look. I want to remember you in this dress. I want to burn it in my brain.* He spun me slowly, and we danced there by the bed.

To be honest, I never really liked weddings. The pageantry. The artifice. It's all acting, but without professional actors. Community theater—and what's worse than that?

I pressed my foot to the gas and sped up toward the gate. The factory came into view over the hump of the hill. I parked my car on the lot farthest from the studio because the main lot had been blocked off by police vehicles trying to keep the crowd at bay.

The show must go on. Not will. *Must.* Both a promise and a threat.

Souvenir vendors had lined their carts along the road, selling yellow visors, and foam fingers, and air horns, and T-shirts airbrushed with photos of Celeste and Vincent. As I walked past, I saw a little girl in a pink dress with a chiffon skirt. "Mommy," she cried. "It's the bride!" I'd committed the ultimate faux pas—I was wearing white to a wedding. I felt the bulge near my ribs.

If anyone had been with me an hour earlier, they'd have seen me step out of my clothing like I was shedding my skin. I stepped into my Earthshine dress, that tattered secondhand wedding costume Halley had bought with me. I slid inside, arm by arm. I twisted my back and managed to zip myself up, then I stood in front of the mirror. Now I was my own bride. If anyone were watching, they would have noted those letters Edith left me were fanned out like a poker hand on my bed. They would have said I looked like a ghost in that antique dress, that I was wearing a necklace that seemed to glow, even in the dimness of my room.

The crowd was a mix of celebrity sighters and protesters, gawkers and journalists. A wiry man had climbed the statue of Bertie and threaded a rope in and out of her bronze arm and was now rappelling down her leg. When he reached the bottom, he doused the rope in lighter fluid, lit a Bic, and set the statue on fire.

I'll admit, an energy seized me as I watched the flame follow the guidance of the gasoline and snake toward the statue. As soon as the fire met the metal, it briefly expanded, disappeared, and was replaced by a long swirl of smoke. I thought of the *Challenger* explosion, and I thought of Christa McAuliffe, and I wondered what she was thinking in the final moments of her life, when she realized she'd never see Earth from space, that she'd, in fact, never see Earth again.

If I allow myself to get into her character, I can access her final thoughts: She was not thinking of immortality. She was not thinking of herself as a hero or the future winner of the Congressional Medal of Honor, or of how breathtakingly beautiful the world appeared, so high up in the sky. If they make a movie of her, I hope they get it right. At moments of crisis, the camera of one's mind narrows. The angles are tight. The shots are close. She was thinking small: detangling her daughter's hair after a bath. Her son's fat hands when he was small. The smell of the mail, of books, of her classroom, of rainy New Hampshire evenings, of her husband when he kissed her goodbye. The sounds of things, too: morning birds and small footsteps from the second floor and pens scratching paper and the radiator when it kicked on in winter and all the details that seem so dull in our regular lives. In the end, I imagine, ordinary details become extraordinary.

"Nona Dixon?" I heard behind me. A woman's voice. I turned. I didn't know her, but I recognized her standing there in her visor, the same braids she wore at the Riverview restaurant. She still had the camcorder strapped against her chest like a purse. I started to backpedal. "No," she said. Her voice wasn't harsh, not like it was when I first met her. "Stay." She held her hands up. She was wearing mittens and a hat. "Aren't you cold?" she asked. She removed her scarf and gave it to me. I wrapped it around my neck.

"I need to get to the front," I said. "I need to get to the studio."

She sized me up, scanned my outfit.

"I thought they wrote you off," she said.

"They did."

"Then what?" She reached for her camera. She took off one of her mittens and put her hand through the strap.

Women have a native clairvoyance. Perhaps it's because of the way we've been trained from an early age to be polite, to observe, to not put words to what we're really thinking.

She didn't ask questions, didn't turn on the camera to film me. "Get her to the front!" She yelled, and moments later, I was hoisted in the air, carried on the shoulders of strangers.

The factory was in front of me, and I tipped my head back. Suspended in the air, I wasn't thinking of drugs in the soap, or my impending divorce, or the way I'd spent most of my life pleasing other people. I wasn't thinking of the Jane Does or Bertie, despite the giant statue of her that gave off smoke because the crowd was still trying to light it on fire. I was thinking of how light my own body felt being carried by those women.

The sky was vast above me, far away and close at once. I reached out my forefinger and thumb to measure the distance between the sun and the moon. Humans are always trying to contain the things they can't. The news had said you'd able to see the comet with your naked eye if conditions were right. But that's the problem with life—the conditions.

I moved shoulder to shoulder, through the heavy crowd, passed from one stranger to the next, until I was set down before the security booth that stood between me and the studio doors. The guard recognized me immediately.

"Well, if it isn't Stella," he said.

"Mr. Security Guard," I said to Mike.

On his hip was a gun, and a walkie-talkie, too, from which I could hear another staticky voice. "You're not on the list," he said, flipping through pages. "At least, I don't think. Didn't you die again?"

"I'm not on the list," I said. "Surprise appearance. Elliot doesn't even know. They wanted Celeste and Vincent to be truly surprised. Something about the Stanislavski Method. Live television, am I right?" I became conscious of my body, the way I held my frame. I grazed his arm. I leaned in close and squeezed my boobs together.

He peeked at my cleavage, then his walkie-talkie buzzed again, just empty static noises, and he turned it down. "Had to call half the police precinct in for backup, just in case."

Someone from the crowd threw something against the building—a glass bottle from the sound of it. A woman's voice rose above the crowd: "Burn it all down!"

He looked past me, and I watched his hand tickle his walkie-talkie.

"All for soap!" I said.

"Next thing you know, they'll be blaming shaving cream," he said, his voice warming. "Or toilet paper!"

"Rubs them the wrong way," I said. "Everyone looking for a cause." I leaned in until I could feel his beard against my cheek. "And those stupid visors," I whispered. "They look like deranged tennis moms."

He laughed. Then, he lifted his walkie-talkie to his lips and said something to the man on the other end. I walked right past him.

"Hey," he called out. I turned. I was prepared for him to stop me, to tackle me, or worse. "Break a leg!"

I hopped one-legged, holding a knee. Then, I opened another set of interior doors, and immediately I could smell it: paint, electricity, hairspray. The set of *Stars and Shadows.*

I was home.

1910

The photo reprinted in the *Inquisitor* was the one Arnold Jenkins had taken in her parlor a month ago. A whole lifetime ago, it seemed. The exposure was all wrong. The high collar of her dress faded into the background, so her body appeared detached from her head completely. Her eyes looked wild, wide, unhinged from their sockets.

Madame de Fleur had told her about scientists who'd studied the mediums of Europe, like Eusapia Palladino and Eva C. The way Madame de Fleur had described it, these women were examined as one might weigh a molting butterfly, not with fear but with wonder at the corporeal transition. Opal remembered the leather straps with nodes and wires she'd seen lying about the Colonel's house. Dixie had called for a public test of Opal's spiritualist abilities, and now she imagined herself lashed to a chair again, an electrified Medusa, wires for snakes.

Tonight, Opal couldn't see a single speck of light in the sky. It was brisk for a spring evening. She wore black to cloak herself in the dark, and she walked twelve city blocks in boots that now felt too small. Only a certain kind of woman travels alone at night. The rest are home, protected in their houses, like delicate eggs that might crack if exposed to darkness.

She paced the entrance of the beer caves until Bertie arrived. There, in the lamplight, Bertie looked different, less herself and yet more so.

Her eyes held the edges of shadow. They didn't speak until they began walking, the movement of their bodies a necessary distraction.

"It's beyond even Charles now," Bertie said.

"Then you'll help me get away? We could go to your country house. Your house girl can help. You said so yourself."

"For two months? Charles would find out."

They made their way through the tunnel and up the stairs through the memorabilia room. It was late, and the strikers had gone home. Through the large windows, the city looked ablaze with light and framed, like a living photograph made just for them. Bertie found a crate of soap, and she unwrapped a bar and held it to her nose.

"The smell—it makes me feel nostalgic."

"For your childhood?"

"I don't know. For the opposite, I suppose. Is there a word for that? Missing what you never had in the first place?"

"I think it's called being a woman," Opal said.

Bertie turned and put her hands to Opal's stomach. Then she withdrew them, and the spot she'd been touching grew cool. Bertie had stuffed her maternity corset with a rubber water bag, and now she adjusted it. From her basket, she produced two pints of milk. The liquid coated Opal's throat, and she couldn't drink more, despite Bertie's urging.

Dixie Ellison had also learned of Bertie's pregnancy. In the papers she referred to Bertie's baby as "The Heir of Suds." She complimented Bertie's tasteful maternity attire. Dixie reported that Bertie's face had grown plumper; she described Bertie's glowing skin, her hair that grew thick and lustrous. Dixie insisted pregnancy makes a woman more beautiful, more vital. *The work of motherhood does the job of a thousand beauty products.*

Outside the windows, Opal observed the city lights; she squinted and imagined they were stars. Bertie helped her climb the stairs to the laboratory. Opal pulled the chain and brightness stung her eyes. Bertie's makeup was heavy. Not a hair was out of place. She wore a maternity gown with a bright blue belt, but the material bunched at the waist.

"No matter what happens, I'll talk to Charles. I'll convince him to talk to the mayor. You're an Earthshine Girl. He's particular about public perception, you know."

Bertie sat at the table, so Opal sat, too. Above them the bare bulb kicked out heat, and between them, on the table, a jar of capsules. Bertie picked it up and examined the contents with curiosity. The woman never said if she did or didn't believe in the Other Side. Opal admired that, how her beliefs didn't affect her ability to understand what she needed or to take it. *A truly self-sustaining woman.*

"Where did you get them—your formulas?"

Opal hesitated a moment, then reached for the formulary she'd hidden in the ceiling, beneath a loose tin tile. The women were intimates now; they knew each other's secrets. Opal took faith in that exchange, how they both wanted something they couldn't have, how they both felt like equals because of it. Opal held the formulary out for Bertie to take, and she took it.

"My husband was a doctor," Opal said.

"And what's this? Oh, that necklace of yours." She pulled the necklace from the crease of the formulary, stuffed with those letters, and dangled it on her finger. "I knew from the start you weren't a simple factory girl." She closed the formulary and pushed it forward on the table. Opal took it, and Bertie watched as she tucked it back into the space behind the ceiling tile.

"Is there no way you can call in your connections? Surely you know someone who can help—" Opal started to say, but Bertie cut her off.

"Think of what you can do within your means. That's always the question I ask of myself—the question every woman must ask herself every day if she wants to survive in this world. What power is yours, even if limited? How can you use it?"

The women sat for a while in silence.

M—, OPAL WROTE LATER THAT night. *I've imagined again and again stepping off that boat in France. Would you be there? Have I understood you correctly? All my life I've been waiting, and when I discovered I was pregnant, the waiting became measurable, finally. A new life would soon arrive. I've never felt so close to death and life at once with this baby inside of me. Maybe every woman dies at some point, and then spends the rest of her life on the Other Side, trying to recover the distance. I know what I want now. Rump roast.*

If this is my last letter, please know how hard I've tried to reach your shore.

1986

Only SweetHeart can relax you, revive you, reward you so well—because only SweetHeart adores you so.

—SWEETHEART SOAP

A clock counted down to showtime. The backdrop of the soundstage was a field with purple lilacs, as if Port Middleton had morphed into a cheap Monet print. Celeste was in full costume and makeup. She was doing a sound check. "One, two, three," she was saying. She spoke with her jaw clenched. Halley used to say she'd be the perfect spokeswoman for Metamucil.

Vincent walked up behind her and touched the small of her back. He was already in character. I could tell by the sound of his voice, too, tinged with old Port Middleton money. "One, two, three," he now joined her.

Across the room, I spotted Charlie, and I was surprised to see him, I don't know why. He was speaking with Elliot, and he wore a tuxedo.

Charlie kept his hands in his pockets. He'd lost weight, and it made him look older, grandfatherly, though he was not a grandfather and never would be now. Finally, he looked in my direction, and I stepped out from behind the curtain where I'd been shrouded.

He crossed the room, weaving among the cameras and reflectors. He had the gait of a military man—even, quick, decisive—though he'd never served. He stopped and studied me, there in that dress. "What the—"

He held up his hands. "An interview, Nona? With the local news station? At least have the dignity to go national."

"You've had me followed," I said. "You tapped my phone. And that hit piece in the *Tempo of the Times*? My life is ruined."

"You're contractually obligated—" He stopped himself. "You've refused to call Gene Longworth, and we need assurances. And what were you doing with those other actresses at that park? Consider the optics."

"What about the optics of the Jane Does? They aren't crazy. I have proof. Halley gave it to me."

"Gene Longworth said—"

"What do *you* say?" The curtain near me started moving, closing. The backstage was being sealed off from the soundstage. The clock behind Charlie read three minutes until lights.

Charlie held up his hands again. "There's a time and place." He shook his head but refused to meet my eyes. "I'll wave Gene off for now. But you have to talk to him. We have new contracts for you to sign. NDAs. Addendums."

"You aren't listening," I said.

"I don't care what Halley gave you. She was *sick*. This is my family's legacy—a hundred and fifty years of history. I won't have this company destroyed. And neither will Bertie."

I scanned the room, but I didn't see Bertie. To me, she'd always be the woman in a pantsuit, her hair clipped back, embracing me as she uttered the words "it's her," words that would set the course of my life and bring me back here, to this same studio, twenty-some years later. My orbit was shorter than the comet's, but predictable all the same.

"Please," he said. "After all we've done for you."

"What about me? What about my life?"

Charlie reached forward and squeezed my wrist. His eyes penetrated my own. For a moment, I saw Halley in them. I saw someone else, too. I thought he might hug me, but then he spoke. His words were sharp. Spittle hit my face. "You ungrateful girl," he said.

At that moment, the producer called for everyone to be silent and take their places. A band began playing the *Stars and Shadows* theme song, but all I could hear was thumping and that sound, calling to me from a distance.

"Roll cameras," Elliot yelled. "Roll sound." The audience hushed. Lights blinked. The soundboard clapped. The actors took their places.

Bianca Dupont and Celeste had forgiven each other, and now Bianca was the maid of honor, gripping a bouquet at the back of the church. The flower girl held a basket of rose petals. A few other actresses adjusted their strapless dresses, hiking up their sagging breasts. The wardrobe director was doing final touches. What most people don't realize is just how crowded a soundstage can be. I could hear Vincent bloviating about how love exists beyond the plane of time and death. The "Bridal Chorus" began to play, and at that moment, I jumped in line.

I loved the exhilaration of the camera, the heat of the lamps. The brightness washes the world with light. It's true that stage lights blind you, but an actress doesn't need sight. She needs imagination. She needs vision. She needs to consider a world that doesn't exist and then will it into existence.

I marched down the aisle with the rest of the bridal party.

At that point, Elliot finally saw me. "What are you doing?" he mouthed from behind the camera. "Get out of the scene." He hitched his thumb.

I shook my head defiantly.

Elliot couldn't do anything—couldn't call security and have me hauled away—unless he wanted to stop a live shot, which he didn't. Primetime, baby.

"You're dead," he mouthed.

I mouth back: "I'm never dead."

1910

At least Colonel Bloodworth had the courtesy to cover the windows. They stood in the librarian's office, eleven stories up. Opal's clothing lay at her feet. Just last month President Taft had spoken here, at the Mercantile Library, to a crowd of six hundred and fifty. She'd seen pictures of him; he was 350 pounds, so big he once got stuck in the White House bathtub. Likely, the president himself occupied this room, but Opal doubted he'd been asked to disrobe before his speech.

She hadn't seen the Colonel since his house, when she'd pushed him too far to help her, and he'd grown cold. Now, because he was also a medical doctor, he'd been tasked with examining Opal to ensure she wasn't hiding any props or special effects, no trumpets to help throw her voice or thread she could use to move objects about the room or waxy ectoplasm that might spill from her mouth or her ears.

The Colonel clutched the lapel of his vest as he circled her. His mannerisms were formal; his face, tight. He smelled of wind and gasoline, of the long drive from Indian Hill to the city. Opal opened her mouth wide. The Colonel peered inside it, then drew his fingers along her gums and teeth. His touch was so different now, cold and clinical. He ran his fingers through her hair and down her neck. He stuck his pinky finger inside her ears, one at a time. She lifted her arms, and he stood face-to-face with her.

She was certain he'd break his silence, soften his touch, admit familiarity with her body. "My darling," she whispered when his ear was close enough.

He cleared his throat.

"It's me—Hazel."

He lifted her breasts, one at a time, and felt beneath each with the back of his hand. He moved some ledger books from the desk, and he motioned for her to sit. She imagined she was President Taft, whose favorite foods were wild game and steak and potatoes. He could eat a pound of meat in a single sitting. She imagined she was Hazel. What foods might she have liked? What foods would she have cooked for her husband as a token of her love? What else might she have given to him except all of her?

Opal spread her legs. The Colonel crouched and lifted her slip. She felt a pulse at her seam. "Hazel Grouse," she whispered. She felt his pooled breath on one knee, then the other. He ran his fingers up and down the insides of her thighs, around to her buttocks, until he was satisfied that she was hiding nothing.

"You may dress," he said.

THE SÉANCE WOULD BEGIN AT eight o'clock. At a quarter till, the large library was already full, buzzing with anticipation. From where she stood, hidden between two shelves of books that smelled like binding glue, Opal tried to count the number of people milling about the room. She counted the velvet-seated chairs arranged in rows. She counted the rows. The counting calmed her nerves. One, two, three. She touched the tip of her tongue to the roof of her mouth as she marked each number to one hundred before she recognized Dixie Ellison. Dixie wore a green peacock hat; her cane was propped on the chair beside her. She hunched forward, scribbling notes. Across the room, near the back, a group of Earthshine Girls huddled together conspiratorially. She saw Maria and Gilly and Pearl. Amanda Mahooney was turned away from the rest of them, watching Charles Tuttle with his wife, Bertie, on his arm.

The elevator dinged again, and another group of patrons arrived, Clara Dowd among them. Tuttle and Bertie greeted her familiarly. The two women hugged and kissed each other's cheeks. They stood next to an alabaster statue of a woman with her index finger pressed to her lips, a replica of a statue a library member had seen in France.

France—how far away it seemed, how impossible.

The windows were covered in black muslin to achieve pitch-darkness. At the front, an oval table. Affixed to one of the chairs was a leather strap attached to wires that led to one of the Colonel's boxes.

The elevator dinged again. Ding. Ding, incessantly, like an unanswered telephone. Like the bell she'd rung in her parlor when the committee first visited her—only she hadn't been the one to ring it.

In the background, piano music played a tune Opal recognized, "By the Light of the Silvery Moon." The lyrics came to her now:

Act two, scene new,
roses blooming all around the place.
Cast, three. You, me,
Preacher with a solemn-looking face.
Choir sings, bell rings,
Preacher: "You are wed forever more."
Act two, all through, every night the same encore.

Opal had always paused at the phrase *same encore*. She'd never heard a more accurate description of her marriage: a show she was stuck performing, day after day.

And yet, here she was, playing a new act altogether.

As darkness fell, the spectators took their seats. Someone extinguished the electrical lights and lit the lamps. The atmosphere softened.

The crowd hushed on its own, sensing the start of the show. Opal's eyes adjusted to the dimness.

She wasn't sure how this would end, only that it would. *I worry about endings,* Madame de Fleur had written.

The table. The stage. How far she had come from Gallipolis. She settled her weight against the bookshelf. She told herself again that it'd be over soon, that she'd done this before. Her ankles swelled inside her boots. She told herself this would be a story to tell to *M.* Just a story.

The mayor rang a bell. "Take your seats, ladies and gentlemen, and please direct your attention to the committee assembled before you." He waited for the final chairs to be occupied, for all eyes to obligingly settle upon him. He took from his breast pocket a piece of paper and unfolded it. He began reading. "We have gathered to witness Madame Doucet as she proves, or disproves, her practice and abilities as a medium capable of communing with the spirit world." The crowd murmured, then hushed. The windows offered a consoling darkness. The room was a tomb. The spirits would soon awaken. "Madame Doucet behaved unlawfully in producing dangerous pharmaceuticals. Comet Pills, so named. Beyond that, we've learned she's prescribed various remedies with neither permit nor licensure. And, yet, the woman claims to commune with the spirit realm."

"A crime!" someone yelled.

"A sin!" yelled another voice.

"To test the veracity of her claims," the mayor continued, gesturing toward that box, "we'll be using scientific monitoring devices specifically designed to capture the frequencies of the astral plane. Leading the experiment will be none other than Colonel Davis Bloodworth, a trained medical doctor known internationally for his cadaverous brains experiments, who has published and lectured widely on the workings of the human mind." The committee members took their seats, except for the Colonel, who remained standing, arranging the wires and nodes. "I'd now like to announce Madame Doucet," the mayor said.

A handful of people in the audience clapped, but most pitched forward in their chairs, waiting to lay eyes on the Witch of Walnut Street.

The only way forward is forward. Opal stepped out of the shadows of the stacks and into the center aisle. The crowd turned toward her, expecting to see a real witch: a pointy hat, a cauldron and broom. She registered their surprise at her appearance, at her simple dress, at the demure way she curtseyed before walking toward the men at the table. The Colonel adjusted and readjusted wires. He opened the headband piece, a strap of leather that buckled like a belt.

The room was stifling. Tuttle and the mayor had already removed their suit jackets and hung them on the backs of their chairs. They loosened their neckties. Opal lifted her skirt and took a few steps forward, slowly, a one-woman procession.

She proceeded to the table at the front of the room, where Colonel Bloodworth occupied himself with manipulating wires, pushing buttons, readying his gauges, adjusting the strap that Opal knew would be fastened to her head. She walked slowly, not wanting to suggest fear or alarm, not wanting to reveal that her heart was a clock wound too tightly. The Colonel motioned her to sit, and so she did.

As she turned to face the crowd, Bertie caught her gaze. She placed her finger to her lips, like that statue near the door. *Silence.*

The Colonel stood behind Opal now, fitting the strap onto her head. He began attaching and tightening the rubber nodes to Opal's forehead, twisting small clamps so that she felt a grip that didn't hurt but made her feel uncomfortably tethered. At that moment, she remembered the eclipse box Oren had set over her head the day they met. She'd tipped forward with the weight of it, and he gently righted her, and they'd grasped hands for a brief, searing moment before he again leveled the box on her head and told her where to look.

"This machine—a Mind Box, I call it," the Colonel said, "can measure the frequencies of the brain. It would be expected that when Madame Doucet embodies the mind of . . . of . . ."—he stuttered—"from the astral plane, the frequency will shift dramatically to reflect such a change." His hands moved quickly, working to adjust the contraption on her head. "Does this feel uncomfortable?" he asked her. "It shouldn't cause any pain."

"I'd rather hear *won't,*" she said. The audience's laughter eased her nerves; she drew energy from it.

The Colonel was momentarily wounded; she could tell by the way he lifted his foot and tapped the toe of his shoe against the floor. He took his seat at the table, the box in front of him. He adjusted a few knobs and took notation of the meter, a leaning needle. "It is ready," he said.

Someone extinguished the remaining electrical lights. Another lit a candle. The committee joined hands. To her right sat Jenkins, whose palm was a dead fish in her own. The Colonel sat to Opal's left. He squeezed her hand three times—a code? A reassurance? Either way, silence fell upon the room like a tangible thing. A candle illuminated her face for all to see.

Opal closed her eyes. The darkness comforted her, released the grip of tension in her head. Were she to make a commotion, throw her voice, perhaps she could create a disturbance enough to make it to the elevator. At that very moment the elevator dinged again, and Opal could hear footsteps and chairs scraping against the floor.

Opal began to hum. She hummed for several minutes, for she was safe here, in this moment before the moment, as her lips buzzed. The leather band squeezed her head; wires fell like hair down her back. Medusa could turn enemies to stone. *You are stone,* Opal thought. *You are stone.*

She sensed the restlessness of the crowd. She tried to listen, like Madame de Fleur had instructed before she'd pulled her so close their hip bones were touching. The thought of the woman settled into her memory, and she warmed, then grew hot, then angry. Why were the things she wanted always out of reach? Her pleasures only fleeting? Why couldn't she seem to hold on to anything? Opal swiveled her neck, as far as the contraption on her head allowed her to move, then she pounded her fist on the table.

Sound carries quickly in a silent room; the thud echoed from the back wall as it bounced. The crowd gasped. Opal heard the shifting of bodies in seats. Though her eyes were still closed, she heard a few people shuffling out of the room, their legs moving quickly, then the ding of the elevator—they'd seen enough. Opal considered the elevator sitting empty on the ground floor. An empty box. How long might it take to call it back? Certainly there must be stairs—but where?

Opal opened her eyes again. The men around the table rolled their sleeves like bankers counting cash, except for the Colonel, who scrutinized his Mind Box, watching the needle.

She channeled Madame de Fleur until her body was Opal's body, her mind Opal's mind. She was two women at once. She remembered how when Oren came through, Madame de Fleur exhaled, a moan, and Opal had wondered if it hurt to hold someone else inside you, even though she already knew the answer.

Her voice turned throaty and low. She slowed her speech. She'd always been consistently measured, not prone to excitability. Now, she allowed anger to settle in her bones: "You mewling, fly-bitten pile of horse manure." The crowd erupted.

"This is a public setting," the mayor said.

"You insufferable minnows. All of you. Cowards. You have no cause, by law. No proof. No legal recourse, and so you resort to public shaming. Go ahead. Arrest her and save her the embarrassment of this spectacle."

More murmuring from the audience. The police officer in the back straightened, but made no attempt to move forward.

"She's interfered with business," said Tuttle, finally. "She's impeded the sale of a company. That's tortious interference."

"This isn't about that, I remind you," said the mayor, impartially. "It's about the medicines. The pills."

For a moment the room grew quiet. Opal heard the rustling of clothing, then the voice of an Earthshine worker from the back.

"We were sick!" Maria yelled, and the other Earthshine Girls echoed in agreement. "She cured us!" They all yelled now.

"Silence!" yelled the mayor, but at that moment, someone hurled a bar of soap toward him. He ducked. As if on cue, the row of Earthshine Girls stood and threw soap in the men's direction, the distinctive lavender smell wafting toward Opal, the soap cakes thudding gently as they landed at her feet.

"Ladies, please," Charles Tuttle now said. He looked toward the Earthshine Girls, toward Amanda Mahooney, and Opal saw it, his quickened breath at the sight of his mistress. His voice softened some. "Let's be reasonable. We don't want anyone to get hurt."

She remembered Bertie's advice: Think of what you can do within your means.

"'Can death be sleep when life is but a dream?'" Opal said. Her voice was not her own. "I've always loved that line. You're familiar with that woman, aren't you? Intimately?" The rest of the Earthshine Girls took their seats, but Amanda remained standing.

"I . . . I . . . No. She works for me. I've never met her personally," Tuttle stammered.

A pause, then Amanda ran toward the elevator, weeping. At that moment, it dinged again, as though it'd been waiting. The sound made the whole of Opal recoil, as though the bell itself had been shoved in her ear. Something told Opal to look, the same way her eyes were drawn to grotesque sights, like to a dead squirrel being picked at by vultures, its innards appearing stretched and rubbery in the beaks of the birds.

The doors slid open.

Jagr emerged.

The air was syrup in her lungs. Jagr held a newspaper. He looked unwell. He stood boulder-like near the door, which isn't to say he was strong or immovable, but that now, once he arrived, he didn't know what to do. Amanda ran past him. The doors of the elevator closed.

Jagr's beard was gone, and in its place a mustache. His suit, which normally hugged his frame, drooped in the legs, so he resembled a boy in his father's clothing. He looked so unfashionable among these city folk, in his barn coat and mud-caked boots that hadn't been scrubbed by her in months.

He set his umbrella in the stand, then lingered next to that statue of that woman, the one with her finger to her lips. What secret was she unwilling to tell?

Jagr took off his hat, revealing thin patches of hair pulled across his head like plow lines. She watched him watch her, but she felt no power in the act. His eyes rolled up and down her body, his wife. The space of time provides clarity, makes one all the more aware of the body's subtle shifts. As she had recognized the changes of his body, so he recognized hers. Still, no one was more familiar with her than that man. She did not need clairvoyance to know he'd made note of her fuller face and her swollen knuckles and her center of gravity that forced her to lean back in the chair.

Opal tried not to move. Perhaps she could become invisible. Evaporate. Travel through the air as tiny unseen particles. The band felt too tight around her head. *You are someone else,* she uttered silently. *You are far away.* And for an instant—a flash of time too small to be recognized—she thought she'd willed herself elsewhere, the same room but a different time. Her body calmed. The room brightened. She heard the clacking of a typewriter. The chairs beside her were empty.

She felt unwell. Her condition—Jagr had convinced her of it.

And now he walked forward, closer to her.

"Sir, have a seat," the mayor said. He stood and threw his arms wide, marking a line with his body.

"She is my wife," Jagr said. "I've come to take her home."

Opal did not remember his voice being so plain. In fact, she didn't remember it at all. The mind can do that, willfully forget. It's what's allowed the human species to survive.

The crowd gasped. Dixie Ellison scribbled in her notebook. Jagr repeated himself, louder this time. "She is my wife!"

Opal could not see the Colonel, but she could sense him. The audience began to murmur. Someone yelled, "She's a widow!" and at that several people screamed.

"I am alive, despite her wishes," he said. He patted his chest as proof. "Stand up, Opal."

Nobody knew what to do. Opal looked toward Bertie, who was studying Jagr with dull eyes like a taxidermized bird, the kind that hung in the Colonel's sitting room. She felt her baby kick. The chair was hard on her bottom, and she had the urge to shift her weight for comfort, but she didn't dare move.

Tuttle spoke next: "What's the meaning of this?" He stood now, too.

"My wife. *Madame,* she calls herself now, I understand from the papers. She's sick. Unwell. She has a condition. I've come to take her home."

"You mean to tell me you are married to Madame Doucet?" Tuttle asked. Jagr corrected his pronunciation. He stood. Was he delighted? Enraged? Opal couldn't read him.

Now Jenkins stood, too. Dixie licked the tip of her pencil and continued writing.

"She ran away. Six months ago," Jagr said. "She tried to poison me. I nearly died."

Opal sat motionless in her chair, tapping her front teeth, concentrating her worry there. Only she could hear the click, click, click of her teeth. She'd read when some women give birth, the midwife places rags in their mouths to bite upon because screaming might startle a baby. A baby startled at birth would be plagued its whole life with a weakened constitution. When her neighbor in Gallipolis gave birth, they'd stuffed her mouth with gauze for just this reason.

From her periphery, Opal watched Bertie rise. The Colonel's gaze was trained on the Mind Box. He took notations, then set down his pencil and adjusted some knobs. He didn't look up, not at Opal, not at Tuttle, who spoke next.

"Arrest her this instant. Police!" he called. "Police!"

Jagr continued forward, down the aisle. He held his hat upside down in his hands now, like it was the offering basket at church. He *was* making an offer: "I won't be pressing charges," he said. "She's sick. She has a condition."

"Is it true?" Jenkins asked.

She tried to stand, but the motion was difficult, not because she was pregnant but because the leather strap encircled her head.

Dixie scribbled. Her pencil sounded like a whip as it scratched the paper. Bertie wiped her brow with her glove. She began stumbling backward toward the door, holding her middle.

"Her condition," Opal heard someone murmur.

"You're married?" Jenkins asked.

She tried to face the Colonel, but the wires impeded her movements. The band was too tight. Her headache was a rock in her skull; if she could unzip her skin, it'd tumble out. She found it hard to concentrate on anything other than the pressure there, and then the pressure migrated lower, to her abdomen.

"To whom?" one of the men asked.

Opal didn't answer. Now her whole body was throbbing, thumping, cramping. What did it matter, to whom? She tried to catch Bertie's attention, but she was heading toward the door. She could feel the heat of the Colonel at her back.

"It's her condition. You see what we're dealing with here." Jagr tried to get closer to Opal, but Jenkins stopped him. "She is lucky I'll allow her to come home at all. Opal," Jagr commanded. "Stand up. Opal."

But she wasn't Opal right then.

I am not Opal. I am not me. Let her be anyone else. Let her be far away. And for a moment again, she felt it—the vacuity, a sense she occupied a different body in a different life.

The Colonel continued to observe readings from the Mind Box, jotting down his findings in a notebook. His eyes darted back and forth. His cheeks were flushed.

"My wife is hysterical, clearly. It must be her pregnancy—the hormones can lead to psychotic stupor," said Jagr. "She has a condition. A nervous condition. Headaches. Blackouts. I've always told her pregnancy would make it worse. I believed her to be sterile. But—" He scratched his beard, calculating an equation in his head.

"Pregnancy?" said Tuttle. More audience members found their way to the exit.

The pressure in her head was now too much for her. Her whole body tightened, and she braced herself. She heard a strange noise in her head, a *waa-waaing*, like the cry of her baby making its way to the light. She still had more than a month, according to her calculations.

"To whom is she married?" the mayor asked. Now the entire committee faced Opal, whose head was bound up with straps and nodes. She couldn't speak for the pain.

The Colonel made a few more notations in his log. He set down his pen and looked up at the men.

"Please," said Jenkins. "Tell us, please."

"To whom are you married?" asked Tuttle.

"Answer immediately," said the mayor.

"A woman who'd lie about this is capable of any sort of lie," said Tuttle.

"Tell us," ordered Jenkins.

The audience waited.

"To me." The voice that spoke came from behind her, from the final committee member who now stood to join his partners. She felt a pair of hands, a warm harness at her shoulders. The Colonel. "And now I have it. Proof. My Mind Box has given it to me." He held up the logbook above his head, like a priest holding a Bible. "She is my wife. And the child is mine."

At that moment, Opal felt it rising up in her—an earthquake that began at her feet. Her whole body began to tremble. She could feel froth at the corners of her mouth. Her body was a foreign object, no longer in her control.

The gasping of the crowd again. Dixie closed her notebook. Chairs toppled to the floor as spectators jumped up. Now Opal was on the floor. Jagr tried to reach her. She could see his boots, caked with mud, drawing near. "My wife," he yelled, but he was blocked by the Earthshine Girls, who'd run to the front. The Colonel peeled the contraption off Opal's head and helped her up.

From his pocket he produced a ring: Hazel's wedding ring. She recognized it from the portrait, the way the artist had drawn it to look like it was catching light. The Colonel now held the ring between two fingers, and he pushed it onto Opal's knuckle. That the ring fit seemed to be of some comfort to the Colonel, who bent over her, weeping. He kissed her neck, her cheek, her eyes once more. His tears were warm and wet against her skin.

"It's me," she whispered.

Outside, Opal's body trembled with exhaustion, with the worry that Jagr was not far behind. He'd produce documents, proof. He'd have the law on his side.

"I will not lose you twice," the Colonel said. "We'll go away."

She imagined her life as Hazel. He'd save her, his wife. They'd leave the next morning, enough time for him to make travel arrangements and get his affairs in order. She touched his arm. He felt solid beneath his coat, immovable. "Did the Mind Box—" Opal said. Her throat was raw. "Give you the truth?"

"Science is incapable of lying," he said.

Yes, she thought, but it can be wrong.

THE NEXT MORNING, SHE GATHERED her trunk and began filling it with her belongings. She folded her clothes; she collected her papers and letters and pens and little trinkets—how easy it is to accumulate effects. From her icebox, she retrieved the coffee tin with her savings.

As she was locking the latch on the trunk, a pain seared through her side, as though the baby were pulling at her ribs. Opal lost her breath and sat on the trunk and covered her eyes and, for the first time since she'd run away from Gallipolis, allowed herself to cry.

She didn't want the neighbors to hear her. She contained her sobs, and it occurred to her that's how she always felt—contained—her whole life: to kitchens and factories and houses and special elixirs and this body of hers, which now doubled her over, thick with discomfort. She wanted to be big, but not in this way. She wanted to be as wide as the world, but here she was in her apartment, dark except for the orange light of the streetlamps that cast long rectangular lines on her wall. The Colonel would be here soon. The baby kicked again.

He told her not to answer to anybody. When he arrived, he'd whistle, as he did now, outside her door. The sidewalks were crowded with evening walkers. The entire city seemed to be outside tonight, sky-gazing, searching for the comet that would swoop into the earth's atmosphere with its toxic tail. May 19. The day the scientists said the world would end.

They walked to the Colonel's car, parked around the corner because the street vendors had set up their food carts. "We'll take a train to Baltimore," he explained. "From there we'll board a boat."

"France?"

"London. I know a doctor there who specializes in—" He stopped talking and looked up toward the sky. Then, Opal saw it, too, smoke from the direction of the Earthshine factory. The plume looked fat and wormlike, gray against the black. She thought of the Earthshine Girls—Maria and Ruth and Gilly and the others. How when the séance had concluded last night, they'd formed a wall of their bodies so Jagr couldn't get to her.

"Take me there," she pleaded. "Something awful's happened. I feel it."

"But, Grouse," he said. He checked his pocket watch. "It could be fireworks."

"Please. Five minutes. It's all I ask. Five minutes and then the rest of my life."

She wondered how far London was from France, and if a boat could take her there quickly. The car moved toward the factory; the fat worm of smoke faded from the sky.

When they arrived, a crowd had gathered outside. The Colonel instructed his driver to get as close as possible, then he opened the door and helped Opal down. From here, they couldn't see any smoke, but they could still smell it, acrid in the air.

"Five minutes," he said. "And be careful."

Opal made her way through the crowd to the entrance of the factory, where a group of Earthshine Girls stood.

The chain on the door had been cut.

She stood on her toes now and spotted the Colonel waiting near his car. He held his hat over his heart; his hair was mussed. She must be quick. "Who did it?" Opal asked.

"Amanda," Maria said. "She's locked it from the inside."

"I saw smoke," Opal said.

"She said it was foolish of us all to fight for some old factory that belonged to his wife. I told her that's not what we're fighting for." Maria gestured toward the building, and if Opal had the powers of clairvoyance, she could see it, what would happen in just a few minutes.

Now the Earthshine workers formed a circle around her. They looked as somber as they did the day Betsy died. A siren blared in the distance. Others must have seen the smoke. Opal strained her neck in the direction of the Colonel's car, but he was no longer there.

Above her, the stars were a thing of beauty, and she searched for the comet beyond the factory, beyond the large chimney that poked at the black fabric of sky. That's when she saw movement in a window, a flash of light, but not the electrical kind.

"Look!" Maria shouted.

"What?" Pearl yelled. "What do you see?"

Just then Opal spotted a hand. In the hand was a yardstick and some rags. The window began to glow.

Smoke soon filled the sky again. Maria knocked out a window with her megaphone, threw her cloak over the ledge, and climbed inside. Within seconds, the door swung open. Gilly and Pearl and a few others raced inside. Opal stumbled forward behind them.

Inside, the smell of smoke and soap. Everywhere. Pungent. Above her, she heard footsteps on the walkway, where the floor manager usually stood. Smoke quickly filled the building, greedy for space. She couldn't see through it. Opal covered her nose and mouth with her shawl. A blur of movement. "Maria! Amanda!" she yelled. She heard Sudsy barking in the distance. She used her hands to guide herself to the stairwell, where she grasped for the railing. Her foot met the first step, and she tried to heave her weight upward, but then a cramp jolted through her body. Her baby. The smoke. She heard footsteps, the quick-ringing sound of boots on metal. "Maria!" Opal yelled again, then more footsteps from above. She remembered Jagr's formulary tucked in the ceiling tile, and now she imagined it darkening around the edges, curling inward to destroy itself.

"Get out!" Opal's middle seized. "Get out!" She heaved one last time. She managed to make her way up one single step, but when she tried to lift herself upward again, the weight of her body pulled her back. She slid off the stair, holding tight to her middle. Smoke caught in her throat. She stumbled backward and clung to a wheeled cart full of uncut soap as she made her way toward the door, coughing. She could barely breathe.

She felt the mild sensation of a balloon popping inside her, then wetness between her legs. A stream of fluid ran down into her shoe.

She'd run out of time.

1986

Isn't it a shame she doesn't know this
lovelier way to avoid offending?

—CASHMERE BOUQUET SOAP

Weddings always leave someone disappointed, don't they? The "Bridal Chorus" played, and I watched Celeste Shadow stride confidently toward Vincent Glass. He licked his lips. Celeste was pretend-trying to contain her emotions. Her eyes were glassy, but she didn't let one tear fall because even stage makeup isn't totally waterproof. A few feet from the altar, she noticed me. She stopped. The bridal march ground to a halt. She gripped my shoulders and squeezed me so tight I felt the bulge of her mic. "Stella, you're alive!" she gasped.

Now the audience applauded. A dramatic pause. Celeste covered her mic. "What the hell are you doing? It's my big scene," she whispered. Then for the audience: "You must be a ghost. A projection of my desires. We had your ashes scattered in Port Middleton forest, and yet here you stand. Don't speak. It's enough that you've come." She turned again to Vincent and reached out her hand. They did what a bride and groom do. He lifted her veil. She stood for a moment to be admired before someone yelled: "Fifteen-second commercial break! Hold places!"

Elliot rushed toward me. "Not so much as a sigh. Do you understand? I've got the writers redoing the script. You're an apparition. A hallucination. A side effect of Celeste's damn medication. I don't know. You just don't speak. Don't say a word."

All my life, distilled into one frame, and I had not a single line.

The lights flashed for a moment, signaling places, and in the dimness I saw her in the audience. She was sitting in her wheelchair, dressed in a loose sequin pantsuit. Her Saint Bernard, Sudsy, sat next to her, his tongue waggling from his mouth. He looked thirsty, poor dog. Bertie's hair was dyed, more orange than amber, pinned back with pearl and diamond clips that glimmered in the reflector beams.

What struck me was how old she looked. Her loose skin mapped an atlas of veins and creases. Her wizened, white hand rested on the dog's neck. Bertie narrowed her eyes on me. She didn't have to say a word for me to know what she was thinking.

She knew I knew. *Something*. Her secret. She'd lied. She'd lied and called it history so nobody would question it.

But, still, I didn't know *everything*—not yet. I hadn't listened to my acting coaches. I hadn't fully accessed my character. I hadn't listened for her pulse, her voice. I hadn't fully allowed her body to rest in my body. Nervously, I played with that necklace.

"And three, two . . ." Elliot yelled. We were live again, and I was safe there in the spotlight. Vincent and Celeste gazed into each other's eyes. Tears streamed down Bianca Dupont's face, and I wondered if she really had feelings for the actor who played Vincent.

"We are gathered here today," said Reverend Peacock, Port Middleton's man of the cloth. He used to be a mercenary. He wore a patch over one eye from an old war wound. In soap operas characters remake themselves all the time. Reverend Peacock continued, ". . . to watch

Celeste and Vincent's public testament of timeless love as they join together as one." Again, the audience applauded. I looked toward the crowd, but I couldn't see anyone, blinded as I was by the stage lights. The reverend continued the speech. "Should anyone present know of any reason why Celeste and Vincent should not be joined in matrimony, speak now or forever hold your peace."

The cast looked around at one another, at me, the woman who'd returned from the dead again and again and again and again. "Don't say a word," Elliot mouthed from off camera. He put an index finger to his lips, like *Silence,* and I thought of her for a moment, standing in that library, like a woman who knows something: secrets.

"'Would you not have me honest?'" I said. It was a line from *As You Like It.* I was Audrey again. I could imagine Halley and Charlie in the front row. Wyatt was in the audience, too. Onstage as Audrey, I hadn't known yet I'd sleep with him that night, that we'd date, that we'd marry, that the arc of my life would land me here, on this soundstage.

"She speaks! The apparition speaks," said Reverend Peacock. "Careful—she could be an instrument of the devil."

"Of course you should be honest," Bianca Dupont said. "We should all be. And that's why I need to tell you, Celeste, I'm still in love with Vincent."

The crowd heaved a collective gasp. A few people cheered, Bianca fans.

"Darling." Celeste turned to Vincent. "Do something. She's a figment of my mind—a side effect of that horrible disease."

"Do I look like me?" I said, a line from that deviated septum commercial.

"You look exactly like you, darling, though a bit frazzled and unkempt," said Vincent. "Perhaps you need a nice soak. A warm bath."

"All systems ready," I said. Now I was Les Nessman's copilot from *WKRP*. I wasn't focused. I wasn't channeling my characters' essences. I was just saying lines. I wasn't Les Nessman's copilot, but I wasn't Nona either. I could feel something deep in my bones, a ripple of anger, a reckoning, something rising up in me. In my ear, that *waa-waaing* began again, but it became sharper, more focused, like a radio had been tuned. I squeezed that necklace to ground myself.

"Good, then let's continue," Reverend Peacock said. As the music started up again, I turned toward the camera, and the beam light followed me. I was hot. I was sweating. An invisible force unstitched a seam along my ribs and a ball of concrete thudded out. I felt light, buoyant. I was no longer anchored by the weight of gravity. I lifted, suspended in air. I could see my whole life from above with startling clarity.

Everyone was looking at me now. Elliot waved his arms to stop me, but I wasn't in control of myself, because I was not myself—no self I'd ever known. I breathed in and out, like I'd been taught to do, in through the feet, up through the head, and the *waa-waaing* died down, or maybe just became clearer, like a dial had been turned again, a frequency tuned. I imagined my mouth a perfect O. I listened for her pulse. I listened for her voice. *I am Opal Doucet. I am Opal Doucet,* I repeated to myself.

I closed my eyes and harnessed my greatest skill as an actress: stillness. *I am Opal Doucet. I am Opal Doucet.* I became her—not just channeling her essence, I tell you—I *was* her. The weight of my stomach. Wetness between my legs. I smelled kerosene, and I watched smoke billowing above me. Screaming. Heat. The sound of bursting glass. *Save her,* people were yelling—not everyone, but the women there, the ones in white.

"What have you done?" I asked. My mouth moved, but it wasn't my voice that spoke.

"Done?" said Celeste. "I'm about to marry Vincent."

I was there and not there—two places at once. The air smelled peculiar. Something acrid tinged with something sweet. Earthshine Soap. Now everyone was looking up, arms raised like they were worshiping the building itself. It was the production crew, but not the production crew. They were not worshiping, they were pointing.

My body buckled. *Pre-telling signs of childbirth,* Dixie Ellison had described. Water between my legs. Confusion and chaos. Burning rubber. Pinpricks of bursting glass on my skin. My body was lifted, pulled back from the fire, and I was safe for a moment. My shoes were wet. Soon, she appeared in front me. Bertie Tuttle.

"What have you done?" I asked again.

I was Nona in this moment, and I was on the soundstage in a wedding dress, but I was Opal Doucet, and I wore widow's black, and the pain seared through me, and I wanted to scream, but, still, I restrained myself as I'd been taught.

A therapist later told me that what happened must have been a fabrication of my mind—the projection of my desires or a way for me to process the trauma of the events. A false memory. Some embellishments become truths after telling and retelling. We can convince ourselves of anything. Wyatt used to like to tell the story of how we met: late summer, that Labor Day cookout. We all jumped into the pool with our clothes on after a few too many gin and tonics. But after repeating the story so many times, he says—no, he really believes—I fell into the pool, and he jumped in to save me. How could I convince him otherwise after so many years? How can I be sure we both jumped in together? My therapist called it confabulation, a sort of memory error. But memory is a way of perceiving, a way of processing, a way of convincing yourself you'd done your best. *You don't need to change your thinking,* she told me. *You need to change your being.* I think she was a Buddhist.

"Why, Bertie?" I asked. I'd disregarded the cardinal rule of television, broken the fourth wall. They call it the fourth wall because it separates fiction from reality, but I think it reminds us that reality can be a fiction to begin with. I was not Les Nessman's copilot or Stella or Audrey or Opal. I was not myself, either. I moved off the stage and toward the audience, but I could feel the camera following my back. I stood in front of her chair, and she blinked at me like I was both familiar and foreign at once, a stranger she used to know. "Why did you do it?" I asked. "You knew what would happen." She smelled like kerosene. I would swear it.

The studio grew quiet. So quiet.

Bertie's eyes flinted. Her body was failing, but her mind was sharp. I gripped the armrests of her chair and leaned forward as I stood above her. In her presence, I almost lost my resolve, wanting to please her above all else, wanting to be a part of her world.

Bertie raised her withered hand and touched my cheek. "I thought you were dead," she said. Tears welled in her eyes.

"I'm not dead," I said.

"Stella!" Celeste was calling, now, trying to save the scene. "Stay away from my grandmother. She's . . . she's . . . contagious."

The band started up again, the *Stars and Shadows* theme song. Bertie's eyelids were thin like paper. Her hands were bony and veiny and shook as she raised one toward me.

Privacy is the opposite of fame. It's what you must be willing to risk for it. That voice returned to me, the one I'd been hearing. The radio dial had been turned in my head. The sound was clearer now, closer. I listened to it, not a horn or a baby's cry, but her voice—Opal Doucet.

My tongue was a slug in my mouth; my throat was dry. I remember how at the conservatory we'd drink olive oil before we went onstage so our voices slipped more easily from our mouths. I got closer to her ear—right up to it—and I spoke again, the name Bertie spent her lifetime trying to forget.

"I am Opal Doucet."

I'm not sure what I expected Bertie to say.

At first, she said nothing.

Actors build tension in a scene not through action, but pauses. Not through words, but silence. Bertie took my hand in her own, and held it there, on her lap. Her skin was warm and soft. Then she pulled me forward, closer, so my ear was to her lips. "It was all I could do. I didn't know," she whispered. "I didn't know." I'd never seen her look so old and so weak.

I remembered the day she emerged from the viewing booth at the studio, and she said to me in her breathy voice: *It's her. It's the Earthshine*

Girl. I stood in that cold studio, in my antique dress and parasol, holding a cardboard canister of Earthshine Soap. *Earthshine Soap,* I'd been asked to say into the camera, again and again. I had a lisp that elocution class eventually resolved, and when I tried to correct myself, hold my tongue behind my teeth like my mother suggested, she said: *No, no, no. In your real voice.*

I had been discovered.

But to be discovered suggests one never existed in the first place. I had a life. I was a girl who played with dolls, who wanted to be a ventriloquist. On Saturdays I helped my mother stir the batter for the cakes she'd sell at church. *More sugar.* All these years later, I stood before Bertie with a different kind of understanding. I was solid. I was liquid. I was gas. I was the tail of a comet, threatening to choke the atmosphere.

I let go of her hand. I owed her nothing.

"It really is you," Bertie said.

"Who?" Bianca asked.

"Her brain has been deprived of oxygen for too long," said Vincent.

Someone's arms wrapped around my middle and began pulling me back. It was Celeste herself, strong from years of Jazzercise.

But Bertie—she had real power. She didn't need a microphone. When she spoke, everyone listened. "My Earthshine Girl," Bertie said.

Then I turned toward the camera. A red light blinked, an angry eye. I was in your living room. I was boxed into your TVs.

I tore at my dress. I stripped to my bra and underwear. Beneath my breasts I'd tucked that formulary. On my body, in paint, I'd written her name: OPAL DOUCET. The red paint had dripped down my leg, like blood, like what those Jane Does described, like a period, like afterbirth, like what whooshed from me now, like the kind of blood nobody wants to acknowledge, and so we keep it discreet, to ourselves, sometimes for years, sometimes against our better judgment. Elliot looked horrified.

I stared into the camera and projected my voice loudly enough to be picked up by the boom mic: "I am not your Earthshine Girl."

The tabloids would later describe what happened next as a meltdown. Melting suggests a gradual shrinking, like a candle that can burn for hours. However, my meltdown did not last for hours. It lasted seven seconds. A burst of rage. Seven seconds of, first, staring just past the camera, followed by a teeth-gritted wail. I was holding that formulary Halley had left me. Halley, who loved me enough to tell me the truth. Halley who, even in death, held up a mirror so I could finally see myself. *Really* see myself. I howled, and I sounded like I was in labor. I felt my vocal cords pop. I screamed, with Opal's voice, which I now recognized in my head, and then I screamed again with my own, because screaming seemed the only useful thing I could do with my body, an action of last resort.

1910

Opal staggered from the burning building, sooty, her dark shawl draped over her face. She was accustomed to over-warmth, to shortness of breath. She reached for the handrail to brace her weight.

"Somebody, help her!" a voice yelled, a woman's voice in front of her, one of the Earthshine workers.

Opal rasped. Her throat felt like she'd swallowed walnut husks.

"Take deep breaths. Keep breathing."

She thought of her laboratory now, engulfed in flames, the vat of powders turned black with smoke and heat. She imagined the combustion, the explosion. She thought of the times she helped Jagr with his work, how he cautioned against breathing in the vapors. Opal had become accustomed to working with a handkerchief tied about her face, her breath held, so her memories of helping Jagr were ones of lightheadedness.

Her skirt was soaked. Her body cramped. The baby was here. *Stay with me, stay with me, stay with me,* Opal silently commanded. *Just a while longer.* If she ever held the ability to commune with the Other Side, let her child hear her words and listen. The police officers were forming a barricade around the scene. She searched for the Colonel in the crowd, but she didn't see him.

Flames now escaped from windows, licking at the brick. The EARTHSHINE SOAP sign toppled. Her legs wobbled like a foal's.

"Madame Doucet, sit. Sit!"

Opal gasped and held her stomach. The smoke had stolen her air. Her eyes stung with needling dryness. Kneeling in front of her now was Ruth. In a horseshoe behind her stood other Earthshine workers. Their outlines glowed from the fire. Their white uniforms were sooty from ash.

Then, the sound of bursting glass. Fragments of crystal rained to the ground. Opal felt her body being lifted again, moved back, away from the building and the heat, which was making her feel fevered. A tightness seized her belly. Where was Amanda? Maria? Gilly? The others? Opal allowed the women to help her to her feet again. She wished she were like the great Houdini who could escape even a sunken milk can. She'd seen advertisements: *Failure means drowning to death.*

She had to hurry.

She searched again for the Colonel, for his hat with a small blue feather she assumed was from a grouse. *I will not lose you twice,* he'd told her. Now he was the one who was lost.

Opal tried to stand, but Ruth wouldn't let her. "You must sit," she was saying.

She tried to see past the row of Earthshine Girls gathering around her, but more immediate concerns drew her attention to her body, to the pain now searing through her, threatening to cleave her in two.

A newspaper man stood too close to the building, taking photographs. A burst of glass drew him back. The world was no longer silent. The sound boomed in layers: the crackling of fire, the chants of the crowd, the wailing of sirens drawing nearer.

Another explosion. Then soon an automobile, then two, then three. A fire engine. The flash of a camera. Maria hung from the window, screaming.

"Save her!" someone yelled.

Opal knew she couldn't save her—or the others—and she couldn't run. She doubled over. A pain seared through her middle and would not release, not until the baby came.

"Save her!" someone yelled again.

The papers had predicted that today would find the citizens gazing skyward. Finally, the yellow press had been right about something. But the comet that blazes by every seventy-some years would be overlooked by the spectacle of the moment, by the earthbound fire that was licking at the sky.

"*Save her!*" the crowd chanted then, not a protest but a plea.

Soon, the crowd formed a wall around her, and from somewhere behind them Bertie Tuttle emerged, her skin glistening with sweat. She held Sudsy on a rope.

"Bertie," Opal whispered. From the factory came a loud boom, then frenzied screams from the onlookers, who were moving backward, away from the building.

Bertie didn't flinch. When she spoke, her voice was breathy, like she was speaking to a man she was trying to seduce. "We can go away. Tonight."

The wind had shifted and pushed the smoke sideways, away from them. Opal crouched forward in pain, then reached for Bertie's arm to brace herself.

Bertie dug into her handbag until she found what she was looking for: Jagr's formulary. She held up the gray notebook for Opal to see, then shoved it back inside her bag. "For you."

Her fingertips were blackened from the matches. She smelled of kerosene. Her eyes held in them a terrifying dullness, like a specimen that'd been pinned to a mounting box. Bertie didn't have to use words to admit it. Opal knew she was the one who set the factory on fire.

"Why, Bertie?" Opal asked.

"It was all I could do," Bertie whispered. "He'd have taken it from me. I didn't know. I didn't know they were inside."

Opal's eyes stung. Everywhere hung smoke like souls that refused to rise. Opal had heard that during yellow fever outbreaks, so many people died that some cities had to bury their dead beneath the streets. Carriages and horses and automobiles ran above them now, unaware of the piles of bones beneath them.

Bertie put on her gloves. She adjusted her barrettes. She looked exactly as she had atop those factory stairs when Opal first laid eyes on her. A mix of loneliness and desire, a woman trapped in the space between.

Time belongs to the dead. For the living, it's an illusion. In Opal's mind, an entire lifetime unfurled. Oren. Madame de Fleur. The Colonel. His warm skin. The scar beneath his eye that would soften as he aged. How when she embodied Hazel he reflected back to her the new person she could be, a new possibility. No choice is final, except death. She'd go with the Colonel to England, then she'd find her way to France. To Madame de Fleur. Eventually, she'd see the woman again.

Another explosion. The heat. The women were pulled back by a group of Earthshine Girls, toward safety. A car pulled up on the street in front of them. The flashes of a camera. The smell of kerosene and rubber and smoke. Tuttle stood before her. Jagr now, too. They'd arrived together, the two men, as though they'd been acquainted all their lives.

At the sight of Jagr, the world went hazy, like Opal was witnessing it from across a vast distance, the vantage point of the Other Side. How small she'd have to fold herself to fit back into that life. How impossible. She doubled over in pain so intense she felt dead already. She searched for the Colonel in the crowd.

She couldn't see past Bertie, who looked at Opal as though to say, *Trust me.*

"It was one of the Earthshine Girls," Bertie said. "I saw her. I tried to stop it, Charles. And, she . . . She helped them. She told them to do it. It was awful. All of it. And in my condition."

Opal wiped ash from her eyes, surprised to find Bertie pointing in her direction.

Tuttle stepped forward and embraced his wife.

"Oh, Charles. All that you've worked for." Her voice contained tears even if her eyes did not.

"Let's get you away from here," he said. He pulled his wife farther back from the flames, then he turned and watched the factory burn.

The pain intensified. Opal listened to sounds of crackling as though she herself were on fire. Her whole body burned in pain. Jagr grabbed hold of her arm. She managed only a grunt of resistance. "We need to get her to a bed," he said.

"She'll face charges," Tuttle said.

"Even so," Jagr said. He eased his grip. "She's in labor. She's sick."

A loud boom forced Tuttle to look toward the factory, toward Maria and Amanda and the other girls now standing at the windows, begging for help. The smoke puffed and curled in the light, like the elaborate hand-painted wallpaper pattern Opal had seen in Bertie's house. There was nothing to be done.

"Those poor girls," Tuttle said. "My God. They'll burn alive."

He stared up toward the window, toward Amanda Mahooney, who waved her cap. The cap looked like a frantic moth, but then the wind shifted, and the smoke grew thick, and the facade of the building was entirely covered in black. They couldn't see the Earthshine Girls after that, but they could still hear their cries.

Opal hadn't thought Tuttle to be the kind of man capable of crying, but he did now, quiet sobs. He squeezed his temples; he fell to his knees.

"Those poor girls," Bertie said to her husband, now kneeling to comfort him. "You'll rebuild." She drew her arms around him and pulled his head to her lap. Now she was crying, too. Sudsy sat down beside them.

The roar of the fire magnified, then Opal's world grew quiet. She couldn't hear the fire or the sirens or the burst glass. Her attention turned inward, toward the pain. Pain has a sound. It sounds like the desperate whooshing of water, like the opening and closing of the rusted hinge of her mail slot, like the mechanical whirring of the soap plodder—all the sounds of the world at once on a pinpoint. She couldn't contain the baby much longer.

A police wagon pulled up. Now the policemen formed a circle around them.

Tuttle extended his arm. "Her," he said. A single sound, no more than a huff of air. "The others are . . ." A policeman moved toward Opal. Now her arms were cuffed, her wrists touching. She could hardly balance.

The details came to her later, not in pictures but in sounds: her heels rough against the pavement. The heavy breath of Jagr who carried her body. Then Bertie's voice above the crowd: *I'll go with her. To help with the baby, Charles. I must. The poor child shouldn't suffer.* As they lifted Opal into wagon, the world went sideways. Finally, she caught a glimpse of the Colonel. He was holding his hat with that small blue feather to his chest, as though he were taking an oath of some sort. The Colonel was a man of science, not poetry, which limited his depth of expression, but not his feeling. He was accustomed to disappointing experiments and results.

They placed her on the blankets in the back of the wooden wagon. Through the smoke and the dark she tried to see Halley's Comet. Opal knew it was up there somewhere, a beautiful ball of gas and dust, an ancient, illuminated rock hurtling across the sky, cold and dirty, but looked to be set aflame. She listened for that voice, but she heard nothing save the sound of her own labored breathing, of her body's own drumming. Her ears filled with noise, and she opened her mouth, but she couldn't speak. Not a word.

IN THE BACK OF THE wagon, it was just the three of them. Soon four.

Jagr instructed her to push. Her spine was a fault line. Her entire body quaked.

Later, somewhere else, Clara Dowd brought medicines.

And then the greatest surprise of all: Her baby was a boy.

A boy.

Who, then, was she to save?

She couldn't think of it now, because the baby rooted for her breasts. Opal named him Halley, after the comet, after Edmond Halley, who hadn't lived to see the truth of his prediction, that this object in the sky would return again and again and again. Opal held the baby and kissed the tufts of hair that felt like willow wisps. She pressed his cheek to her own, and she'd never felt anything softer in her life.

Her body responded to his presence. Her nipples stung with the urge to be useful. He was wrapped in a blanket. He brooded in his sleep. The baby was so warm against her skin. All she could feel in this moment was love, as potent as any drug she'd ever taken. She wished she could bottle it. He clawed her breasts because he wanted something that only she had. He wanted Opal. He wanted her very existence.

Years later, moments before her death, this is the memory she chose to hold in her mind: the baby. He looked like Madame de Fleur. Wide brow. Eyes dark and deep. In this way, she saw the woman again. She'd held her to her chest. She felt the relief of her presence as she stepped off the ledge of the hospital's turret and jumped. For an instant, she believed she was flying. Free.

In the other room, voices. Bertie's.

A child needs a mother.

I'll pay you. Name your price.

More drugs to take. Darkness again, and in the morning Opal awoke, bumping along in the back of Bertie's Franklin next to Jagr. Her shirt was wet. She'd bled through her skirt. She looked out the windows, up ahead. She recognized the sandstone towers in the distance, the turrets rising up like an ancient castle. That hospital where her husband worked, where Oren once lived.

The vehicle came to a stop near the doors. Two nurses stood at the ready. Jagr wiped his hands on a handkerchief. Opal heard something, a sound that saturated the world, a noise so loud it forced her to draw her fingers to plug her ears. She finally recognized that voice, *the* voice. The same voice she'd heard in the river. Not someone else's voice, but her own.

She was screaming.

1986

Because innocence is sexier than you think.

—LOVE'S BABY SOFT FOAMING WASH

I could feel the strain at the back of my throat. I screamed again, then took a few steps backward, until I bumped into the camera dolly.

I turned. I studied myself on the camera's viewfinder. I blinked. I watched the others in the room blink back at me: Bertie and Charlie and the security guards and the strangers. All eyes were on me.

Actresses are drawn to the spotlight because it completes us in some way, electrifies our blood, springs us to life. My body is my art, true, but so is my mind. So are my experiences. So are my memories. So is my life and the choices I have made. The light gives us compound vision, the ability to see all this at once. I was Nona Dixon and Opal Doucet and every role I had ever played. I was a squadron of women. The camera's spotlight followed me as I scooted away from the crowd, back to the soundstage, to the altar made of fake shrubbery. I couldn't see past the light, but I didn't need to.

The studio was dark now. Commercial break. I felt metal on my wrists, the twisting of my limbs behind my back. I could hear the scraping of my shoes as they raked across the floor. I tried to wrangle away, to jerk myself free, but there were two officers, one of me.

As they dragged me out, Bertie looked at me like she was witnessing something familiar, like I was a vision haunting her, but then her attendant wheeled her away, and she was barricaded by the crowd. I could hear the band playing "Endless Love" through the studio doors as they loaded me into the police cruiser. I could hear Vincent say, "Darling, let's not let this ruin our special day." I could hear Celeste: "Love, I'm tired of waiting."

I watched the sky through the window as they drove me away. All I could see was a cover of clouds, the police cruiser's bouncing light. I knew the comet was up there, made of ice and dust and cosmic dirt, and I imagined Halley sitting atop it, riding it, laughing, her head tipped back, her mouth wide, like she was about to swallow the entire universe.

THE HAMILTON COUNTY COURTHOUSE RESEMBLED something of a church and a museum. Maroon-speckled carpet. Brass railings. Long rows of wooden pews faced the judge's bench, behind which was a large oil painting depicting soldiers atop horses, revolutionaries of some sort, though I wasn't sure of which war.

Mr. Longworth sat at the table opposite me, talking about violation of gag orders, libel, attempted assault, tortious interference. "Considering the gravity of these charges," he was arguing, "and the defendant's mental state . . ." He was flanked by another set of lawyers, men holding brown accordion folders. So much of the law profession is pageantry and paperwork, one person speaking louder than the other. "The damage to the Earthshine brand is incalculable."

Mr. Longworth kept talking, and the judge looked bored; his cheek sagged against his fist. At some point, I looked behind me. The courtroom was packed. The rows of benches were full and bodies pressed against the walls, three people deep. I saw Edith standing by the door.

I saw the librarian seated near the aisle. The rest, I didn't recognize: women in yellow visors, or not. Some were old or young or held babies or held hands with one another. Some were tall or short or wearing T-shirts or business attire or ripped jeans or dresses or coats still buttoned up because they weren't sure if they should stay, if they should be there in the first place. Jane Does, each one.

"How do you plead?" the judge asked. My lawyer nudged my arm. She was young, eager, ambitious, working pro bono because she'd gone to high school with one of the original Jane Does. I bent the mic toward my lips.

I'd said the same words before on camera when I played a bit part on the local cops-and-robbers show. And now I said them again, this time playing me: "Not guilty, Your Honor."

The judge looked typecast: white hair. Thin lips. Sharp features. Wire-rimmed glasses that slipped down his nose as he read the files in front of him. "The defendant has violated the terms of her contract—and I agree that immeasurable damage has been done to the brand in question . . ." He looked up at me over the rims of his glasses. "However, the defendant had been summoned by federal court to testify in a deposition. And that, coupled with the media exposure to these unusual allegations that predates the defendant's accusations, could be construed as participation in a public forum, the right to which cannot be denied to any free man." He removed his glasses. "Or woman." He continued: "While I'm not absolving the defendant of her actions, which are serious in nature, I'll remand this case to federal jurisdiction where I believe it belongs."

The judge released me until the next hearing, and the courtroom emptied, and after a meeting with my lawyer and some paperwork to sign, I made my way outside, to the courthouse steps, where I knew a crowd would be waiting.

I paused before I opened the door to the steps of the courthouse, because I could already hear it: "Nona Dixon! Nona Dixon!" the chant of my name from the crowd. My *real* name—not Stella or the

Earthshine Girl or some role I played. I opened the door and immediately a circle began to form around me, so I was forced to take a step back, the heel of my shoe catching the edge of concrete. Someone grabbed my wrist to keep me from falling.

It was Wyatt.

He'd shaved his beard. I recognized his chin, the little divot I hadn't seen in years, the one I used to press, claiming it held my fingerprint. The daylight disoriented me after being inside so long. I had to blink to bring him into focus. His hands reached out to catch me, and I recognized them, too, the way they felt when they clasped my own, as they did those years ago before we jumped into that pool with our clothes on. Before he pulled me to the surface. I would remember these details later, when I'd tell the story—not to a camera or legal counsel, but privately, to him. I'd tell him the story again and again, understanding it a little more with each telling, how I'd lost myself but then found myself again. And this is who I was now. This is who I am.

I planted myself into the cave of Wyatt, who in the end, like the comet itself, had returned.

This is how I tell it.

That day we were swept up in the crowd as it moved toward the Earthshine factory. Police had blocked off all the entrances, so we took to the paths among the trees. As we neared, I could hear the crowd. My body brushed against Wyatt's, and I felt something between us still. History. Stories. Muscle memory, perhaps, but memory all the same. Our brains are trained to want the familiar, but this crowd was like nothing I'd ever seen.

Were there ten thousand people there? Fifty thousand? A million? The news outlets reported *two thousand*, but I can tell you, it felt like the whole world was there in front of the Earthshine Factory. It felt like the whole world was chanting now.

We are not your Earthshine Girls. We are not your Earthshine Girls.

A gangly man clambered to the top of Bertie's statue again and roped her thick, bronze body. He stood on her shoulders, working the rope, like a cowboy tying up a hog. Then he threw two long ends of the rope down to the people below. From where I stood with Wyatt, I could see the strain of the rope, pulled taut like a V. I thought of the first time I'd seen that statue, as a young girl. I hadn't met Bertie yet, but I imagined her to be a giant of some sort, and in a way I suppose she was.

I remembered this moment, just the other day, when the Earthshine trial *finally* began, more than ten years after the first Jane Does came forward. Now, of course, we know all their names. Now we know how lawyers from the class-action lawsuit hired chemists to reverse engineer the soap, and how they linked it to those Comet Pills in the formulary I'd turned over to the authorities. In her sworn affidavit, Bertie claimed she hadn't known the effect of the chemicals in the soap. She believed Earthshine helped women. Her whole life had been a testament to women's rights. She had always done what she could within her means. She'd always used her powers for good. She'd cited passages from *The Juggernaut*. The company could not be reached for further comment.

I watched the opening arguments from our living room. Wyatt was with me, and I asked him if he remembered right before the statue fell, before the protesters scattered and the police arrived to make arrests, and we held hands and ran as fast as we could back to his car. How after the protesters dislodged two of the statue's anchors, and the casting of Bertie began to tilt, Bertie hovered above the earth, her arms outstretched, a giant bird frozen midflight, and her shadow cast a momentary darkness over the crowd. Then, we heard the deafening boom.

"I don't remember it making a sound," Wyatt said.

Was I happy to see that statue fall?

No. I was not.

Dozens of police cars and ambulances arrived, parked at an angle, like a closing scene from *Miami Vice*. Nobody in Cincinnati saw the comet in 1986. It was too cloudy. Nothing but low-hanging clouds—a typical Midwestern winter day. I'll be dead when the comet comes again. I missed my only chance to see it.

What will the world look like in 2061? I wonder.

A few years ago, Charlie hired a private investigator to do some research. He used his connections and money to exhume the body of Opal Doucet and to obtain a DNA test. He'd found out the truth about his biological mother—but his other parent remained a mystery. After all that he called me up to apologize. It was the first time we'd spoken since my arrest and my legal troubles that followed me for years, until finally I'd won a settlement.

"They say her brain was damaged by the effects of narcotics. That's why she took her own life."

"Do you believe that?"

"It was all there in her hospital records. But—" he paused. "I know the feeling of being pinned in, like all your choices have already been made for you." I'd handed those old letters from Madame de Fleur over to the authorities, too, and I could only assume Charlie had read them.

"You seem to have everything you want," I said.

Charlie laughed, but it was a sad one. "Not everything. Maybe that's where Halley got it; maybe longing, like addiction, in our genes."

"She was more than her genes." My words did not come out as anger, just a statement, a reminder not to reduce her to a single fact. "Look at what she did—how she helped people—despite her pain, despite the fact nobody believed her. That wasn't an easy thing to do."

"The world wants what is easy," Charlie said.

And then I knew he had read those letters.

Charlie had long since stepped down as chairman of the board. Under new leadership, they pulled Earthshine Soap from the market, citing low sales. But everyone knew this was a preemptive move as the company readied for the trial. They'd refused to settle.

"I miss her," he said.

"Me, too," I said, and we sat on the phone a long while after that.

Bertie died at 103. Her death was announced on the front page of the *Inquisitor*. Her family held a private burial. I was not invited. I still wonder if her choices were misdeeds or mistakes—or what the paper had called *the consequences of her ambition*.

I guess the trial will try to answer that.

Or maybe there are no easy answers.

"What do you want for dinner?" I asked Wyatt. That old dance. Well, you have to eat!

"Pizza," he said. He always suggests pizza—says he can't cook. *Selective incompetence,* I tell him. We used paper plates and drank beer right out of the can. When we finished, he pitched everything in the garbage, and I dug out the recycling and tried not to get annoyed. He unmuted the television. "Don't you want to watch the trial?" he asked.

"I'll watch the highlights later," I said. I've grown my hair long again. I've let it go gray, and people love to tell me how brave this is, as if aging is an act of courage and not a fact of biology.

We bought a new house, with new memories, with a deck that overlooks the Ohio River. We sit out there in the mornings with our coffee, listening for birds. In the evenings, barges float by carrying coal. We cut a path down to the water. I can't quite explain my pull toward the river except to say it's supernatural.

It's summer now, and I roll up my pants, and I wade out until the brown water is up to my calves. I stop when a branch floats past, a remnant of yesterday's storm. When I was younger, I used to tell my agent, find me a role that matters, one that involves war or espionage or politics, not domestic trifles. A big role.

My life is simple now. I play a small role. I've taken up baking. I find calm in a well-organized house. I've become my mother's daughter, but that's a statement of scale, not worth.

I haven't acted in years. Not for the camera or stage, anyway. Instead, I teach acting classes from time to time. I tell my students: *You must understand your own essence before you can assume another's with any authority*. I tell them: *The core of every character is your own compassion.* I tell them: *Never lose yourself to any part.*

And, yet, I can't help but think a piece of me is still missing, that there's more to life than this, that I've got some bigger role to play. Maybe everyone thinks that.

I dare myself farther into the river. The hems of my pants turn dark with water. When I'm deep enough, I tip myself back. I can see a yellow bridge from here and roads snaking through lush green hills above. I can see Wyatt looking down at me from the deck wondering what I'm doing. He's calling my name, but I ignore it. I pretend I don't hear.

Water fills my ears. I hear a whirling and a whooshing, the sounds of submerged quiet. I move with the current, and for a moment my whole body lifts, and I feel weightless, free.

Then, I remember Halley and the time we crossed this frozen river on foot. We'd walked on water, and Wyatt got mad, saying, *You could've died.*

We could have died, but we didn't. We arrived safely to the other side.

ACKNOWLEDGMENTS

During the years it took to write this book, I'd often dream of arriving here, to this very page where I can finally, rhapsodically, thank those who supported me along the way.

First, boundless gratitude to my brilliant editor, Caroline Bleeke, for your wise, patient guidance. Thank you equally for helping me envision the story and for trusting me to find my way. I'm immensely grateful to my whole dream team at Flatiron Books, including Mary Retta and Cat Kenney; to Michelle Brower, agent extraordinaire, who believed in me from the start; to Amelia Possanza for a round two; and to Danya Kukafka and other early readers of this book.

The Sewanee Writers' Conference provided support and the gift of community. Special thanks to friends and teachers I met there: Leah Stewart, Chris Bachelder, Katie Kitamura, Michelle Hart, Erika Wurth, Stephanie Glazier, and Alyssa Konermann (and Charlie!). And to Brenda Peynado for your rallying Zooms and your encouragement.

The support of the Sustainable Arts Foundation, and Caroline and Tony Grant, meant so much to me, psychically and literally. Thank you for acknowledging that parenting as an artist is both a challenge and a reward, but always important.

The Mercantile Library in Cincinnati, Ohio, is a mystical, magical place for me. Thank you to Amy Hunter for your serendipitous fact-finding and for your mutual fangirling over *Silencia*.

Thank you to my Hillside Writing community, especially to the ever-sage Allan Reeder and Cara Feinberg for teaching me to take care of the writing by taking care of the writer. I did just that. And to Kate Leary, whose song "Easy to Be Good" inspired me during my revision process.

My Savannah friends sustained me from the earliest days of motherhood and through a pandemic, when writing seemed impossible and also the only way to make sense of the world. Thank you, especially, to Katie Griffith, Sarah Jackson, and Suzette Pioske. Y'all have my heart.

To others who supported me as friends, mentors, listeners, advice givers, readers, blurbers, cheerleaders, joke-tellers, and/or stellar human beings: Jill Christman (whose accountability check-ins kept this novel alive), Katy Didden, Meaghan Gerard, Jen Burns, Susan Steinkamp, Kathy Bradley, Kate Bishop, Liz Tilton, Nicola Mason, Brock Clarke, Clare Beams, Erika Swyler, Kathleen Rooney—and to Christie Pfalzgraf for helping me tell my own story which, in turn, helped me tell this one.

To my students and colleagues at the University of North Carolina Wilmington, a place that makes me believe a little bit in destiny—and a big bit in finding one's place. Special thanks to Emily Smith and Kimi Faxon Hemingway for commiserating with me in the teaching and motherhood trenches, and to Nina de Gramont, David Gessner, Jason Mott, and Leigh Kresge. Extra special thanks to Michael Ramos and KaToya Fleming for your camaraderie and your memes. And to Melissa Crowe for your lamplight, your timing, and your trophies. We can do anything. I believe it.

Thank you to the women who, for many years, have carried me: To Lauren Bailey for your steadiness and strength. To Kelcey Parker for your pep talks and path-blazing. To Natalie Lamberjack for your humor and acceptance. To Julie Hernandez for the vault of your friendship that continues to awe me. (And to Odessa and Viosa, too.)

My late grandmothers, Blanch Obermeyer and Mary Domet, both worked in factories—and both women loomed large in my mind as I wrote this book. Thank you for your sacrifices that made my life possible. I hope I've made you proud.

What freedom to know I'm unconditionally supported by my family. Abundant gratitude to my parents, Luke and Sally, and to the other wonderous members of my family whose love and influence I'm lucky to carry with me every single day: Mary Ann, Shelby, Ian, Angelina, Eli, Luke, April, Evelyn, and to Laura, who makes me laugh and makes me brave.

Thank you, always, to Saskia and Buchanan. I love you infinity plus one (plus one). I'd eat an octopus sandwich for you. Buchanan and Saskia, this is my truest wish: May you always hear your own voice. May you always follow it.

Finally, to all the women who have felt the need to howl. Go on, howl.

ABOUT THE AUTHOR

Sarah Domet is the author of *The Guineveres.* She is a professor and the coordinator of the MFA program in creative writing at the University of North Carolina Wilmington. A Cincinnati native, Sarah now lives in coastal North Carolina.